Parable of
the Sower

BOOKS BY OCTAVIA E. BUTLER

Fledgling
Parable of the Talents
Parable of the Sower
Lilith's Brood
Dawn
Adulthood Rites
Imago
Seed to Harvest
Wild Seed
Mind of My Mind
Clay's Ark
Patternmaster
Kindred
Survivor
Bloodchild and Other Stories

OCTAVIA E. BUTLER

Parable of the Sower

GLORIA STEINEM
introduction

Seven Stories Press
NEW YORK • OAKLAND

Copyright © 1993 by Octavia E. Butler
Introduction © 2016 by Gloria Steinem. Reprinted by permission.

Seven Stories Press
140 Watts Street
New York, NY 10013
www.sevenstories.com

Library of Congress Cataloging-in-Publication Data

Names: Butler, Octavia E., author.
Title: Parable of the sower : a novel / Octavia E. Butler.
Description: Seven Stories Press edition. | New Yokr : Seven Stories Press, [2016]
Identifiers: LCCN 2016033091 | ISBN 9781609807191 (hardcover)
Subjects: LCSH: African Americans--Fiction. | Twenty-first century--Fiction. | California, Southern--Fiction. | BISAC: FICTION / Science Fiction / General. | FICTION / Literary. | GSAFD: Science fiction.
Classification: LCC PS3552.U827 P37 2016 | DDC 813/.54--dc23
LC record available at https://lccn.loc.gov/2016033091

Printed in the USA.

Introduction

by Gloria Steinem

If there is one thing scarier than a dystopian novel about the future, it's one written in the past that has already begun to come true. This is what makes *Parable of the Sower* even more impressive than it was when first published.

Twenty-five years ago, the great Octavia Butler wrote this first volume of what was to be a trilogy. She died at the tragically early age of fifty-eight, but we are lucky to have this novel and its sequel, *Parable of the Talents*. Its title refers to the biblical verse that describes not the seed, but the differing grounds it falls on; a challenge to readers who will be the ground for seeds of warning.

Its story begins in a future California that has become divided into three overlapping worlds: the powerful who own and control water, electricity, and the growth of food; the struggling middle population of those who live in walled communities, protect themselves with guns, and do their best to hang on to an order of the past; and the homeless, illiterate, dying, and prostituted of the city streets and countryside who rob the living and scavenge among unburied corpses that lie wherever they fell.

In all these worlds, water costs more than gasoline, police and firefighters serve only those who can pay, literacy is rare enough to be a marketable skill, designer drugs compel an obsession with fire, and no one is safe from robbery or rape or burning despite arms, walls, locked gates, and layers of protection.

It is in this middle population in walled communities, struggling to preserve a past order, that we meet a teenager named Lauren. She is our narrator. She is smart and subject to hope and fear, friends and betrayals. She is also afflicted with hyperempathy syndrome, something she inherited from her drug-addicted mother. It causes her to

5

feel the pain of any living being around her, including animals, yet the pain may be so great that it immobilizes her and she cannot help the one who is suffering. Hyperempathy can become so painful that she helps the sufferer to die; Butler is no romantic about the cost of empathy. In Lauren's own complicated life, we see her first with her family, then, as she loses them and begins to walk north through lawless territory, with a lover and disparate friends, then, as a leader who not only keeps the group together, but refuses to abandon them in order to be safer herself. She also is a poet who imagines the future. In a book called *Earthseed: The Book of the Living*, she tells us what was to be the theme of Butler's book: "The destiny of the human race is to migrate to other planets and star systems."

This does not mean I'm giving away the story. Events will hook you anyway by their immediacy, intimacy, and odd resonance with what we are already experiencing. In fact, you may find yourself carrying the plot forward in your mind long after you put the book down. For Butler, the future depends not only on a mega-force like global warming—which is depicted here in gradual and frightening reality of long droughts and then floods—but also on human behavior. She makes very clear that human behavior caused global warming, not the other way around; at least, not until it was almost too late. Unlike many in science fiction, but like such feminist science fiction writers as Joanna Russ, Ursula LeGuin, and Marge Piercy, Butler doesn't just create a future based on new science and new technology, she also shows the results of old human behavior that guides them.

In a science fiction world that was, in her lifetime, mostly by and for white male writers and readers, Octavia Butler has always been considered an oddity. She herself felt uniquely well suited. As she explained: "I'm black, I'm solitary, I've always been an outsider." Her characters are young and old, Latina, African American, and more, all in the most natural and uniquely American of ways.

When young Lauren starts walking cross-country to save her future life, for instance, there is an echo of enslaved Africans walking north to save their lives in the past. In defining God, her characters come up with the idea that God is Change, the Truth of Life.

It's not surprising that Octavia Butler became the first science fiction writer ever to receive a MacArthur "Genius" Award; or that she inspired millions of readers who had never seen themselves in science fiction or future fantasy before; or that African American science fiction writers, mostly but not only women, cite her as their almost sole inspiration; or that the science fiction books she read as a child were given to her mother by families who employed her as a maid; or that she now has been translated and read in countries around the world; or that her own life sounds like science fiction.

But as she often pointed out, what she wrote was neither science nor fiction, because "All struggles are essentially power struggles. Who will rule? Who will lead? Who will define, refine, confine, design?"

Octavia Butler was playing out our very real possibilities as humans. I think she can help each of us to do the same.

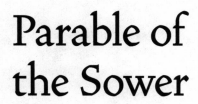

Parable of
the Sower

2024

◻ ◻ ◻

Prodigy is, at its essence, adaptability and persistent, positive obsession. Without persistence, what remains is an enthusiasm of the moment. Without adaptability, what remains may be channeled into destructive fanaticism. Without positive obsession, there is nothing at all.

EARTHSEED: THE BOOKS OF THE LIVING
by Lauren Oya Olamina

1

□ □ □

All that you touch
You Change.

All that you Change
Changes you.

The only lasting truth
Is Change.

God
Is Change.

EARTHSEED: THE BOOKS OF THE LIVING
SATURDAY, JULY 20, 2024

I had my recurring dream last night. I guess I should have expected it. It comes to me when I struggle—when I twist on my own personal hook and try to pretend that nothing unusual is happening. It comes to me when I try to be my father's daughter.

Today is our birthday—my fifteenth and my father's fifty-fifth. Tomorrow, I'll try to please him—him and the community and God. So last night, I dreamed a reminder that it's all a lie. I think I need to write about the dream because this particular lie bothers me so much.

I'm learning to fly, to levitate myself. No one is teaching me. I'm just learning on my own, little by little, dream lesson by dream lesson. Not a very subtle image, but a persistent one. I've had many lessons, and I'm better at flying than I used to be. I trust my ability more now, but I'm still afraid. I can't quite control my directions yet.

I lean forward toward the doorway. It's a doorway like the one between my room and the hall. It seems to be a long way from me, but I lean toward it. Holding my body stiff and tense, I let go of whatever I'm grasping, whatever has kept me from rising or falling so far. And I lean into the air, straining upward, not moving upward, but not quite falling down either. Then I do begin to move, as though to slide on the air drifting a few feet above the floor, caught between terror and joy.

I drift toward the doorway. Cool, pale light glows from it. Then I slide a little to the right; and a little more. I can see that I'm going to miss the door and hit the wall beside it, but I can't stop or turn. I drift away from the door, away from the cool glow into another light.

The wall before me is burning. Fire has sprung from nowhere, has eaten in through the wall, has begun to reach toward me, reach for me. The fire spreads. I drift into it. It blazes up around me. I thrash and scramble and try to swim back out of it, grabbing handfuls of air and fire, kicking, burning! Darkness.

Perhaps I awake a little. I do sometimes when the fire swallows me. That's bad. When I wake up all the way, I can't get back to sleep. I try, but I've never been able to.

This time I don't wake up all the way. I fade into the second part of the dream—the part that's ordinary and real, the part that did happen years ago when I was little, though at the time it didn't seem to matter.

Darkness.

Darkness brightening.

Stars.

Stars casting their cool, pale, glinting light.

"We couldn't see so many stars when I was little," my stepmother says to me. She speaks in Spanish, her own first language. She stands still and small, looking up at the broad sweep of the Milky Way. She

OCTAVIA E. BUTLER

and I have gone out after dark to take the washing down from the clothesline. The day has been hot, as usual, and we both like the cool darkness of early night. There's no moon, but we can see very well. The sky is full of stars.

The neighborhood wall is a massive, looming presence nearby. I see it as a crouching animal, perhaps about to spring, more threatening than protective. But my stepmother is there, and she isn't afraid. I stay close to her. I'm seven years old.

I look up at the stars and the deep, black sky. "Why couldn't you see the stars?" I ask her. "Everyone can see them." I speak in Spanish, too, as she's taught me. It's an intimacy somehow.

"City lights," she says. "Lights, progress, growth, all those things we're too hot and too poor to bother with anymore." She pauses. "When I was your age, my mother told me that the stars—the few stars we could see—were windows into heaven. Windows for God to look through to keep an eye on us. I believed her for almost a year." My stepmother hands me an armload of my youngest brother's diapers. I take them, walk back toward the house where she has left her big wicker laundry basket, and pile the diapers atop the rest of the clothes. The basket is full. I look to see that my stepmother is not watching me, then let myself fall backward onto the soft mound of stiff, clean clothes. For a moment, the fall is like floating.

I lie there, looking up at the stars. I pick out some of the constellations and name the stars that make them up. I've learned them from an astronomy book that belonged to my father's mother.

I see the sudden light streak of a meteor flashing westward across the sky. I stare after it, hoping to see another. Then my stepmother calls me and I go back to her.

"There are city lights now," I say to her. "They don't hide the stars."

She shakes her head. "There aren't anywhere near as many as there were. Kids today have no idea what a blaze of light cities used to be—and not that long ago."

"I'd rather have the stars," I say.

"The stars are free." She shrugs. "I'd rather have the city lights back myself, the sooner the better. But we can afford the stars."

2

□ □ □

**A gift of God
May sear unready fingers.**

EARTHSEED: THE BOOKS OF THE LIVING
SUNDAY, JULY 21, 2024

At least three years ago, my father's God stopped being my God. His church stopped being my church. And yet, today, because I'm a coward, I let myself be initiated into that church. I let my father baptize me in all three names of that God who isn't mine anymore.

My God has another name.

We got up early this morning because we had to go across town to church. Most Sundays, Dad holds church services in our front rooms. He's a Baptist minister, and even though not all of the people who live within our neighborhood walls are Baptists, those who feel the need to go to church are glad to come to us. That way they don't have to risk going outside where things are so dangerous and crazy. It's bad enough that some people—my father for one—have to go out to work at least once a week. None of us goes out to school anymore. Adults get nervous about kids going outside.

But today was special. For today, my father made arrangements with another minister—a friend of his who still had a real church building with a real baptistery.

Dad once had a church just a few blocks outside our wall. He began it before there were so many walls. But after it had been slept in by the homeless, robbed, and vandalized several times, someone poured gasoline in and around it and burned it down. Seven of the homeless people sleeping inside on that last night burned with it.

But somehow, Dad's friend Reverend Robinson has managed to keep his church from being destroyed. We rode our bikes to it this morning—me, two of my brothers, four other neighborhood kids who were ready to be baptized, plus my father and some other neighborhood adults riding shotgun. All the adults were armed. That's the rule. Go out in a bunch, and go armed.

The alternative was to be baptized in the bathtub at home. That would have been cheaper and safer and fine with me. I said so, but no one paid attention to me. To the adults, going outside to a real church was like stepping back into the good old days when there were churches all over the place and too many lights and gasoline was for fueling cars and trucks instead of for torching things. They never miss a chance to relive the good old days or to tell kids how great it's going to be when the country gets back on its feet and good times come back.

Yeah.

To us kids—most of us—the trip was just an adventure, an excuse to go outside the wall. We would be baptized out of duty or as a kind of insurance, but most of us aren't that much concerned with religion. I am, but then I have a different religion.

"Why take chances," Silvia Dunn said to me a few days ago. "Maybe there's something to all this religion stuff." Her parents thought there was, so she was with us.

My brother Keith who was also with us didn't share any of my beliefs. He just didn't care. Dad wanted him to be baptized, so what the hell. There wasn't much that Keith did care about. He liked to hang out with his friends and pretend to be grown up, dodge work and dodge school and dodge church. He's only twelve, the oldest of my three brothers. I don't like him much, but he's my stepmother's favorite. Three smart sons and one dumb one, and it's the dumb one she loves best.

Keith looked around more than anyone as we rode. His ambition, if you could call it that, is to get out of the neighborhood and go to

Los Angeles. He's never too clear about what he'll do there. He just wants to go to the big city and make big money. According to my father, the big city is a carcass covered with too many maggots. I think he's right, though not all the maggots are in L.A. They're here, too.

But maggots tend not to be early-morning types. We rode past people stretched out, sleeping on the sidewalks, and a few just waking up, but they paid no attention to us. I saw at least three people who weren't going to wake up again, ever. One of them was headless. I caught myself looking around for the head. After that, I tried not to look around at all.

A woman, young, naked, and filthy stumbled along past us. I got a look at her slack expression and realized that she was dazed or drunk or something.

Maybe she had been raped so much that she was crazy. I'd heard stories of that happening. Or maybe she was just high on drugs. The boys in our group almost fell off their bikes, staring at her. What wonderful religious thoughts they would be having for a while.

The naked woman never looked at us. I glanced back after we'd passed her and saw that she had settled down in the weeds against someone else's neighborhood wall.

A lot of our ride was along one neighborhood wall after another; some a block long, some two blocks, some five. . . . Up toward the hills there were walled estates—one big house and a lot of shacky little dependencies where the servants lived. We didn't pass anything like that today. In fact we passed a couple of neighborhoods so poor that their walls were made up of unmortared rocks, chunks of concrete, and trash. Then there were the pitiful, unwalled residential areas. A lot of the houses were trashed—burned, vandalized, infested with drunks or druggies or squatted in by homeless families with their filthy, gaunt, half-naked children. Their kids were wide awake and watching us this morning. I feel sorry for the little ones, but the ones my age and older make me nervous. We ride down the middle of the cracked street, and the kids come out and stand along the curb to stare at us. They just stand and stare. I think if there were only one or two of us, or if they couldn't see our guns, they might try to pull us down and steal our bikes, our clothes, our shoes, whatever. Then what? Rape? Murder? We could wind up like that naked woman, stumbling along, dazed, maybe hurt, sure to attract dangerous attention unless she could steal some clothing. I wish we could have given her something.

My stepmother says she and my father stopped to help an injured woman once, and the guys who had injured her jumped out from behind a wall and almost killed them.

And we're in Robledo—20 miles from Los Angeles, and, according to Dad, once a rich, green, unwalled little city that he had been eager to abandon when he was a young man. Like Keith, he had wanted to escape the dullness of Robledo for big city excitement. L.A. was better then—less lethal. He lived there for 21 years. Then in 2010, his parents were murdered and he inherited their house. Whoever killed them had robbed the house and smashed up the furniture, but they didn't torch anything. There was no neighborhood wall back then.

Crazy to live without a wall to protect you. Even in Robledo, most of the street poor—squatters, winos, junkies, homeless people in general—are dangerous. They're desperate or crazy or both. That's enough to make anyone dangerous.

Worse for me, they often have things wrong with them. They cut off each other's ears, arms, legs. . . . They carry untreated diseases and festering wounds. They have no money to spend on water to wash with so even the unwounded have sores. They don't get enough to eat so they're malnourished—or they eat bad food and poison themselves. As I rode, I tried not to look around at them, but I couldn't help seeing—collecting—some of their general misery.

I can take a lot of pain without falling apart. I've had to learn to do that. But it was hard, today, to keep pedaling and keep up with

OCTAVIA E. BUTLER

the others when just about everyone I saw made me feel worse and worse.

My father glanced back at me every now and then. He tells me, "You can beat this thing. You don't have to give in to it." He has always pretended, or perhaps believed, that my hyperempathy syndrome was something I could shake off and forget about. The sharing isn't real, after all. It isn't some magic or ESP that allows me to share the pain or the pleasure of other people. It's delusional. Even I admit that. My brother Keith used to pretend to be hurt just to trick me into sharing his supposed pain. Once he used red ink as fake blood to make me bleed. I was eleven then, and I still bled through the skin when I saw someone else bleeding. I couldn't help doing it, and I always worried that it would give me away to people outside the family.

I haven't shared bleeding with anyone since I was twelve and got my first period. What a relief that was. I just wish all the rest of it had gone away, too. Keith only tricked me into bleeding that once, and I beat the hell out of him for it. I didn't fight much when I was little because it hurt me so. I felt every blow that I struck, just as though I'd hit myself. So when I did decide that I had to fight, I set out to hurt the other kid more than kids usually hurt one another. I broke Michael Talcott's arm and Rubin Quintanilla's nose. I knocked out four of Silvia Dunn's teeth. They all earned what I did to them two or three times over. I got punished every time, and I resented it. It was double punishment, after all, and my father and stepmother knew it. But knowing didn't stop them. I think they did it to satisfy the other kids' parents. But when I beat up Keith, I knew that Cory or Dad or both of them would punish me for it—my poor little brother, after all. So I had to see that my poor little brother paid in advance. What I did to him had to be worthwhile in spite of what they would do to me.

It was.

We both got it later from Dad—me for hurting a younger kid and

Keith for risking putting "family business" into the street. Dad is big on privacy and "family business." There's a whole range of things we never even hint about outside the family. First among these is anything about my mother, my hyperempathy, and how the two are connected. To my father, the whole business is shameful. He's a preacher and a professor and a dean. A first wife who was a drug addict and a daughter who is drug damaged is not something he wants to boast about. Lucky for me. Being the most vulnerable person I know is damned sure not something I want to boast about.

I can't do a thing about my hyperempathy, no matter what Dad thinks or wants or wishes. I feel what I see others feeling or what I believe they feel. Hyperempathy is what the doctors call an "organic delusional syndrome." Big shit. It hurts, that's all I know. Thanks to Paracetco, the small pill, the Einstein powder, the particular drug my mother chose to abuse before my birth killed her, I'm crazy. I get a lot of grief that doesn't belong to me, and that isn't real. But it hurts.

I'm supposed to share pleasure *and* pain, but there isn't much pleasure around these days. About the only pleasure I've found that I enjoy sharing is sex. I get the guy's good feeling and my own. I almost wish I didn't. I live in a tiny, walled fish-bowl cul-de-sac community, and I'm the preacher's daughter. There's a real limit to what I can do as far as sex goes.

Anyway, my neurotransmitters are scrambled and they're going to stay scrambled. But I can do okay as long as other people don't know about me. Inside our neighborhood walls I do fine. Our rides today, though, were hell. Going and coming, they were all the worst things I've ever felt—shadows and ghosts, twists and jabs of unexpected pain.

If I don't look too long at old injuries, they don't hurt me too much. There was a naked little boy whose skin was a mass of big red sores; a man with a huge scab over the stump where his right hand used to be; a little girl, naked, maybe seven years old with blood running down her bare thighs. A woman with a swollen, bloody, beaten face. . . .

I must have seemed jumpy. I glanced around like a bird, not letting my gaze rest on anyone longer than it took me to see that they weren't coming in my direction or aiming anything at me.

Dad may have read something of what I was feeling in my expression. I try not to let my face show anything, but he's good at reading me. Sometimes people say I look grim or angry. Better to have them think that than know the truth. Better to have them think anything than let them know just how easy it is to hurt me.

Dad had insisted on fresh, clean, potable water for the baptism. He couldn't afford it, of course. Who could? That was the other reason for the four extra kids:

Silvia Dunn, Hector Quintanilla, Curtis Talcott, and Drew Balter, along with my brothers Keith and Marcus. The other kids' parents had helped with costs. They thought a proper baptism was important enough to spend some money and take some risks. I was the oldest by about two months. Curtis was next. As much as I hated being there, I hated even more that Curtis was there. I care about him more than I want to. I care what he thinks of me. I worry that I'll fall apart in public some day and he'll see. But not today.

By the time we reached the fortress-church, my jaw-muscles hurt from clinching and unclinching my teeth, and overall, I was exhausted.

There were only five or six dozen people at the service—enough to fill up our front rooms at home and look like a big crowd. At the church, though, with its surrounding wall and its security bars and Lazor wire and its huge hollowness inside, and its armed guards, the crowd seemed a tiny scattering of people. That was all right. The last thing I wanted was a big audience to maybe trip me up with pain.

The baptism went just as planned. They sent us kids off to the bathrooms ("men's," "women's," "please do not put paper of any kind into toilets," "water for washing in bucket at left. . . .") to undress and put on white gowns. When we were ready, Curtis's father took us to an anteroom where we could hear the preaching—from the first chapter of Saint John and the second chapter of The Acts—and wait our turns.

My turn came last. I assume that was my father's idea. First the neighbor kids, then my brothers, then me. For reasons that don't make a lot of sense to me, Dad thinks I need more humility. I think my particular biological humility—or humiliation—is more than enough.

What the hell? Someone had to be last. I just wish I could have been courageous enough to skip the thing altogether.

So, "In the name of the Father, the Son, and the Holy Ghost. . . ."

Catholics get this stuff over with when they're babies. I wish Baptists did. I almost wish I could believe it was important the way a lot of people seem to, the way my father seems to. Failing that, I wish I didn't care.

But I do. The idea of God is much on my mind these days. I've been paying attention to what other people believe—whether they believe, and if so what kind of God they believe in. Keith says God is just the adults' way of trying to scare you into doing what they want. He doesn't say that around Dad, but he says it. He believes in what he sees, and no matter what's in front of him, he doesn't see much. I suppose Dad would say that about me if he knew what I believe. Maybe he'd be right. But it wouldn't stop me from seeing what I see.

A lot of people seem to believe in a big-daddy-God or a big-cop-God or a big-king-God. They believe in a kind of super-person. A few believe God is another word for nature. And nature turns out to mean just about anything they happen not to understand or feel in control of.

Some say God is a spirit, a force, an ultimate reality. Ask seven people what all of that means and you'll get seven different answers. So what is God? Just another name for whatever makes you feel special and protected?

There's a big, early-season storm blowing itself out in the Gulf of

Mexico. It's bounced around the Gulf, killing people from Florida to Texas and down into Mexico. There are over 700 known dead so far. One hurricane. And how many people has it hurt? How many are going to starve later because of destroyed crops? That's nature. Is it God? Most of the dead are the street poor who have nowhere to go and who don't hear the warnings until it's too late for their feet to take them to safety. Where's safety for them anyway? Is it a sin against God to be poor? We're almost poor ourselves. There are fewer and fewer jobs among us, more of us being born, more kids growing up with nothing to look forward to. One way or another, we'll all be poor some day. The adults say things will get better, but they never have. How will God—my father's God—behave toward us when we're poor?

Is there a God? If there is, does he (she? it?) care about us? Deists like Benjamin Franklin and Thomas Jefferson believed God was something that made us, then left us on our own.

"Misguided," Dad said when I asked him about Deists. "They should have had more faith in what their Bibles told them."

I wonder if the people on the Gulf Coast still have faith. People have had faith through horrible disasters before. I read a lot about that kind of thing. I read a lot period. My favorite book of the Bible is Job. I think it says more about my father's God in particular and gods in general than anything else I've ever read.

In the book of Job, God says he made everything and he knows everything so no one has any right to question what he does with any of it. Okay. That works. That Old Testament God doesn't violate the way things are now. But that God sounds a lot like Zeus—a super-powerful man, playing with his toys the way my youngest brothers play with toy soldiers. Bang, bang! Seven toys fall dead. If they're yours, you make the rules. Who cares what the toys think. Wipe out a toy's family, then give it a brand new family. Toy children, like Job's children, are interchangeable.

Maybe God is a kind of big kid, playing with his toys. If he is, what difference does it make if 700 people get killed in a hurricane—or if seven kids go to church and get dipped in a big tank of expensive water?

But what if all that is wrong? What if God is something else altogether?

3

□ □ □

We do not worship God.
We perceive and attend God.
We learn from God.
With forethought and work,
We shape God.
In the end, we yield to God.
We adapt and endure,
For we are Earthseed
And God is Change.

EARTHSEED: THE BOOKS OF THE LIVING
TUESDAY, JULY 30, 2024

One of the astronauts on the latest Mars mission has been killed. Something went wrong with her protective suit and the rest of her team couldn't get her back to the shelter in time to save her. People here in the neighborhood are saying she had no business going to Mars, anyway. All that money wasted on another crazy space trip when so many people here on earth can't afford water, food, or shelter.

The cost of water has gone up again. And I heard on the news today that more water peddlers are being killed. Peddlers sell water to squatters and the street poor—and to people who've managed to hold on to their homes, but not to pay their utility bills. Peddlers are being found with their throats cut and their money and their handtrucks stolen. Dad says water now costs several times as much as gasoline. But, except for arsonists and the rich, most people have given up buying gasoline. No one I know uses a gas-powered car, truck, or cycle. Vehicles like that are rusting in driveways and being cannibalized for metal and plastic.

It's a lot harder to give up water.

Fashion helps. You're supposed to be dirty now. If you're clean, you make a target of yourself. People think you're showing off, trying to be better than they are. Among the younger kids, being clean is a great way to start a fight. Cory won't let us stay dirty here in the neighborhood, but we all have filthy clothes to wear outside the walls. Even inside, my brothers throw dirt on themselves as soon as they get away from the house. It's better than getting beaten up all the time.

Tonight the last big Window Wall television in the neighborhood went dark for good. We saw the dead astronaut with all of red, rocky Mars around her. We saw a dust-dry reservoir and three dead water peddlers with their dirty-blue armbands and their heads cut halfway off. And we saw whole blocks of boarded up buildings burning in Los Angeles. Of course, no one would waste water trying to put such fires out.

Then the Window went dark. The sound had flickered up and down for months, but the picture was always as promised—like looking through a vast, open window.

The Yannis family has made a business of having people in to look through their Window. Dad says that kind of unlicensed business isn't legal, but he let us go to watch sometimes because he didn't see any harm in it, and it helped the Yannises. A lot of small businesses are illegal, even though they don't hurt anyone, and they keep a household or two alive. The Yannis Window is about as old as I am. It covers the long west wall of their living room. They must have had plenty of money back when they bought it. For the past couple of years, though, they've been charging admission—only letting in people from the neighborhood—and selling fruit, fruit juice, acorn bread, or walnuts. Whatever they had too much of in their garden, they found a way to sell. They showed movies from their library and let us watch news and whatever else was broadcast. They couldn't afford to subscribe to any of the new multisensory stuff, and their old Window couldn't have received most of it, anyway.

They have no reality vests, no touch-rings, and no headsets. Their setup was just a plain, thin-screened Window.

All we have left now are three small, ancient, murky little TV sets scattered around the neighborhood, a couple of computers used for work, and radios. Every household still has at least one working radio. A lot of our everyday news is from radio.

I wonder what Mrs. Yannis will do now. Her two sisters have moved in with her, and they're working so maybe it will be all right. One is a pharmacist and the other is a nurse. They don't earn much, but Mrs. Yannis owns the house free and clear. It was her parents' house.

All three sisters are widows and between them they have twelve kids, all younger than I am. Two years ago, Mr. Yannis, a dentist, was killed while riding his electric cycle home from the walled, guarded clinic where he worked. Mrs. Yannis says he was caught in a crossfire, hit from two directions, then shot once more at close range. His bike was stolen. The police investigated, collected their fee, and couldn't find a thing. People get killed like that all the time. Unless it happens in front of a police station, there are never any witnesses.

SATURDAY, AUGUST 3, 2024

The dead astronaut is going to be brought back to Earth. She wanted to be buried on Mars. She said that when she realized she was dying. She said Mars was the one thing she had wanted all her life, and now she would be part of it forever.

But the Secretary of Astronautics says no. He says her body might be a contaminant. Idiot.

Can he believe that any microorganism living in or on her body would have a prayer of surviving and going native in that cold, thin, lethal ghost of an atmosphere? Maybe he can. Secretaries of Astronautics don't have to know much about science. They have to know about politics. Theirs is the youngest Cabinet department, and already it's fighting for its life. Christopher Morpeth Donner, one of the men running for President this year, has promised to abolish it if he's elected. My father agrees with Donner.

"Bread and circuses," my father says when there's space news on the radio. "Politicians and big corporations get the bread, and we get the circuses."

"Space could be our future," I say. I believe that. As far as I'm concerned, space exploration and colonization are among the few things left over from the last century that can help us more than they hurt us. It's hard to get anyone to see that, though, when there's so much suffering going on just outside our walls.

Dad just looks at me and shakes his head. "You don't understand," he says. "You don't have any idea what a criminal waste of time and money that so-called space program is." He's going to vote for Donner. He's the only person I know who's going to vote at all. Most people have given up on politicians. After all, politicians have been promising to return us to the glory, wealth, and order of the twentieth century ever since I can remember. That's what the space program is about these days, at least for politicians. Hey, we can run a space station, a station on the moon, and soon, a colony on Mars. That proves we're still a great, forward-looking, powerful nation, right?

Yeah.

Well, we're barely a nation at all anymore, but I'm glad we're still in space. We have to be going some place other than down the toilet.

And I'm sorry that astronaut will be brought back from her own chosen heaven. Her name was Alicia Catalina Godinez Leal. She was a chemist. I intend to remember her. I think she can be a kind of model for me. She spent her life heading for Mars—preparing herself, becoming an astronaut, getting on a Mars crew, going to Mars,

OCTAVIA E. BUTLER

beginning to figure out how to terraform Mars, beginning to create sheltered places where people can live and work now. . . .

Mars is a rock—cold, empty, almost airless, dead. Yet it's heaven in a way. We can see it in the night sky, a whole other world, but too nearby, too close within the reach of the people who've made such a hell of life here on Earth.

MONDAY, AUGUST 12, 2024

Mrs. Sims shot herself today—or rather, she shot herself a few days ago, and Cory and Dad found her today. Cory went a little crazy for a while afterward.

Poor, sanctimonious, old Mrs. Sims. She used to sit in our front-room church every Sunday, large-print Bible in hand, and shout out her responses: "Yes, Lord!" "Hallelujah!" "Thank you, Jesus!" "Amen!" During the rest of the week she sewed, made baskets, took care of her garden, sold what she could from it, took care of pre-school children, and talked about everyone who wasn't as holy as she thought she was.

She was the only person I've ever known who lived alone. She had a whole big house to herself because she and the wife of her only son hated each other. Her son and his family were poor, but they wouldn't live with her. Too bad.

Different people frightened her in some deep, hard, ugly way. She didn't like the Hsu family because they were Chinese and His-panic, and the older Chinese generation is still Buddhist. She's lived a couple of doors up from them for longer than I've been alive, but they were still from Saturn as far as she was concerned.

"Idolaters," she would call them if none of them were around. At least she cared enough about neighborly relations to do her talking about them behind their backs. They brought her peaches and figs and a length of good cotton cloth last month when she was robbed.

That robbery was Mrs. Sims's first major tragedy. Three men

climbed over the neighborhood wall, cutting through the strands of barbed wire and Lazor wire on top. Lazor wire is terrible stuff. It's so fine and sharp that it slices into the wings or feet of birds who either don't see it or see it and try to settle on it. People, though, can always find a way over, under, or through.

Everyone brought Mrs. Sims things after the robbery, in spite of the way she is. Was. Food, clothing, money. . . . We took up collections for her at church. The thieves had tied her up and left her—after one of them raped her. An old lady like that! They grabbed all her food, her jewelry that had once belonged to her mother, her clothes, and worst of all, her supply of cash. It turns out she kept that—all of it—in a blue plastic mixing bowl high up in her kitchen cabinet. Poor, crazy old lady. She came to my father, crying and carrying on after the robbery because now she couldn't buy the extra food she needed to supplement what she grew. She couldn't pay her utility bills or her upcoming property taxes. She would be thrown out of her house into the street! She would starve!

Dad told her over and over that the church would never let that happen, but she didn't believe him. She talked on and on about having to be a beggar now, while Dad and Cory tried to reassure her. The funny thing is, she didn't like us either because Dad had gone and married "that Mexican woman Cory-ah-zan." It just isn't that hard to say "Corazon" if that's what you choose to call her. Most people just call her Cory or Mrs. Olamina.

Cory never let on that she was offended. She and Mrs. Sims were sugary sweet to one another. A little more hypocrisy to keep the peace.

Last week Mrs. Sims's son, his five kids, his wife, her brother, and her brother's three kids all died in a house fire—an arson fire. The son's house had been in an unwalled area north and east of us, closer to the foothills. It wasn't a bad area, but it was poor. Naked. One night someone torched the house. Maybe it was a vengeance fire set by some enemy of a family member or maybe some crazy just set it

OCTAVIA E. BUTLER

for fun. I've heard there's a new illegal drug that makes people want to set fires.

Anyway, no one knows who did it to the Sims/Boyer families. No one saw anything, of course.

And no one got out of the house. Odd, that. Eleven people, and no one got out.

So about three days ago, Mrs. Sims shot herself. Dad said he'd heard from the cops that it was about three days ago. That would have been just two days after she heard about her son's death. Dad went to see her this morning because she missed church yesterday. Cory forced herself to go along because she thought she should. I wish she hadn't. To me, dead bodies are disgusting. They stink, and if they're old enough, there are maggots. But what the hell? They're dead. They aren't suffering, and if you didn't like them when they were alive, why get so upset about their being dead? Cory gets upset. She jumps on me for sharing pain with the living, but she tries to share it with the dead.

I began writing this about Mrs. Sims because she killed herself. That's what's upset me. She believed, like Dad, that if you kill yourself, you go to hell and burn forever. She believed in a literal acceptance of everything in the Bible. Yet, when things got to be too much for her, she decided to trade pain for eternal pain in the hereafter.

How could she do that?

Did she really believe in anything at all? Was it all hypocrisy?

Or maybe she just went crazy because her God was demanding too much of her. She was no Job. In real life, how many people are?

SATURDAY, AUGUST 17, 2024

I can't get Mrs. Sims out of my mind. Somehow, she and her suicide have gotten tangled up with the astronaut and her death and her expulsion from heaven. I need to write about what I believe. I need to begin to put together the scattered verses that I've been writing about God since I was twelve. Most of them aren't much good. They say what I need to say, but they don't say it very well. A few are the way they should be. They press on me, too, like the two deaths. I try to hide in all the work there is to do here for the household, for my father's church, and for the school Cory keeps to teach the neighborhood kids. The truth is, I don't care about any of those things, but they keep me busy and make me tired, and most of the time, I sleep without dreaming. And Dad beams when people tell him how smart and industrious I am.

I love him. He's the best person I know, and I care what he thinks. I wish I didn't, but I do.

For whatever it's worth, here's what I believe. It took me a lot of time to understand it, then a lot more time with a dictionary and a thesaurus to say it just right—just the way it has to be. In the past year, it's gone through twenty-five or thirty lumpy, incoherent rewrites. This is the right one, the true one. This is the one I keep coming back to:

> *God is Power—*
> *Infinite,*
> *Irresistible,*
> *Inexorable,*
> *Indifferent.*
> *And yet, God is Pliable—*
> *Trickster,*
> *Teacher,*
> *Chaos,*
> *Clay.*
> *God exists to be shaped.*
> *God is Change.*

This is the literal truth.

God can't be resisted or stopped, but can be shaped and focused.

This means God is not to be prayed to. Prayers only help the person doing the praying, and then, only if they strengthen and focus that person's resolve. If they're used that way, they can help us in our only real relationship with God. They help us to shape God and to accept and work with the shapes that God imposes on us. God is power, and in the end, God prevails.

But we can rig the game in our own favor if we understand that God exists to be shaped, and will be shaped, with or without our forethought, with or without our intent.

That's what I know. That's some of it anyway. I'm not like Mrs. Sims. I'm not some kind of potential Job, long suffering, stiff necked, then, at last, either humble before an all-knowing almighty, or destroyed. My God doesn't love me or hate me or watch over me or know me at all, and I feel no love for or loyalty to my God. My God just is.

Maybe I'll be more like Alicia Leal, the astronaut. Like her, I believe in something that I think my dying, denying, backward-looking people need. I don't have all of it yet. I don't even know how to pass on what I do have. I've got to learn to do that. It scares me how many things I've got to learn. How will I learn them?

Is any of this real?

Dangerous question. Sometimes I don't know the answer. I doubt myself. I doubt what I think I know. I try to forget about it. After all, if it's real, why doesn't anyone else know about it? Everyone knows that change is inevitable. From the second law of thermodynamics to Darwinian evolution, from Buddhism's insistence that nothing is permanent and all suffering results from our delusions of permanence to the third chapter of Ecclesiastes ("To everything there is a season . . . ."), change is part of life, of existence, of the common wisdom. But I don't believe we're dealing with all that that means. We haven't even begun to deal with it.

We give lip service to acceptance, as though acceptance were enough. Then we go on to create super-people—super-parents, super-kings and queens, super-cops—to be our gods and to look after us—to stand between us and God. Yet God has been here all along, shaping us and being shaped by us in no particular way or in too many ways at once like an amoeba—or like a cancer. Chaos.

Even so, why can't I do what others have done—ignore the obvious. Live a normal life. It's hard enough just to do that in this world.

But this thing (this idea? Philosophy? New religion?) won't let me alone, won't let me forget it, won't let me go. Maybe. . . . Maybe it's like my sharing: One more weirdness; one more crazy, deep-rooted delusion that I'm stuck with. I am stuck with it. And in time, I'll have to do something about it. In spite of what my father will say or do to me, in spite of the poisonous rottenness outside the wall where I might be exiled, I'll have to do something about it.

That reality scares me to death.

WEDNESDAY, NOVEMBER 6, 2024

President William Turner Smith lost yesterday's election. Christopher Charles Morpeth Donner is our new President—President-elect. So what are we in for? Donner has already said that as soon as possible after his inauguration next year, he'll begin to dismantle the "wasteful, pointless, unnecessary" moon and Mars programs. Near space programs dealing with communications and experimentation will be privatized—sold off.

Also, Donner has a plan for putting people back to work. He hopes to get laws changed, suspend "overly restrictive" minimum wage, environmental, and worker protection laws for those employers willing to take on homeless employees and provide them with training and adequate room and board.

What's adequate, I wonder: A house or apartment? A room? A bed in a shared room? A barracks bed? Space on a floor? Space on the ground? And what about people with big families? Won't they be seen as bad investments? Won't it make much more sense for companies to hire single people, childless couples, or, at most, people with only one or two kids? I wonder.

And what about those suspended laws? Will it be legal to poison, mutilate, or infect people—as long as you provide them with food, water, and space to die?

Dad decided not to vote for Donner after all. He didn't vote for anyone. He said politicians turned his stomach.

2025

□ □ □

Intelligence is ongoing, individual adaptability.
Adaptations that an intelligent species may make in
a single generation, other species make over many
generations of selective breeding and selective dying.
Yet intelligence is demanding. If it is misdirected by
accident or by intent, it can foster its own orgies of
breeding and dying.

EARTHSEED: THE BOOKS OF THE LIVING

4

□ □ □

A victim of God may,
Through learning adaption,
Become a partner of God,
A victim of God may,
Through forethought and planning,
Become a shaper of God.
Or a victim of God may,
Through shortsightedness and fear,
Remain God's victim,
God's plaything,
God's prey.

EARTHSEED: THE BOOKS OF THE LIVING
SATURDAY, FEBRUARY 1, 2025

We had a fire today. People worry so much about fire, but the little kids will play with it if they can. We were lucky with this fire. Amy Dunn, three years old, managed to start it in her family's garage.

Once the fire began to crawl up the wall, Amy got scared and ran into the house. She knew she had done something bad, so she didn't tell anyone. She hid under her grandmother's bed.

Out back, the dry wood of the garage burned fast and hot. Robin Balter saw the smoke and rang the emergency bell on the island in our street. Robin's only ten, but she's a bright little kid—one of my stepmother's star students. She keeps her head. If she hadn't alerted people as soon as she saw the smoke, the fire could have spread.

I heard the bell and ran out like everyone else to see what was wrong. The Dunns live across the street from us, so I couldn't miss the smoke.

The fire plan worked the way it was supposed to. The adult men and women put the fire out with garden hoses, shovels, wet towels and blankets. Those without hoses beat at the edges of the fire and smothered them with dirt. Kids my age helped out where we were needed and put out any new fires started by flying embers. We brought buckets to fill with water, and shovels, blankets, and towels of our own. There were a lot of us, and we kept our eyes open. The very old people watched the little kids and kept them out of the way and out of trouble.

No one missed Amy. No one had seen her in the Dunn backyard, so no one thought about her. Her grandmother found her much later and got the truth out of her.

The garage was a total loss. Edwin Dunn salvaged some of his garden and carpentry equipment, but not much. The grapefruit tree next to the garage and the two peach trees behind it were half-burned, too, but they might survive. The carrot, squash, collard, and potato plants were a trampled mess.

Of course, no one called the fire department. No one would take on fire service fees just to save an unoccupied garage. Most of our households couldn't afford another big bill, anyway. The water wasted on putting out the fire was going to be hard enough to pay for.

What will happen, I wonder, to poor little Amy Dunn. No one cares about her. Her family feeds her and, now and then, cleans her up, but they don't love her or even like her. Her mother Tracy is only a year older than I am. She was 13 when Amy was born. She was 12 when her 27-year-old uncle who had been raping her for years managed to make her pregnant.

Problem: Uncle Derek was a big, blond, handsome guy, funny and bright and well-liked. Tracy was, is, dull and homely, sulky and dirty-looking. Even when she's clean, she looks splotchy, dirty. Some of her problems might have come from being raped by Uncle Derek

OCTAVIA E. BUTLER

for years. Uncle Derek was Tracy's mother's youngest brother, her favorite brother, but when people realized what he had been doing, the neighborhood men got together and suggested he go live somewhere else. People didn't want him around their daughters. Irrational as usual, Tracy's mother blamed Tracy for his exile, and for her own embarrassment. Not many girls in the neighborhood have babies before they drag some boy to my father and have him unite them in holy matrimony. But there was no one to marry Tracy, and no money for prenatal care or an abortion. And poor Amy, as she grew, looked more and more like Tracy: scrawny and splotchy with sparse, stringy hair. I don't think she'll ever be pretty.

Tracy's maternal instincts didn't kick in, and I doubt that her mother Christmas Dunn has any. The Dunn family has a reputation for craziness. There are sixteen of them living in the Dunn house, and at least a third are nuts. Amy isn't crazy, though. Not yet. She's neglected and lonely, and like any little kid left on her own too much, she finds ways to amuse herself.

I've never seen anyone hit Amy or curse her or anything like that. The Dunns do care what people think of them. But no one pays any attention to her, either. She spends most of her time playing alone in the dirt. She also eats the dirt and whatever she finds in it, including bugs. But not long ago, just out of curiosity, I took her to our house, sponged her off, taught her the alphabet, and showed her how to write her name. She loved it. She's got a hungry, able little mind, and she loves attention.

Tonight I asked Cory if Amy could start school early. Cory doesn't take kids until they're five or close to five, but she said she'd let Amy in if I would take charge of her. I expected that, though I don't like it. I help with the five- and six-year-olds, anyway. I've been taking care of little kids since I was one, and I'm tired of it. I think, though, that if someone doesn't help Amy now, someday she'll do something a lot worse than burning down her family's garage.

Some cousins of old Mrs. Sims have inherited her house. They're lucky there's still a house to inherit. If it weren't for our wall, the house would have been gutted, taken over by squatters, or torched as soon as it was empty. As it was, all people did was take back things they had given to Mrs. Sims after she was robbed, and take whatever food she had in the house. No sense letting it rot. We didn't take her furniture or her rugs or her appliances. We could have, but we didn't. We aren't thieves.

Wardell Parrish and Rosalee Payne think otherwise. They're both small, rust-brown, sour-looking people like Mrs. Sims. They're the children of a first cousin that Mrs. Sims had managed to keep contact and good relations with. He's a widower twice over, no kids, and she's been widowed once, seven kids. They're not only brother and sister, but twins. Maybe that helps them get along with each other. They damn sure won't get along with anyone else.

They're moving in today. They've been here a couple of times before to look the place over, and I guess they must have liked it better than their parents' house. They shared that with 18 other people. I was busy in the den with my class of younger school kids, so I didn't meet them until today, though I've heard Dad talking to them—heard them sit in our living room and insinuate that we had cleaned out Mrs. Sims's house before they arrived.

Dad kept his temper. "You know she was robbed during the month before she died," he said. "You can check with the police about that—if you haven't already. Since then the community has protected the house. We haven't used it or stripped it. If you choose to live among us, you should understand that. We help each other, and we don't steal."

"I wouldn't expect you to say you did," Wardell Parrish muttered.

His sister jumped in before he could say more. "We're not accusing anyone of anything," she lied. "We just wondered. . . . We knew

Cousin Marjorie had some nice things—jewelry that she inherited from her mother. . . . Very valuable. . . ."

"Check with the police," my father said.

"Well, yes, I know, but. . . ."

"This is a small community," my father said. "We all know each other here. We depend on each other."

There was a silence. Perhaps the twins were getting the message.

"We're not very social," Wardell Parrish said. "We mind our own business."

Again his sister jumped in before he could go on. "I'm sure everything will be all right," she said. "I'm sure we'll get along fine."

I didn't like them when I heard them. I liked them even less when I met them. They look at us as though we smell and they don't. Of course, it doesn't matter whether I like them or not. There are other people in the neighborhood whom I don't like. But I don't trust the Payne-Parrishes. The kids seem all right, but the adults. . . . I wouldn't want to have to depend on them. Not even for little things.

Payne and Parrish. What perfect names they have.

SATURDAY, FEBRUARY 22, 2025

We ran into a pack of feral dogs today. We went to the hills today for target practice—me, my father, Joanne Garfield, her cousin and boyfriend Harold—Harry—Balter, my boyfriend Curtis Talcott, his brother Michael, Aura Moss and her brother Peter. Our other adult Guardian was Joanne's father Jay. He's a good guy and a good shot. Dad likes to work with him, although sometimes there are problems. The Garfields and the Balters are white, and the rest of us are black. That can be dangerous these days. On the street, people are expected to fear and hate everyone but their own kind, but with all of us armed and watchful, people stared, but they let us alone. Our neighborhood is too small for us to play those kinds of games.

Everything went as usual at first. The Talcotts got into an argument first with each other, then with the Mosses. The Mosses are always blaming other people for whatever they do wrong, so they tend to have disputes outstanding with most of us. Peter Moss is the worst because he's always trying to be like his father, and his father is a total shit. His father has three wives. All at once, Karen, Natalie, and Zahra. They've all got kids by him, though so far, Zahra, the youngest and prettiest, only has one. Karen is the one with the marriage license, but she let him get away with bringing first one, then another new woman into the house and calling them his wives. I guess the way things are, she didn't think she could make it on her own with three kids when he brought in Natalie and five by the time he found Zahra.

The Mosses don't come to church. Richard Moss has put together his own religion—a combination of the Old Testament and historical West African practices. He claims that God wants men to be patriarchs, rulers and protectors of women, and fathers of as many children as possible. He's an engineer for one of the big commercial water companies, so he can afford to pick up beautiful, young homeless women and live with them in polygamous relationships. He could pick up twenty women like that if he could afford to feed them. I hear there's a lot of that kind of thing going on in other neighborhoods. Some middle class men prove they're men by having a lot of wives in temporary or permanent relationships. Some upper class men prove they're men by having one wife and a lot of beautiful, disposable young servant girls. Nasty. When the girls get pregnant, if their rich employers won't protect them, the employers' wives throw them out to starve.

Is that the way it's going to be, I wonder? Is that the future: Large numbers of people stuck in either President-elect Donner's version of slavery or Richard Moss's?

We rode our bikes to the top of River Street past the last neighborhood walls, past the last ragged, unwalled houses, past the last stretch of broken asphalt and rag and stick shacks of squatters and street poor who stare at us in their horrible, empty way, and then higher into the hills along a dirt road. At last we dismounted and

OCTAVIA E. BUTLER

walked our bikes down the narrow trail into one of the canyons that we and others use for target practice. It looked all right this time, but we always have to be careful. People use canyons for a lot of things. If we find corpses in one, we stay away from it for a while. Dad tries to shield us from what goes on in the world, but he can't. Knowing that, he also tries to teach us to shield ourselves.

Most of us have practiced at home with BB guns on homemade targets or on squirrel and bird targets. I've done all that. My aim is good, but I don't like it with the birds and squirrels. Dad was the one who insisted on my learning to shoot them. He said moving targets would be good for my aim. I think there was more to it than that. I think he wanted to see whether or not I could do it—whether shooting a bird or a squirrel would trigger my hyperempathy.

It didn't, quite. I didn't like it, but it wasn't painful. It felt like a big, soft, strange ghost blow, like getting hit with a huge ball of air, but with no coolness, no feeling of wind. The blow, though still soft, was a little harder with squirrels and sometimes rats than with birds. All three had to be killed, though. They ate our food or ruined it. Tree-crops were their special victims: Peaches, plums, figs, persimmons, nuts. . . . And crops like strawberries, blackberries, grapes . . . Whatever we planted, if they could get at it, they would. Birds are particular pests because they can fly in, yet I like them. I envy their ability to fly. Sometimes I get up and go out at dawn just so I can watch them without anyone scaring them or shooting them. Now that I'm old enough to go target shooting on Saturdays, I don't intend to shoot anymore birds, no matter what Dad says. Besides, just because I can shoot a bird or a squirrel doesn't mean I could shoot a person—a thief like the ones who robbed Mrs. Sims. I don't know whether I could do that. And if I did it, I don't know what would happen to me. Would I die?

It's my father's fault that we pay so much attention to guns and shooting. He carries a nine millimeter automatic pistol whenever he leaves the neighborhood. He carries it on his hip where people can see it. He says that discourages mistakes. Armed people do get killed—most often in crossfires or by snipers—but unarmed people get killed a lot more often.

Dad also has a silenced nine millimeter submachine gun. It stays at home with Cory in case something happens there while he's away. Both guns are German—Heckler & Koch. Dad has never said where he got the submachine gun. It's illegal, of course, so I don't blame him. It must have cost a hell of a lot. He's only had it away from home a few times so he, Cory, and I could get the feel of it. He'll do the same for the boys when they're older.

Cory has an old Smith & Wesson .38 revolver that she's good with. She's had it since before she married Dad. She loaned that one to me today. Ours aren't the best or the newest guns in the neighborhood, but they all work. Dad and Cory keep them in good condition. I have to help with that now. And they spend the necessary time on practice and money on ammunition.

At neighborhood association meetings, Dad used to push the adults of every household to own weapons, maintain them, and know how to use them. "Know how to use them so well," he's said more than once, "that you're as able to defend yourself at two a.m. as you are at two p.m."

At first there were a few neighbors who didn't like that—older ones who said it was the job of the police to protect them, younger ones who worried that their little children would find their guns, and religious ones who didn't think a minister of the gospel should need guns. This was several years ago.

"The police," my father told them, "may be able to avenge you, but they can't protect you. Things are getting worse. And as for your children. . . . Well, yes, there is risk. But you can put your guns out of their reach while they're very young, and train them as they grow older. That's what I mean to do. I believe they'll have a better chance of growing up if you can protect them." He paused, stared at the people, then went on. "I have a wife and five children," he said. "I will pray for them all. I'll also see to it that they know how to defend themselves. And for as long as I can, I will stand between my family and any intruder." He paused again. "Now that's what I have to do. You all do what you have to do."

By now there are at least two guns in every household. Dad says he suspects that some of them are so well hidden—like Mrs. Sims's gun—that they wouldn't be available in an emergency. He's working on that.

All the kids who attend school at our house get gun handling instruction. Once they've passed that and turned fifteen, two or three of the neighborhood adults begin taking them to the hills for target practice. It's a kind of rite of passage for us. My brother Keith has been whining to go along whenever someone gets a shooting group together, but the age rule is firm.

I worry about the way Keith wants to get his hands on the guns. Dad doesn't seem to worry, but I do.

There are always a few groups of homeless people and packs of feral dogs living out beyond the last hillside shacks. People and dogs hunt rabbits, possums, squirrels, and each other. Both scavenge whatever dies. The dogs used to belong to people—or their ancestors did. But dogs eat meat. These days, no poor or middle class person who had an edible piece of meat would give it to a dog. Rich people still keep dogs, either because they like them or because they use them to guard estates, enclaves, and businesses. The rich have plenty of other security devices, but the dogs are extra insurance. Dogs scare people.

I did some shooting today, and I was leaning against a boulder, watching others shoot, when I realized there was a dog nearby, watching me. Just one dog—male, yellow-brown, sharp-eared, short-haired. He wasn't big enough to make a meal of me, and I still had the Smith & Wesson, so while he was looking me over, I took a good look at him. He was lean, but he didn't look starved. He looked alert and curious. He sniffed the air, and I remembered that dogs were supposed to be oriented more toward scent than sight.

"Look at that," I said to Joanne Garfield who was standing nearby.

She turned, gasped, and jerked her gun up to aim at the dog. The dog vanished into the dry brush and boulders. Turning, Joanne tried to look everywhere as though she expected to see more dogs stalking us, but there was nothing. She was shaking.

"I'm sorry," I said. "I didn't know you were afraid of them."

She drew a deep breath and looked at the place where the dog had been. "I didn't know I was either," she whispered. "I've never been so close to one before. I . . . I wish I had gotten a better look at it."

At that moment, Aura Moss screamed and fired her father's Llama automatic.

I pushed away from the boulder and turned to see Aura pointing her gun toward some rocks and babbling.

"It was over there!" she said, her words tumbling over one another. "It was some kind of animal—dirty yellow with big teeth. It had its mouth open. It was huge!"

"You stupid bitch, you almost shot me!" Michael Talcott shouted. I could see now that he had ducked down behind a boulder. He would have been in Aura's line of fire, but he didn't seem to be hurt.

"Put your gun away, Aura," my father said. He kept his voice low, but he was angry. I could see that, whether Aura could or not.

"It was an animal," she insisted. "A big one. It might still be around."

"Aura!" My father raised his voice and hardened it.

Aura looked at him, then seemed to realize that she had more than a dog to worry about. She looked at the gun in her hand, frowned, fumbled it safe, and put it back into her holster.

"Mike?" my father said.

"I'm okay," Michael Talcott said. "No thanks to her!"

"It wasn't my fault," Aura said, right on cue. "There was an animal. It could have killed you! It was sneaking up on us!"

"I think it was just a dog," I said. "There was one watching us over here. Joanne moved and it ran away."

"You should have killed it," Peter Moss said. "What do you want to do? Wait until it jumps someone."

"What was it doing?" Jay Garfield asked. "Just watching?"

"That's all," I said. "It didn't look sick or starved. It wasn't very big. I don't think it was a danger to anyone here. There are too many of us, and we're all too big."

"The thing I saw was huge," Aura insisted. "It had its mouth open!"

I went over to her because I'd had a sudden thought. "It was panting," I said. "They pant when they're hot. It doesn't mean they're angry or hungry." I hesitated, watching her. "You've never seen one before, have you?"

She shook her head.

"They're bold, but they're not dangerous to a group like this. You don't have to worry."

She didn't look as though she quite believed me, but she seemed to relax a little. The Moss girls were both bullied and sheltered. They were almost never allowed to leave the walls of the neighborhood. They were educated at home by their mothers according to the religion their father had assembled, and they were warned away from the sin and contamination of the rest of the world. I'm surprised that Aura was allowed to come to us for gun handling instruction and target practice. I hope it will be good for her—and I hope the rest of us will survive.

"All of you stay where you are," Dad said. He glanced at Jay Garfield, then went a short way up among the rocks and scrub oaks to see whether Aura had shot anything. He kept his gun in his hand and the safety off. He was out of our sight for no more than a minute.

He came back with a look on his face that I couldn't read. "Put your guns away," he said. "We're going home."

"Did I kill it?" Aura demanded.

"No. Get your bikes." He and Jay Garfield whispered together for a moment, and Jay Garfield sighed. Joanne and I watched them, wondering, knowing we wouldn't hear anything from them until they were ready to tell us.

"This is not about a dead dog," Harold Balter said behind us. Joanne moved back to stand beside him.

"It's about either a dog pack or a human pack," I said, "or maybe it's a corpse."

It was, as I found out later, a family of corpses: A woman, a little boy of about four years, and a just-born infant, all partly eaten. But Dad didn't tell me that until we got home. At the canyon, all we knew was that he was upset.

"If there were a corpse around here, we would have smelled it," Harry said.

"Not if it were fresh," I countered.

Joanne looked at me and sighed the way her father sighs. "If it's that, I wonder where we'll go shooting next time. I wonder when there'll be a next time."

Peter Moss and the Talcott brothers had gotten into an argument over whose fault it was that Aura had almost shot Michael, and Dad had to break it up. Then Dad checked with Aura to see that she was all right. He said a few things to her that I couldn't hear, and I saw a tear slide down her face. She cries easily. She always has.

Dad walked away from her looking harassed. He led us up the path out of the canyon. We walked our bikes, and we all kept looking around. We could see now that there were other dogs nearby. We were being watched by a big pack. Jay Garfield brought up the rear, guarding our backs.

"He said we should stick together," Joanne told me. She had seen me looking back at her father.

"You and I?"

"Yeah, and Harry. He said we should look out for one another."

"I don't think these dogs are stupid enough or hungry enough to attack us in daylight. They'll go after some lone street person tonight."

OCTAVIA E. BUTLER

"Shut up, for godsake."

The road was narrow going up and out of the canyon. It would have been a bad place to have to fight off dogs. Someone could trip and step off the crumbling edge. Someone could be knocked off the edge by a dog or by one of us. That would mean falling several hundred feet.

Down below, I could hear dogs fighting now. We may have been close to their dens or whatever they lived in. I thought maybe we were just close to what they were feeding on.

"If they come," my father said in a quiet, even voice, "freeze, aim, and fire. That will save you. Nothing else will. Freeze, aim, and fire. Keep your eyes open and stay calm."

I replayed the words in my mind as we went up the switchbacks. No doubt Dad wanted us to replay them. I could see that Aura was still leaking tears and smearing and streaking her face with dirt like a little kid. She was too wrapped up in her own misery and fear to be of much use.

We got almost to the top before anything happened. We were beginning to relax, I think. I hadn't seen a dog for a while. Then, from the front of our line, we heard three shots.

We all froze, most of us unable to see what had happened.

"Keep moving," my father called. "It's all right. It was just one dog getting too close."

"Are you okay?" I called.

"Yes," he said. "Just come on and keep your eyes open."

One by one, we came abreast of the dog that had been shot and walked past it. It was a bigger, grayer animal than the one I had seen. There was a beauty to it. It looked like pictures I had seen of wolves. It was wedged against a hanging boulder just a few steps up the steep canyon wall from us.

It moved.

I saw its bloody wounds as it twisted. I bit my tongue as the pain I knew it must feel became my pain. What to do? Keep walking? I couldn't. One more step and I would fall and lie in the dirt, helpless against the pain. Or I might fall into the canyon.

"It's still alive," Joanne said behind me. "It's moving."

Its forefeet were making little running motions, its claws scraping against the rock.

I thought I would throw up. My belly hurt more and more until I felt skewered through the middle. I leaned on my bike with my left arm. With my right hand, I drew the Smith & Wesson, aimed, and shot the beautiful dog through its head.

I felt the impact of the bullet as a hard, solid blow—something beyond pain. Then I felt the dog die. I saw it jerk, shudder, stretch its body long, then freeze. I saw it die. I felt it die. It went out like a match in a sudden vanishing of pain. Its life flared up, then went out. I went a little numb. Without the bike, I would have collapsed.

People had crowded close before and behind me. I heard them before I could see them clearly.

"It's dead," I heard Joanne say. "Poor thing."

"What?" my father demanded. "Another one?"

I managed to focus on him. He must have skirted close to the cliff-edge of the road to have gotten all the way back to us. And he must have run.

"The same one," I said, managing to straighten up. "It wasn't dead. We saw it moving."

"I put three bullets into it," he said.

"It was moving, Reverend Olamina," Joanne insisted. "It was suffering. If Lauren hadn't shot it, someone else would have had to."

Dad sighed. "Well, it isn't suffering now. Let's get out of here." Then he seemed to realize what Joanne had said. He looked at me. "Are you all right?"

I nodded. I don't know how I looked. No one was reacting to me as though I looked odd, so I must not have shown much of what I had gone through. I think only Harry Balter, Curtis Talcott, and Joanne had seen me shoot the dog. I looked at them and Curtis grinned at me. He leaned against his bike and in a slow, lazy motion, he drew an imaginary gun, took careful aim at the dead dog, and fired an imaginary shot.

"Pow," he said. "Just like she does stuff like that every day. Pow!"

"Let's go," my father said.

We began walking up the path again. We left the canyon and made our way down to the street. There were no more dogs.

I walked, then rode in a daze, still not quite free of the dog I had killed. I had felt it die, and yet I had not died. I had felt its pain as though it were a human being. I had felt its life flare and go out, and I was still alive.

Pow.

5

□ □ □

Belief
Initiates and guides action—
Or it does nothing.

EARTHSEED: THE BOOKS OF THE LIVING

SUNDAY, MARCH 2, 2025

It's raining.

We heard last night on the radio that there was a storm sweeping in from the Pacific, but most people didn't believe it. "We'll have wind," Cory said. "Wind and maybe a few drops of rain, or maybe just a little cool weather. That would be welcome. It's all we'll get."

That's all there has been for six years. I can remember the rain six years ago, water swirling around the back porch, not high enough to come into the house, but high enough to attract my brothers who wanted to play in it. Cory, forever worried about infection, wouldn't let them. She said they'd be splashing around in a soup of all the waste-water germs we'd been watering our gardens with for years. Maybe she was right, but kids all over the neighborhood covered themselves with mud and earthworms that day, and nothing terrible happened to them.

But that storm was almost tropical—a quick, hard, warm, September rain, the edge of a hurricane that hit Mexico's Pacific coast. This is a colder, winter storm. It began this morning as people were coming to church.

In the choir we sang rousing old hymns accompanied by Cory's piano playing and lightning and thunder from outside. It was wonderful. Some people missed part of the sermon, though, because they went home to put out all the barrels, buckets, tubs, and pots they could find to catch the free water. Other went home to put pots and buckets inside where there were leaks in the roof.

I can't remember when any of us have had a roof repaired by a professional. We all have Spanish tile roofs, and that's good. A tile roof is, I suspect, more secure and lasting than wood or asphalt shingles. But time, wind, and earthquakes have taken a toll. Tree limbs have done some damage, too. Yet no one has extra money for anything as nonessential as roof repair. At best, some of the neighborhood men go up with whatever materials they can scavenge and create makeshift patches. No one's even done that for a while. If it only rains once every six or seven years, why bother?

Our roof is all right so far, and the barrels and things we put out after services this morning are full or filling. Good, clean, free water from the sky. If only it came more often.

MONDAY, MARCH 3, 2025

Still raining.

No thunder today, though there was some last night. Steady drizzle, and occasional, heavy showers all day. All day. So different and beautiful. I've never felt so overwhelmed by water. I went out and walked in the rain until I was soaked. Cory didn't want me to, but I did it anyway. It was so wonderful. How can she not understand that? It was so incredible and wonderful.

TUESDAY, MARCH 4, 2025

Amy Dunn is dead.

Three years old, unloved, and dead. That doesn't seem reasonable or even possible. She could read simple words and count to thirty. I taught her. She so much loved getting attention that she stuck to me during school hours and drove me crazy. Didn't want me to go to the bathroom without her.

Dead.

I had gotten to like her, even though she was a pest.

Today I walked her home after class. I had gotten into the habit of walking her home because the Dunns wouldn't send anyone for her.

"She knows the way," Christmas said. "Just send her over. She'll get here all right."

I didn't doubt that she could have. She could look across the street, and across the center island, and see her house from ours, but Amy had a tendency to wander. Sent home alone, she might get there or she might wind up in the Montoya garden, grazing, or in the Moss rabbit house, trying to let the rabbits out. So I walked her across, glad for an excuse to get out in the rain again. Amy loved it, too, and we lingered for a moment under the big avocado tree on the island. There was a navel orange tree at the back end of the island, and I picked a pair of ripe oranges—one for Amy and one for me. I peeled both of them, and we ate them while the rain plastered Amy's scant colorless hair against her head and made her look bald.

I took her to her door and left her in the care of her mother.

"You didn't have to get her so wet," Tracy complained.

"Might as well enjoy the rain while it lasts," I said, and I left them.

I saw Tracy take Amy into the house and shut the door. Yet somehow Amy wound up outside again, wound up near the front gate, just opposite the Garfield/Balter/Dory house. Jay Garfield found her there when he came out to investigate what he thought was another bundle that someone had thrown over the gate. People toss us things sometimes—gifts of envy and hate: A maggoty, dead animal, a bag of shit, even an occasional severed human limb or a dead child. Dead adults have been left lying just beyond our wall. But these were all outsiders. Amy was one of us.

Someone shot Amy right through the metal gate. It had to be an accidental hit because you can't see through our gate from the outside. The shooter either fired at someone who was in front of the gate or fired at the gate itself, at the neighborhood, at us and our supposed wealth and privilege. Most bullets wouldn't have gotten through the gate. It's supposed to be bulletproof. But it's been penetrated a couple of times before, high up, near the top. Now we have six new bullet holes in the lower portion—six holes and a seventh dent, a long, smooth gauge where a bullet had glanced off without breaking through.

We hear so much gunfire, day and night, single shots and odd bursts of automatic weapons fire, even occasional blasts from heavy artillery or explosions from grenades or bigger bombs. We worry most about those last things, but they're rare. It's harder to steal big weapons, and not many people around here can afford to buy the illegal ones—or that's what Dad says. The thing is, we hear gunfire so much that we don't hear it. A couple of the Balter kids said they heard shooting, but as usual, they paid no attention to it. It was outside, beyond the wall, after all. Most of us heard nothing except the rain.

Amy was going to turn four in a couple of weeks. I had planned to give her a little party with my kindergartners.

God, I hate this place.

I mean, I love it. It's home. These are my people. But I hate it. It's like an island surrounded by sharks—except that sharks don't bother you unless you go in the water. But our land sharks are on their way in. It's just a matter of how long it takes for them to get hungry enough.

WEDNESDAY, MARCH 5, 2025

I walked in the rain again this morning. It was cold, but good. Amy has already been cremated. I wonder if her mother is relieved. She doesn't look relieved. She never liked Amy, but now she cries. I don't think she's faking. The family has spent money it could not afford to get the police involved to try to find the killer. I suspect that the only good this will do will be to chase away the people who live on the sidewalks and streets nearest to our wall. Is that good? The street poor will be back, and they won't love us for siccing the cops on them. It's illegal to camp out on the street the way they do—the way they must—so the cops knock them around, rob them if they have anything worth stealing, then order them away or jail them. The miserable will be made even more miserable. None of that can help Amy. I suppose, though, that it will make the Dunns feel better about the way they treated her.

On Saturday, Dad will preach Amy's funeral. I wish I didn't have to be there. Funerals have never bothered me before, but this one does.

"You cared about Amy," Joanne Garfield said to me when I complained to her. We had lunch together today. We ate in my bedroom because it's still raining off and on, and the rest of the house was full of all the kids who hadn't gone home to eat lunch. But my room is still mine. It's the one place in the world where I can go and not be followed by anyone I don't invite in. I'm the only person I know who has a bedroom to herself. These days, even Dad and Cory knock before they open my door. That's one of the best things about being the only daughter in the family. I have to kick my brothers out of here all the time, but at least I can kick them out. Joanne is an only child, but she shares a room with three younger girl cousins—whiny Lisa, always demanding and complaining; smart, giggly Robin with her near-genius I.Q.; and invisible Jessica who whispers and stares at her feet and cries if you give her a dirty look. All three are Balters— Harry's sisters and the children of Joanne's mother's sister. The two adult sisters, their husbands, their eight children, and their parents Mr. and Mrs. Dory are all squeezed into one five-bedroom house. It isn't the most crowded house in the neighborhood, but I'm glad I don't have to live like that.

"Almost no one cared about Amy," Joanne said. "But you did."

"After the fire, I did," I said. "I got scared for her then. Before that, I ignored her like everyone else."

"So now you're feeling guilty?"

"No."

"Yes, you are."

I looked at her, surprised. "I mean it. No. I hate that she's dead, and I miss her, but I didn't cause her death. I just can't deny what all this says about us."

"What?"

I felt on the verge of talking to her about things I hadn't talked about before. I'd written about them. Sometimes I write to keep from going crazy. There's a world of things I don't feel free to talk to anyone about.

But Joanne is a friend. She knows me better than most people, and she has a brain. Why not talk to her? Sooner or later, I have to talk to someone.

"What's wrong?" she asked. She had opened a plastic container of bean salad. Now she put it down on my night table.

"Don't you ever wonder if maybe Amy and Mrs. Sims are the lucky ones?" I asked. "I mean, don't you ever wonder what's going to happen to the rest of us?"

There was a clap of dull, muffled thunder, and a sudden heavy shower. Radio weather reports say today's rain will be the last of the four-day series of storms. I hope not.

"Sure I think about it," Joanne said. "With people shooting little kids, how can I not think about it?"

"People have been killing little kids since there've been people," I said.

"Not in here, they haven't. Not until now."

"Yes, that's it, isn't it? We got a wake-up call. Another one."

"What are you talking about?"

"Amy was the first of us to be killed like that. She won't be the last."

OCTAVIA E. BUTLER

Joanne sighed, and there was a little shudder in the sigh. "So you think so, too."

"I do. But I didn't know you thought about it at all."

"Rape, robbery, and now murder. Of course I think about it. Everyone thinks about it. Everyone worries. I wish I could get out of here."

"Where would you go?"

"That's it, isn't it? There's nowhere to go."

"There might be."

"Not if you don't have money. Not if all you know how to do is take care of babies and cook."

I shook my head. "You know much more than that."

"Maybe, but none of it matters. I won't be able to afford college. I won't be able to get a job or move out of my parents' house because no job I could get would support me and there are no safe places to move. Hell, my parents are still living with their parents."

"I know," I said. "And as bad as that is, there's more."

"Who needs more? That's enough!" She began to eat the bean salad. It looked good, but I thought I might be about to ruin it for her.

"There's cholera spreading in southern Mississippi and Louisiana," I said. "I heard about it on the radio yesterday. There are too many poor people—illiterate, jobless, homeless, without decent sanitation or clean water. They have plenty of water down there, but a lot of it is polluted. And you know that drug that makes people want to set fires?"

She nodded, chewing.

"It's spreading again. It was on the east coast. Now it's in Chicago. The reports say that it makes watching a fire better than sex. I don't know whether the reporters are condemning it or advertising it." I drew a deep breath. "Tornadoes are smashing hell out of Alabama, Kentucky, Tennessee, and two or three other states. Three hundred people dead so far. And there's a blizzard freezing the northern midwest, killing even more people. In New York and New Jersey, a measles epidemic is killing people. Measles!"

"I heard about the measles," Joanne said. "Strange. Even if people can't afford immunizations, measles shouldn't kill."

"Those people are half dead already," I told her. "They've come through the winter cold, hungry, already sick with other diseases. And, no, of course they can't afford immunizations. We're lucky our parents found the money to pay for all our immunizations. If we have kids, I don't see how we'll be able to do even that for them."

"I know, I know." She sounded almost bored. "Things are bad. My mother is hoping this new guy, President Donner, will start to get us back to normal."

"Normal," I muttered. "I wonder what that is. Do you agree with your mother?"

"No. Donner hasn't got a chance. I think he would fix things if he could, but Harry says his ideas are scary. Harry says he'll set the country back a hundred years."

"My father says something like that. I'm surprised that Harry agrees."

"He would. His own father thinks Donner is God. Harry wouldn't agree with him on anything."

I laughed, distracted, thinking about Harry's battles with his father. Neighborhood fireworks—plenty of flash, but no real fire.

"Why do you want to talk about this stuff?" Joanne asked, bringing me back to the real fire. "We can't do anything about it."

"We have to."

"Have to what? We're fifteen! What can we do?"

"We can get ready. That's what we've got to do now. Get ready for what's going to happen, get ready to survive it, get ready to make a life afterward. Get focused on arranging to survive so that we can do more than just get batted around by crazy people, desperate people, thugs, and leaders who don't know what they're doing!"

She just stared at me. "I don't know what you're talking about."

I was rolling—too fast, maybe. "I'm talking about this place, Jo, this cul-de-sac with a wall around it. I'm talking about the day a big gang of those hungry, desperate, crazy people outside decide to come in. I'm talking about what we've got to do before that happens so that we can survive and rebuild—or at least survive and escape to be something other than beggars."

"Someone's going to just smash in our wall and come in?"

"More likely blast it down, or blast the gate open. It's going to happen some day. You know that as well as I do."

"Oh, no I don't," she protested. She sat up straight, almost stiff, her lunch forgotten for the moment. I bit into a piece of acorn bread that was full of dried fruit and nuts. It's a favorite of mine, but I managed to chew and swallow without tasting it.

"Jo, we're in for trouble. You've already admitted that."

"Sure," she said. "More shootings, more break-ins. That's what I meant."

"And that's what will happen for a while. I wish I could guess how long. We'll be hit and hit and hit, then the big hit will come. And if we're not ready for it, it will be like Jericho."

She held herself rigid, rejecting. "You don't know that! You can't read the future. No one can."

"You can," I said, "if you want to. It's scary, but once you get past the fear, it's easy. In L.A. some walled communities bigger and stronger than this one just aren't there anymore. Nothing left but ruins, rats, and squatters. What happened to them can happen to us. We'll die in here unless we get busy now and work out ways to survive."

"If you think that, why don't you tell your parents? Warn them and see what they say."

"I intend to as soon as I think of a way to do it that will reach them. Besides . . . I think they already know. I think my father does, anyway. I think most of the adults know. They don't want to know, but they do."

"My mother could be right about Donner. He really could do some good."

"No. No, Donner's just a kind of human banister."

"A what?"

"I mean he's like . . . like a symbol of the past for us to hold on to as we're pushed into the future. He's nothing. No substance. But having him there, the latest in a two-and-a-half-century-long line of American Presidents, makes people feel that the country, the culture that they grew up with is still here—that we'll get through these bad times and back to normal."

"We could," she said. "We might. I think someday we will." No, she didn't. She was too bright to take anything but the most superficial comfort from her denial. But even superficial comfort is better than none, I guess. I tried another tactic.

"Did you ever read about bubonic plague in medieval Europe?" I asked.

She nodded. She reads a lot the way I do, reads all kinds of things. "A lot of the continent was depopulated," she said. "Some survivors thought the world was coming to an end."

"Yes, but once they realized it wasn't, they also realized there was a lot of vacant land available for the taking, and if they had a trade, they realized they could demand better pay for their work. A lot of things changed for the survivors."

"What's your point?"

"The changes." I thought for a moment. They were slow changes compared to anything that might happen here, but it took a plague to make some of the people realize that things *could* change."

"So?"

"Things are changing now, too. Our adults haven't been wiped out by a plague so they're still anchored in the past, waiting for the good old days to come back. But things have changed a lot, and they'll change more. Things are always changing. This is just one of the big jumps instead of the little step-by-step changes that are easier to take. People have changed the climate of the world. Now they're waiting for the old days to come back."

OCTAVIA E. BUTLER

"Your father says he doesn't believe people changed the climate in spite of what scientists say. He says only God could change the world in such an important way."

"Do you believe him?"

She opened her mouth, looked at me, then closed it again. After a while, she said, "I don't know."

"My father has his blind spots," I said. "He's the best person I know, but even he has blind spots."

"It doesn't make any difference," she said. "We can't make the climate change back, no matter why it changed in the first place. You and I can't. The neighborhood can't. We can't do anything."

I lost patience. "Then let's kill ourselves now and be done with it!"

She frowned, her round, too serious face almost angry. She tore bits of peel from a small navel orange. "What then?" she demanded. "What can we do?"

I put the last bite of my acorn bread down and went around her to my night table. I took several books from the deep bottom drawer and showed them to her. "This is what I've been doing—reading and studying these over the past few months. These books are old like all the books in this house. I've also been using Dad's computer when he lets me—to get new stuff."

Frowning, she looked them over. Three books on survival in the wilderness, three on guns and shooting, two each on handling medical emergencies, California native and naturalized plants and their uses, and basic living: log-cabin-building, livestock raising, plant cultivation, soap making—that kind of thing. Joanne caught on at once.

"What are you doing?" she asked. "Trying to learn to live off the land?"

"I'm trying to learn whatever I can that might help me survive out there. I think we should all study books like these. I think we should bury money and other necessities in the ground where thieves won't find them. I think we should make emergency packs—grab and run packs—in case we have to get out of here in a hurry. Money, food, clothing, matches, a blanket. . . . I think we should fix places outside where we can meet in case we get separated. Hell, I think a lot of things. And I know—I know!—that no matter how many things I think of, they won't be enough. Every time I go outside, I try to imagine what it might be like to live out there without walls, and I realize I don't know anything."

"Then why—"

"I intend to survive."

She just stared.

"I mean to learn everything I can while I can," I said. "If I find myself outside, maybe what I've learned will help me live long enough to learn more."

She gave me a nervous smile. "You've been reading too many adventure stories," she said.

I frowned. How could I reach her? "This isn't a joke, Jo."

"What is it then?" She ate the last section of her orange. "What do you want me to say?"

"I want you to be serious. I realize I don't know very much. None of us knows very much. But we can all learn more. Then we can teach one another. We can stop denying reality or hoping it will go away by magic."

"That's not what I'm doing."

I looked out for a moment at the rain, calming myself.

"Okay. Okay, what are you doing?"

She looked uncomfortable. "I'm still not sure we can really do anything."

"Jo!"

"Tell me what I can do that won't get me in trouble or make everyone think I'm crazy. Just tell me something."

At last. "Have you read all your family's books?"

"Some of them. Not all. They aren't all worth reading. Books aren't going to save us."

"Nothing is going to save us. If we don't save ourselves, we're dead.

Now use your imagination. Is there anything on your family book-shelves that might help you if you were stuck outside?"

"No."

"You answer too fast. Go home and look again. And like I said, use your imagination. Any kind of survival information from ency-clopedias, biographies, anything that helps you learn to live off the land and defend ourselves. Even some fiction might be useful."

She gave me a sidelong glance. "I'll bet," she said.

"Jo, if you never need this information, it won't do you any harm. You'll just know a little more than you did before. So what? By the way, do you take notes when you read?"

Guarded look. "Sometimes."

"Read this." I handed her one of the plant books. This one was about California Indians, the plants they used, and how they used them—an interesting, entertaining little book. She would be sur-prised. There was nothing in it to scare her or threaten her or push her. I thought I had already done enough of that.

"Take notes," I told her. "You'll remember better if you do."

"I still don't believe you," she said. "Things don't have to be as bad as you say they are."

I put the book into her hands. "Hang on to your notes," I said. "Pay special attention to the plants that grow between here and the coast and between here and Oregon along the coast. I've marked them."

"I said I don't believe you."

"I don't care."

She looked down at the book, ran her hands over the black cloth-and-cardboard binding. "So we learn to eat grass and live in the bushes," she muttered.

"We learn to survive," I said. "It's a good book. Take care of it. You know how my father is about his books."

The rain stopped. My windows are on the north side of the house, and I can see the clouds breaking up. They're being blown over the mountains toward the desert. Surprising how fast they can move. The wind is strong and cold now. It might cost us a few trees.

I wonder how many years it will be before we see rain again.

6

□ □ □

Drowning people
Sometimes die
Fighting their rescuers.

EARTHSEED: THE BOOKS OF THE LIVING
SATURDAY, MARCH 8, 2025

Joanne told.

She told her mother who told her father who told my father who had one of those serious talks with me.

Damn her. *Damn her!*

I saw her today at the service we had for Amy and yesterday at school. She didn't say a word about what she had done. It turns out she told her mother on Thursday. Maybe it was supposed to be a secret between them or something. But, oh, Phillida Garfield was so concerned for me, so worried. And she didn't like my scaring Joanne. Was Joanne scared? Not scared enough to use her brain, it seems. Joanne always seemed so sensible. Did she think getting me into trouble would make the danger go away? No, that's not it. This is just more denial: A dumb little game of "If we don't talk about bad things, maybe they won't happen." Idiot! I'll never be able to tell her anything important again.

What if I'd been more open? What if I'd talked religion with her? I'd wanted to. How will I ever be able to talk to anyone about that?

What I did say worked its way back to me tonight. Mr. Garfield talked to Dad after the funeral. It was like the whispering game that little kids play. The message went all the way from, "We're in danger here and we're going to have to work hard to save ourselves,"

71

to "Lauren is talking about running away because she's afraid that outsiders are going to riot and tear down the walls and kill us all."

Well, I had said *some* of that, and Joanne had made it clear that she didn't agree with me. But I hadn't just let the bad predictions stand alone: "We're going to die, boo-hoo." What would be the point of that? Still, only the negative stuff came home to me.

"Lauren, what did you say to Joanne?" my father demanded. He came to my room after dinner when he should have been doing his final work on tomorrow's sermon. He sat down on my one chair and stared at me in a way that meant, "Where is your mind, girl? What's the matter with you?" That look plus Joanne's name told me what had happened, what this was about. My friend Joanne. *Damn her!*

I sat on my bed and looked back at him. "I told her we were in for some bad, dangerous times," I said. "I warned her we ought to learn what we could now so we could survive."

That was when he told me how upset Joanne's mother was, how upset Joanne was, and how they both thought I needed to "talk to someone," because I thought our world was coming to an end.

"Do you think our world is coming to an end?" Dad asked, and with no warning at all, I almost started crying. I had all I could do to hold it back. What I thought was, "No, I think *your* world is coming to an end, and maybe you with it." That was terrible. I hadn't thought about it in such a personal way before. I turned and looked out a window until I felt calmer. When I faced him again, I said, "Yes. Don't you?"

He frowned. I don't think he expected me to say that. "You're fifteen," he said. "You don't really understand what's going on here. The problems we have now have been building since long before you were born."

"I know."

He was still frowning. I wondered what he wanted me to say. "What were you doing, then?" he asked. "Why did you say those things to Joanne?"

I decided to go on telling the truth for as long as I could. I hate to lie to him. "What I said was true," I insisted.

"You don't have to say everything you think you know," he said. "Haven't you figured that out yet?"

"Joanne and I were friends," I said. "I thought I could talk to her."

He shook his head. "These things frighten people. It's best not to talk about them."

"But, Dad, that's like . . . like ignoring a fire in the living room because we're all in the kitchen, and, besides, house fires are too scary to talk about."

"Don't warn Joanne or any of your other friends," he said. "Not now. I know you think you're right, but you're not doing anyone any good. You're just panicking people."

I managed to suppress a surge of anger by shifting the subject a little. Sometimes the way to move Dad is to go at him from several directions.

"Did Mr. Garfield give you back your book?" I asked.

"What book?"

"I loaned Joanne a book about California plants and the ways Indians used them. It was one of your books. I'm sorry I loaned it to her. It's so neutral, I didn't think it could cause trouble. But I guess it has."

He looked startled, then he almost smiled. "Yes, I will have to have that one back, all right. You wouldn't have the acorn bread you like so much without that one—not to mention a few other things we take for granted."

"Acorn bread . . . ?"

He nodded. "Most of the people in this country don't eat acorns, you know. They have no tradition of eating them, they don't know how to prepare them, and for some reason, they find the idea of eating them disgusting. Some of our neighbors wanted to cut down all our big live oak trees and plant something useful. You wouldn't believe the time I had changing their minds."

"What did people eat before?"

"Bread made of wheat and other grains—corn, rye, oats . . . things like that."

"Too expensive!"

"Didn't use to be. You get that book back from Joanne." He drew a deep breath. "Now, let's get off the side track and back onto the main track. What were you planning? Did you try to talk Joanne into running away?"

Then I sighed. "Of course not."

"Her father says you did."

"He's wrong. This was about staying alive, learning to live outside so that we'd be able to if we ever had to."

He watched me as though he could read the truth in my mind. When I was little, I used to think he could. "All right," he said. "You may have meant well, but no more scare talk."

"It wasn't scare talk. We do need to learn what we can while there's time."

"That's not up to you, Lauren. You don't make decisions for this community."

Oh hell. If I could just find a balance between holding back too much and pushing, poaching. " Yes, sir."

He leaned back and looked at me. "Tell me exactly what you told Joanne. All of it."

I told him. I was careful to keep my voice flat and passionless, but I didn't leave anything out. I wanted him to know, to understand what I believed. The nonreligious part of it, anyway. When I finished, I stopped and waited. He seemed to expect me to say more. He just sat there for a while and stared at me. I couldn't tell what he felt. Other people never could if he didn't want them to, but I've been able to most of the time. Now I felt shut out, and there was nothing I could do about it. I waited.

At last he let his breath out as though he had been holding it. "Don't talk about this anymore," he said in a voice that didn't invite argument.

I looked back at him, not wanting to give a promise that would be a lie.

"Lauren."

"Dad."

"I want your promise that you won't talk about this anymore."

What to say? I wouldn't promise. I couldn't. "We could make earthquake packs," I suggested. "Emergency kits that we can grab in case we have to get out of the house fast. If we call them earthquake packs, the idea might not bother people so much. People are used to worrying about earthquakes." All this came out in a rush.

"I want your promise, daughter."

I slumped. "Why? You know I'm right. Even Mrs. Garfield must know it. So why?"

I thought he would yell at me or punish me. His voice had had that warning edge to it that my brothers and I had come to call the rattle—as in a rattlesnake's warning sound. If you pushed him past the rattle, you were in trouble. If he called you "son" or "daughter" you were close to trouble.

"Why?" I insisted.

"Because you don't have any idea what you're doing," he said. He frowned and rubbed his forehead. When he spoke again, the edge went out of his voice. "It's better to teach people than to scare them, Lauren. If you scare them and nothing happens, they lose their fear, and you lose some of your authority with them. It's harder to scare them a second time, harder to teach them, harder to win back their trust. Best to begin by teaching." His mouth crooked into a little smile. "It's interesting that you chose to begin your efforts with the book you lent to Joanne. Did you ever think of teaching from that book?"

"Teaching . . . my kindergartners?"

"Why not. Get them started on the right foot. You could even put together a class for older kids and adults. Something like Mr. Ibarra's wood carving class, Mrs. Balter's needlework classes, and young Robert Hsu's astronomy lectures. People are bored. They wouldn't mind another informal class now that they've lost the Yannis television. If you can think of ways to entertain them and teach them at the same time, you'll get your information out. And all without making anyone look down."

"Look down . . . ?"

"Into the abyss, daughter." But I wasn't in trouble anymore. Not at the moment. "You've just noticed the abyss," he continued. "The adults in this community have been balancing at the edge of it for more years than you've been alive."

I got up, went over to him and took his hand. "It's getting worse, Dad."

"I know."

"Maybe it's time to look down. Time to look for some hand and foot holds before we just get pushed in."

"That's why we have target practice every week and Lazor wire and our emergency bell. Your idea for emergency packs is a good one. Some people already have them. For earthquakes. Some will assemble them if I suggest it. And, of course, some won't do anything at all. There are always people who won't do anything."

"Will you suggest it?"

"Yes. At the next neighborhood association meeting."

"What else can we do? None of this is fast enough."

"It will have to be." He stood up, a tall, broad wall of a man. "Why don't you ask around, see if anyone in the neighborhood knows anything about martial arts. You need more than a book or two to learn good dependable unarmed combat."

I blinked. "Okay."

"Check with old Mr. Hsu and Mr. and Mrs. Montoya."

"Mr. *and* Mrs.?"

"I think so. Talk to them about classes, not about Armageddon."

I looked up at him, and he looked more like a wall than ever, standing and waiting. And he had offered me a lot—all I would get, I suspected. I sighed. "Okay, Dad, I promise. I'll try not to scare anyone else. I just hope things hold together long enough for us to do it your way."

And he echoed my sigh. "At last. Good. Now come out back with me. There are some important things buried in the yard in sealed containers. It's time for you to know where they are—just in case."

SUNDAY, MARCH 9, 2025

Today, Dad preached from Genesis six, Noah and the ark: "And God saw that the wickedness of man was great in the earth, and that every imagination of the thoughts and of his heart was only evil continually. And it repented the Lord that he had made man on the earth, and it grieved him at his heart. And the Lord said, I will destroy man whom I have created from the face of the earth; both man, and beast, and the creeping thing and the fowls of the air; for it repenteth me that I have made them. But Noah found grace in the eyes of the Lord."

And then, of course, later God says to Noah, "Make thee an ark of gopher wood; rooms shalt thou make in the ark, and shalt pitch it within and without with pitch."

Dad focused on the two-part nature of this situation. God decides to destroy everything except Noah, his family, and some animals. But if Noah is going to be saved, he has plenty of hard work to do.

Joanne came to me after church and said she was sorry for all the craziness.

"Okay," I said.

"Still friends?" she asked.

And I hedged: "Not enemies, anyway. Get my father's book back to me. He wants it."

"My mother took it. I didn't know she'd get so upset."

"It isn't hers. Get it back to me. Or have your dad give it to mine. I don't care. But he wants his book."

"All right."

I watched her leave the house. She looks so trustworthy—tall and straight and serious and intelligent—I still feel inclined to trust her.

But I can't. I don't. She has no idea how much she could have hurt me if I had given her just a few more words to use against me. I don't think I'll ever trust her again, and I hate that. She was my best friend. Now she isn't.

WEDNESDAY, MARCH 12, 2025

Garden thieves got in last night. They stripped citrus trees of fruit in the Hsu yard and the Talcott yard. In the process, they trampled what was left of winter gardens and much of the spring planting.

Dad says we have to set up a regular watch. He tried to call a neighborhood association meeting for tonight, but it's a work night for some people, including Gary Hsu who sleeps over at his job whenever he has to report in person. We're supposed to get together for a meeting on Saturday. Meanwhile, Dad got Jay Garfield, Wyatt and Kayla Talcott, Alex Montoya, and Edwin Dunn together to patrol the neighborhood in shifts in armed pairs. That meant that except for the Talcotts who are already a pair (and who are so angry about their garden that I pity any thief who gets in their way), the others have to find partners among the other adults of the neighborhood.

"Find someone you trust to protect your back," I heard Dad tell the little group. Each pair was to patrol for two hours from just before dark to just after dawn. The first patrol, walking through or looking into all the backyards, would get people used to the idea of watchers while they were still awake enough to understand.

"Make sure they see you if you get first watch," Dad said. "The sight of you will remind them that there will be watchers all through the night. We don't want any of them mistaking you for thieves."

Sensible. People go to bed soon after dark to save electricity, but between dinner and darkness they spend time on their porches or in their yards where it isn't so hot. Some listen to their radio on front or back porches. Now and then people get together to play music, sing, play board games, talk, or get out on the paved part of the street for volleyball, touch football, basketball, or tennis. People used to play baseball, but we just can't afford what that costs in windows. A few people just find a corner and read a book while there's still daylight. It's a good, comfortable, recreational time. What a pity to spoil it with reminders of reality. But it can't be helped.

"What will you do if you catch a thief?" Cory asked my father before he went out. He was on the second shift, and he and Cory were having a rare cup of coffee together in the kitchen while he waited. Coffee was for special occasions. I couldn't miss the good smell of it in my room where I lay awake.

I eavesdrop. I don't put drinking glasses to walls or crouch with my ear against doors, but I do often lie awake long after dark when we kids are all supposed to be asleep. The kitchen is across the hall from my room, the dining room is nearby at the end of the hall, and my parents' room is next door. The house is old and well insulated. If there's a shut door between me and the conversation, I can't hear much. But at night with all or most of the lights out, I can leave my door open a crack, and if other doors are also open, I can hear a lot. I learn a lot.

"We'll chase him off, I hope," Dad said. "We've agreed to that. We'll give him a good scare and let him know there are easier ways to get a dollar."

"A dollar . . . ?"

"Yes, indeed. Our thieves didn't steal all that food because they were hungry. They stripped those trees—took everything they could."

"I know," Cory said. "I took some lemons and grapefruits to both the Hsus and the Wyatts today and told them they could pick from our trees when they needed more. I took them some seed, too. They both had a lot of young plants trampled, but this early in the season, they should be able to repair the damage."

"Yes." My father paused. "But you see my point. People steal that way for money. They're not desperate. Just greedy and dangerous. We might be able to scare them into looking for easier pickings."

"But what if you can't?" Cory asked, almost whispering. Her voice fell so low that I was afraid I would miss something.

"If you can't, will you shoot them?"

"Yes," he said.

". . . yes?" she repeated in that same small voice. "Just . . . 'yes?'" She was like Joanne all over again—denial personified. What planet do people like that live on?

"Yes," my father said.

"Why!"

There was a long silence. When my father spoke again, his own voice had gone very soft. "Baby, if these people steal enough, they'll force us to spend more than we can afford on food—or go hungry. We live on the edge as it is. You know how hard things are."

"But . . . couldn't we just call the police?"

"For what? We can't afford their fees, and anyway, they're not interested until after a crime has been committed. Even then, if you call them, they won't show up for hours—maybe not for two or three days."

"I know."

"What are you saying then? You want the kids to go hungry? You want thieves coming into the house once they've stripped the gardens?"

"But they haven't done that."

"Of course they have. Mrs. Sims was only their latest victim."

"She lived alone. We always said she shouldn't do that."

"You want to trust them not to hurt you or the kids just because there are seven of us? Baby, we can't live by pretending this is still twenty or thirty years ago."

"But you could go to jail!" She was crying—not sobbing, but speaking with that voice-full-of-tears that she can manage sometimes.

"No," Dad said. "If we have to shoot someone, we're together in it. After we've shot him we carry him into the nearest house. It's still legal to shoot housebreakers. After that we do a little damage and get our stories straight."

OCTAVIA E. BUTLER

Long, long silence. "You could still get in trouble."

"I'll risk it."

Another long silence. "Thou shalt not kill," Cory whispered.

"Nehemiah four," Dad said. "Verse 14."

There was nothing more. A few minutes later, I heard Dad leave. I waited until I heard Cory go to her room and shut the door. Then I got up, shut my door, moved my lamp so the light wouldn't show under the door, then turned it on and opened my grandmother's Bible. She had had a lot of Bibles and Dad had let me keep this one.

Nehemiah, chapter four, Verse 14: "And I looked and rose up and said unto the nobles, and to the rulers, and to the rest of the people, be not afraid of them: remember the Lord which is great and terrible, and fight for your brethren, your sons, and your daughters, your wives and your houses."

Interesting. Interesting that Dad had that verse ready, and that Cory recognized it. Maybe they've had this conversation before.

SATURDAY, MARCH 15, 2025

It's official.

Now we have a regular neighborhood watch—a roster of people from every household who are over eighteen, good with guns—their own and others'—and considered responsible by my father and by the people who have already been patrolling the neighborhood. Since none of the watchers have ever been cops or security guards, they'll go on working in pairs, watching out for each other as well as for the neighborhood. They'll use whistles to call for help if they need it. Also, they'll meet once a week to read, discuss, and practice martial arts and shoot-out techniques. The Montoyas will give their martial arts classes, all right, but not at my suggestion. Old Mr. Hsu is having back problems, and he won't be teaching anything for a while, but the Montoyas seem to be enough. I plan to sit in on the classes as often as I can stand to share everyone's practice pains.

Dad has collected all his books from me this morning. All I have left are my notes. I don't mind. Thanks to the garden thieves, people are preparing themselves for the worst. I feel almost grateful to the thieves.

They haven't come back, by the way—our thieves. When they do, we should be able to give them something they don't expect.

SATURDAY, MARCH 29, 2025

Our thieves paid us another visit last night.

Maybe they weren't the same ones, but their intentions were the same: To take away what someone else has sweated to grow and very much needs.

This time they were after Richard Moss's rabbits. Those rabbits are the neighborhood's only livestock except for some chickens the Cruz and Montoya families tried to raise a few years ago. Those were stolen as soon as they were old enough to make noise and let outsiders know they were there. The Moss rabbits have been our secret until this year when Richard Moss insisted on selling meat and whatever his wives could make from raw or tanned rabbit hides out beyond the wall. The Mosses had been selling to us all along, of course, meat, hides, fertilizer, everything except live rabbits. Those he hoarded as breeding stock. But now, stubborn, arrogant, and greedy, he had decided he could earn more if he peddled his merchandise outside. So, now the word is out on the street about the damned rabbits, and last night someone came to get them.

The Moss rabbit house is a converted three-car garage added to the property in the 1980s according to Dad. It's hard to believe any household once had three cars, and gas fueled cars at that. But I remember the old garage before Richard Moss converted it. It was huge with three black oil spots on the floor where three cars had once been housed. Richard Moss repaired the walls and roof, put in windows for cross ventilation, and in general, made the place almost

OCTAVIA E. BUTLER

fit for people to live in. In fact, it's much better than what a lot of people live in now on the outside. He built rows and tiers of cages—hutches—and put in more electric lights and ceiling fans. The fans can be made to work on kid power. He's hooked them up to an old bicycle frame, and every Moss kid who's old enough to manage the pedals sooner or later gets drafted into powering the fans. The Moss kids hate it, but they know what they'll get if they don't do it.

I don't know how many rabbits the Mosses have now, but it seems they're always killing and skinning and doing disgusting things to pelts. Even a little monopoly is worth a lot of trouble.

The two thieves had managed to stuff 13 rabbits into canvas sacks by the time our watchers spotted them. The watchers were Alejandro Montoya and Julia Lincoln, one of Shani Yannis's sisters. Mrs. Montoya has two kids sick with the flu so she's off the watch roster for a while.

Mrs. Lincoln and Mr. Montoya followed the plan that the group of watchers had put together at their meetings. Without a word of command or warning, they fired their guns into the air two or three times each, at the same time, blowing their whistles full blast. They kept to cover, but inside the Moss house, someone woke up and turned on the rabbit house lights. That could have been a lethal mistake for the watchers, but they were hidden behind pomegranate bushes.

The two thieves ran like rabbits.

Abandoning sacks, rabbits, pry bars, a long coil of rope, wire cutters, and even an excellent long aluminum ladder, they scrambled up that ladder and over the wall in seconds. Our wall is three meters high and topped off with pieces of broken glass as well as the usual barbed wire and the all but invisible Lazor wire. All the wire had been cut in spite of our efforts. What a pity we couldn't afford to electrify it or set other traps. But at least the glass—the oldest, simplest of our tricks—had gotten one of them. We found a broad stream of dried blood down the inside of the wall this morning.

We also found a Glock 19 pistol where one of the thieves had dropped it. Mrs. Lincoln and Mr. Montoya could have been shot. If the thieves hadn't been scared out of their minds, there could have been a gun battle. Someone in the Moss house or a neighboring house could have been hurt or killed.

Cory went after Dad about that once they were alone in the kitchen tonight.

"I know," Dad said. He sounded tired and miserable. "Don't think we haven't thought about those things. That's why we want to scare the thieves away. Even shooting into the air isn't safe. Nothing's safe."

"They ran away this time, but they won't always run."

"I know."

"So what, then? You protect rabbits or oranges, and maybe get a child killed?"

Silence.

"*We can't live this way!*" Cory shouted. I jumped. I've never heard her sound like that before.

"We do live this way," Dad said. There was no anger in his voice, no emotional response at all to her shouting. There was nothing. Weariness. Sadness. I've never heard him sound so tired, so ... almost beaten. And yet he had won. His idea had beaten off a pair of armed thieves without our having to hurt anyone. If the thieves had hurt themselves, that was their problem.

Of course they would come back, or others would come. That would happen no matter what. And Cory was right. The next thieves might not lose their guns and run away. So what? Should we lie in our beds and let them take all we had and hope they were content with stripping our gardens? How long does a thief stay content? And what's it like to starve?

"We couldn't make it without you," Cory was saying. She wasn't shouting now. "That could have been you out there, facing criminals. Next time it might be you. You could be shot, protecting the neighbors' rabbits."

OCTAVIA E. BUTLER

"Did you notice," Dad said, "that every off-duty watcher answered the whistles last night? They came out to defend their community."

"I don't care about them! It's you I'm worried about!"

"No," he said. "We can't think that way anymore. Cory, there's nobody to help us but God and ourselves. I protect Moss's place in spite of what I think of him, and he protects mine, no matter what he thinks of me. We all look out for one another." He paused. "I've got plenty of insurance. You and the kids should be able to make it all right if—"

"No!" Cory said. "Do you think that's all it is? Money? Do you think—?"

"No, babe. No." Pause. "I know what it is to be left alone. This is no world to be alone in."

There was a long silence, and I didn't think they would say anymore. I lay on my bed, wondering if I should get up and shut my door so I could turn on my lamp and write. But there was a little more.

"What are we supposed to do if you die?" she demanded, and I think she was crying. "What do we do if they shoot you over some damn rabbits?"

"Live!" Dad said. "That's all anybody can do right now. Live. Hold out. Survive. I don't know whether good times are coming back again. But I know that won't matter if we don't survive these times."

That was the end of their talk. I lay in the dark for a long time, thinking about what they had said. Cory was right again. Dad might get hurt. He might get killed. I don't know how to think about that. I can write about it, but I don't feel it. On some deep level, I don't believe it. I guess I'm as good at denial as anyone.

So Cory is right, but it doesn't matter. And Dad is right, but he doesn't go far enough. God is Change, and in the end, God prevails. But God exists to be shaped. It isn't enough for us to just survive, limping along, playing business as usual while things get worse and worse. If that's the shape we give to God, then someday we must become too weak—too poor, too hungry, too sick—to defend ourselves. Then we'll be wiped out.

There has to be more that we can do, a better destiny that we can shape. Another place. Another way. Something!

7

□ □ □

We are all Godseed, but no more or less so than any
other aspect of the universe, Godseed is all there
is—all that Changes. Earthseed is all that spreads
Earthlife to new earths. The universe is Godseed. Only
we are Earthseed. And the Destiny of Earthseed is to
take root among the stars.

EARTHSEED: THE BOOKS OF THE LIVING
SATURDAY, APRIL 26, 2025

Sometimes naming a thing—giving it a name or discovering its
name—helps one to begin to understand it. Knowing the name of
a thing *and* knowing what that thing is for gives me even more of a
handle on it.

The particular God-is-Change belief system that seems right to
me will be called Earthseed. I've tried to name it before. Failing that,
I've tried to leave it unnamed. Neither effort has made me comfortable. Name plus purpose equals focus for me.

Well, today, I found the name, found it while I was weeding the
back garden and thinking about the way plants seed themselves,
windborne, animalborne, waterborne, far from their parent plants.
They have no ability at all to travel great distances under their own
power, and yet, they do travel. Even they don't have to just sit in one
place and wait to be wiped out. There are islands thousands of miles
from anywhere—the Hawaiian Islands, for example, and Easter
Island—where plants seeded themselves and grew long before any
humans arrived.

Earthseed.

I am Earthseed. Anyone can be. Someday, I think there will be a lot of us. And I think we'll have to seed ourselves farther and farther from this dying place.

I've never felt that I was making any of this up—not the name, Earthseed, not any of it. I mean, I've never felt that it was anything other than real: discovery rather than invention, exploration rather than creation. I wish I could believe it was all supernatural, and that I'm getting messages from God. But then, I don't believe in that kind of God. All I do is observe and take notes, trying to put things down in ways that are as powerful, as simple, and as direct as I feel them. I can never do that. I keep trying, but I can't. I'm not good enough as a writer or poet or whatever it is I need to be. I don't know what to do about that. It drives me frantic sometimes. I'm getting better, but so slowly.

The thing is, even with my writing problems, every time I understand a little more, I wonder why it's taken me so long—why there was ever a time when I didn't understand a thing so obvious and real and true.

Here's the only puzzle in it all, the only paradox, or bit of illogic or circular reasoning or whatever it should be called:

> *Why is the universe?*
> *To shape God.*
>
> *Why is God?*
> *To shape the universe.*

I can't get rid of it. I've tried to change it or dump it, but I can't. I *cannot.* It feels like the truest thing I've ever written. It's as mysterious and as obvious as any other explanation of God or the universe that I've ever read, except that to me the others feel inadequate, at best.

All the rest of Earthseed is explanation—what God is, what God

does, what we are, what we should do, what we can't help doing. . . .
Consider: Whether you're a human being, an insect, a microbe, or a
stone, this verse is true.

> *All that you touch,*
> *You Change.*

> *All that you Change,*
> *Changes you.*

> *The only lasting truth*
> *Is Change.*

> *God*
> *Is Change.*

I'm going to go through my old journals and gather the verses
I've written into one volume. I'll put them into one of the exercise
notebooks that Cory hands out to the older kids now that there are
so few computers in the neighborhood. I've written plenty of useless
stuff in those books, getting my high school work out of the way.
Now I'll put one to better use. Then, someday when people are able
to pay more attention to what I say than to how old I am, I'll use
these verses to pry them loose from the rotting past, and maybe push
them into saving themselves and building a future that makes sense.

That's if everything will just hold together for a few more years.

SATURDAY, JUNE 7, 2025

I've finally assembled a small survival pack for myself—a grab-
and-run pack. I've had to dig some things I need out of the garage
and the attic so that no one complains about my taking things they
need. I've collected a hatchet, for instance, and two small, light, all-

metal pots. There's plenty of stuff like that around because no one throws anything away that has any possibility of someday being useful or salable.

I packed my few hundred dollars in savings—almost a thousand. It *might* feed me for two weeks if I'm allowed to keep it, and if I'm very careful what I buy and where I buy it. I've kept up with prices, questioning Dad when he and the other neighborhood men do the essential shopping. Food prices are insane, always going up, never down. Everyone complains about them.

I found an old canteen and a plastic bottle both for water, and I resolved to keep them clean and full. I packed matches, a full change of clothing, including shoes in case I have to get up at night and run, comb, soap, toothbrush and toothpaste, tampons, toilet paper, bandages, pins, needles and thread, alcohol, aspirin, a couple of spoons and forks, a can opener, my pocket knife, packets of acorn flour, dried fruit, roasted nuts and edible seeds, dried milk, a little sugar and salt, my survival notes, several plastic storage bags, large and small, a lot of plantable raw seed, my journal, my Earth-seed notebook, and lengths of clothesline. I stowed all this in a pair of old pillowcases, one inside the other for strength. I rolled the pillowcases into a blanket pack and tied it with some of the clothesline so that I could grab it and run without losing things, but I made it easy to open at the top so that I could get my journal in and out, change the water to keep it fresh, and less often, change the food and check on the seed. The last thing I wanted to find out was that instead of carrying plantable seed or edible food, I had a load of bugs and worms.

I wish I could take a gun. I don't own one and Dad won't let me keep one of his in my room. I mean to try to grab one if trouble comes, but I may not be able to. It would be crazy to wind up outside with nothing but a knife and a scared look, but it could happen. Dad and Wyatt Talcott took us out for target practice today, and afterward I tried to talk Dad into letting me keep one of the guns in my room.

"No," he said, sitting down, tired and dusty, behind his desk in his cluttered office. "You don't have anywhere to keep it safe during the day, and the boys are always in and out of your room."

I hesitated, then told him about the emergency pack that I had put together.

He nodded. "I thought it was a good idea back when you first suggested it," he said. "But, think, Lauren. It would be like a gift to a burglar. Money, food, water, a gun. . . . Most burglars don't find what they want all bundled up and waiting for them. I think we'd better make it a little harder for any burglar who comes here to get hold of a gun."

"It will just be a rolled up blanket mixed in with some other rolled or folded bed clothes in my closet," I said. "No one will even notice it."

"No." He shook his head. "No, the guns stay where they are."

And that's that. I think he's more worried about the boys snooping around than about burglars. My brothers have been taught how to behave around guns all their lives, but Greg is only eight and Ben is nine. Dad just isn't ready to put temptation in their paths yet. Marcus at 11 is more trustworthy than a lot of adults, but Keith at almost 13 is a question mark. He wouldn't steal from Dad. He wouldn't dare. But he has stolen from me—only little things so far. He wants a gun, though, the way thirsty people want water. He wants to be all grown up—yesterday. So maybe Dad's right. I hate his decision, but maybe he's right.

"Where would you go?" I asked him, changing the subject. "If we were forced out of here, where would you take us?"

He blew out a breath, puffing up his cheeks for a second. "To the neighbors or to the college," he said. "The college has temporary emergency accommodations for employees who are burned or driven out of their homes."

"And then?"

"Rebuilding, fortifying, doing whatever we can do to live and be safe."

"Would you ever think about leaving here, heading north to where water isn't such a problem and food is cheaper?"

"No." He stared into space. "My job down here is as secure as a job can be. There are no jobs up there. Newcomers work for food if they work at all. Experience doesn't matter. Education doesn't matter. There are just too many desperate people. They work their lives away for a sack of beans and they live on the streets."

"I heard it was easier up there," I said. "Oregon, Washington, Canada."

"Closed," he said. "You've got to sneak into Oregon if you get in at all. Even harder to sneak into Washington. People get shot every day trying to sneak into Canada. Nobody wants California trash."

"But people do leave. People are always moving north."

"They try. They're desperate and they have nothing to lose. But I do. This is my home. Beyond taxes, I don't owe a penny on it. You and your brothers have never known a hungry day here, and God willing, you never will."

In my Earthseed notebook, I've written,

> *A tree*
> *Cannot grow*
> *In its parents' shadows.*

Is it necessary to write things like that? Everyone knows them. What do they mean now, anyway? What does this one mean if you live in a cul-de-sac with a wall around it? What does it mean if you're damned lucky to live in a cul-de-sac with a wall around it?

MONDAY, JUNE 16, 2025

There was a long report on the radio today about the findings of the big Anglo-Japanese cosmological station on the moon. The station, with its vast array of telescopes and some of the most sensitive spectroscopic equipment ever made, has detected more planets orbiting nearby stars. That station has been detecting new worlds for a dozen years now, and there's even evidence that a few of the discovered

OCTAVIA E. BUTLER

worlds may be life-bearing. I've listened to and read every scrap of information I could find on this subject, and I've noticed that there's less and less argument against the likelihood that some of these worlds are alive. The idea is gaining scientific acceptance. Of course, no one has any idea whether the extrasolar life is anything more than a few trillion microbes. People speculate about intelligent life, and it's fun to think about, but no one is claiming to have found anyone to talk to out there. I don't care. Life alone is enough. I find it . . . more exciting and encouraging than I can explain, more important than I can explain. There *is* life out there. There are living worlds just a few light years away, and the United States is busy drawing back from even our nearby dead worlds, the moon and Mars. I understand why they are, but I wish they weren't.

I suspect that a living world might be easier for us to adapt to and live on without a long, expensive umbilical to Earth. *Easier* but not easy. Still, that's something, because I don't think there could be a multi-light-year umbilical. I think people who traveled to extrasolar worlds would be on their own—far from politicians and business people, failing economies and tortured ecologies—and far from help. Well out of the shadow of their parent world.

SATURDAY, JULY 19, 2025

Tomorrow, I'll be sixteen. Only sixteen. I feel older. I want to be older. I need to be older. I hate being a kid. Time drags!

Tracy Dunn has disappeared. She's been depressed since Amy was killed. When she talked at all, it was about dying and wanting to die and deserving to die. Everyone kept hoping she would get over her grief—or her guilt—and get on with her life. Maybe she couldn't. Dad talked with her several times, and I know he was worried about her. Her crazy family hasn't been any help. They treat her the way she treated Amy: They ignore her.

The rumor is that she went outside sometime yesterday. A group of Moss and Payne kids say they saw her go out of the gate just after they left school. No one has seen her since.

SUNDAY, JULY 20, 2025

Here's the birthday gift that came into my mind this morning as I woke up—just two lines:

> *The Destiny of Earthseed*
> *Is to take root among the stars.*

This is what I was reaching for a few days ago when the story of the new planets being discovered caught my attention. It's true, of course. It's obvious.

Right now, it's also impossible. The world is in horrible shape. Even rich countries aren't doing as well as history says rich countries used to do. President Donner isn't the only one breaking up and selling off science and space projects. No one is expanding the kind of exploration that doesn't earn an immediate profit, or at least promise big future profits. There's no mood now for doing anything that could be considered unnecessary or wasteful. And yet,

> *The Destiny of Earthseed*
> *Is to take root among the stars.*

I don't know how it will happen or when it will happen. There's so much to do before it can even begin. I guess that's to be expected. There's always a lot to do before you get to go to heaven.

8

□ □ □

To get along with God,
Consider the consequences of your behavior.

EARTHSEED: THE BOOKS OF THE LIVING
SATURDAY, JULY 26, 2025

Tracy Dunn has not come home and has not been found by the police. I don't think she will be. She's only been gone for a week, but a week outside must be like a week in hell. People vanish outside. They go through our gate like Mr. Yannis did, and everyone waits for them, but they never come back—or they come back in an urn. I think Tracy Dunn is dead.

Bianca Montoya is pregnant. It isn't just gossip, it's true, and it matters to me, somehow. Bianca is 17, unmarried, and out of her mind about Jorge Iturbe who lives at the Ibarra house and is Yolanda Ibarra's brother.

Jorge admits to being the father. I don't know why they didn't just get married before everything got so public. Jorge is 23, and he, at least, ought to have some sense. Anyway, they're going to get married now. The Ibarra and Iturbe families have been feuding with the Montoyas for a week over this. So stupid. You'd think they had nothing else to do. At least they're both Latino. No interracial feud this time. Last year when Craig Dunn who's white and one of the saner members of the Dunn family was caught making love to Siti Moss who's black and Richard Moss's oldest daughter to boot, I thought someone was going to get killed. Crazy.

But my point isn't who's sleeping with whom or who's feuding.

My point is—my question is—how in the world can anyone get married and make babies with things the way they are now?

I mean, I know people have always gotten married and had kids, but now.... Now there's nowhere to go, nothing to do. A couple gets married, and if they're lucky, they get a room or a garage to live in—with no hope of anything better and every reason to expect things to get worse.

Bianca's chosen life is one of my options. It's not one that I intend to exercise, but it is pretty much what the neighborhood expects of me—of anyone my age. Grow up a little more, get married, have babies. Curtis Talcott says the new Iturbe family will get half-a-garage to live in after they marry. Jorge's sister Celia Iturbe Cruz and her husband and baby have the other half. Two couples, and not one paying job among them. The best they could hope for would be to move into some rich people's compound as domestic servants and work for room and board. There's no way to save any money or ever do any better.

And what if they wanted to go north, try for a better life in Oregon or Washington or Canada? It would be much harder to travel with a baby or two, and much more dangerous to try to sneak past hostile guards and over state lines or international borders with babies.

I don't know whether Bianca is brave or stupid. She and her sister are busy altering their mother's old wedding dress, and everyone's cooking and getting ready for a party as though these were the good old days. *How can they?*

I like Curtis Talcott a lot. Maybe I love him. Sometimes I think I do. He says he loves me. But if all I had to look forward to was marriage to him and babies and poverty that just keeps getting worse, I think I'd kill myself.

SATURDAY, AUGUST 2, 2025

We had a target practice today, and for the first time since I killed the dog, we found another corpse. We all saw it this time—an old woman, naked, maggoty, half-eaten, and beyond disgusting.

That did it for Aura Moss. She says she won't do anymore target shooting. Not ever. I tried talking to her, but she says it's the men's job to protect us anyway. She says women shouldn't have to practice with guns.

"What if you have to protect your younger sisters and brothers?" I asked her. She has to babysit them often enough.

"I already know enough to do that," she said.

"You get rusty without practice," I said.

"I'm not going out again," she insisted. "It's none of your business. I don't have to go!"

I couldn't move her. She was afraid, and that made her defensive. Dad said I should have waited until the memory of the corpse faded, then tried to convince her. He's right, I guess. It's the Moss attitude that gets me. Richard Moss lets his wives and daughters pull things like this. He works them like slaves in his gardens and rabbit raising operation and around the house, but he lets them pretend they're "ladies" when it comes to any community effort. If they don't want to do their part, he always backs them up. This is dangerous and stupid. It's a breeding ground for resentment. No Moss woman has ever stood a watch. I'm not the only one who's noticed.

The two oldest Payne kids went with us for the first time. Bad luck for them. They weren't scared off, though. Doyle and Margaret. There's a toughness to them. They're all right. Their uncle Wardell Parrish hadn't wanted them to go. He had made nasty comments about Dad's ego, about private armies and vigilantes, and about his taxes—how he had paid enough in his life to have a right to depend on the police to protect him. Blah, blah, blah. He's a strange, solitary, whiny man. I've heard that he used to be wealthy. Dad agrees with me that he can't be trusted. But he's not Doyle and Margaret's father, and their mother Rosalee Payne doesn't like anyone telling her how to raise her five kids. The only power she has in the world is her authority over her children and her money. She does have a little money, inherited from her parents. Her brother has somehow lost his. So his trying to tell her what to do or what she shouldn't let her kids do was a dumb move. He should have known better—though for the kids' sake, I'm glad he didn't.

My brother Keith begged to go with us as usual. He'll turn thirteen in a few days—August 14—and the thought of waiting two more years until he's 15 must seem impossible to him. I understand that. Waiting is terrible. Waiting to be older is worse than other kinds of waiting because there's nothing you can do to make it happen faster. Poor Keith. Poor me.

At least Dad lets Keith shoot at birds and squirrels with the family BB gun, but Keith still complains. "It's not fair," he said today for the twentieth or thirtieth time. "Lauren's a girl and you let her go. You always let her do things. I could learn to help you guard and scare off robbers. . . ." He had once made the mistake of offering to help "shoot robbers" instead of scaring them off, and Dad all but preached him a sermon. Dad almost never hits us, but he can be scary without lifting a finger.

Keith didn't go today, of course. And our practice went all right until we found the corpse. We didn't see any dogs this time. Most upsetting to me, though, there were a few more rag, stick, cardboard, and palm frond shacks along the way into the hills along River Street. There always seem to be more. They've never bothered us beyond begging and cursing, but they always stare so. It gets harder to ride past them. They're living skeletons, some of them. Skin and bones and a few teeth. They eat whatever they can find up there.

Sometimes I dream about the way they stare at us.

Back at home, my brother Keith slipped out of the neighborhood— out through the front gates and away. He stole Cory's key and took off on his own. Dad and I didn't know until we got home. Keith was still gone, and by then Cory knew he must be outside. She had checked with others in the neighborhood and two of the Dunn kids, twins

Allison and Marie, age six, said they saw him go out the gate. That was when Cory went home and discovered that her key was gone.

Dad, tired and angry and scared, was going to go right back out to look for him, but Keith got home just as Dad was leaving. Cory, Marcus, and I had gone to the front porch with Dad, all three of us speculating about where Keith had gone, and Marcus and I volunteering to go with Dad to help search. It was almost dark.

"You get back in that house and stay there," Dad said. "It's bad enough to have one of you out there." He checked the submachine gun, made sure it was fully loaded.

"Dad, look," I said. I had spotted something moving three houses down—quick, shadowy movement alongside the Garfield porch. I didn't know it was Keith. I was attracted by its furtiveness. Someone was sneaking around, trying to hide.

Dad was quick enough to see the movement before it was hidden by the Garfield house. He got up at once, took the gun, and went to check. The rest of us watched and waited.

Moments later Cory said she heard an odd noise in the house. I was too focused on Dad and what was going on outside to hear what she heard, or to pay any attention to her. She went in. Marcus and I were still on the porch when she screamed.

Marcus and I glanced at each other, then at the front door. Marcus lunged for the door. I yelled for Dad. Dad was out of sight, but I heard him answer my call.

"Come quick," I shouted, then I ran into the house.

Cory, Marcus, Bennett, and Gregory were in the kitchen, clustered around Keith. Keith was sprawled, panting, on the floor, wearing only his underpants. He was scraped and bruised, bleeding, and filthy. Cory knelt beside him, examining him, questioning him, crying.

"What happened to you? Who did this? Why did you go outside? Where are your clothes? What—?"

"Where's the key you stole?" Dad cut in. "Did they take it from you?"

Everyone jumped, looked up at Dad, then down at Keith.

"I couldn't help it," Keith said, still panting. "I couldn't, Daddy. There were five guys."

"So they got the key."

Keith nodded, careful not to meet Dad's eyes.

Dad turned and strode out of the house, almost at a run. It was too late now to get George or Brian Hsu to change the gate lock. That would have to be done tomorrow, and new keys made and passed out. I thought Dad must be going out to warn people and to put more watchers on duty. I wanted to offer to help alert people, but I didn't. Dad looked too angry to accept help from one of his kids right then. And when he got back, Keith was in for it. Was he ever in for it. A pair of pants gone, and a shirt and *a pair of shoes*. Cory had never been willing to let us run around barefoot the way a lot of kids did, except in the house. Her definitions of being civilized did not involve dirty, heavily callused feet anymore than they involved dirty, diseased skin. Shoes were expensive, and we were always growing out of ours, but Cory insisted. Each of us had at least one pair of wearable shoes, in spite of what they cost, and they cost a lot. Now money would have to be found to get an extra pair for Keith.

Keith curled up on the floor, smudging the tile with blood from his nose and mouth, hugging himself and crying now that Dad was gone. It took Cory two or three minutes to get him up and half carry him to the bathroom. I tried to help her, but she stared at me like I was the one who beat him up, so I let them alone. It wasn't as though I wanted to help. I just thought I should. Keith was in real pain, and it was hard for me to endure sharing it.

I cleaned up the blood so no one would slip in it or track it around. Then I fixed dinner, ate, fed the three younger boys, and put the rest aside for Dad, Cory, and Keith.

Keith had to confess what he had done this morning at church. He had to stand up in front of the whole congregation and tell them everything, including what the five thugs had done to him. Then he had to apologize—to God, to his parents, and to the congregation that he had endangered and inconvenienced. Dad made him do that over Cory's objections.

Dad never hit him, though last night he must have been tempted. "Why would you do such a thing!" he kept demanding. "How could any son of mine be so stupid! Where are your brains, boy? What did you think you were doing? I'm talking to you! Answer me!"

Keith answered and answered and answered, but the answers never seemed to make much sense to Dad. "I ain't no baby no more," he wept. Or, "I wanted to show you. Just wanted to show you! You always let Lauren do stuff!" Or, "I'm a man! I shouldn't be hiding in the house, hiding in the wall; I'm a man!"

It went on and on because Keith refused to admit he had done anything wrong. He wanted to show he was a man, not a scared girl. It wasn't his fault that a gang of guys jumped him, beat him, robbed him. He didn't do anything. It wasn't his fault.

Dad stared at him in utter disgust. "You disobeyed," he said. "You stole. You endangered the lives and the property of everyone here, including your mother, your sister, and your little brothers. If you were the man you think you are, I'd beat the hell out of you!"

Keith stared straight ahead. "Bad guys come in even if they don't have a key," he muttered. "They come in and steal stuff. It's not my fault!"

It took Dad two hours to get Keith to admit that it was his fault, no excuses. He'd done wrong. He wouldn't do it again.

My brother isn't very smart, but he makes up for it in pure stubbornness. My father is smart and stubborn. Keith didn't have a chance, but he made Dad work for his victory. The next morning,

Dad had his revenge. I don't believe he thought of Keith's forced confession that way, but Keith's expression told me that he did.

"How do I get out of this family," Marcus muttered to me as we watched. I sympathized. He had to share a room with Keith, and the two of them, only a year apart in age, fought all the time. Now things would be worse.

Keith is Cory's favorite. If you asked her, she would say she didn't have a favorite, but she does. She babies him and lets him get away with skipping chores, a little lying, a little stealing.. . . Maybe that's why Keith thinks when he screws up, it's okay.

This morning's sermon was on the ten commandments with extra emphasis on "Honor thy father and thy mother," and "Thou shalt not steal." I think Dad got rid of a lot of anger and frustration, preaching that sermon. Keith, tall, stone-faced, looking older than his thirteen years, kept his anger. I could see him keeping it inside, holding it down, choking on it.

9

□ □ □

All struggles
Are essentially
power struggles.
Who will rule,
Who will lead,
Who will define,
refine,
confine,
design,
Who will dominate.
All struggles
Are essentially
power struggles,
And most
are no more intellectual
than two rams
knocking their heads together.

EARTHSEED: THE BOOKS OF THE LIVING
SUNDAY, AUGUST 17, 2025

My parents' usual good judgement failed them this week on my brother Keith's birthday. They gave him his own BB gun. It wasn't new, but it worked, and it looked much more dangerous than it was. And it was his. He didn't have to share it. I suppose it was intended to make him feel better about the two years he still had to wait until he got his hands on the Smith & Wesson, or better yet, the Heckler & Koch. And, of course, it was supposed to help him get over his stupid desire to sneak out, and the humiliation of his public confession.

Keith shot a few more pigeons and crows, threatened to shoot Marcus—Marcus just told me about that tonight—then yesterday, he took off for parts unknown. He took the BB gun with him, of course. No one has seen him for about eighteen hours, and there's not much doubt that he's gone outside again.

MONDAY, AUGUST 18, 2025

Dad went out looking for Keith today. He even called in the police. He says he doesn't know how we'll afford the fee, but he's scared. The longer Keith is gone, the more likely he is to get hurt or killed. Marcus says he thinks Keith went looking for the guys who beat him up. I don't believe it. Not even Keith would go looking for five guys—or even one guy—with nothing but a BB gun.

Cory's even more upset than Dad. She's scared and jumpy and sick to her stomach, and she keeps crying. I talked her into going back to bed, then taught her classes myself. I've done that four or five times before when she was sick, so it wasn't too weird for the kids. I just used Cory's lesson plans, and during the first part of the day, I partnered the older kids with my kindergartners and let everyone get a taste of teaching or learning from someone different. Some of my students are my age and older, and a couple of these—Aura Moss and Michael Talcott—got up and left. They knew I understood the work. I got the last of my high school work and tests out of the way almost two years ago. Since then I've done uncredited (free) college work with Dad. Michael and Aura know all that, but they're much too grown up to learn anything from the likes of me. The hell with them. It's a pity, though, that my Curtis has to have a brother like Michael—not that any of us gets to choose our brothers.

OCTAVIA E. BUTLER

No sign of Keith. I think Cory has gone into mourning for him. I handled classes again today, and Dad went out searching again. He came home looking exhausted tonight, and Cory wept and shouted at him.

"You didn't try!" she said with me and all three of my brothers looking on. We'd all come to see whether Dad had brought Keith back. "You could have found him if you'd tried!"

Dad tried to go to her, but she backed away, still shouting: "If it were your precious Lauren out there alone, you would have found her by now! You don't care about Keith."

She's never said anything like that before.

I mean, we were always Cory and Lauren. She never asked me to call her "mother," and I never thought to do it. I always knew she was my stepmother. But still . . . I always loved her. It mystified me that Keith was her favorite, but it didn't make me love her any less. I was her kid, but not her kid. Not quite. Not really. But I always thought she loved me.

Dad shooed us all off to bed. He quieted Cory and took her back to their room. A few minutes ago, he came to see me.

"She didn't mean it," he said. "She loves you as though you were her daughter, Lauren."

I just looked at him.

"She wants you to know she's sorry."

I nodded, and after a few more assurances, he went.

Is she sorry? I don't think so.

Did she mean it. She did. Oh, yes, she meant it.

Shit.

THURSDAY, AUGUST 30, 2025

Keith came back last night.

He just walked into the house during dinner, as though he'd been outside playing football instead of gone since Saturday. And this time he looked fine. Not a mark on him. He was wearing a clean new set of clothing—even new shoes. All of it was of much better quality than he had when he left, and much more expensive than we could have afforded.

He still had the BB gun until Dad took it away from him and smashed it.

Keith wouldn't say where he'd been or how he'd gotten the new things, so Dad beat him bloody.

I've only seen Dad like that once before—when I was 12. Cory tried to stop him, tried to pull him off Keith, screamed at him in English, then in Spanish, then without words.

Gregory threw up on the floor, and Bennett started to cry. Marcus backed away from the whole scene, and slipped out of the house.

Then it was over.

Keith was crying like a two-year-old and Cory was holding him. Dad stood over both of them, looking dazed.

I followed Marcus out the back door and stumbled and almost fell down the back steps. I didn't know what I was doing. Marcus wasn't around. I sat on the steps in the warm darkness and let my body shake and hurt and vomit in helpless empathy with Keith. Then I guess I passed out.

I came to sometime later with Marcus shaking me and whispering my name.

I got up with Marcus hanging on to my arm, trying to steady me, and I got to my bedroom.

"Let me sleep in here," he whispered once I was sitting on my bed, dazed and still in pain. "I'll sleep on the floor, I don't care."

"All right," I said, not caring where he slept. I lay down on the bed without taking off even my shoes, and drew my body into a fetal ball on top of the bedclothes. I either fell asleep that way or I passed out again.

SATURDAY, OCTOBER 25, 2025

Keith has gone outside again. He went yesterday afternoon. Cory didn't admit until tonight that he took not only her key this time, but her gun. He took the Smith & Wesson.

Dad refused to go out and look for him. Dad slept in his office last night. He's sleeping there again tonight.

I never liked my brother much. I hate him now for what he's doing to the family—for what he's doing to my father. I hate him. Damn, I hate him.

MONDAY, NOVEMBER 3, 2025

Keith came home tonight while Dad was visiting over at the Talcott house. I suspect that Keith hung around and watched the house and waited until Dad left. He had come to see Cory. He brought her a lot of money done up in a fat roll.

She stared at it, then took it, dazed. "So much, Keith," she whispered. "Where did you get it?"

"It's for you," he said. "All for you, not him."

He took her hand and closed it around the money—and she let him do it, though she had to know it must be stolen money or drug money or worse.

Keith gave Bennett and Gregory big, expensive bars of milk chocolate with peanuts. He just smiled at Marcus and me—an obvious "fuck you" smile. Then, before Dad could come home and find him here, he left again. Cory hadn't realized that he was leaving again, and she all but screamed and clung to him.

"No! You'll be killed out there! What's the matter with you? Stay home!"

"Mama, I won't let him beat me again," he said. "I don't need him hitting me and telling me what to do. Pretty soon, I'll be able to make more money in a day than he can in a week—maybe in a month."

"You'll be killed!"

"No I won't. I know what I'm doing." He kissed her, then, with surprising ease, took her arms from around him. "I'll come back and see you," he said. "I'll bring you presents."

And he vanished out the back door, and was gone.

2026

□ □ □

Civilization is to groups what intelligence is to individuals. It is a means of combining the intelligence of many to achieve ongoing group adaptation.

Civilization, like intelligence, may serve well, serve adequately, or fail to serve its adaptive function. When civilization fails to serve, it must disintegrate unless it is acted upon by unifying internal or external forces.

EARTHSEED: THE BOOKS OF THE LIVING

10

□ □ □

When apparent stability disintegrates,
As it must—
God is Change—
People tend to give in
To fear and depression,
To need and greed.
When no influence is strong enough
To unify people
They divide.
They struggle,
One against one,
Group against group,
For survival, position, power.
They remember old hates and generate new ones,
They create chaos and nurture it.
They kill and kill and kill,
Until they are exhausted and destroyed,
Until they are conquered by outside forces,
Or until one of them becomes
A leader
Most will follow,
Or a tyrant
Most fear.

EARTHSEED: THE BOOKS OF THE LIVING

Keith came home yesterday, bigger than ever, as tall and lean as Dad is tall and broad. He's not quite 14, but he already looks like the man he wants so much to be. We're like that, we Olaminas—tall, sturdy, fast growing people. Except for Gregory who is only nine, we all tower over Cory. I'm still the tallest, but my height seems to annoy her these days. She loves Keith's size, though—her big son. She just hates the fact that he doesn't live with us anymore.

"I got a room," he said to me yesterday. We talked, he and I. Cory was with Dorotea Cruz who is one of her best friends and who had just had another baby. The other boys were playing in the street and on the island. Dad had gone to the college, and would be gone overnight. Now, more than ever, it's safest to go out just at dawn, and not to try coming home until just at dawn the next morning. That's if you have to go outside at all, which Dad does about once a week. The worst parasites still prowl at night and sleep late into the morning. Yet Keith lives outside.

"I got a room in a building with some other people," he said. Translation: He and his friends were squatting in an abandoned building. Who were his friends? A gang? A flock of prostitutes? A bunch of *astronauts*, flying high on drugs? A den of thieves? All of the above? Whenever he came to see us he brought money to Cory and little gifts to Bennett and Gregory.

How could he get money? There's no honest way.

"Do your friends know how old you are?" I asked.

He grinned. "Hell, no. Why should I tell them that?"

I nodded. "It does help to look older sometimes."

"You want something to eat?"

"You going to cook for me?"

"I've cooked for you hundreds of times. Thousands."

"I know. But you always had to before."

"Don't be stupid. You think I couldn't act the way you did: Skip out on my responsibilities if I felt like it? I don't feel like it. You want to eat or not?"

"Sure."

I made rabbit stew and acorn bread—enough for Cory and all the boys when they came in. He hung around and watched me work for a while, then began to talk to me. He's never done that before. We've never, never liked each other, he and I. But he had information I wanted, and he seemed to want to talk. I must have been the safest person he could talk to. He wasn't afraid of shocking me. He didn't much care what I thought. And he wasn't afraid I'd tell Dad or Cory anything he said. Of course, I wouldn't. Why cause them pain? I've never been much for tattling on people, anyway.

"It's just a nasty old building on the outside," he was saying of his new home. "You wouldn't believe how great it looks once you go in, though."

"Whorehouse or spaceship?" I asked.

"It's got stuff like you never saw," he evaded. "TV windows you go through instead of just sitting and looking at. Headsets, belts, and touchrings . . . you see and feel everything, do anything. Anything! There's places and things you can get into with that equipment that are insane! You don't ever have to go into the street except to get food."

"And whoever owns this stuff took you in?" I asked.

"Yeah."

"Why?"

He looked at me for a long time, then started to laugh. "Because I can read and write," he said at last. "And none of them can. They're all older than me, but not one of them can read or write anything. They stole all this great stuff and they couldn't even use it. Before I got there they even broke some of it because they couldn't read the instructions."

Cory and I had had a hell of a struggle, teaching him to read and write. He had been bored, impatient, anything but eager.

"So you read for a living—help your new friends learn to use their stolen equipment," I said.

"Yeah."

"And what else?"

"Nothin' else."

What a piss-poor liar he is. Always was. He's got no conscience. He just isn't smart enough to tell convincing lies. "Drugs, Keith?" I asked. "Prostitution? Robbery?"

"I said nothing else! You always think you know everything."

I sighed. "You're not done causing Dad and Cory pain are you? Not by a long shot."

He looked as though he wanted to shout back at me or hit me. He might have done one or the other if I hadn't mentioned Cory.

"I don't give a shit about him," he said, his voice low and ugly. He had a man's voice already. He had everything but a man's brain. "I do more for her than he does. I bring her money and nice things. And my friends . . . my friends know she lives here, and they let this place alone. He's nothing!"

I turned and looked at him and saw my father's face, lighter-skinned, younger, thinner, but my father's face, unmistakable. "He's you," I whispered. "Every time I look at you, I see him. Every time you look at him, you see yourself."

"Dogshit!"

I shrugged.

It was a long time before he spoke again. At last he said, "Did he ever hit you?"

"Not for about five years."

"Why'd he hit you—back then?"

I thought about that, and decided to tell him. He was old enough. "He caught me and Rubin Quintanilla in the bushes together."

Keith shouted with abrupt laughter. "You and Rubin? Really? You were doing it with him? You're kidding."

"We were twelve. What the hell."

OCTAVIA E. BUTLER

"You're lucky you didn't get pregnant."

"I know. Twelve can be a dumb age."

He looked away. "Bet he didn't beat you as bad as he beat me!"

"He sent you boys over to play with the Talcotts." I gave him a glass of cold orange juice and poured one for myself.

"I don't remember," he said.

"You were nine," I said. "Nobody was going to tell you what was going on. As I remember, I told you I fell down the back steps."

He frowned, perhaps remembering. My face had been memorable. Dad hadn't beaten me as badly as he beat Keith, but I looked worse. He should remember that.

"He ever beat up Mama?"

I shook my head. "No. I've never seen any sign of it. I don't think he would. He loves her, you know. He really does."

"Bastard!"

"He's our father, and he's the best man I know."

"Did you think that when he beat you?"

"No. But later when I figured out how stupid I'd been, I was just glad he was so strict. And back when it happened, I was just glad he didn't quite kill me."

He laughed again—twice in just a few minutes, and both times at things I'd said. Maybe he was ready to open up a little now.

"Tell me about the outside," I said. "How do you live out there?"

He drained the last of his second glass of juice. "I told you. I live real good out there."

"But how did you live when you first went out—when you went to stay."

He looked at me and smiled. He smiled like that years ago when he used red ink to trick me into bleeding in empathy with a wound he didn't have. I remember that particular nasty smile.

"You want to go out yourself, don't you?" he demanded.

"Someday."

"What, instead of marrying Curtis and having a bunch of babies?"

"Yeah. Instead of that."

"I wondered why you were being so nice to me."

The food smelled just about ready, so I got up and took the bread from the oven and bowls from the cupboard. I was tempted to tell him to dish up his own stew, but I knew he would spoon all the meat out of the stew and leave nothing but potatoes and vegetables for the rest of us. So I served him and myself, covered the pot, left it on the lowest possible fire, and put a towel over the bread.

I let him eat in peace for a while, though I thought the boys would be coming in any time now, starving.

Then I was afraid to wait any longer. "Talk to me, Keith," I said. "I really want to know. How did you survive when you first went out there."

His smile this time was less evil. Maybe the food had mellowed him. "Slept in a cardboard box for three days and stole food," he said. "I don't know why I kept going back to that box. Could have slept in any old corner. Some kids carry a piece of cardboard to sleep on—so they won't be right down on the ground, you know.

"Then I got a sleepsack from an old man. It was new, like he never used it. Then I—"

"You stole it?"

He gave me a look of scorn. "What you think I was going to do? I didn't have no money. Just had that gun—Mama's .38."

Yes. He had brought it back to her three visits ago, along with two boxes of ammunition. Of course he never said how he got the ammunition—or how he got his replacement gun—a Heckler & Koch nine millimeter just like Dad's. He just showed up with things and claimed that if you had the money, you could buy anything outside. He had never admitted how he got the money.

"Okay," I said. "So you stole a sleepsack. And you kept stealing food? It's a wonder you didn't get caught."

"The old guy had some money. I used it to buy food. Then I started walking toward L.A."

That old dream of his. For reasons that make sense to him alone, he's always wanted to go to L.A. Any sane person would be thankful for the twenty miles that separate us from that oozing sore.

"There's people all over the freeway coming away from L.A.," he said. "There's even people walking up from way down in San Diego. They don't know where they're going. I talked to this guy, he said he was going to Alaska. Goddamn. Alaska!"

"Good luck to him," I said. "He's got a lot of guns to face before he gets there."

"He won't get there. Alaska must be a thousand miles from here!"

I nodded. "More than that, and with hostile state lines and borders along the way. But good luck to him anyhow. It's a goal that makes sense."

"He had twenty-three thousand dollars in his pack."

I didn't say anything. I just froze, stared at him in disgust and renewed dislike. But of course. Of course.

"You wanted to know," he said. "That's what it's like outside. If you got a gun, you're somebody. If you don't, you're shit. And a lot of people out there don't have guns."

"I thought most of them did—except the ones too poor to be worth robbing."

"I thought so too. But guns cost a lot. And it's easier to get one if you already got one, you know?"

"What if that Alaska guy had had one. You'd be dead."

"I sneaked up on him while he was sleeping. Just sort of followed him until he went off the road to go to sleep. Then I got him. He led me away from L.A., though."

"You shot him?"

The nasty smile again.

"He talked to you. He was friendly to you. And you shot him."

"What was I supposed to do? Wait for God to come and give me some money? What was I supposed to do?"

"Come home."

"Shit."

"Doesn't it even bother you that you took someone's life—you killed a man?"

He seemed to think about that for a while. Then he shook his head. "It don't bother me," he said. "I was scared at first, but then . . . after I did it, I didn't feel nothing. Nobody saw me do it. I just took his stuff and left him there. Besides, maybe he wasn't dead. People don't always die just because you shoot them."

"You didn't check?"

"I just wanted his stuff. He was crazy anyway. Alaska!"

I didn't say anymore to him, didn't ask anymore questions. He talked a little about meeting some guys and joining up with them, then discovering that even though they were all older than he was, none of them could read or write. He was a help to them. He made their lives pleasanter. Maybe that's why they didn't just wait until he was asleep and kill him and take his loot for themselves.

After a while, he noticed that I wasn't saying anything, and he laughed. "You better marry Curtis and make babies," he said. "Out there, outside, you wouldn't last a day. That hyperempathy shit of yours would bring you down even if nobody touched you."

"You think that," I said.

"Hey, I saw a guy get both of his eyes gouged out. After that, they set him on fire and watched him run around and scream and burn. You think you could stand to see that?"

"Your new friends did that?" I asked.

"Hell no! Crazies did that. Paints. They shave off all their hair—even their eyebrows—and they paint their skin green or blue or red or yellow. They eat fire and kill rich people."

"They do what?"

"They take that drug that makes them like to watch fires. Sometimes a camp fire or a trash fire or a house fire. Or sometimes they grab a rich guy and set him on fire."

"*Why?*"

OCTAVIA E. BUTLER

"I don't know. They're crazy. I heard some of them used to be rich kids, so I don't know why they hate rich people so much. That drug is bad, though. Sometimes the paints like the fire so much they get too close to it. Then their friends don't even help him. They just watch them burn. It's like . . . I don't know, it's like they were fucking the fire, and like it was the best fuck they ever had."

"You've never tried it?"

"Hell no! I told you. Those guys are crazy. You know, even the girls shave their heads. Damn, they look ugly!"

"They're mostly kids, then?"

"Yeah. Your age up to maybe twenty. There's a few old ones, twenty-five, even thirty. I hear most of them don't live that long though."

Cory and the boys came in at that moment, Gregory and Bennett excited because their side in soccer had won. Cory was happy and wistful, talking to Marcus about Dorotea Cruz's new baby girl. Things changed when they all saw Keith, of course, but the evening wasn't too bad. Keith had presents for the little boys, of course, and money for Cory and nothing for Marcus and me. This time, though, he was a little shamefaced with me.

"Maybe I'll bring you something next time," he said.

"No, don't," I said, thinking of the Alaska-bound traveler. "It's all right. I don't want anything."

He shrugged and turned to talk to Cory.

MONDAY, JULY 20, 2026

Keith came to see me today just before dark. He found me walking home from the Talcott house where Curtis had been wishing me a very happy birthday. We've been very careful, Curtis and I, but from somewhere or other, he's gotten a supply of condoms. They're old fashioned, but they work. And there's an unused darkroom in a corner of the Talcott garage.

Keith scared me out of a very sweet mood. He came from behind two houses without making a sound. He had almost reached me before I realized someone was there and turned to face him.

He raised his hands, smiling, "Brought you a birthday present," he said. He put something into my left hand. Money.

"Keith, no, give it to Cory."

"You give it to her. You want her to have it, you give it to her. I gave it to you."

I walked him to the gate, concerned that one of the watchers might spot him and shoot him. He was that much taller than he had been when he stopped living with us. Dad was home so he wouldn't come in. I thanked him for the money and told him I would give it to Cory. I wanted him to know that because I didn't want him to bring me anything else, ever.

He seemed not to mind. He kissed the side of my face said, "Happy birthday," and went out. He still had Cory's key, and although Dad knew he had it, he hadn't had the lock changed again.

WEDNESDAY, AUGUST 26, 2026

Today, my parents had to go downtown to identify the body of my brother Keith.

SATURDAY, AUGUST 29, 2026

I haven't been able to write a word since Wednesday. I don't know what to write. The body was Keith's. I never saw it, of course. Dad said he tried to keep Cory from seeing it. The things someone had done to Keith before he died. . . . I don't want to write about this, but I need to. Sometimes writing about a thing makes it easier to stand.

Someone had cut and burned away most of my brother's skin. Everywhere except his face. They burned out his eyes, but left the rest of his face intact—like they wanted him to be recognized. They cut and they cauterized and they cut and they cauterized. . . . Some of the wounds were days old. Someone had an endless hatred of my brother.

Dad got us all together and described to us what had been done. He told it in a flat, dead monotone. He wanted to scare us, to scare Marcus, Bennett, and Gregory in particular. He wanted us to understand just how dangerous the outside is.

The police said drug dealers torture people the way Keith was tortured. They torture people who steal from them and people who compete with them. We don't know whether Keith was doing either of these things. We just know he's dead. His body was dumped across town from here in front of a burned-out old building that was once a nursing home. It was dumped on the broken concrete and abandoned several hours after Keith died. It could have been dumped in one of the canyons and only the dogs would have found it. But someone wanted it to be found, wanted it to be recognized. Had one of his victims' relatives or friends managed to get even at last?

The police seemed to think we should know who killed him. I got the feeling from their questions that they would have been happy to arrest Dad or Cory or both of them. But they both lead very public lives, and neither had any unexplained absences or other breaks in routine. Dozens of people could give them alibis. Of course, I said nothing about what Keith had told me he had been doing. What good would that do? He was dead, and in a horrible way. By accident or by intent, all his victims were avenged.

Wardell Parrish felt called upon to tell the police about the big fight Dad and Keith had had last year. He'd heard it, of course. Half the neighborhood had heard it. Family fights are neighborhood theater—and Dad, the minister, after all!

I know Wardell Parrish was the one who told the cops. His youngest niece Tanya let that much slip. "Uncle Ward said he hated to mention it but . . ."

Oh, I'll bet he hated to mention it. Damned bastard! But nobody backed him up. The cops went nosing around the neighborhood, but no one else admitted knowing anything about a fight. After all, they knew Dad didn't kill Keith. And they knew the cops liked to solve cases by "discovering" evidence against whomever they decided must be guilty. Best to give them nothing. They never helped when people called for help. They came later, and more often than not, made a bad situation worse.

We had the service today. Dad asked his friend Reverend Robinson to take care of it. Dad just sat with Cory and the rest of us and looked bent and old. So old.

Cory cried all day, most of the time without making a sound. She's been crying off and on since Wednesday. Marcus and Dad tried to comfort her. Even I tried, though the way she looked at me . . . as though I had had something to do with Keith's death, as though she almost hated me. I keep reaching out to her. I don't know what else to do. Maybe in time, she'll be able to forgive me for not being her daughter, for being alive when her son is dead, for being Dad's daughter by someone else . . . ? I don't know.

Dad never shed a tear. I've never seen him cry in my life. Today, I wish he would. I wish he could.

Curtis Talcott sort of hung around with me today, and we talked and talked. I guess I needed to talk, and Curtis was willing to put up with me.

He said I should cry. He said no matter how bad things had gotten between Keith and me or Keith and the family, I should let myself cry. Odd. Until he brought it up, I hadn't thought about my own absence of tears. I hadn't cried at all. Maybe Cory had noticed. Maybe my dry face was just one more grudge she held against me.

It wasn't that I was holding back, being stoic. It's just that I hated Keith at least as much as I loved him. He was my brother—half-brother—but he was also the most sociopathic person I've ever been close to. He would have been a monster if he had been allowed to grow up. Maybe he was one already. He never cared what he did. If he wanted to do something and it wouldn't cause him immediate physical pain, he did it, fuck the earth.

He messed up our family, broke it into something less than a family. Still, I would never have wished him dead. I would never wish anyone dead in that horrible way. I think he was killed by monsters much worse than himself. It's beyond me how one human being could do that to another. If hyperempathy syndrome were a more common complaint, people couldn't do such things. They could kill if they had to, and bear the pain of it or be destroyed by it. But if everyone could feel everyone else's pain, who would torture? Who would cause anyone unnecessary pain? I've never thought of my problem as something that might do some good before, but the way things are, I think it would help. I wish I could give it to people. Failing that, I wish I could find other people who have it, and live among them. A biological conscience is better than no conscience at all.

But as for me crying, if I were going to cry, I think I would have done it back when Dad beat Keith—when the beating was over and Dad saw what he had done, and we all saw how both Keith and Cory looked at him. I knew then that neither of them would ever forgive him. Not ever. That was the end of something precious in the family.

I wish Dad could cry for his son, but I don't feel any need at all to cry for my brother. May he rest in peace—in his urn, in heaven, wherever.

11

□ □ □

Any Change may bear seeds of benefit.
Seek them out.
Any Change may bear seeds of harm.
Beware.
God is infinitely malleable.
God is Change.

EARTHSEED: THE BOOKS OF THE LIVING
SATURDAY, OCTOBER 17, 2026

We are coming apart.

The community, the families, individual family members. . . .
We're a rope, breaking, a single strand at a time.

There was another robbery last night—or an attempted robbery.
I wish that was all. No garden theft this time. Three guys came over
the wall and crowbarred their way into the Cruz house. The Cruz
family, of course, has loud burglar alarms, barred windows, and security gates at all the doors just like the rest of us, but that doesn't seem
to matter. When people want to come in, they come in. The thieves
used simple hand tools—crowbars, hydraulic jacks, things anyone
can get. I don't know how they disabled the burglar alarm. I know
they cut the electrical and phone lines to the house. That shouldn't
have mattered since the alarm had back-up batteries. Whatever else
they did, or whatever went wrong, the alarm didn't go off. And
after the thieves used the crowbar on the door, they walked into the
kitchen and used it on Dorotea Cruz's seventy-five-year-old grandmother. The old lady was a light sleeper and had gotten into the
habit of getting up at night and brewing herself a cup of lemon grass

tea. Her family says that's what she was coming into the kitchen to do when the thieves broke in.

Then Dorotea's brothers Hector and Rubin Quintanilla, came running, guns in hand. They had the bedroom nearest to the kitchen and they heard all the noise—the break-in itself and Mrs. Quintanilla being knocked against the kitchen table and chairs. They killed two of the thieves. The third got away, perhaps wounded. There was a lot of blood. But old Mrs. Quintanilla was dead.

This is the seventh incident since Keith was killed. More and more people are coming over our wall to take what we have, or what they think we have. Seven intrusions into house or garden in less than two months—in an 11-household community. If this is what's happening to us, what must it be like for people who are really rich—although perhaps with their big guns, private armies of security guards, and up to date security equipment, they're better able to fight back. Maybe that's why we're getting so much attention. We have a few stealables and we're not that well protected. Of the seven intrusions, three were successful. Thieves got in and out with something—a couple of radios, a sack of walnuts, wheat flour, corn meal, pieces of jewelry, an ancient TV, a computer. . . . If they could carry it, they made off with it. If what Keith told me is true, we're getting the poorer class of thieves here. No doubt the tougher, smarter, more courageous thieves hit stores and businesses. But our lower-class thugs are killing us slowly.

Next year, I'll be 18—old enough, according to Dad, to stand a regular night watch. I wish I could do it now. As soon as I can do it, I will. But it won't be enough.

It's funny. Cory and Dad have been using some of the money Keith brought us to help the people who've been robbed. Stolen money to help victims of theft. Half the money is hidden in our back yard in case of disaster. There has always been some money hidden out there. Now there's enough to make a difference. The other half has gone into the church fund to help our neighbors in emergencies. It won't be enough.

OCTAVIA E. BUTLER

Something new is beginning—or perhaps something old and nasty is reviving. A company called Kagimoto, Stamm, Frampton, and Company—KSF—has taken over the running of a small coastal city called Olivar. Olivar, incorporated in the 1980s, is just one more beach/bedroom suburb of Los Angeles, small and well- to-do. It has little industry, much hilly, vacant land and a short, crumbling coastline. Its people, like some here in our Robledo neighborhood, earn salaries that would once have made them prosperous and comfortable. In fact, Olivar is a lot richer than we are, but since it's a coastal city, its taxes are higher, and since some of its land is unstable, it has extra problems. Parts of it sometimes crumble into the ocean, undercut or deeply saturated by salt water. Sea level keeps rising with the warming climate and there is the occasional earthquake. Olivar's flat, sandy beach is already just a memory. So are the houses and businesses that used to sit on that beach. Like coastal cities all over the world, Olivar needs special help. It's an upper middle class, white, literate community of people who once had a lot of weight to throw around. Now, not even the politicians it's helped to elect will stand by it. The whole state, the country, the world needs help, it's been told. What the hell is tiny Olivar whining about?

Somewhat richer and less geologically active communities are getting help—dikes, sea walls, evacuation assistance, whatever's appropriate. Olivar, located between the sea and Los Angeles, is getting an influx of salt water from one direction and desperate poor people from the other. It has a solar powered desalination plant on some of its flatter, more stable land, and that provides its people with a dependable supply of water.

But it can't protect itself from the encroaching sea, the crumbling earth, the crumbling economy, or the desperate refugees. Even getting back and forth to work, for those few who can't work at home, was becoming as dangerous for them as it is for our people—a kind of terrible gauntlet that has to be run over and over again.

Then the people of KSF showed up. After many promises, much haggling, suspicion, fear, hope, and legal wrangling, the voters and the officials of Olivar permitted their town to be taken over, bought out, privatized. KSF will expand the desalination plant to vast size. That plant will be the first of many. The company intends to dominate farming and the selling of water and solar and wind energy over much of the southwest—where for pennies it's already bought vast tracts of fertile, waterless land. So far, Olivar is one of its smaller coastal holdings, but with Olivar, it gets an eager, educated work force, people a few years older than I am whose options are very limited. And there's all that formerly public land that they now control. They mean to own great water, power, and agricultural industries in an area that most people have given up on. They have long-term plans, and the people of Olivar have decided to become part of them—to accept smaller salaries than their socio-economic group is used to in exchange for security, a guaranteed food supply, jobs, and help in their battle with the Pacific.

There are still people in Olivar who are uncomfortable with the change. They know about early American company towns in which the companies cheated and abused people.

But this is to be different. The people of Olivar aren't frightened, impoverished victims. They're able to look after themselves, their rights and their property. They're educated people who don't want to live in the spreading chaos of the rest of Los Angeles County. Some of them said so on the radio documentary we all listened to last night—as they made a public spectacle of selling themselves to KSF.

"Good luck to them," Dad said. "Not that they'll have much luck in the long run."

"What do you mean?" Cory demanded. "I think the whole idea is wonderful. It's what we need. Now if only some big company would want to do the same thing with Robledo."

"No," Dad said. "Thank God, no."

"You don't know! Why shouldn't they?"

"Robledo's too big, too poor, too black, and too Hispanic to be of interest to anyone—and it has no coastline. What it does have is street poor, body dumps, and a memory of once being well-off—of shade trees, big houses, hills, and canyons. Most of those things are still here, but no company will want us."

At the end of the program it was announced that KSF was looking for registered nurses, credentialed teachers, and a few other skilled professionals who would be willing to move to Olivar and work for room and board. The offer wasn't put that way, of course, but that's what it meant. Yet Cory recorded the phone number and called it at once. She and Dad are both teachers, both Ph.D.'s. She was desperate to get in ahead of the crowd. Dad just shrugged and let her call.

Room and board. The offered salaries were so low that if Dad and Cory both worked, they wouldn't earn as much as Dad is earning now with the college. And out of it they'd have to pay rent as well as the usual expenses. In fact, when you add everything up, it's clear that with the six of us, they couldn't earn enough to meet expenses. It might work if I could find a job of some kind, but in Olivar they don't need me. They've got hundreds of me, at least—maybe thousands. Every surviving community is full of unemployed, half-educated kids or unemployed, uneducated kids.

Anyone KSF hired would have a hard time living on the salary offered. In not very much time, I think the new hires would be in debt to the company. That's an old company-town trick—get people into debt, hang on to them, and work them harder. Debt slavery. That might work in Christopher Donner's America. Labor laws, state and federal, are not what they once were.

"We could *try*," Cory insisted to Dad. "We could be safe in Olivar. The kids could go to a real school and later get jobs with the company. After all, where can they go from here except outside?"

Dad shook his head. "Don't hope for it, Cory. There's nothing safe about slavery."

Marcus and I were still up, listening. The two younger boys had been sent to bed, but we four were still clustered around the radio. Now Marcus spoke up.

"Olivar doesn't sound like slavery," he said. "Those rich people would never let themselves be slaves."

Dad gave him a sad smile. "Not now," he said. "Not at first." He shook his head. "Kagimoto, Stamm, Frampton: Japanese, German, Canadian. When I was young, people said it would come to this. Well, why shouldn't other countries buy what's left of us if we put it up for sale. I wonder how many of the people in Olivar have any idea what they're doing."

"I don't think many do," I said. "I don't think they'd dare let themselves know."

He looked at me, and I looked back. I'm still learning how dogged people can be in denial, even when their freedom or their lives are at stake. He's lived with it longer. I wonder how.

Marcus said, "Lauren, you ought to want to go to some place like Olivar more than anyone. You share pain every time you see someone get hurt. There'd be a lot less pain in Olivar."

"And there would be all those guards," I said. "I've noticed that people who have a little bit of power tend to use it. All those guards KSF is bringing in—they won't be allowed to bother the rich people, at least at first. But new, bare-bones, work-for-room-and-board employees. . . . I'll bet they'll be fair game."

"There's no reason to believe the company would allow that kind of thing," Cory said. "Why do you always expect the worst of everyone?"

"When it comes to strangers with guns," I told her, "I think suspicion is more likely to keep you alive than trust."

She made a sharp, wordless sound of disgust. "You know nothing about the world. You think you have all the answers but you know nothing!"

I didn't argue. There wasn't much point in my arguing with her.

"I doubt that Olivar is looking for families of blacks and Hispanics, anyway," Dad said. "The Balters or the Garfields or even some of the Dunns might get in, but I don't think we would. Even if I were trusting enough to put my family into KSF's hands, they wouldn't have us."

"We could try it," Cory insisted. "We should! We wouldn't be any worse off than we are now if they turn us down. And if we got in and we didn't like it, we could come back here. We could rent the house to one of the big families here—charge them just a little, then—"

"Then come back here jobless and penniless," Dad said. "No, I mean it. This business sounds half antebellum revival and half science fiction. I don't trust it. Freedom is dangerous, Cory, but it's precious, too. You can't just throw it away or let it slip away. You can't sell it for bread and pottage."

Cory stared at him—just stared. He refused to look away. Cory got up and went to their bedroom. I saw her there a few minutes later, sitting on the bed, cradling the urn of Keith's ashes, and crying.

SATURDAY, OCTOBER 24, 2026

Marcus tells me the Garfields are trying to get into Olivar. He's been spending a lot of time with Robin Balter and she told him. She hates the idea because she likes her cousin Joanne a lot better than she does her two sisters. She's afraid that if Joanne goes away to Olivar, she'll never see her again. I suspect she's right.

I can't imagine this place without the Garfields. Joanne, Jay, Phillida. . . . We've lost individuals before, of course, but we've never lost a whole family. I mean . . . they'll be alive, but . . . they'll be gone.

I hope they're refused. I know it's selfish, but I don't care. Not that it makes any difference what I hope. Oh hell. I hope they get whatever will be best for their survival. I hope they'll be all right.

At 13, my brother Marcus has become the only person in the family whom I would call beautiful. Girls his age stare at him when they think he's not looking. They giggle a lot around him and chase him like crazy, but he sticks to Robin. She's not pretty at all—all skin and bones and brains—but she's funny and sensible. In a year or two, she'll start to fill out and my brother will get beauty along with all those brains. Then, if the two of them are still together, their lives will get a lot more interesting.

I've changed my mind. I used to wait for the explosion, the big crash, the sudden chaos that would destroy the neighborhood. Instead, things are unraveling, disintegrating bit by bit. Susan Talcott Bruce and her husband have applied to Olivar. Other people are talking about applying, thinking about it. There's a small college in Olivar. There are lethal security devices to keep thugs and the street poor out. There are more jobs opening up. . . .

Maybe Olivar is the future—one face of it. Cities controlled by big companies are old hat in science fiction. My grandmother left a whole bookcase of old science fiction novels. The company-city subgenre always seemed to star a hero who outsmarted, overthrew, or escaped "the company." I've never seen one where the hero fought like hell to get taken in and underpaid by the company. In real life, that's the way it will be. That's the way it is.

And what should I be doing? What can I do? In less than a year, I'll be 18, an adult—an adult with no prospects except life in our disintegrating neighborhood. Or Earthseed.

To begin Earthseed, I'll have to go outside. I've known that for a long time, but the idea scares me just as much as it always has.

Next year when I'm 18, I'll go. That means now I have to begin to plan how I'll handle it.

I'm going to go north. My grandparents once traveled a lot by car. They left us old road maps of just about every county in the state plus several of other parts of the country. The newest of them is 40 years old, but that doesn't matter. The roads will still be there. They'll just be in worse shape than they were back when my grandparents drove a gas-fueled car over them. I've put maps of the California counties north of us and the few I could find of Washington and Oregon counties into my pack.

I wonder if there are people outside who will pay me to teach them reading and writing—basic stuff—or people who will pay me to read or write for them. Keith started me thinking about that. I might even be able to teach some Earthseed verses along with the reading and writing. Given any chance at all, teaching is what I would choose to do. Even if I have to take other kinds of work to get enough to eat, I can teach. If I do it well, it will draw people to me—to Earthseed.

> *All successful life is*
> *Adaptable,*
> *Opportunistic,*
> *Tenacious,*
> *Interconnected, and*
> *Fecund.*
> *Understand this.*
> *Use it.*
> *Shape God.*

I wrote that verse a few months ago. It's true like all the verses. It seems more true than ever now, more useful to me when I'm afraid.

I've finally got a title for my book of Earthseed verses—Earthseed: The Book of the Living. There are the Tibetan and the Egyptian Books of the Dead. Dad has copies of them. I've never heard of anything called a book of the living, but I wouldn't be surprised to discover that there is something. I don't care. I'm trying to speak—to write—the truth. I'm trying to be clear. I'm not interested in being fancy, or even original. Clarity and truth will be plenty, if I can only achieve them. If it happens that there are other people outside somewhere preaching my truth, I'll join them. Otherwise, I'll adapt where I must, take what opportunities I can find or make, hang on, gather students, and teach.

OCTAVIA E. BUTLER

12

□ □ □

We are Earthseed
The life that perceives itself
Changing.

EARTHSEED: THE BOOKS OF THE LIVING
SATURDAY, NOVEMBER 14, 2026

The Garfields have been accepted at Olivar.

They'll be moving next month. That soon. I've known them all my life, and they'll be gone. Joanne and I have had our differences, but we grew up together. I thought somehow that when I left, she would still be here. Everyone would still be here, frozen in time just as I left them. But no, that's fantasy. God is Change.

"Do you want to go?" I asked her this morning. We had gotten together to pick a few early lemons and navel oranges and some persimmons, almost ripe and brilliant orange. We picked at my house, and then at hers, enjoying the work. The weather was cool. It was good to be outside.

"I have to go," she said. "What else is there for me—for anyone. It's all going to hell here. You know it is."

I stared at her. I guess discussing such things is all right now that she has a way out. "So you move into another fortress," I said.

"It's a better fortress. It won't have people coming over the walls, killing old ladies."

"Your mother says all you'll have is an apartment. No yard. No garden. You'll have less money, but you'll have to use more of it to buy food."

"We'll manage!" There was a brittle quality to her voice.

I put down the old rake I was using as a fruit picker. It worked fine on the lemons and oranges. "Scared?" I asked.

She put down her own real fruit picker with its awkward extension handle and small fruit-catching basket. It was best for persimmons. She hugged herself. "I've lived here, lived with trees and gardens all my life. I . . . don't know how it will be to be shut up in an apartment. It does scare me, but we'll manage. We'll have to."

"You can come back here if things aren't what you hope. Your grandparents and your aunt's family will still be here."

"Harry will still be here," she whispered, looking toward her house. I would have to stop thinking of it as the Garfield house. Harry and Joanne were at least as close as Curtis and I. I hadn't thought about her leaving him—what that must be like. I like Harry Balter. I remember being surprised when he and Joanne first started going together. They'd lived in the same house all their lives. I had thought of Harry almost as her brother. But they were only first cousins, and against the odds, they had managed to fall in love. Or I thought they had. They hadn't gone with anyone else for years. Everyone assumed they would get around to marrying when they were a little older.

"Marry him and take him with you," I said.

"He won't go," she said in that same whisper. "We've talked and talked about it. He wants me to stay here with him, get married soon and go north. Just . . . go with no prospects. Nothing. It's crazy."

"Why won't he go to Olivar?"

"He thinks the way your father does. He thinks Olivar's a trap. He's read about nineteenth and early twentieth century company towns, and he says no matter how great Olivar looks, all we'll get from it in the end is debt and loss of freedom."

I knew Harry had sense. "Jo," I said, "you'll be of age next year. You could stay here with the Balters until then and marry. Or you could talk your father into letting you marry now."

"And then what? Go join the street poor? Stay and stuff more babies into that crowded house. Harry doesn't have a job, and there's no real chance of his getting one that pays money. Are we supposed to live on what Harry's parents earn? What kind of future is that? None! None at all!"

Sensible. Conservative and sensible and mature and *wrong*. Very much in character with Joanne.

Or maybe I was the one who was wrong. Maybe the security Joanne will find in Olivar is the only kind of security to be had for anyone who isn't rich. To me, though, security in Olivar isn't much more attractive than the security Keith has finally found in his urn.

I picked a few more lemons and some oranges and wondered what she would do if she knew I was also planning to leave next year. Would she run to her mother again, frightened for me, and eager to have someone protect me from myself? She might. She wants a future she can understand and depend on—a future that looks a lot like her parents' present. I don't think that's possible. Things are changing too much, too fast. Who can fight God?

We put baskets of fruit inside my back door on the porch, then headed for her house.

"What will you do?" she asked me as we walked. "Are you just going to stay here? I mean . . . are you going to stay and marry Curtis?"

I shrugged and lied. "I don't know. If I marry anyone, it will be Curtis. But I don't know about marrying. I don't want to have children here anymore than you do. I know we'll be staying here for a while longer, though. Dad won't let Cory even apply to Olivar. I'm glad of that because I don't want to go there. But there'll be other Olivars. Who knows what I might wind up doing?" That last didn't feel like a lie.

"You think there'll be more privatized cities?" she asked.

"Bound to be if Olivar succeeds. This country is going to be parceled out as a source of cheap labor and cheap land. When people like those in Olivar beg to sell themselves, our surviving cities are bound to wind up the economic colonies of whoever can afford to buy them."

"Oh, God, there you go again. You've always got a disaster up your sleeve."

"I see what's out there. You see it too. You just deny it."

"Remember when you thought starving hordes were going to come crawling over our walls and we would have to run away to the mountains and eat grass?"

Did I remember? I turned to face her, first angry—furious—then to my own surprise, sad. "I'll miss you," I said.

She must have read my feelings. "I'm sorry," she whispered.

We hugged each other. I didn't ask her what she was sorry for, and she didn't say anymore.

TUESDAY, NOVEMBER 17, 2026

Dad didn't come home today. He was due this morning.

I don't know what that means. I don't know what to think. I'm scared to death.

Cory called the college, his friends, fellow ministers, co-workers, the cops, the hospitals. . . .

Nothing. He isn't under arrest or sick or injured or dead—at least not as far as anyone knows. None of his friends or colleagues had seen him since he left work early this morning. His bike was working all right. He was all right.

He had ridden off toward home with three co-workers who lived in other neighborhoods in our area. Each of these said the same thing: That they had left him as usual at River Street where it intersects Durant Road. That's only five blocks from here. We're at the tip-end of Durant Road.

So where is he?

Today a group of us, all armed, rode bicycles from home to River Street and down River Street to the college. Five miles in all. We checked side streets, alleys, vacant buildings, every place we could think of. I went. I took Marcus with me because if I hadn't, he would have gone out alone. I had the Smith & Wesson. Marcus had only his knife. He's quick and agile with it, and strong for his age, but he's never used it on anything alive. If anything had happened to him, I don't think I would have dared to go home. Cory is already out of her mind with worry. All this on top of losing Keith. . . . I don't know. Everyone helped. Jay Garfield will be leaving soon, but that didn't stop him from leading the search. He's a good man. He did everything he could think of to find Dad.

Tomorrow we're going into the hills and canyons. We have to. No one wants to, but what else can we do?

WEDNESDAY, NOVEMBER 18, 2026

I've never seen more squalor, more human remains, more feral dogs than I saw today. I have to write. I have to dump this onto paper. I can't keep it inside of me. Seeing the dead has never bothered me before, but this . . .

We were looking for Dad's body, of course, though no one said so. I couldn't deny that reality or avoid thinking about it. Cory checked with the police again, with the hospitals, with everyone we could think of who knew Dad.

Nothing.

So we had to go to the hills. When we go for target practice, we don't look around, except to ensure safety. We don't look for what we'd rather not find. Today in groups of three or four, we combed through the area nearest to the top of River Street. I kept Marcus with me—which was not easy. What is it in young boys that makes them want to wander off alone and get killed? They get two chin hairs and they're trying to prove they're men.

"You watch my back and I'll watch yours," I said. "I'm not going to let you get hurt. Don't you let me down."

He gave me the kind of near-smile that said he knew exactly what I was trying to do, and that he was going to do as he pleased. I got mad and grabbed him by the shoulders.

"Dammit, Marcus, how many sisters have you got? How many fathers have you got!" I never used even mild profanity with him unless things were very serious. Now, it got his attention.

"Don't worry," he muttered. "I'll help."

Then we found the arm. Marcus was the one who spotted it—something dark lying just off the trail we were following. It was hung up in the low branches of a scrub oak.

The arm was fresh and whole—a hand, a lower, and an upper arm. A black man's arm, just the color of my father's where color could be seen. It was slashed and cut all over, yet still powerful looking—long-boned, long-fingered, yet muscular and massive. . . . Familiar?

Smooth, white bone stuck out at the shoulder end. The arm had been cut off with a sharp knife. The bone wasn't broken. And, yes. It could have been his.

Marcus threw up when he saw it. I made myself examine it, search it for something familiar, for certainty. Jay Garfield tried to stop me, and I shoved him away and told him to go to hell. I'm sorry for that, and I told him so later. But I had to know. And yet, I still don't know. The arm was too slashed and covered in dried blood. I couldn't tell. Jay Garfield took fingerprints in his pocket notebook, but we left the arm itself. How could we take that back to Cory?

And we kept searching. What else could we do? George Hsu found a rattlesnake. It didn't bite anyone and we didn't kill it. I don't think anyone was in a mood to kill things.

We saw dogs, but they kept away from us. I even saw a cat watching us from under a bush. Cats either run like hell or crouch and freeze. They're interesting to watch, somehow. Or, at any other time, they'd be interesting.

Then someone began to scream. I've never heard screams like that before—on and on. A man, screaming, begging, praying: "No! No more! Oh, God, no more, please. Jesus, Jesus, Jesus, *please!*" Then there were wordless, grating cries and high, horrible mewling.

It was a man's voice, not like my father's but not that different from his. We couldn't locate the source. The echoes bounced around the canyon, confusing us, sending us first in one direction, then in another. The canyon was full of loose rock and spiny,

OCTAVIA E. BUTLER

vicious plants that kept us on the pathways where there were pathways.

The screaming stopped, then began again as a kind of horrible, bubbling noise.

I had let myself fall back to the end of the line of us by then. I wasn't in trouble. Sound doesn't trigger my sharing. I have to see another person in pain before I do any sharing. And this was one I'd do *anything* to avoid seeing.

Marcus dropped back beside me and whispered, "You okay?"

"Yeah," I said. "I just don't want to know anything about what's happening to that man."

"Keith," he said.

"I know," I agreed.

We walked our bikes behind the others, watching the back trail. Kayla Talcott dropped back to see if we were all right. She hadn't wanted us to come, but since we had come, she had come, she had kept an eye on us. She's like that.

"It doesn't sound like your daddy," she said. "Doesn't sound like him at all." Kayla is from Texas like my biological mother. Sometimes she sounded as though she'd never left, and sometimes she sounded as though she'd never been near any part of the south. She seemed to be able to turn the accent on and off. She tended to turn it on for comforting people, and for threatening to kill them. Sometimes when I'm with Curtis, I see her in his face and wonder what kind of relative—what kind of mother-in-law—she would make. Today I think both Marcus and I were glad she was there. We needed to be close to someone with her kind of mothering strength.

The horrible noise ended. Maybe the poor man was dead and out of his misery. I hope so.

We never found him. We found human bones and animal bones. We found the rotting corpses of five people scattered among the boulders. We found the cold remains of a fire with a human femur and two human skulls lying among the ashes.

At last, we came home and wrapped our community wall around us and huddled in our illusions of security.

SUNDAY, NOVEMBER 22, 2026

No one has found my father. Almost every adult in the neighborhood has spent some time looking. Richard Moss didn't, but his oldest son and daughter did. Wardell Parrish didn't, but his sister and oldest nephew did. I don't know what else people could have done. If I did know, I would be out doing it.

And yet nothing, nothing, nothing! The police never came up with any sign of him. He never turned up anywhere. He's vanished, gone. Even the severed arm's fingerprints weren't his.

Every night since Wednesday, I've dreamed that horrible screaming. I've gone out twice more with teams hunting through the canyons. We've found nothing but more of the dead and the poorest of the living—people who are all staring eyes and visible bones. My own bones ached in empathy. Sometimes if I sleep for a while without hearing the screaming, I see these—the living dead. I've always seen them. I've never seen them.

A team I wasn't with found a living child being eaten by dogs. The team killed the dogs, then watched, helpless as the boy died.

I spoke at services this morning. Maybe it was my duty. I don't know. People came for church, all uncertain and upset, not knowing what they should do. I think they wanted to draw together, and they had years of habit drawing them together at our house on Sunday morning. They were uncertain and hesitant, but they came.

Both Wyatt Talcott and Jay Garfield offered to speak. Both did say a few words, both informally eulogizing my father, though neither admitted that that was what they were doing. I was afraid everyone would do that and the service would become an impossible impromptu funeral. When I stood up, it wasn't just to say a couple of words. I meant to give them something they could take home—

something that might make them feel that enough had been said for today.

I thanked them all for the ongoing—emphasize ongoing—efforts to find my father. Then . . . well, then I talked about perseverance. I preached a sermon about perseverance if an unordained kid can be said to preach a sermon. No one was going to stop me. Cory was the only one who might have tried, but Cory was in a kind of walking coma. She wasn't doing anything she didn't have to do.

So I preached from Luke, chapter eighteen, verses one through eight: the parable of the importunate widow. It's one I've always liked. A widow is so persistent in her demands for justice that she overcomes the resistance of a judge who fears neither God nor man. She wears him down.

Moral: The weak can overcome the strong if the weak persist. Persisting isn't always safe, but it's often necessary.

My father and the adults present had created and maintained our community in spite of the scarcity and the violence outside. Now, with my father or without him, that community had to go on, hold together, survive. I talked about my nightmares and the source of those nightmares. Some people might not have wanted their kids to hear things like that, but I didn't care. If Keith had known more, maybe he would still be alive. But I didn't mention Keith. People could say what happened to Keith was his own fault. No one could say that about Dad. I didn't want anyone to be able to say it about this community some day.

"Those nightmares of mine are our future if we fail one another," I said, winding up. "Starvation, agony at the hands of people who aren't human anymore. Dismemberment. Death.

"We have God and we have each other. We have our island community, fragile, and yet a fortress. Sometimes it seems too small and too weak to survive. And like the widow in Christ's parable, its enemies fear neither God nor man. But also like the widow, it persists. *We persist.* This is our place, no matter what."

That was my message. I left it there, hanging before them with an unfinished feel to it. I could feel them expecting more, then realizing that I wasn't going to say more, then biting down on what I had said.

At just the right moment, Kayla Talcott began an old song. Others took it up, singing slowly, but with feeling: "We shall not, we shall not be moved. . . ."

I think this might have sounded weak or even pitiful somehow if it had been begun by a lesser voice. I think I might have sang it weakly. I'm only a fair singer. Kayla, on the other hand, has a big voice, beautiful, clear, and able to do everything she asks of it. Also, Kayla has a reputation for not moving unless she wants to.

Later, as she was leaving, I thanked her.

She looked at me. I'd grown past her years ago, and she had to look up. "Good job," she said, and nodded and walked away toward her house. I love her.

I got other compliments today, and I think they were sincere. Most said, in one way or another, "You're right," and "I didn't know you could preach like that," and "Your father would be proud of you."

Yeah, I hope so. I did it for him. He built this bunch of houses into a community. And now, he's probably dead. I wouldn't let them bury him, but I know. I'm no good at denial and self-deception. That was Dad's funeral that I was preaching—his and the community's. Because as much as I want all that I said to be true, it isn't. We'll be moved, all right. It's just a matter of when, by whom, and in how many pieces.

13

□ □ □

There is no end
To what a living world
Will demand of you.

EARTHSEED: THE BOOKS OF THE LIVING
SATURDAY, DECEMBER 19, 2026

Today Reverend Matthew Robinson in whose church I was baptized came to preach my father's funeral. Cory made the arrangements. There was no body, no urn. No one knows what happened to my father. Neither we nor the police have been able to find out. We're sure he's dead. He would find a way to come home if he were alive, so we're certain he's dead.

No, we're not certain. We're not certain at all. Is he sick somewhere? Hurt? Held against his will for who knows what reason by who knows what monsters?

This is worse than when Keith died. So much worse. As horrible as that was, we knew he was dead. Whatever he suffered, we knew he wasn't suffering anymore. Not in this world, anyway. We *knew*. Now, we don't know anything. He is dead. But we don't *know!*

The Dunns must of felt this when Tracy vanished. Crazy as they are, crazy as she was, they must have felt this. What do they feel now? Tracy never came back. If she's not dead, what must be happening to her outside? A girl alone only faced one kind of future outside. I intend to go out posing as a man when I go.

How will they feel when I go? I'll be dead to them—to Cory, the boys, the neighborhood. They'll hope I'm dead, considering the supposed alternative. Thank Dad for my tallness and my strength.

I won't have to leave Dad now. He's already left me. He was 57. What reason would strangers have for keeping a 57-year-old man alive? Once they'd robbed him, they would either let him go or kill him. If they let him go, he'd come home, walking, limping, crawling.

So he's dead.

That's that.

It has to be.

TUESDAY, DECEMBER 22, 2026

The Garfields left for Olivar today—Phillida, Jay, and Joanne. An armored KSF truck came from Olivar to collect them and their belongings. The adults of the community had all they could do to keep the little kids from climbing all over the truck and pestering the drivers to death. Most kids my brothers' ages have never been close to a truck that runs. Some of the younger Moss kids have never seen a truck of any kind. The Moss kids weren't even allowed to visit the Yannis house back when the Yannis television still worked.

The two guys from KSF were patient once they realized the kids weren't thieves or vandals. Those two guys with their uniforms, pistols, whips, and clubs, looked more like cops than movers. No doubt they had even more substantial weapons in the truck. My brother Bennett said he saw bigger guns mounted inside the truck when he climbed onto the hood. But when you consider how much a truck that size is worth, and how many people might want to relieve them of it and its contents, I guess the weaponry isn't surprising.

The two movers were a black and a white, and I could see that Cory considered that hopeful. Maybe Olivar wouldn't be the white enclave that Dad had expected.

Cory cornered the black guy and talked to him for as long as he would let her. Will she try now to get us into Olivar? I think she will. After all, without Dad's salary, she'll have to do something. I don't think we have a prayer of being accepted. The insurance company isn't going to pay—or not for a long time. Its people choose not to believe that Dad is dead. Without proof he can't be declared legally dead for seven years. Can they hold on to our money for that long? I don't know, but it wouldn't surprise me. We could starve many times over in seven years. And Cory must know she alone can't earn enough in Olivar to feed and house us. Is she hoping to get work for me, too? I don't know what we're going to do.

Joanne and I cried all over each other, saying good-bye. We promised to phone each other, to stay in touch. I don't think we'll be able to. It costs extra to call Olivar. We won't be able to afford it. I don't think she will either. Chances are, I'll never see her again. The people I've grown up with are falling out of my life, one by one.

After the truck pulled away, I found Curtis and took him back to the old darkroom to make love. We hadn't done it for a long time, and I needed it. I wish I could imagine just marrying Curtis, staying here, and having a decent life with him.

It isn't possible. Even if there were no Earthseed, it wouldn't be possible. I would almost be doing the family a favor if I left now—one less mouth to feed. Unless I could somehow get a job. . . .

"We've got to get out of here, too," Curtis said as we lay together afterward, lingering, tempting fate, not wanting to lose the feel of each other so soon. But that wasn't what he had meant. I turned my head to look at him.

"Don't you want to go?" he asked. "Wouldn't you like to get out of this dead end neighborhood, out of Robledo."

I nodded. "I was just thinking that. But—"

"I want you to marry me, and I want us to get out of here," he said in a near whisper. "This place is dying."

I raised myself to my elbows and looked down at him. The only light in the room came from a single window up near the ceiling. Nothing covered it anymore, and the glass was broken out of it, but still, only a little light came in. Curtis's face was full of shadows.

"Where do you want to go?" I asked him.

"Not Olivar," he said. "That could turn out to be a bigger dead end than living here."

"Where, then?"

"I don't know. Oregon or Washington? Canada? Alaska?"

I don't think I gave any sign of sudden excitement. People tell me my face doesn't show them what I'm feeling. My sharing has been a hard teacher. But he saw something.

"You've already been thinking about leaving, haven't you," he demanded. "That's why you won't talk about getting married."

I rested my hand on his smooth chest.

"You were thinking about going alone!" He grasped my wrist, seemed ready to push it away. Then he held on to it, kept it. "You were just going to walk away from here and leave me."

I turned so that he couldn't see my face because now I had a feeling my emotions were all too obvious: Confusion, fear, hope. . . . Of course I had intended to go alone, and of course I hadn't told anyone that I was leaving. And I had not decided yet how Dad's disappearance would affect my going. That raised frightening questions. What are my responsibilities? What will happen to my brothers if I leave them to Cory? They're her sons, and she'll move the earth to take care of them, keep them fed and clothed and housed. But can she do it alone? How?

"I want to go," I admitted, moving around, trying to be comfortable on the pallet of old sleepsacks that we had put down on the concrete floor. "I planned to go. Don't tell anyone."

"How can I if I go with you?"

I smiled, loving him. But. . . "Cory and my brothers are going to need help," I said. "When my father was here, I planned to go next year when I'm eighteen. Now . . . I don't know."

"Where were you going?"

"North. Maybe as far as Canada. Maybe not."

"Alone?"

"Yeah."

"Why?" Why alone, he meant.

I shrugged. "I could get killed as soon as I leave here. I could starve. The cops could pick me up. Dogs could get me. I could catch a disease. Anything could happen to me; I've thought about it. I haven't named half the bad possibilities."

"That's why you need help!"

"That's why I couldn't ask anyone else to walk away from food and shelter and as much safety as there is in our world. To just start walking north, and hope you wind up some place good. How could I ask that of you?"

"It's not that bad. Farther north, we can get work."

"Maybe. But people have been flooding north for years. Jobs are scarce up there, too. And statelines and borders are closed."

"There's nothing down there!"

"I know."

"So how can you help Cory and your brothers?"

"I don't know. We haven't figured out what to do. So far, nothing I've thought of will work."

"They'd have more of everything if you left."

"Maybe. But, Curtis, how can I leave them? Could you walk away and leave your family, not knowing how they would manage to survive?"

"Sometimes I think so," he said.

I ignored that. He didn't get along very well with his brother Michael, but his family was probably the strongest unit in the neighborhood. Take on one of them and you've got to deal with them all. He would never walk away from them if they were in trouble.

"Marry me now," he said. "We'll stay here and help your family get on its feet. Then we'll leave."

"Not now," I said. "I can't see how anything is going to work out now. Everything's too crazy."

"And what? You think it's going to get sane? It's never been sane. You just have to go ahead and live, no matter what."

I didn't know what to say, so I kissed him. But I couldn't distract him.

"I hate this room," he said. "I hate hiding to be with you and I hate playing games." He paused. "But I do love you. Damn! Sometimes I almost wish I didn't."

"Don't wish that," I said. He knew so little about me, and he thought he knew everything. I'd never told him about my sharing, for instance. I'll have to before I marry him. If I don't, when he finds out, he'll know I didn't trust him enough to be honest with him. And not much is known about sharing. Suppose I pass it on to my kids?

Then there's Earthseed. I'll have to tell him about that. What will he think? That I've gone crazy? I can't tell him. Not yet.

"We could live at your house," he said. "My parents would help out with food. Maybe I could find some kind of job. . . ."

"I want to marry you," I said. I hesitated, and there was absolute silence. I couldn't believe I'd heard myself say such a thing, but it was true. Maybe I was just feeling bereft. Keith, my father, the Garfields, Mrs. Quintanilla. . . . People could disappear so easily. I wanted someone with me who cared about me, and who wouldn't disappear. But my judgment wasn't entirely gone.

"When my family is back on its feet, we'll marry," I said. "Then we can get out of here. I just have to know that my brothers will be all right."

"If we're going to marry anyway, why not do it now?"

Because I have things to tell you, I thought. Because if you reject me or make me reject you with your reactions, I don't want to have to hang around and watch you with someone else.

"Not now," I said. "Wait for me."

He shook his head in obvious disgust. "What the hell do you think I've been doing?"

It's Christmas Eve.

Last night someone set fire to the Payne-Parrish house. While the community tried to put out the fire, and then tried to keep it from spreading, three other houses were robbed. Ours was one of the three:

Thieves took all our store-bought food: wheat flour, sugar, canned goods, packaged goods. . . . They took our radio—our last one. The crazy thing is, before we went to bed we had been listening to a half-hour news feature about increasing arson. People are setting more fires to cover crimes—although why they would bother these days, I don't know. The police are no threat to criminals. People are setting fires to do what our arsonist did last night—to get the neighbors of the arson victim to leave their own homes unguarded. People are setting fires to get rid of whomever they dislike from personal enemies to anyone who looks or sounds foreign or racially different. People are setting fires because they're frustrated, angry, hopeless. They have no power to improve their lives, but they have the power to make others even more miserable. And the only way to prove to yourself that you have power is to use it.

Then there's that fire drug with it's dozen or so names: Blaze, fuego, flash, sunfire. . . . The most popular name is pyro—short for pyromania. It's all the same drug, and it's been around for a while. From what Keith said, it's becoming more popular. It makes watching the leaping, changing patterns of fire a better, more intense, longer-lasting high than sex. Like Paracetco, my biological mother's drug of choice, pyro screws around with people's neurochemistry. But Paracetco began as a legitimate drug intended to help victims of Alzheimer's disease. Pyro was an accident. It was a homebrew—a basement drug invented by someone who was trying to assemble one of the other higher-priced street drugs. The inventor made a very small chemical mistake, and wound up with pyro. That happened on the east coast and caused an immediate increase in the number of senseless arson fires, large and small.

Pyro worked its way west without making nearly as much trouble as it could have. Now its popularity is growing. And in dry-as-straw Southern California, it can cause a real orgy of burning.

"My God," Cory said when the radio report was over. And in a small, whispery voice, she quoted from the Book of Revelation: " 'Babylon the great is fallen, is fallen, and is become the habitation of devils . . .'"

And the devils set fire to the Payne-Parrish house.

At about two a.m. I woke to the jangling of the bell: Emergency! Earthquake? Fire? Intruders?

But there was no shaking, no unfamiliar noise, no smoke. Whatever was happening, it wasn't at our house. I got up, threw clothing on, debated for a second whether to snatch my survival pack, then left it. Our house didn't seem to be in immediate danger. My pack was safe in the closet, mixed in among blankets and bundles of old clothes. If I had to have it, I could come back and snatch it in seconds.

I ran outside to see what was needed, and saw at once. The Payne-Parrish house was fully involved, surrounded by fire. One of the watchers on duty was still sounding the alarm. People spilled from all the houses, and must have seen as I did that the Parrish house was a total loss. Neighbors were already wetting down the houses on either side. A live oak tree—one of our huge, ancient ones—was afire. There was a light wind blowing, swirling bits of burning leaves and twigs into the air and scattering them. I joined the people who were beating and wetting the grounds.

Where were the Paynes? Where was Wardell Parrish? Had anyone called the fire department? A house full of people, after all, it wasn't like a burning garage.

I asked several people. Kayla Talcott said she had called them. I was grateful and ashamed. I wouldn't have asked if Dad were still with us. One of us would have just called. Now we couldn't afford to call.

No one had seen any of the Paynes. Wardell Parrish I found in the Yannis yard where Cory and my brother Bennett were wrapping him

OCTAVIA E. BUTLER

in a blanket. He was coughing so much that he couldn't talk, and wearing only pajama pants.

"Is he okay?" I asked.

"He breathed a lot of smoke," Cory said. "Has someone called—"

"Kayla Talcott called the fire department."

"Good. But no one's at the gate to let them in."

"I'll go." I turned away, but she caught my arm.

"The others?" she whispered. She meant the Paynes, of course.

"I don't know."

She nodded and let me go.

I went to the gate, borrowing Alex Montoya's key on the way. He always seemed to have his gate key in his pocket. It was because of him that I didn't go back into our house and maybe interrupt a robbery and be killed for my trouble.

Firefighters arrived in no great hurry. I let them in, locked the gate after them, and watched as they put out the fire.

No one had seen the Paynes. We could only assume they had never gotten out. Cory tried to take Wardell Parrish to our house, but he refused to leave until he found out one way or the other about his twin sister and his nieces and nephews.

When the fire was almost out, the bell began to ring again. We all looked around. Caroline Balter, Harry's mother, was jerking and pushing at the bell and screaming.

"Intruders!" she shouted. "Thieves! They've broken into the houses!"

And we all rushed without thinking back to our houses. Wardell Parrish came along with my family, still coughing, and wheezing, and as useless—as weaponless—as the rest of us. We could have been killed, rushing in that way. Instead, we were lucky. We scared away our thieves.

Along with our store-bought food and the radio, the thieves got some of Dad's tools and supplies—nails, wire, screws, bolts, that kind of thing. They didn't get the phone, the computer, or anything in Dad's office. In fact, they didn't get into Dad's office at all. I suppose we scared them away before they could search the whole house.

They stole clothing and shoes from Cory's room, but didn't touch my room or the boys'. They got some of our money—the kitchen money, Cory calls it. She had hidden it in the kitchen in a box of detergent. She had thought no one would steal such a thing. In fact, the thieves might have stolen it for resale without realizing that it wasn't just detergent. It could have been worse. The kitchen money was only about a thousand dollars for minor emergencies.

The thieves did not find the rest of our money, some of it hidden out by our lemon tree, and some hidden with our two remaining guns under the floor in Cory's closet. Dad had gone to a lot of trouble to make a kind of floor safe, not locked, but completely concealed beneath a rug and a battered chest of drawers filled with sewing things—salvaged bits of cloth, buttons, zippers, hooks, things like that. The chest of drawers could be moved with one hand. It slid from one side of the closet to the other if you pushed it right, and in seconds you could have the money and the guns in your hands. The concealment trick wouldn't have defeated people who had time to make a thorough search, but it had defeated our thieves. They had dumped some of the drawers onto the floor, but they had not thought to look under the chest.

The thieves did take Cory's sewing machine. It was a compact, sturdy old machine with its own carrying case. Both case and machine were gone. That was a real blow. Cory and I both use that machine to make, alter, and repair clothing for the family. I had thought I might even be able to earn some money with the machine, sewing for other people in the neighborhood. Now the machine is gone. Sewing for the family will have to be done by hand. It will take much more time, and may not look like what we're used to. Bad. Hard. But not a fatal blow. Cory cried over the loss of her machine, but we can get along without it. She's just being worn down by one blow after another.

OCTAVIA E. BUTLER

We'll adapt. We'll have to. God is Change.

Strange how much it helps me to remember that.

Curtis Talcott just came to my window to tell me that the firemen have found charred bodies and bones in the ashes of the Payne-Parrish house. The police are here, taking reports of the robberies and the obvious arson. I told Cory. She can tell Wardell Parrish or let the cops tell him. He's lying down on one of our living room couches. I doubt that he's sleeping. Even though I've never liked him, I feel sorry for him. He's lost his house and his family. He's the only survivor. What must that be like?

TUESDAY, DECEMBER 29, 2026

I don't know how long it can last, but in some way that I suspect is not quite legal, Cory has taken over part of the job Dad held for so long. She'll give the classes Dad gave. With the computer hookups we have already in place, she'll issue assignments, receive homework, and be available for phone and compu-conferences. The administrative part of Dad's work will be handled by someone else who can use the extra money, and who is willing to show up at the college more often than once or twice a month. It will be as though Dad were still teaching, but had decided to give up his other responsibilities.

Cory has arranged this by pleading and begging, by crying and cajoling and calling in every favor and every friend she could think of. People at the college know her. She taught there before Bennett's birth, before she saw the need here and began the front-room school that serves all the children of the neighborhood. Dad was all for her quitting the college because he didn't want her going back and forth outside, exposed to all the dangers that involved. The neighbors pay a per-kid fee, but it isn't much. No one could support a household on it.

Now Cory will have to go outside again. She's already drafting men and older boys in the neighborhood to escort her when she has to go out. There are plenty of unemployed men here, and Cory will be paying them a small fee.

So in a few days, the new term will start and Cory will do Dad's work—while I do her work. I'll handle the school with help from her and from Russel Dory, Joanne and Harry's grandfather. He used to be a highschool math teacher. He's been retired for years, but he's still sharp. I don't think I need his help, but Cory does, and he's willing, so that's that.

Alex Montoya and Kayla Talcott will take over Dad's preaching and other church work. Neither is ordained, but both have substituted for Dad in the past. Both have authority in the community and the church. And, of course, both know their Bible.

This is how we will survive and hold together. It will work. I don't know how long it will last, but for now, it will work.

WEDNESDAY, DECEMBER 30, 2026

Wardell Parrish has finally dragged himself back to his people—to the part of his family that he lived with before he and his sister inherited the Sims house. He's stayed with us since his sister and all her children were killed. Cory gave him some of Dad's clothes which were too big for him. Much too big.

He wandered around, not talking, not seeming to see anything, not eating enough. . . . Then yesterday he said, like a little boy, "I want to go home. I can't stay here. I hate it here; everyone's dead! I have to go home."

So today Wyatt Talcott, Michael, and Curtis escorted him home. Poor man. He's years older than he was a week ago. I think he may not live much longer.

2027

□ □ □

We are Earthseed. We are flesh—self aware, quest-
ing, problem-solving flesh. We are that aspect of
Earthlife best able to shape God knowingly. We are
Earthlife maturing, Earthlife preparing to fall away
from the parent world. We are Earthlife preparing
to take root in new ground, Earthlife fulfilling its
purpose, its promise, its Destiny.

14

□ □ □

In order to rise
From its own ashes
A phoenix
First
Must
Burn.

EARTHSEED: THE BOOKS OF THE LIVING
SATURDAY, JULY 31, 2027 — MORNING

Last night, when I escaped from the neighborhood, it was burning. The houses, the trees, the people: Burning.

Smoke awoke me, and I shouted down the hall to Cory and the boys. I grabbed my clothes and emergency pack and followed Cory as she herded the boys out.

The bell never rang. Our watchers must have been killed before they could reach it.

Everything was chaos. People running, screaming, shooting. The gate had been destroyed. Our attackers had driven an ancient truck through it. They must have stolen a truck just to crash it through our gate.

I think they must have been pyro addicts—bald people with painted heads, faces, and hands. Red faces; blue faces; green faces; screaming mouths; avid, crazy eyes, glittering in the firelight.

They shot us and shot us and shot us. I saw Natalie Moss, running, screaming, then pitching backward, her face half gone, her body still impelled forward. She fell flat on her back, and did not move again.

I fell with her, caught up in her death. I lay there, dazed, strug-

159

gling to move, to get up. Cory and the boys, running ahead of me never noticed. They ran on.

I got up, felt for my pack, found it, and ran. I tried not to see what was happening around me. Hearing the gunfire and the screams didn't stop me. A dead body—Edwin Dunn—didn't stop me. I bent, snatched up his gun, and kept running.

Someone screamed near me, then tackled me, pulled me down. I fired the gun in reflexive terror, and took the terrible impact in my own stomach. A green face hung above mine, mouth open, eyes wide, not yet feeling all his pain. I shot him again, terrified that his pain would immobilize me when he did feel it. It seemed that he took a long time to die.

When I could move again, I pushed his body off me. I got up, still holding the gun, and ran for the wrecked gate.

Best to be in the darkness outside. Best to hide.

I ran up Meredith Street away from Durant Road, away from the fires and the shooting. I had lost track of Cory and the boys. I thought they would go toward the hills and not toward the center of town. Every direction was dangerous, but there was more danger where there were more people. In the night, a woman and three kids might look like a gift basket of food, money, and sex.

North toward the hills. North through the dark streets to where the nearby hills and mountains blotted out the stars.

And then what?

I didn't know. I couldn't think. I had never been outside the walls when it was so dark. My only hope of staying alive was to listen, hear any movement before it got too close to me, see what I could by starlight, be as quiet as I could.

I walked down the middle of the street looking and listening and trying to avoid potholes and chunks of broken asphalt. There was little other trash. Anything that would burn, people would use as fuel. Anything that could be reused or sold had been gathered. Cory used to comment on that. Poverty, she said, had made the streets cleaner.

Where was she? Where had she taken my brothers? Were they all right? Had they even gotten out of the neighborhood?

I stopped. Were my brothers back there? Was Curtis? I hadn't seen him at all—though if anyone were going to survive this insanity, it would be the Talcotts. But we had no way of finding each other.

Sound. Footsteps. Two pairs of running footsteps. I stayed where I was, frozen in place. No sudden moves to draw attention to me. Had I already been seen? Could I be seen—a figure of darker darkness in an otherwise empty street?

The sound was behind me. I listened and knew that it was off to one side, approaching, passing. Two people running down a side street, indifferent to the noise they made, indifferent to woman-shaped shadows.

I let out a breath and drew another through my mouth because I could get more air with less sound that way. I couldn't go back to the fires and the pain. If Cory and the boys were there, they were dead or worse, captive. But they had been ahead of me. They must have gotten out. Cory wouldn't let them come back to look for me. There was a bright glow in the air over what had been our neighborhood. If she had gotten the boys away, all she had to do was look back to know that she didn't want to go back.

Did she have her Smith & Wesson? I wished I had it and the two boxes of ammunition that went with it. All I had was the knife in my pack and Edwin Dunn's old .45 automatic. And all the ammunition I had for it was in it. If it wasn't empty. I knew the gun. It held seven rounds. I'd fired it twice. How many times had Edwin Dunn fired it before someone shot him? I didn't expect to find out until morning. I had a flashlight in my pack, but I didn't intend to use it unless I could be certain I wouldn't be making a target of myself.

During the day the sight of the bulge in my pocket would be enough to make people think twice about robbing or raping me. But during the night the blue gun would be all but invisible even in my hand. If it were empty, I could only use it as a club. And the moment

I hit someone with it, I might as well hit myself. If I lost conscious-ness for any reason during a fight, I would lose all my possessions if not my life. Tonight I had to hide.

Tomorrow I would have to try to bluff as much as possible. Most people wouldn't insist on my shooting them just to test whether or not the gun was loaded. For the street poor, unable to afford medical care, even a minor wound might be fatal.

I am one of the street poor, now. Not as poor as some, but home-less, alone, full of books and ignorant of reality. Unless I meet someone from the neighborhood, there's no one I can afford to trust. No one to back me up.

Three miles to the hills. I kept to the starlit back streets, listening and looking around. The gun was in my hand. I meant to keep it there. I could hear dogs barking and snarling, fighting somewhere not far away.

I was in a cold sweat. I had never been more terrified in my life. Yet nothing attacked me. Nothing found me.

I didn't go all the way to the hills. Instead I found a burned out, unwalled house a few blocks before the end of Meredith Street. Fear of dogs had made me keep an eye open for anything that might pro-vide shelter.

The house was a ruin, a plundered ruin. It wasn't safe to walk into with or without a light. It was a roofless collection of upright black bones. But it had been built up off the ground. Five con crete steps led up to what had been the front porch. There should be a way under the house.

What if other people were under it?

I walked around it, listening, trying to see. Then, instead of daring to crawl under, I settled in what was left of the attached garage. A corner of it was still standing, and there was enough rubble in front of that corner to conceal me if I didn't show a light. Also, if I were surprised, I could get out of the garage faster than I could crawl out from under a house. The concrete floor could not collapse under me as the wooden floor might in what was left of the house proper. It was as good as I was going to get, and I was exhausted. I didn't know whether I could sleep, but I had to rest.

Morning now. What shall I do? I did sleep a little, but I kept startling awake. Every sound woke me—the wind, rats, insects, then squirrels, and birds. . . . I don't feel rested, but I'm a little less exhausted. So what shall I do?

How is it that we had never established an outside meeting place—somewhere where the family could reunite after disaster. I remember suggesting to Dad that we do that, but he had never done anything about it, and I hadn't pushed the idea as I should have. (Poor Godshaping. Lack of forethought.)

What now!

Now, I have to go home. I don't want to. The idea scares me to death. It's taken me a long time just to write the word: Home. But I have to know about my brothers, and about Cory and Curtis. I don't know how I can help if they're hurt or being held by someone. I don't know what might be waiting for me back at the neighborhood. More painted faces? The police? I'm in trouble either way. If the police are there, I'll have to hide my gun before I go in—my gun, and my small amount of money. Carrying a gun can win you a lot of unwanted attention from the police if you catch them in the wrong mood. Yet everyone who has one carries it. The trick, of course, is not to get caught carrying it.

On the other hand, if the painted faces are still there, I can't go in at all. How long do those people stay high on pyro and fire? Do they hang around after their fun to steal whatever's left and maybe kill a few more people?

No matter. I have to go and see.

I have to go home.

I have to write. I don't know what else to do. The others are asleep now, but it isn't dark. I'm on watch because I couldn't sleep if I tried. I'm jittery and crazed. I can't cry. I want to get up and just run and run. . . . Run away from everything. But there isn't any away.

I have to write. There's nothing familiar left to me but the writing. God is Change. I hate God. I have to write.

There were no unburned houses back in the neighborhood, although some were burned worse than others. I don't know whether police or firefighters ever came. If they had come, they were gone when I got there. The neighborhood was wide open and crawling with scavengers.

I stood at the gate, staring in as strangers picked among the black bones of our homes. The ruins were still smoking, but men, women, and children were all over them, digging through them, picking fruit from the trees, stripping our dead, quarreling or fighting over new acquisitions, stashing things away in clothing or bundles. . . . Who were these people?

I put my hand on the gun in my pocket—it had four rounds left in it—and I went in. I was grimy from lying in dirt and ashes all night. I might not be noticed.

I saw three women from an unwalled part of Durant Road, digging through what was left of the Yannis house. They were laughing and throwing around chunks of wood and plaster.

Where were Shani Yannis and her daughters? Where were her sisters?

I walked through the neighborhood, looking past the human maggots, trying to find some of the people I had grown up with. I found dead ones. Edwin Dunn lay where he had when I took his gun, but now he was shirtless and shoeless. His pockets had been turned out.

The ground was littered with ash-covered corpses, some burned or half blown apart by automatic weapons fire. Dried or nearly dried blood had pooled in the street. Two men were prying loose our emergency bell. The bright, clear, early morning sunlight made the whole scene less real somehow, more nightmarelike. I stopped in front of our house and stared at the five adults and the child who were picking through the ruins of it. Who were these vultures? Did the fire draw them? Is that what the street poor do? Run to fire and hope to find a corpse to strip?

There was a dead green face on our front porch. I went up the steps and stood looking at him—at her. The green face was a woman— tall, lean, bald, but female. And what had she died for? What was the point of all this?

"Leave her alone." A woman who had a pair of Cory's shoes in her hand strode up to me. "She died for all of us. Leave her alone."

I've never in my life wanted more to kill another human being. "Get the hell out of my way," I said. I didn't raise my voice. I don't know how I looked, but the thief backed away.

I stepped over the green face and went into the carcass of our home. The other thieves looked at me, but none of them said anything. One pair, I noticed, was a man with a small boy. The man was dressing the boy in a pair of my brother Gregory's jeans. The jeans were much too big, but the man belted them and rolled them up.

And where was Gregory, my clownish smartass of a baby brother? Where was he? Where was everyone?

The roof of our house had fallen in. Most things had burned— kitchen, living room, dining room, my room. . . . The floor wasn't safe to walk on. I saw one of the scavengers fall through, give a surprised yell, then climb, unhurt, onto a floor joist.

Nothing left in my room could be salvaged. Ashes. A heat-distorted metal bedframe, the broken metal and ceramic remains of my lamp, bunches of ashes that had been clothing or books. Many books were not burned through. They were useless, but they had been packed so tightly together that the fire had burned in deeply from the edges and the spines. Rough circles of un-burned paper remained, surrounded by ash. I didn't find a single whole page.

The back two bedrooms had survived better. That was where the scavengers were, and where I headed.

I found bundled pairs of my father's socks, folded shorts and T-shirts, and an extra holster that I could use for the .45. All this I found in or under the unpromising-looking remains of Dad's chest of drawers. Most things were burned beyond use, but I stuffed the best of what I found into my pack. The man with the child came over to scavenge beside me, and somehow, perhaps because of the child, because this stranger in his filthy rags was someone's father, too, I didn't mind. The little boy watched the two of us, his small brown face expressionless. He did look a little like Gregory.

I dug a dried apricot out of my pack and held it out to him. He couldn't have been more than six, but he wouldn't touch the food until the man told him to. Good discipline. But at the man's nod, he snatched the apricot, bit off a tiny taste, then stuffed the rest into his mouth whole.

So, in company with five strangers, I plundered my family's home. The ammunition under the closet floor in my parents' room had burned, had no doubt exploded. The closet was badly charred. So much for the money hidden there.

I took dental floss, soap, and a jar of petroleum jelly from my parents' bathroom. Everything else was already gone.

I managed to gather one set of outer clothing each for Cory and my brothers. In particular, I found shoes for them. There was a woman scavenging among Marcus's shoes, and she glared at me, but she kept quiet. My brothers had run out of the house in their pajamas. Cory had thrown on a coat. I had been the last to get out of the house because I had risked stopping to grab jeans, a sweatshirt, and shoes as well as my emergency pack. I could have been killed. If I had thought about what I was doing, if I had had to think, no doubt I would have been killed. I reacted the way I had trained myself to react—though my training was far from up to date—more memory than anything else. I hadn't practiced late at night for ages. Yet my self-administered training had worked.

Now, if I could get these clothes to Cory and my brothers, I might be able to make up for their lack of training. Especially if I could get the money under the rocks by the lemon tree.

I put clothes and shoes into a salvaged pillow case, looked around for blankets, and couldn't find one. They must have been grabbed early. All the more reason to get the lemon-tree money.

I went out to the peach tree, and, being tall, managed to reach a couple of nearly-ripe peaches that other scavengers had missed. Then I looked around as though for something more to take, and surprised myself by almost crying at the sight of Cory's big, well-tended back garden, trampled into the ground. Peppers, tomatoes, squashes, carrots, cucumbers, lettuce, melons, sunflowers, beans, corn. . . . Much of it wasn't ripe yet, but what hadn't been stolen had been destroyed.

I scavenged a few carrots, a couple of handfuls of sunflower seeds from flower heads that lay on the ground, and a few bean pods from vines Cory had planted to run up the sunflower stalks and corn plants. I took what was left the way I thought a late-arriving scavenger would. And I worked my way toward the lemon tree. When I reached it, heavy with little green lemons, I hunted for any with even a hint of paling, of yellow. I took a few from the tree, and from the ground. Cory had planted shade-loving flowers at the base of the tree, and they had thrived there. She and my father had scattered small, rounded boulders among these in a way that seemed no more than decorative. A few of these had been turned over, crushing the flowers near them. In fact, the rock with the money under it had been turned over. But the two or three inches of dirt over the money packet, triple wrapped and heat-sealed in plastic, was undisturbed.

I snatched the packet in no more time than it had taken to pick up a couple of lemons a moment before. First I spotted the hiding place, then I snatched up the money packet along with a hand full of dirt.

Then, eager to leave, but terrified of drawing attention to myself, I picked up a few more lemons and hunted around for more food.

The figs were hard and green instead of purple, and the persimmons were yellow-green instead of orange. I found a single ear of corn left on a downed stalk and used it to stuff the money packet deeper into my blanket pack. Then I left.

With my pack on my back and the pillow case in my left arm, resting on my hip like a baby, I walked down the driveway to the street. I kept my right hand free for the gun still in my pocket. I had not taken time to put on the holster.

There were more people within the walls than there had been when I arrived. I had to walk past most of them to get out. Others were leaving with their loads, and I tried to follow them without quite attaching myself to any particular group. This meant that I moved more slowly than I would have chosen to. I had time to look at the corpses and see what I didn't want to see.

Richard Moss, stark naked, lying in a pool of his own blood. His house, closer to the gate than ours, had been burned to the ground. Only the chimney stuck up blackened and naked from the rubble. Where were his two surviving wives Karen and Zahra? Or had they survived? Where were all his many children?

Little Robin Balter, naked, filthy, bloody between her legs, cold, bony, barely pubescent. Yet she might have married my brother Marcus someday. She might have been my sister. She had always been such a bright, sharp, great little kid, all serious and knowing. Twelve going on thirty-five, Cory used to say. She always smiled when she said it.

Russell Dory, Robin's grandfather. Only his shoes had been taken. His body had been almost torn apart by automatic weapons fire. An old man and a child. What had the painted faces gotten for all their killing?

"She died for us," the scavenger woman had said of the green face. Some kind of insane burn-the-rich movement, Keith had said. We've

OCTAVIA E. BUTLER

never been rich, but to the desperate, we looked rich. We were surviving and we had our wall. Did our community die so that addicts
could make a help-the-poor political statement?

There were other corpses. I didn't get a close look at most of them.
They littered the front yards, the street, and the island. There was no
sign of our emergency bell now. The men who had wanted it had
carried it away—perhaps to be sold for its metal.

I saw Layla Yannis, Shani's oldest daughter. Like Robin, she had
been raped. I saw Michael Talcott, one side of his head smashed in.
I didn't look around for Curtis. I was terrified that I might see him
lying nearby. I was almost out of control as it was, and I couldn't
draw attention to myself. I couldn't be anything more than another
scavenger hauling away treasure.

Bodies passed under my eyes: Jeremy Balter, one of Robin's
brothers, Philip Moss, George Hsu, his wife and his oldest son, Juana
Montoya, Rubin Quintanilla, Lidia Cruz. . . . Lidia was only eight
years old. She had been raped, too.

I made it back through the gate. I didn't break down. I hadn't seen
Cory or my brothers in the carnage. That didn't mean they weren't
there, but I hadn't seen them. They might be alive. Curtis might be
alive. Where could I look for them?

The Talcotts had relatives living in Robledo, but I didn't know
where. Somewhere on the other side of River Street. I couldn't look
for them, though Curtis might have gone to them. Why hadn't
anyone else stayed to salvage what they could?

I circled the neighborhood, keeping the wall in sight, then made
a greater circle. I saw no one—or at least no one I knew. I saw other
street poor who stared at me.

Then because I didn't know what else to do, I headed back toward
my burned out garage on Meredith Street. I couldn't call the police.
All the phones I knew of were slag. No strangers would let me use
their phone if they had phones, and I didn't know anyone whom I
could pay to call and trust to make the call. Most people would avoid

me or be tempted to keep my money and never call. And anyway, if the police have ignored what's been done to my neighborhood so far, if such a fire and so many corpses can be ignored, why should I go to them? What would they do? Arrest me? Take my cash as their fee? I wouldn't be surprised. Best to stay clear of them.

But *where* was my family!

Someone called my name.

I turned around, my hand in my pocket, and saw Zahra Moss and Harry Balter—Richard Moss's youngest wife and Robin Balter's oldest brother. They were an unlikely pair, but they were definitely together. They managed, without touching each other, to give the appearance of all but clinging together. Both were blood-spattered and ragged. I looked at Harry's battered swollen face and remembered that Joanne had loved him—or thought she had—and that he wouldn't marry her and go with her to Olivar because he believed what Dad believed about Olivar.

"Are you all right?" he asked me.

I nodded, remembering Robin. Did he know? Russell Dory, Robin, and Jeremy. . . . "They beat you up?" I asked, feeling stupid and awkward. I didn't want to tell him his grandfather, brother, and sister were dead.

"I had to fight my way out last night. I was lucky they didn't shoot me." He swayed, looked around. "Let's sit on the curb."

Both Zahra and I looked around, made sure no one else was near by. We sat with Harry between us. I sat on my pillowcase of clothing. Zahra and Harry were fully dressed, in spite of their coating of blood and dirt, but they carried nothing. Did they have nothing, or had they left their things somewhere—perhaps with whatever was left of their families. And where was Zahra's little girl Bibi? Did she know that Richard Moss was dead?

"Everyone's dead," Zahra whispered as though speaking into my thoughts. "Everyone. Those painted bastards killed them all!"

"No!" Harry shook his head. "We got out. There'll be some others."

He sat with his face in his hands, and I wondered whether he was more hurt than I had thought. I wasn't sharing any serious pain with him.

"Have either of you seen my brothers or Cory?" I asked. "Dead," Zahra whispered. "Like my Bibi. All dead."

I jumped. "No! Not all of them. No! Did you see them?"

"I saw most of the Montoya family," Harry said. He wasn't talking to me as much as musing aloud. "We saw them last night. They said Juana was dead. The rest of them were going to walk to Glendale where their relatives live."

"But—" I began.

"And I saw Laticia Hsu. She had been stabbed forty or fifty times."

"But did you see my brothers?" I had to ask.

"They're all dead, I told you," Zahra said. "They got out, but the paints caught them and dragged them back and killed them. I saw. One of them had me down, and he . . . I saw."

She was being raped when she saw my family dragged back and killed? Was that what she meant? Was it true?

"I went back this morning," I said. "I didn't see their bodies. Didn't see any of them." Oh, no. Oh, no. Oh, no. . . .

"I saw. Your mother. All of them. I saw." Zahra hugged herself. "I didn't want to see, but I saw."

We all sat without talking. I don't know how long we sat there. Now and then someone walked past us and looked at us, some dirty, ragged person with bundles. Cleaner people in little bunches rode past us on bikes. A group of three rode past on motorcycles, their electric hum and whine strange in the quiet street.

When I got up, the other two looked at me. For no reason except habit, I picked up my pillowcase. I don't know what I meant to do with the things in it. It had occurred to me, though, that I should get back to my garage before someone else settled there. I wasn't thinking very well. It was as though that garage was home now, and all I wanted in the world was to be there.

Harry got up and almost fell down again. He bent and threw up into the gutter. The sight of his throwing up grabbed at me, and I only just managed to look away in time to avoid joining him. He finished, spat, turned to face Zahra and me, and coughed.

"I feel like hell," he said.

"They hit him in the head last night," Zahra explained. "He got me away from the guy who was . . . Well, you know. He got me away, but they hurt him."

"There's a burned out garage where I slept last night," I said. "It's a long walk, but he can rest there. We can all rest there."

Zahra took my pillowcase and carried it. Maybe something in it could do her some good. We walked on either side of Harry and kept him from stopping or wandering off or staggering too much. Somehow, we got him to the garage.

15

□ □ □

Kindness eases Change

EARTHSEED: THE BOOKS OF THE LIVING
SUNDAY, AUGUST 1, 2027

Harry slept most of the day today. Zahra and I took turns staying with him. He has a concussion, at least, and he needs time to heal. We haven't talked about what we'll do if he gets sicker instead of healing. Zahra doesn't want to abandon him because he fought to save her. I don't want to abandon him because I've known him all my life. He's a good guy. I wonder if there's some way to get in touch with the Garfields. They would give him a home, or at least see that he has medical care.

But he doesn't seem to be getting worse. He totters out to the fenced back yard to urinate. He eats the food and drinks the water that I give him. With no need for discussion, we're eating and drinking sparingly from my supplies. They're all we have. Soon we'll have to risk going out to buy more. But today, Sunday, is a day of rest and healing for us.

The pain of Harry's headache and his bruised, beaten body are almost welcome to me. They're distractions. Along with Zahra's talking and crying for her dead daughter, they fill my mind.

Their misery eases my own, somehow. It gives me moments when I don't think about my family. Everyone is dead. But how can they be? Everyone?

Zahra has a soft, little-girl voice that I used to think was phony. It's real, but it takes on a sandpaper roughness when she's upset. It sounds painful, as though it's abrading her throat as she speaks.

173

She had seen her daughter killed, seen the blue face who shot Bibi as Zahra ran, carrying her. She believed the blue face was enjoying himself, shooting at all the moving targets. She said his expression reminded her of a man having sex.

"I fell down," she whispered. "I thought I was dead. I thought he had killed me. There was blood. Then I saw Bibi's head drop to one side. A red face grabbed her from me. I didn't see where he came from. He grabbed her and threw her into the Hsu house. The house was burning everywhere. He threw her into the fire.

"I went crazy then. I don't know what I did. Somebody grabbed me, then I was free, then somebody shoved me down and fell on me. I couldn't get my breath, and he tore my clothes. Then he was on me, and I couldn't do anything. That's when I saw your mother, your brothers. . . .

"Then Harry was there, and he pulled the bastard off me. He told me later that I was screaming. I don't know what I was doing. He was beating up the guy he'd pulled off me when a new guy jumped him. I hit the new guy with a rock and Harry knocked the other one out. Then we got away. We just ran. We didn't sleep. We hid between two unwalled houses down the street away from the fire until a guy came out with an ax and chased us away. Then we just wandered until we found you. We didn't even really know each other before. You know, Richard never wanted us to have much to do with the neighbors—especially the white ones."

I nodded, remembering Richard Moss. "He's dead, you know," I said. "I saw him." I wanted to take the words back as soon as I'd said them. I didn't know how to tell someone her husband was dead, but there must be a better, gentler way than that.

She stared at me, stricken. I wanted to apologize for my bluntness, but I didn't think it would help. "I'm sorry," I said in a kind of generic apology for everything. She began to cry, and I repeated, "I'm sorry."

I held her and let her cry. Harry woke up, drank a little water, and listened while Zahra told how Richard Moss had bought her from her homeless mother when she was only fifteen—younger than I had thought—and brought her to live in the first house she had ever known. He gave her enough to eat and didn't beat her, and even when her co-wives were hateful to her, it was a thousand times better than living outside with her mother and starving. Now she was outside again. In six years, she had gone from nothing to nothing.

"Do you have someplace to go?" she asked us at last. "Do you know anybody who still has a house?"

I looked at Harry. "You might be able to get into Olivar if you can walk there from here. The Garfields would take you in."

He thought about that for a while. "I don't want to," he said. "I don't think there's anymore future in Olivar than there was in our neighborhood. But at least in our neighborhood, we had the guns."

"For all the good it did us," Zahra muttered.

"I know. But they were our guns, not hired gunmen. No one could turn them against us. In Olivar, from what Joanne said, no one's allowed to have a gun except the security force. And who the hell are they?"

"Company people," I said. "People from outside Olivar."

He nodded. "That's what I heard, too. Maybe it will be all right, but it doesn't sound all right."

"It sounds better than starving," Zahra said. "You guys have never missed a meal, have you?"

"I'm going north," I said. "I planned to go anyway once my family was back on its feet. Now I have no family, and I'm going."

"North where?" Zahra demanded.

"Up toward Canada. The way things are now, I may not be able to get that far. But I'll get to a place where water doesn't cost more than food, and where work brings a salary. Even a small one. I'm not going to spend my life as some kind of twenty-first century slave."

"North is where I'm headed, too," Harry said. "There's nothing here. I've tried for over a year to get a job here—any job that pays money. There's nothing. I want to work for money, and get some college. The only jobs that pay serious money are the kind our parents had, the kind that require college degrees."

I looked at him, wanting to ask something, hesitating, plunging. "Harry, what about your parents?"

"I don't know," he said. "I didn't see them killed. Zahra says she didn't. I don't know where anyone is. We got separated."

I swallowed. "I didn't see your parents," I said, "but I did see some of your other relatives—dead."

"Who?" he demanded.

I guess there really isn't any way to tell people that their close relatives are dead except to say it—no matter how much you don't want to. "Your grandfather," I said, "and Jeremy and Robin."

"Robin and Jeremy? Kids? Little kids?"

Zahra took his hand. "They kill little kids," she said. "Out here in the world, they kill kids every day."

He didn't cry. Or maybe he cried when we were asleep. First, though, he closed himself up, stopped talking, stopped responding, stopped doing anything until it was nearly dark. By then, Zahra had gone out and come back with my brother Bennett's shirt full of ripe peaches.

"Don't ask me where I got them," she said.

"I assume you stole them," I said. "Not from anyone around here, I hope. No sense making the neighbors mad."

She lifted an eyebrow. "I don't need you to tell me how to live out here. I was born out here. Eat your peaches."

I ate four of them. They were delicious, and too ripe to travel well anyway.

"Why don't you try on some of those clothes," I said. "Take what fits you."

She fit not only into Marcus's shirt and jeans—though she had to roll the jeans legs up—but into his shoes. Shoes are expensive. Now she has two pair.

"You let me do it, I'll trade these little shoes for some food," she said.

I nodded. "Tomorrow. Whatever you get, we'll split it. Then I'm leaving."

"Going north?"

"Yes."

"Just north. Do you know anything about the roads and towns and where to buy stuff or steal it? Have you got money?"

"I have maps," I said. "They're old, but I think they're still good. No one's been building new roads lately."

"Hell no. Money?"

"A little. Not enough, I suspect."

"No such thing as enough money. What about him?" She gestured toward Harry's unmoving back. He was lying down. I couldn't tell whether he was asleep or not.

"He has to decide for himself," I said. "Maybe he wants to hang around to look for his family before he goes."

He turned over slowly. He looked sick, but fully aware. Zahra put the peaches she had saved for him next to him.

"I don't want to wait for anything," he said. "I wish we could start now. I hate this place."

"You going with her?" Zahra asked, jabbing a thumb at me.

He looked at me. "We might be able to help each other," he said. "At least we know each other, and . . . I managed to grab a few hundred dollars as I ran out of the house." He was offering trust. He meant we could trust each other. That was no small thing.

"I was thinking of traveling as a man," I said to him.

He seemed to be repressing a smile. "That will be safer for you. You're at least tall enough to fool people. You'll have to cut your hair, though."

Zahra grunted. "Mixed couples catch hell whether people think they're gay or straight. Harry'll piss off all the blacks and you'll piss off all the whites. Good luck."

I watched her as she said it, and realized what she wasn't saying. "You want to come?" I asked.

She sniffed. "Why should I? I won't cut my hair!"

"No need," I said. "We can be a black couple and their white friend. If Harry can get a reasonable tan, maybe we can claim him as a cousin."

She hesitated, then whispered, "Yeah, I want to go." And she started to cry. Harry stared at her in surprise.

"Did you think we were going to just dump you?" I asked. "All you had to do was let us know."

"I don't have any money," she said. "Not a dollar."

I sighed. "Where did you get those peaches?"

"You were right. I stole them."

"You have a useful skill, then, and information about living out here." I faced Harry. "What do you think?"

"Her stealing doesn't bother you?" he asked.

"I mean to survive," I said.

"'Thou shalt not steal,'" he quoted. "Years and years—a lifetime of Thou shalt not steal.'"

I had to smother a flash of anger before I could answer. He wasn't my father. He had no business quoting scripture at me. He was nobody. I didn't look at him. I didn't speak until I knew my voice would sound normal. Then, "I said I mean to survive," I told him. "Don't you?"

He nodded. "It wasn't a criticism. I'm just surprised."

"I hope it won't ever mean getting caught or leaving someone else to starve," I said. And to my own surprise, I smiled. "I've thought about it. That's the way I feel, but I've never stolen anything."

"You're kidding!" Zahra said.

I shrugged. "It's true. I grew up trying to set a good example for my brothers and trying to live up to my father's expectations. That seemed like what I should be doing."

"Oldest kid," Harry said. "I know." He was the oldest in his family.

"Oldest, hell," Zahra said, laughing. "You're both babies out here."

And that wasn't offensive, somehow. Perhaps because it was true.

"I'm inexperienced," I admitted. "But I can learn. You're going to be one of my teachers."

"One?" she said. "Who have you got but me?"

"Everyone."

She looked scornful. "No one."

"Everyone who's surviving out here knows things that I need to know," I said. "I'll watch them, I'll listen to them, I'll learn from them. If I don't, I'll be killed. And like I said, I intend to survive."

"They'll sell you a bowl of shit," she said.

I nodded. "I know. But I'll buy as few of those as possible."

She looked at me for a long time, then sighed. "I wish I'd known you better before all this happened," she said. "You're a weird preacher's kid. If you still want to play man, I'll cut your hair for you."

MONDAY, AUGUST 2, 2027
(FROM NOTES EXPANDED SUNDAY, AUGUST 8)

We're on our way.

This morning Zahra took us to Hanning Joss, the biggest secure store complex in Robledo. We could get all we needed there. Hanning vendors sell everything from gourmet food to delousing cream, prostheses to homebirthing kits, guns to the latest in touchrings, headsets, and recordings. I could have spent days just wandering through the aisles, staring at the stuff I couldn't afford. I had never been to Hanning before, had never seen anything like it in person.

But we had to go into the complex one at a time, leaving two outside to guard our bundles—including my gun. Hanning, as I had heard many times on the radio, was one of the safest places in the city. If you didn't like their sniffers, metal detectors, package restrictions, armed guards, and willingness to strip-search anyone they thought was suspicious on the way in or out, you could shop somewhere else. The store was full of people eager to put up with the inconvenience and invasion of privacy if only they could buy the things they needed in peace.

No one strip-searched me, though I was required to prove that I wasn't a deadbeat.

"Show your Hanning disc or money," an armed guard demanded at the massive gates. I was terrified that he would steal my money, but I showed the bills that I intended to spend, and he nodded. He never touched them. No doubt we were both being watched, and our behaviors recorded. Such a security conscious store wouldn't want its guards stealing the customers' money.

"Shop in peace," the guard said with no hint of a smile.

I bought salt, a small tube of honey, and the cheapest of dried foods—oats, fruit, nuts, bean flour, lentils, plus a little dried beef—all that I thought Zahra and I could carry. And I bought more water and a few odd items: water purification tablets—just in case—and sun blocker, which even Zahra and I would need, some stuff for insect bites, and an ointment Dad used for muscle aches. We would have plenty of those. I bought more toilet paper, tampons, and lip balm. I bought myself a new notebook, two more pens, and an expensive supply of ammunition for the .45. I felt better once I had that.

I bought three of the cheap, multipurpose sleepsacks—big, tough storage bags, and the preferred bedding of all the more affluent homeless. The country was full of people who could earn or steal food and water, but could not rent even a cot. These might sleep on the street or in makeshift shacks, but if they could, they put a sleep-sack between their bodies and the ground. The sacks, with their own strapping, fold to serve as packs during the day. They're light, tough, and able to survive most abuse. They're warm even if you have to sleep on the concrete, but they're thin—more useful than comfortable. Curtis and I used to make love on a pallet of them.

And I bought three oversized jackets of the same thin, breathing synthetic as the sleepsacks. They'll finish the job of keeping us warm at night as we moved north. They look cheap and ugly, and that's good. They might not be stolen.

OCTAVIA E. BUTLER

That was the end of my money—the money I had packed in my emergency pack. I haven't touched the money I took from the foot of the lemon tree. That I had split in half and put in two of my father's socks. I kept it pinned inside my jeans, invisible and unavailable to pickpockets.

It isn't a lot of money, but it's more than I've ever had before—more than anyone could expect me to have. I pinned it where it is, rewrapped in plastic and secure in the socks on Saturday night when I had finished writing and still couldn't stop thinking and remembering and knowing there was nothing I could do about the past.

Then I had a kind of tactile memory of grabbing the money packet and a handful of dirt and stuffing both into my pack. I had an incredible amount of nervous energy that was spending itself in jitteriness. My hands shook so that I could hardly find the money—by feel, in darkness. I made it an exercise in concentration to find the money, socks, and pins, divide the money in half, or as close to in half as I could without seeing, put it into the socks, and pin it in place. I checked it when I went out to urinate the next morning. I'd done a good job. The pins didn't show at all on the outside. I'd put them through the seams down near my ankles. Nothing dangling, no problems.

I took my many purchases out to what was once the ground floor of a parking structure, and was now a kind of semienclosed flea market. Many of the things dug out of ash heaps and landfills wind up for sale here. The rule is that if you buy something in the store, you can sell something of similar value in the structure. Your receipt, coded and dated, is your peddler's license.

The structure was patrolled, though more to check these licenses than to keep anyone safe. Still, the structure was safer than the street.

I found Harry and Zahra sitting on our bundles, Harry waiting to go into the store, and Zahra waiting for her license. They had put their backs against a wall of the store at a spot away from the street and away from the biggest crowd of buyers and sellers. I gave Zahra the receipt and began to separate and pack our new supplies. We would leave as soon as Zahra and Harry finished their buying and selling.

We walked down to the freeway—the 118—and turned west. We would take the 118 to the 23 and the 23 to U.S. 101. The 101 would take us up the coast toward Oregon. We became part of a broad river of people walking west on the freeway. Only a few straggled east against the current—east toward the mountains and the desert. Where were the westward walkers going? To something, or just away from here?

We saw a few trucks—most of them run at night—swarms of bikes or electric cycles, and two cars. All these had plenty of room to speed along the outer lanes past us. We're safer if we keep to the left lanes away from the on and off ramps. It's against the law in California to walk on the freeways, but the law is archaic. Everyone who walks walks on the freeways sooner or later. Freeways provide the most direct routes between cities and parts of cities. Dad walked or bicycled on them often. Some prostitutes and peddlers of food, water, and other necessities live along the freeways in sheds or shacks or in the open air. Beggars, thieves, and murderers live here, too.

But I've never walked a freeway before today. I found the experience both fascinating and frightening. In some ways, the scene reminded me of an old film I saw once of a street in mid-twentieth-century China—walkers, bicyclers, people carrying, pulling, pushing loads of all kinds. But the freeway crowd is a heterogenous mass—black and white, Asian and Latin, whole families are on the move with babies on backs or perched atop loads in carts, wagons or bicycle baskets, sometimes along with an old or handicapped person. Other old, ill, or handicapped people hobbled along as best they could with the help of sticks or fitter companions. Many were armed with sheathed knives, rifles, and, of course, visible, holstered handguns. The occasional passing cop paid no attention.

Children cried, played, squatted, did everything except eat. Almost no one ate while walking. I saw a couple of people drink from canteens. They took quick, furtive gulps, as though they were doing something shameful—or something dangerous.

A woman alongside us collapsed. I got no impression of pain from her, except at the sudden impact of her body weight on her knees. That made me stumble, but not fall. The woman sat where she had fallen for a few seconds, then lurched to her feet and began walking again, leaning forward under her huge pack.

Almost everyone was filthy. Their bags and bundles and packs were filthy. They stank. And we, who have slept on concrete in ashes and dirt, and who have not bathed for three days—we fitted in pretty well. Only our new sleepsack packs gave us away as either new to the road or at least in possession of new stealables. We should have dirtied the packs a little before we got started. We will dirty them tonight. I'll see to it.

There were a few young guys around, lean and quick, some filthy, some not dirty at all. Keiths. Today's Keiths. The ones who bothered me most weren't carrying much. Some weren't carrying anything except weapons.

Predators. They looked around a lot, stared at people, and the people looked away. I looked away. I was glad to see that Harry and Zahra did the same. We didn't need trouble. If trouble came, I hoped we could kill it and keep walking.

The gun was fully loaded now, and I wore it holstered, but half covered by my shirt. Harry bought himself a knife. The money he had snatched up as he ran from his burning house had not been enough to buy a gun. I could have bought a second gun, but it would have taken too much of my money, and we have a long way to go.

Zahra used the shoe money to buy herself a knife and a few personal things. I had refused my share of that money. She needed a few dollars in her pocket.

The day she and Harry use their knives, I hope they kill. If they don't, I might have to, to escape the pain. And what will they think of that?

They deserve to know that I'm a sharer. For their own safety, they should know. But I've never told anyone. Sharing is a weakness, a shameful secret. A person who knows what I am can hurt me, betray me, disable me with little effort.

I can't tell. Not yet. I'll have to tell soon, I know, but not yet. We're together, the three of us, but we're not a unit yet. Harry and I don't know Zahra very well, nor she us. And none of us know what will happen when we're challenged. A racist challenge might force us apart. I want to trust these people. I like them, and . . . they're all I have left. But I need more time to decide. It's no small thing to commit yourself to other people.

"You okay?" Zahra asked.

I nodded.

"You look like hell. And you're so damned poker-faced most of the time. . . ."

"Just thinking," I said. "There's so much to think about now."

She sighed her breath out in a near whistle. "Yeah. I know. But keep your eyes open. You get too wrapped up in your thinking, and you'll miss things. People get killed on freeways all the time."

16

□ □ □

Earthseed
Cast on new ground
Must first perceive
That it knows nothing.

EARTHSEED: THE BOOKS OF THE LIVING
MONDAY, AUGUST 2, 2027
(CONT. FROM NOTES EXPANDED AUGUST 8)

Here are some of the things I've learned today:

Walking hurts. I've never done enough walking to learn that before, but I know it now. It isn't only the blisters and sore feet, although we've got those. After a while, everything hurts. I think my back and shoulders would like to desert to another body. Nothing eases the pain except rest. Even though we got a late start, we stopped twice today to rest. We went off the freeway, into the hills or bushes to sit down, drink water, eat dried fruit and nuts. Then we went on. The days are long this time of year.

Sucking on a plum or apricot pit all day makes you feel less thirsty. Zahra told us that.

"When I was a kid," she said, "there were times when I would put a little rock in my mouth. Anything to feel better. It's a cheat, though. If you don't drink enough water, you'll die no matter how you feel."

All three of us walked along with seeds in our mouths after our first stop, and we felt better. We drank only during our stops in the hills. It's safer that way.

Also, cold camps are safer than cheery campfires. Yet tonight we cleared some ground, dug into a hillside, and made a small fire in the hollow. There we cooked some of my acorn meal with nuts and fruit. It was wonderful. Soon we'll run out of it and we'll have to survive on beans, cornmeal, oats—expensive stuff from stores. Acorns are home-food, and home is gone.

Fires are illegal. You can see them flickering all over the hills, but they are illegal. Everything is so dry that there's always a danger of campfires getting away from people and taking out a community or two. It does happen. But people who have no homes will build fires. Even people like us who know what fire can do will build them. They give comfort, hot food, and a false sense of security.

While we were eating, and even after we'd finished, people drifted over and tried to join us. Most were harmless and easily gotten rid of. Three claimed they just wanted to get warm. The sun was still up, red on the horizon, and it was far from cold.

Three women wanted to know whether two studs like Harry and me didn't need more than one woman. The women who asked this may have been cold, considering how few clothes they had on. It's going to be strange for me, pretending to be a man.

"Couldn't I just roast this potato in your coals?" an old man asked, showing us a withered potato.

We gave him some fire and sent him away—and watched to see where he went, since a burning brand could be either a weapon or a major distraction if he had friends hiding. It's crazy to live this way, suspecting helpless old people. Insane. But we need our paranoia to keep us alive. Hell, Harry wanted to let the old guy sit with us. It took Zahra and me together to let him know that wasn't going to happen. Harry and I have been well-fed and protected all our lives. We're strong and healthy and better educated than most people our age. But we're stupid out here. We want to trust people. I fight against the impulse. Harry hasn't learned to do that yet. We argued about it afterward, low voiced, almost whispering.

"Nobody's safe," Zahra told him. "No matter how pitiful they look, they can steal you naked. Little kids, skinny and big-eyed will make off with all your money, water, and food! I know. I used to do it to people. Maybe they died, I don't know. But I didn't die."

Harry and I both stared at her. We knew so little about her life. But to me, at that moment, Harry was our most dangerous question mark.

"You're strong and confident," I said to him. "You think you can take care of yourself out here, and maybe you can. But think what a stab wound or a broken bone would mean out here: Disablement, slow death from infection or starvation, no medical care, nothing."

He looked at me as though he wasn't sure he wanted to know me anymore. "What, then?" he asked. "Everyone's guilty until proven innocent? Guilty of what? And how do they prove themselves to you?"

"I don't give a piss whether they're innocent or not," Zahra said. "Let them tend to their own business."

"Harry, your mind is still back in the neighborhood," I said. "You still think a mistake is when your father yells at you or you break a finger or chip a tooth or something. Out here a mistake—one mistake—and you may be dead. Remember that guy today? What if that happened to us?"

We had seen a man robbed—a chubby guy of 35 or 40 who was walking along eating nuts out of a paper bag. Not smart. A little kid of 12 or 13 snatched the nuts and ran off with them. While the victim was distracted by the little kid, two bigger kids tripped him, cut his pack straps, dragged the pack off his back, and ran off with it. The whole thing happened so fast that no one could have interfered if they'd wanted to. No one tried. The victim was unhurt except for bruises and abrasions—the sort of thing I had to put up with every day back in the neighborhood. But the victim's supplies were gone. If he had a home nearby and other supplies, he would be all right. Otherwise, his only way of surviving might be to rob someone else—if he could.

"Remember?" I asked Harry. "We don't have to hurt anyone unless they push us into it, but we don't dare let our guard down. We can't trust people."

Harry shook his head. "What if I thought that way when I pulled that guy off Zahra?"

I held on to my temper. "Harry, you know I don't mean we shouldn't trust or help each other. We know each other. We've made a commitment to travel together."

"I'm not sure we do know each other."

"I am. And we can't afford your denial. You can't afford it."

He just stared at me.

"Out here, you adapt to your surroundings or you get killed," I said. "That's obvious!"

Now he did look at me as though I were a stranger. I looked back, hoping I knew him as well as I thought I did. He had a brain and he had courage. He just didn't want to change.

"Do you want to break off with us," Zahra asked, "go your own way without us?"

His gaze softened as he looked at her. "No," he said. "Of course not. But we don't have to turn into animals, for godsake."

"In a way, we do," I said. "We're a pack, the three of us, and all those other people out there aren't in it. If we're a good pack, and we work together, we have a chance. You can be sure we aren't the only pack out here."

He leaned back against a rock, and said with amazement, "You damn sure talk macho enough to be a guy."

I almost hit him. Maybe Zahra and I would be better off without him. But no, that wasn't true. Numbers mattered. Friendship mattered. One real male presence mattered.

"Don't repeat that," I whispered, leaning close to him. "Never say that again. There are other people all over these hills; you don't know who's listening. You give me away and you weaken yourself!"

That reached him. "Sorry," he said.

"It's bad out here," Zahra said. "But most people make it if they're careful. People weaker than us make it—if they're careful."

Harry gave a wan smile. "I hate this world already," he said.

"It's not so bad if people stick together."

He looked from her to me and back to her again. He smiled at her and nodded. It occurred to me then that he liked her, was attracted to her. That could be a problem for her later. She was a beautiful woman, and I would never be beautiful—which didn't bother me. Boys had always seemed to like me. But Zahra's looks grabbed male attention. If she and Harry get together, she could wind up carrying two heavy loads northward.

I was lost in thought about the two of them when Zahra nudged me with her foot.

Two big, dirty-looking guys were standing nearby, watching us, watching Zahra in particular.

I stood up, feeling the others stand with me, flanking me. These guys were too close to us. They meant to be too close. As I stood up, I put my hand on the gun.

"Yeah?" I said. "What do you want?"

"Not a thing," one of them said, smiling at Zahra. Both wore big holstered knives which they fingered.

I drew the gun. "Good deal," I said.

Their smiles vanished. "What, you going to shoot us for standing here?" the talkative one said.

I thumbed the safety. I would shoot the talker, the leader. The other one would run away. He already wanted to run away. He was staring, open-mouthed, at the gun. By the time I collapsed, he would be gone.

"Hey, no trouble!" the talker raised his hands, backing away. "Take it easy, man."

I let them go. I think it would have been better to shoot them. I'm afraid of guys like that—guys looking for trouble, looking for victims. But it seems I can't quite shoot someone just because I'm afraid of him. I killed a man on the night of the fire, and I haven't thought much about it. But this was different. It was like what Harry said about stealing. I've heard, "Thou shalt not kill," all my life, but when you have to, you kill. I wonder what Dad would say about that. But then, he was the one who taught me to shoot.

"We'd better keep a damn good watch tonight," I said. I looked at Harry, and was glad to see that he looked the way I probably had a moment before: mad and worried. "Let's pass your watch and my gun around," I told him. "Three hours per watcher."

"You would have done it, wouldn't you?" he asked. It sounded like a real question.

I nodded. "Wouldn't you?"

"Yes. I wouldn't have wanted to, but those guys were out for fun. Their idea of fun, anyway." He glanced at Zahra. He had pulled one man off her, and taken a beating for it. Maybe the obvious threat to her would keep him alert. Anything that would keep him alert couldn't be all bad.

I looked at Zahra, kept my voice very low. "You never went shooting with us, so I have to ask. Do you know how to use this?"

"Yeah," she said. "Richard let his older kids go out, but he wouldn't let me. Before he bought me, though, I was a good shot."

Her alien past again. It distracted me for a moment. I had been waiting to ask her how much a person costs these days. And she had been sold by her mother to a man who couldn't have been much more than a stranger. He could have been a maniac, a monster. And my father used to worry about future slavery or debt slavery. Had he known? He couldn't have.

"Have you used a gun like this before?" I asked. I reengaged the safety and handed it to her.

"Hell, yeah," she said, examining it. "I like this. It's heavy, but if you shoot somebody with it, they go down." She released the clip, checked it, reinserted it, rammed it home, and handed it back. "I wish I could have practiced with you all," she said. "I always wanted to."

Without warning, I felt a pang of loneliness for the burned neighborhood. It was almost a physical pain. I had been desperate to leave it, but I had expected it still to be there—changed, but surviving. Now that it was gone, there were moments when I couldn't imagine how I was going to survive without it.

"You guys get some sleep," I said. "I'm too wound up to sleep now. I'll take the first watch."

"We should gather more wood for the fire first," Harry said. "It's burning low."

"Let it go out," I said. "It's a spotlight on us, and it messes up our night vision. Other people can see us long before we see them."

"And sit here in the dark," he said. It wasn't a protest. At worst, it was grudging agreement. "I'll take the watch after you," he said, lying back and pulling up his sleepsack and positioning the rest of his gear to serve as a pillow. As an afterthought, he took off his wrist watch and gave it to me. "It was a gift from my mother," he said.

"You know I'll take care of it," I told him.

He nodded. "You be careful," he said, and closed his eyes.

I put the watch on, pulled the elastic of my sleeve down over it so that the glow of the dial wouldn't be visible by accident, and sat back against the hill to make a few quick notes. While there was still some natural light, I could write and watch.

Zahra watched me for a while, then laid her hand on my arm. "Teach me to do that," she whispered.

I looked at her, not understanding.

"Teach me to read and write."

I was surprised, but I shouldn't have been. Where, in a life like hers, had there been time or money for school. And once Richard Moss bought her, her jealous co-wives wouldn't have taught her.

"You should have come to us back in the neighborhood," I said. "We would have set up lessons for you."

"Richard wouldn't let me. He said I already knew enough to suit him."

I groaned. "I'll teach you. We can start tomorrow morning if you want."

"Okay." She gave me an odd smile and began ordering her bag and her few possessions, bundled in my scavenged pillowcase. She lay down in her bag and turned on her side to look at me. "I didn't think I'd like you," she said. "Preacher's kid, all over the place, teaching, telling everybody what to do, sticking your damn nose in everything. But you ain't bad."

I went from surprise into amusement of my own. "Neither are you," I said.

"You didn't like me either?" Her turn to be surprised.

"You were the best looking woman in the neighborhood. No, I wasn't crazy about you. And remember a couple of years ago when you tried your hardest to make me throw up while I was learning to clean and skin rabbits?"

"Why'd you want to learn that, anyway?" she asked. "Blood, guts, worms. . . . I just figured, 'There she goes again, sticking her nose where it don't belong. Well, let her have it!' "

"I wanted to know that I could do that—handle a dead animal, skin it, butcher it, treat its hide to make leather. I wanted to know how to do it, and that I could do it without getting sick."

"Why?"

"Because I thought someday I might have to. And we might out here. Same reason I put together an emergency pack and kept it where I could grab it."

"I wondered about that—about you having all that stuff from home, I mean. At first I thought maybe you got it all when you went back. But no, you were ready for all the trouble. You saw it coming."

"No." I shook my head, remembering. "No one could have been ready for that. But . . . I thought something would happen someday. I didn't know how bad it would be or when it would come. But everything was getting worse: the climate, the economy, crime, drugs, you know. I didn't believe we would be allowed to sit behind our walls, looking clean and fat and rich to the hungry, thirsty, homeless, jobless, filthy people outside."

She turned again and lay on her back, staring upward at the stars. "I should have seen some of that stuff," she said. "But I didn't. Those big walls. And everybody had a gun. There were guards every night. I thought . . . I thought we were so strong."

I put my notebook and pen down, sat on my sleepsack, and put my own pillowcased bundle behind me. Mine was lumpy and uncomfortable to lean on. I wanted it uncomfortable. I was tired. Everything ached. Given a little comfort, I would fall asleep.

The sun was down now, and our fire had gone out except for a few glowing coals. I drew the gun and held it in my lap. If I needed it at all, I would need it fast. We weren't strong enough to survive slowness or stupid mistakes.

I sat where I was for three weary, terrifying hours. Nothing happened to me, but I could see and hear things happening. There were people moving around the hills, sometimes silhouetting themselves against the sky as they ran or walked over the tops of hills. I saw groups and individuals. Twice I saw dogs, distant, but alarming. I heard a lot of gunfire—individual shots and short bursts of automatic weapons fire. That last and the dogs worried me, scared me. A pistol would be no protection against a machine gun or automatic rifle. And dogs might not know enough to be afraid of guns. Would a pack keep coming if I shot two or three of its members? I sat in a cold sweat, longing for walls—or at least for another magazine or two for the gun.

It was nearly midnight when I woke Harry, gave him the gun and the watch, and made him as uncomfortable as I could by warning him about the dogs, the gunfire, and the many people who wandered around at night. He did look awake and alert enough when I lay down.

I fell asleep at once. Aching and exhausted, I found the hard ground as welcoming as my bed at home.

A shout awoke me. Then I heard gunfire—several single shots, thunderous and nearby. Harry?

Something fell across me before I could get out of my sleep-sack—something big and heavy. It knocked the breath out of me. I struggled to get it off me, knowing that it was a human body, dead or unconscious. As I pushed at it and felt its heavy beard stubble and long hair, I realized it was a man, and not Harry. Some stranger.

I heard scrambling and thrashing near me. There were grunts and sounds of blows. A fight. I could see them in the darkness—two figures struggling on the ground. The one on the bottom was Harry.

He was fighting someone over the gun, and he was losing. The muzzle was being forced toward him.

That couldn't happen. We couldn't lose the gun or Harry. I took a small granite boulder from our fire pit, set my teeth, and brought it down with all my strength on the back of the intruder's head. And I brought myself down.

It wasn't the worst pain I had ever shared, but it came close. I was worthless after delivering that one blow. I think I was unconscious for a while.

Then Zahra appeared from somewhere, feeling me, trying to see me. She wouldn't find a wound, of course.

I sat up, fending her off, and saw that Harry was there, too.

"Are they dead?" I asked.

"Never mind them," he said. "Are you all right?"

I got up, swaying from the residual shock of the blow. I felt sick and dizzy, and my head hurt. A few days before, Harry had made me feel that way and we'd both recovered. Did that mean the man I'd hit would recover?

I checked him. He was still alive, unconscious, not feeling any pain now. What I was feeling was my own reaction to the blow I'd struck.

"The other one's dead," Harry said. "This one. . . Well, you caved in the back of his head. I don't know why he's still alive."

"Oh, no," I whispered. "Oh hell." And then to Harry, "Give me the gun."

"Why?" he asked.

My fingers had found the blood and broken skull, soft and pulpy at the back of the stranger's head. Harry was right. He should have been dead.

"Give me the gun," I repeated, and held out a bloody hand for it. "Unless you want to do this yourself."

"You can't shoot him. You can't just . . ."

"I hope you'd find the courage to shoot me if I were like that, and out here with no medical care to be had. We shoot him, or leave him here alive. How long do you think it will take him to die?"

"Maybe he won't die."

I went to my pack, struggling to navigate without throwing up. I pulled it away from the dead man, groped within it, and found my knife. It was a good knife, sharp and strong. I flicked it open and cut the unconscious man's throat with it.

Not until the flow of blood stopped did I feel safe. The man's heart had pumped his life away into the ground. He could not regain consciousness and involve me in his agony.

But, of course, I was far from safe. Perhaps the last two people from my old life were about to leave me. I had shocked and horrified them. I wouldn't blame them for leaving.

"Strip the bodies," I said. "Take what they have, then we'll put them into the scrub oaks down the hill where we gathered wood."

I searched the man I had killed, found a small amount of money in his pants pocket and a larger amount in his right sock. Matches, a packet of almonds, a packet of dried meat, and a packet of small, round, purple pills. I found no knife, no weapon of any kind. So this was not one of the pair that sized us up earlier in the night. I hadn't thought so. Neither of them had been long-haired. Both of these were.

I put the pills back in the pocket I had taken them from. Everything else, I kept. The money would help sustain us. The food might or might not be edible. I would decide that when I could see it clearly.

I looked to see what the others were doing, and was relieved to find them stripping the other body. Harry turned it over, then kept watch as Zahra went through the clothing, shoes, socks, and hair. She was even more thorough than I had been. With no hint of squeamishness, she hauled off the man's clothing and examined its greasy pockets, seams, and hems. I got the feeling she had done this before.

"Money, food, and a knife," she whispered at last.

"The other one didn't have a knife," I said, crouching beside them. "Harry, what—?"

"He had one," Harry whispered. "He pulled it when I yelled for them to stop. It's probably on the ground somewhere. Let's put these two down in the oaks."

"You and I can do it," I said. "Give Zahra the gun. She can guard us."

I was glad to see him hand her the gun without protest. He had not made a move to hand it to me when I asked, but that had been different.

We took the bodies down to the scrub oaks and rolled them into cover. Then we kicked dirt over all the blood that we could see and the urine that one of the men had released.

That wasn't enough. By mutual consent, we moved camp. This meant nothing more than gathering our bundles and sleepsacks and carrying them over the next low ridge and out of sight of where we had been.

If you camped on a hill between any two of the many low, rib-like ridges, you could have, almost, the privacy of a big, open-topped, three-walled room. You were vulnerable from hill or ridge tops, but if you camped on the ridges, you would be noticed by far more people. We chose a spot between two ridges, settled and sat silent for some time. I felt set-apart. I knew I had to speak, and I was afraid that nothing I could say would help. They might leave me. In disgust, in distrust, in fear, they might decide that they couldn't travel with me any longer. Best to try to get ahead of them.

"I'm going to tell you about myself," I said. "I don't know whether it will help you to understand me, but I have to tell you. You have a right to know."

And in low whispers, I told them about my mother—my biological mother—and about my sharing.

When I finished, there was another long silence. Then Zahra spoke, and I was so startled by the sound of her soft voice that I jumped.

"So when you hit that guy," she said, "it was like you hitting yourself."

"No," I said. "I don't get the damage. Just the pain."

"But, I mean it felt like you hit yourself?"

I nodded. "Close enough. When I was little, I used to bleed along with people if I hurt them or even if I saw them hurt. I haven't done that for a few years."

"But if they're unconscious or dead, you don't feel anything."

"That's right."

"So that's why you killed that guy?"

"I killed him because he was a threat to us. To me in a special way, but to you, too. What could we have done about him? Abandon him to the flies, the ants, and the dogs? You might have been willing to do that, but would Harry? Could we stay with him? For how long? To what purpose? Or would we dare to hunt up a cop and try to report seeing a guy hurt without involving ourselves. Cops are not trusting people. I think they would want to check us out, hang on to us for a while, maybe charge us with attacking the guy and killing his friend." I turned to look at Harry who had not said a word. "What would you have done?" I asked.

"I don't know," he said, his voice hard with disapproval. "I only know I wouldn't have done what you did."

"I wouldn't have asked you to do it," I said. "I didn't ask you. But, Harry, I would do it again. I might have to do it again. That's why I'm telling you this." I glanced at Zahra. "I'm sorry I didn't tell you before. I knew I should, but talking about it is . . . hard. Very hard. I've never told anyone before. Now . . ." I took a deep breath. "Now everything's up to you."

"What do you mean?" Harry demanded.

I looked at him, wishing I could see his expression well enough to know whether this was a real question. I didn't think it was. I decided to ignore him.

"So what do you think?" I asked, looking at Zahra.

Neither of them said anything for a minute. Then Zahra began to speak, began to say such terrible things in that soft voice of hers. After a moment, I wasn't sure she was talking to us.

"My mama took drugs, too," she said. "Shit, where I was born, everybody's mama took drugs—and whored to pay for them. And had babies all the time, and threw them away like trash when they died. Most of the babies did die from the drugs or accidents or not having enough to eat or being left alone so much . . . or from being sick. They were always getting sick. Some of them were born sick. They had sores all over or big things on their eyes—tumors, you know—or no legs or fits or can't breathe right. . . . All kinds of things. And some of the ones who lived were dumb as dirt. Can't think, can't learn, just sit around nine, ten years old, peeing in their pants, rocking back and forth, and dripping spit down their chins. There's a lot of them."

She took my hand and held it. "You ain't got nothing wrong with you, Lauren—nothing worth worrying about. That Paracetco shit was baby milk."

How was it that I had not gotten to know this woman back in the neighborhood? I hugged her. She seemed surprised, then hugged back.

We both looked at Harry.

He sat still, near us, but far from us—from me. "What would you do," he asked, "if that guy only had a broken arm or leg?"

I groaned, thinking about pain. I already knew more than I wanted to about how broken bones feel. "I think I'd let him go," I said, "and I'm sure I would be sorry for it. It would be a long time before I stopped looking over my shoulder."

"You wouldn't kill him to escape the pain?"

"I never killed anyone back in the neighborhood to escape pain."

"But a stranger . . ."

"I've said what I would do."

"What if I broke my arm?"

"Then I might not be much good to you. I would be having trouble with my arm, too, after all. But we'd have two good arms between us." I sighed. "We grew up together, Harry. You know me. You know what kind of person I am. I might fail you, but if I could help myself, I wouldn't betray you."

"I thought I knew you."

I took his hands, looked at their big, pale, blunt fingers. They had a lot of strength in them, I knew, but I had never seen him use it to bully anyone. He was worth some trouble, Harry was.

"No one is who we think they are," I said. "That's what we get for not being telepathic. But you've trusted me so far—and I've trusted you. I've just put my life in your hands. What are you going to do?"

Was he going to abandon me now to my "infirmity"—instead of me maybe abandoning him at some future time due to a theoretical broken arm. And I thought: One oldest kid to another, Harry; would that be responsible behavior?

He took his hands back. "Well, I did know you were a manipulative bitch," he said.

Zahra smothered a laugh. I was surprised. I'd never heard him use the word before. I heard it now as a sound of frustration. He wasn't going to leave. He was a last bit of home that I didn't have to give up yet. How did he feel about that? Was he angry with me for almost breaking up the group? He had reason to be, I suppose.

"I don't understand how you could have been like this all the time," he said. "How could you hide your sharing from everyone?"

"My father taught me to hide it," I told him. "He was right. In this world, there isn't any room for housebound, frightened, squeamish people, and that's what I might have become if everyone had known about me—all the other kids, for instance. Little kids are vicious. Haven't you noticed?"

"But your brothers must have known."

"My father put the fear of God into them about it. He could do that. As far as I know, they never told anyone. Keith used to play 'funny' tricks on me, though."

"So . . . you faked everyone out. You must be a hell of an actor."

"I *had* to learn to pretend to be normal. My father kept trying to convince me that I was normal. He was wrong about that, but I'm glad he taught me the way he did."

"Maybe you are normal. I mean if the pain isn't real, then maybe—"

"Maybe this sharing thing is all in my head? Of course it is! And I can't get it out. Believe me, I'd love to."

There was a long silence. Then he asked, "What do you write in your book every night?" Interesting shift.

"My thoughts," I said. "The day's events. My feelings."

"Things you can't say?" he asked. "Things that are important to you?"

"Yes."

"Then let me read something. Let me know something about the you that hides. I feel as though . . . as though you're a lie. I don't know you. Show me something of you that's real."

What a request! Or was it a demand? I would have given him money to read and digest some of the Earthseed portions of my journal. But he had to be eased into them. If he read the wrong thing, it would just increase the distance between us.

"The risks you ask me to take, Harry. . . . But, yes, I'll show you some of what I've written. I want to. It'll be another first for me. All I ask is that you read what I show you aloud so Zahra can hear it. As soon as it's light, I'll show you."

When it was light, I showed him this:

> *"All that you touch*
> *You Change.*

All that you Change
Changes you.

The only lasting truth
Is Change.

God
Is Change."

Last year, I chose these lines to the first page of the first book of *Earthseed: The Books of the Living.* These lines say everything. Everything!

Imagine him asking me for it.

I must be careful.

17

□ □ □

Embrace diversity.
Unite —
Or be divided,
robbed,
ruled,
killed
By those who see you as prey.
Embrace diversity
Or be destroyed.

EARTHSEED: THE BOOKS OF THE LIVING
TUESDAY, AUGUST 3, 2027
(FROM NOTES EXPANDED AUGUST 8)

There's a big fire in the hills to the east of us. We saw it begin as a thin, dark column of smoke, rising into an otherwise clear sky. Now it's massive—a hillside or two? Several buildings? Many houses? Our neighborhood again?

We kept looking at it, then looking away. Other people dying, losing their families, their homes. . . . Even when we had walked past it, we looked back.

Had the people with painted faces done this, too? Zahra was crying as she walked along, cursing in a voice so soft that I could hear only a few of the bitter words.

Earlier today we left the 118 freeway to look for and finally connect with the 23. Now we're on the 23 with charred overgrown wilderness on one side and neighborhoods on the other. We can't see the fire itself now. We've passed it, come a long way from it, put hills between it and us as we head southward toward the coast. But we can still see the smoke. We didn't stop for the night until it was almost dark and we were all tired and hungry.

We've camped away from the freeway on the wilderness side of it, out of sight, but not out of hearing of the shuffling hoards of people on the move. I think that's a sound we'll hear for the whole of our journey whether we stop in Northern California or go through to Canada. So many people hoping for so much up where it still rains every year, and an uneducated person might still get a job that pays in money instead of beans, water, potatoes, and maybe a floor to sleep on.

But it's the fire that holds our attention. Maybe it was started by accident. Maybe not. But still, people are losing what they may not be able to replace. Even if they survive, insurance isn't worth much these days.

People on the highway, shadowy in the darkness, had begun to reverse the flow, to drift northward to find a way to the fire. Best to be early for the scavenging.

"Should we go?" Zahra asked, her mouth full of dried meat. We built no fire tonight. Best for us to vanish into the darkness and avoid guests. We had put a tangle of trees and bushes at our backs and hoped for the best.

"You mean go back and rob those people?" Harry demanded.

"Scavenge," she said. "Take what people don't need no more. If you're dead, you don't need much."

"We should stay here and rest," I said. "We're tired, and it will be a long time before things are cool enough over there to allow scavenging. It's a long way off, anyway."

Zahra sighed. "Yeah."

"We don't have to do things like that, anyway," Harry said.

Zahra shrugged. "Every little bit helps."

"You were crying about that fire a while ago."

"Uh-uh," Zahra drew her knees up against her body. "I wasn't crying about that fire. I was crying about our fire and my Bibi and thinking about how much I hate people who set fires like that. I wish they would burn. I wish I could burn them. I wish I could just take them and throw them in the fire . . . like they did my Bibi." And she began to cry again, and he held her, apologizing and, I think, shedding a few tears himself.

Grief hit like that. Something would remind us of the past, of home, of a person, and then we would remember that it was all gone. The person was dead or probably dead. Everything we'd known and treasured was gone. Everything except the three of us. And how well were we doing?

"I think we should move," Harry said sometime later. He was still sitting with Zahra, one arm around her, and she seemed to welcome the contact.

"Why?" she asked.

"I want to be higher, closer to the level of the freeway or above it. I want to be able to see the fire if it jumps the freeway and spreads toward us. I want to see it before it gets too close. Fire moves fast."

I groaned. 'You're right," I said, "but moving now that it's dark is risky. We could lose this place and find nothing better."

"Wait here," he said, and got up and walked away into the darkness. I had the gun, so I hoped he kept his knife handy—and I hoped he wouldn't need it. He was still raw about what had happened the night before. He had killed a man. That bothered him. I had killed a man in a much more cold-blooded way, according to him, and it didn't bother me. But my "cold-bloodedness" bothered him. He wasn't a sharer. He didn't understand that to me pain was the evil. Death was an end to pain. No Bible verses were going to change that as far as I was concerned. He didn't understand sharing. Why should he? Most people knew little or nothing about it.

On the other hand, my Earthseed verses had surprised him, and, I think, pleased him a little. I wasn't sure whether he liked the writing or the reasoning, but he liked having something to read and talk about.

"Poetry?" he said this morning as he looked through the pages I showed him—pages of my Earthseed notebook, as it happened. "I never knew you cared about poetry."

"A lot of it isn't very poetical," I said. "But it's what I believe, and I've written it as well as I could." I showed him four verses in all—gentle, brief verses that might take hold of him without his realizing it and live in his memory without his intending that they should. Bits of the Bible had done that to me, staying with me even after I stopped believing.

I gave to Harry, and through him to Zahra, thoughts I wanted them to keep. But I couldn't prevent Harry from keeping other things as well: His new distrust of me, for instance, almost his new dislike. I was not quite Lauren Olamina to him any longer. I had seen that in his expression off and on all day. Odd. Joanne hadn't liked her glimpse of the real me either. On the other hand, Zahra didn't seem to mind. But then, she hadn't known me very well at home. What she learned now, she could accept without feeling lied to. Harry did feel lied to, and perhaps he wondered what lies I was still telling or living. Only time could heal that—if he let it.

We moved when he came back. He had found us a new campsite, near the freeway and yet private. One of the huge freeway signs had fallen or been knocked down, and now lay on the ground, propped up by a pair of dead sycamore trees. With the trees, it formed a massive lean-to. The rock and ash leavings of a campfire showed us that the place had been used before. Perhaps there had been people here tonight, but they had gone away to see what they could scavenge from the fire. Now we're here, happy to get a little privacy, a view of the hills back where the fire is, and the security, for what it was worth, of at least one wall.

"Good deal!" Zahra said, unrolling her sleepsack and settling down on top of it. "I'll take the first watch tonight, okay?"

It was okay with me. I gave her the gun and lay down, eager for sleep. Again I was amazed to find so much comfort in sleeping on the ground in my clothes. There's no narcotic like exhaustion.

Sometime in the night I woke up to soft, small sounds of voices and breathing. Zahra and Harry were making love. I turned my head and saw them at it, though they were too much involved with each other to notice me.

And, of course, no one was on watch.

I got caught up in their lovemaking, and had all I could do to lie still and keep quiet. I couldn't escape their sensation. I couldn't keep an efficient watch. I could either writhe with them or hold myself rigid. I held rigid until they finished—until Harry kissed Zahra, then got up to put his pants on and began his watch.

And I lay awake afterward, angry and worried. How in hell could I talk to either of them about this? It would be none of my business except for the time they chose for doing it. But look when that was! We could all have been killed.

Still sitting up, Harry began to snore.

I listened for a couple of minutes, then sat up, reached over Zahra, and shook him.

He jumped awake, stared around, then turned toward me. I couldn't see more than a moving silhouette.

"Give me the gun and go back to sleep," I said.

He just sat there.

"Harry, you'll get us killed. Give me the gun and the watch and lie down. I'll wake you later."

He looked at the watch.

"Sorry," he said. "Guess I was more tired than I thought." His voice grew less sleep-fogged. "I'm all right. I'm awake. Go back to sleep."

His pride had kicked in. It would be almost impossible to get the gun and the watch from him now.

I lay down. "Remember last night," I said. "If you care about her at all, if you want her to live, remember last night."

He didn't answer. I hoped I had surprised him. I supposed I had also embarrassed him. And maybe I had made him feel angry and defensive. Whatever I'd done, I didn't hear him doing anymore snoring.

WEDNESDAY, AUGUST 4, 2027

Today we stopped at a commercial water station and filled ourselves and all our containers with clean, safe water. Commercial stations are best for that. Anything you buy from a water peddler on the freeway ought to be boiled, and still might not be safe. Boiling kills disease organisms, but may do nothing to get rid of chemical residue—fuel, pesticide, herbicide, whatever else has been in the bottles that peddlers use. The fact that most peddlers can't read makes the situation worse. They sometimes poison themselves.

Commercial stations let you draw whatever you pay for—and not a drop more—right out of one of their taps. You drink whatever the local householders are drinking. It might taste, smell, or look bad, but you can depend on it not to kill you.

There aren't enough water stations. That's why water peddlers exist. Also, water stations are dangerous places. People going in have money. People coming out have water, which is as good as money. Beggars and thieves hang around such places—keeping the whores and drug dealers company. Dad warned us all about water stations, trying to prepare us in case we ever went out and got caught far enough from home to be tempted to stop for water. His advice: "Don't do it. Suffer. Get your rear end home."

Yeah.

Three is the smallest comfortable number at a water station. Two to watch and one to fill up. And it's good to have three ready for trouble on the way to and from the station. Three would not stop determined thugs, but it would stop opportunists—and most predators are opportunists. They prey on old people, lone women or women with young kids, handicapped people. . . . They don't want to get hurt. My father used to call them coyotes. When he was being polite, he called them coyotes.

OCTAVIA E. BUTLER

We were coming away with our water when we saw a pair of two-legged coyotes grab a bottle of water from a woman who was carrying a sizable pack and a baby. The man with her grabbed the coyote who had taken the water, the coyote passed the water to his partner, and his partner ran straight into us.

I tripped him. I think it was the baby who attracted my attention, my sympathy. The tough plastic bubble that held the water didn't break. The coyote didn't break either. I set my teeth, sharing the jolt as he fell and the pain of his scraped forearms. Back home, the younger kids hit me with that kind of thing every day.

I stepped back from the coyote and put my hand on the gun. Harry stepped up beside me. I was glad to have him there. We looked more intimidating together.

The husband of the woman had thrown off his attacker, and the two coyotes, finding themselves outnumbered, scampered away. Skinny, scared little bastards out to do their daily stealing.

I picked up the plastic bubble of water and handed it to the man. He took it and said, "Thanks man. Thanks a lot."

I nodded and we went on our way. It still felt strange to be called "man." I didn't like it, but that didn't matter.

"All of a sudden you're a Good Samaritan," Harry said. But he didn't mind. There was no disapproval in his voice.

"It was the baby, wasn't it?" Zahra asked.

"Yes," I admitted. "The family, really. All of them together." All of them together. They had been a black man, a Hispanic-looking woman, and a baby who managed to look a little like both of them. In a few more years, a lot of the families back in the neighborhood would have looked like that. Hell, Harry and Zahra were working on starting a family like that. And as Zahra had once observed, mixed couples catch hell out here.

Yet there were Harry and Zahra, walking so close together that they couldn't help now and then brushing against each other. But they kept alert, looked around. We were on U.S.101 now, and there were even more walkers. Even clumsy thieves would have no trouble losing themselves in this crowd.

But Zahra and I had had a talk this morning during her reading lesson. We were supposed to be working on the sounds of letters and the spelling of simple words. But when Harry went off to the bushes of our designated toilet area, I stopped the lesson.

"Remember what you said to me a couple of days ago?" I asked her. "My mind was wandering and you warned me. 'People get killed on freeways all the time,' you said."

To my surprise, she saw where I was headed at once. "Damn you," she said, looking up from the paper I had given her. "You don't sleep sound enough, that's all." She smiled as she said it.

"You want privacy, I'll give it to you," I said. "Just let me know, and I'll guard the camp from someplace a short distance away. You two can do what you want. But no more of this shit when you're on watch!"

She looked surprised. "Didn't think you said words like that."

"And I didn't think you did things like last night. Dumb!"

"I know. Fun, though. He's a big strong boy." She paused. "You jealous?"

"Zahra!"

"Don't worry," she said. "Things took me by surprise last night. I . . . I needed something, someone. It won't be like that no more."

"Okay."

"You jealous?" she repeated.

I made myself smile. "I'm as human as you are," I said. "But I don't think I would have yielded to temptation out here with no prospects, no idea what's going to happen. The thought of getting pregnant would have stopped me cold."

"People have babies out here all the time." She grinned at me. "What about you and that boyfriend of yours."

"We were careful. We used condoms."

Zahra shrugged. "Well Harry and me didn't. If it happens, it happens."

OCTAVIA E. BUTLER

It had apparently happened to the couple whose water we had saved. Now they had a baby to lug north.

They stayed near us today, that couple. I saw them every now and then. Tall, stocky, velvet-skinned, deep-black man carrying a huge pack; short, pretty, stocky, light-brown woman with baby and pack; medium brown baby a few months old—huge-eyed baby with curly black hair.

They rested when we rested. They're camped now not far behind us. They look more like potential allies than potential dangers, but I'll keep an eye on them.

THURSDAY, AUGUST 5, 2027

Late today we came within sight of the ocean. None of us have ever seen it before, and we had to go closer, look at it, camp within sight and sound and smell of it. Once we had decided to do that, we walked shoeless in the waves, pants legs rolled up. Sometimes we just stood and stared at it: the Pacific Ocean—the largest, deepest body of water on earth, almost half-a-world of water. Yet, as it was, we couldn't drink any of it.

Harry stripped down to his underwear and waded out until the cool water reached his chest. He can't swim, of course. None of us can swim. We've never before seen water enough to swim in. Zahra and I watched Harry with a lot of concern. Neither of us felt free to follow him. I'm supposed to be a man and Zahra attracts enough of the wrong kind of attention with all her clothes on. We decided to wait until after sundown and go in fully clothed, just to wash away some of the grime and stink. Then we could change clothes. We both had soap and we were eager to make use of it.

There were other people on the beach. In fact, the narrow strip of sand was crowded with people, though they managed to stay out of each other's way. They had spread themselves out and seemed far more tolerant of one another than they had during our night in the hills. I didn't hear any shooting or fighting. There were no dogs, no obvious thefts, no rape. Perhaps the sea and the cool breeze lulled them. Harry wasn't the only one to strip down and go into the water. Quite a few women had gone out, wearing almost nothing. Maybe this was a safer place than any we'd seen so far.

Some people had tents, and several had built fires. We settled in against the remnants of a small building. We were always, it seemed, looking for walls to shield us. Was it better to have them and perhaps get trapped against them or to camp in the open and be vulnerable on every side? We didn't know. It just felt better to have at least one wall.

I salvaged a flat piece of wood from the building, went a few yards closer to the ocean, and began to dig into the sand. I dug until I found dampness. Then I waited.

"What's supposed to happen?" Zahra asked. Until now she had watched me without saying anything.

"Drinkable water," I told her. "According to a couple of books I read, water is supposed to seep up through the sand with most of the salt filtered out of it."

She looked into the damp hole. "When?" she asked.

I dug a little more. "Give it time," I said. "If the trick works, we ought to know about it. It might save our lives someday."

"Or poison us or give us a disease," she said. She looked up to see Harry coming toward us, dripping wet. Even his hair was wet.

"He don't look bad naked," she said.

He was still wearing his underwear, of course, but I could see what she meant. He had a nice, strong-looking body, and I don't think he minded our looking at it. And he looked clean and he didn't stink.

I couldn't wait to get into the water.

"Go ahead," he said. "It's sundown. I'll watch our stuff. Go."

We got our soap out, gave him the gun, took off shoes and socks, and went. It was wonderful. The water was cold and it was hard to stand up in the waves and the sand kept being drawn away from our feet, even drawn from under our feet. But we threw water on each other and washed everything—clothing, bodies, and hair—let the waves knock us around, and laughed like crazy people. Best time I've had since we left home.

Quite a lot of water had seeped into the hole I dug by the time we got back to Harry. I tasted it—took a little up in my hand while Harry criticized me.

"Look at all the people in this damned place!" he said. "Do you see any bathrooms? What do you think they do out here. You ought to at least have the sense to use a water purification tablet!"

That thought was enough to make me spit out the mouthful of water that I had taken. He was right, of course. But that one mouthful had told me what I wanted to know. The water had been a little brackish, but not bad—drinkable. It should be boiled or a water purification tablet should be added to it, as Harry had said, and before that, according to my book, it could be strained through sand to get rid of more of the salt. That meant if we stayed near the coast, we could survive even if we ran short of water. That was good to know.

We still had our shadows. The couple with the baby had camped near us, and the woman was now sitting on the sand nursing her baby while the man knelt beside his pack, rummaging through it.

"Do you think they want to wash?" I asked Harry and Zahra.

"What are you going to do?" Zahra responded. "Offer to babysit?"

I shook my head. "No, I think that would be too much. Do either of you mind if I invite them over?"

"Aren't you afraid they'll rob us?" Harry demanded. "You're afraid of everyone else."

"They have better gear than we do," I said. "And they have no natural allies around here except us. Mixed couples or groups are rare out here. No doubt that's why they've kept close to us."

"And you helped them," Zahra said. "People don't help strangers too much out here. And you gave them back their water. That means you have enough so you don't have to rob them."

"So do you mind?" I asked again.

They looked at each other.

"I don't mind," Zahra said. "Long as we keep an eye on them."

"Why do you want them?" Harry asked, watching me.

"They need us more than we need them," I said.

"That's not a reason."

"They're potential allies."

"We don't need allies."

"Not now. But we'd be damned fools to wait and try to get them when we do need them. By then, they might not be around."

He shrugged and sighed. "All right. Like Zahra says, as long as we watch them."

I got up and went over to the couple. I could see them straighten and go tense as I approached. I was careful not to go too close or move too fast.

"Hello," I said. "If you two would like to take turns bathing, you can come over and join us. That might be safer for the baby."

"Join you?" the man said. "You're asking us to join you?"

"Inviting you."

"Why?"

"Why not. We're natural allies—the mixed couple and the mixed group."

"Allies?" the man said, and he laughed.

I looked at him, wondering why he laughed.

"What the hell do you really want?" he demanded.

I sighed. "Come join us if you want to. You're welcome, and in a pinch, five is better than two." I turned and left them. Let them talk it over and decide.

"They coming?" Zahra asked when I got back.

"I think so," I said. "Although maybe not tonight."

We built a fire and had a hot meal last night, but the mixed family did not join us. I didn't blame them. People stay alive out here by being suspicious. But they didn't go away either. And it was no accident that they had chosen to stay near us. It was a good thing for them that they were near us. The peaceful beach scene changed late last night. Dogs came onto the sand.

They came during my watch. I saw movement far down the beach and I focused on it. Then there was shouting, screams. I thought it was a fight or a robbery. I didn't see the dogs until they broke away from a group of humans and ran inland. One of them was carrying something, but I couldn't tell what it was. I watched them until they vanished inland. People chased them for a short distance, but the dogs were too fast. Someone's property was lost—someone's food, no doubt.

I was on edge after that. I got up, moved to the inland end of our wall, sat there where I could see more of the beach. I was there, sitting still with the gun in my lap when I spotted movement perhaps a long city block up the beach. Dark forms against pale sand. More dogs. Three of them. They nosed around the sand for a moment, then headed our way. I sat as still as I could, watching. So many people slept without posting watches. The three dogs wandered among the camps, investigating what they pleased, and no one tried to drive them away. On the other hand, people's oranges, potatoes, and grain meal couldn't be very tempting to a dog. Our small supply of dried meat might be another matter. But no dog would get it.

But the dogs stopped at the camp of the mixed couple. I remembered the baby and jumped up. At the same moment, the baby began to cry. I shoved Zahra with my foot and she came awake all at once. She could do that.

"Dogs," I said. "Wake Harry." Then I headed for the mixed couple. The woman was screaming and beating at a dog with her hands. A second dog was dodging the man's kicks and going for the baby. Only the third dog was clear of the family.

I stopped, slipped the safety, and as the third dog went in toward the baby, I shot it.

The dog dropped without a sound. I dropped, too, gasping, feeling kicked in the chest. It surprised me how hard the loose sand was to fall on.

At the crack of the shot, the other two dogs took off inland. From my prone position, I sighted on them as they ran. I might have been able to pick off one more of them, but I let them go. I hurt enough already. I couldn't catch my breath, it seemed. As I gasped, though, it occurred to me that prone was a good shooting position for me. Sharing would be less able to incapacitate me at once if I shot two-handed and prone. I filed the knowledge away for future use. Also, it was interesting that the dogs had been frightened by my shot. Was it the sound that scared them or the fact that one of them had been hit? I wish I knew more about them. I've read books about them being intelligent, loyal pets, but that's all in the past. Dogs now are wild animals who will eat a baby if they can.

I felt that the dog I had shot was dead. It wasn't moving. But by now a lot of people were awake and moving around. A living dog, even wounded, would be frantic to get away.

The pain in my chest began to ebb. When I could breathe without gasping, I stood up and walked back to our camp. There was so much confusion by then that no one noticed me except Harry and Zahra.

Harry came out to meet me. He took the gun from my hand, then took my arm and steered me back to my sleepsack.

"So you hit something," he said as I sat gasping again from the small exertion.

I nodded. "Killed a dog. I'll be okay soon."

"You need a keeper," he said.

"Dogs were after the baby!"

"You've adopted those damned people."

I smiled in spite of myself, liking him, thinking that I'd pretty much adopted him and Zahra, too. "What's wrong with that?" I asked.

He sighed. "Get in your bag and go to sleep, will you. I'll take the next watch,"

"Some people just came and carried off the dog you killed," Zahra said. "We should have got it."

"I'm not ready to eat a dog yet," Harry told her. "Go to sleep."

The names of the members of the mixed family are Travis Charles Douglas, Gloria Natividad Douglas, and six-month-old Dominic Douglas, also called Domingo. They gave in and joined us tonight after we made camp. We've detoured away from the highway to make camp on another beach, and they've followed. Once we were settled, they came over to us, uncertain and suspicious, offering us small pieces of their treasure: milk chocolate full of almonds. Real milk chocolate, not carob candy. It was the best thing I'd tasted since long before leaving Robledo.

"It was you last night?" Natividad asked Harry. The first thing she had told us was to call her Natividad.

"It was Lauren," Harry said, gesturing toward me.

She looked at me. "Thank you."

"Is your baby all right?" I asked.

"He had scratches and sand in his eyes and mouth from being dragged." She stroked the sleeping baby's black hair. "I put salve on the scratches and washed his eyes. He's all right now. He's so good. He only cried a little bit."

"Hardly ever cries," Travis said with quiet pride. Travis has an unusual deep-black complexion—skin so smooth that I can't believe he has ever in his life had a pimple. Looking at him makes me want to touch him and see how all that perfect skin feels. He's young, good looking, and intense—a stocky, muscular man, tall, but a little shorter and a little heavier than Harry. Natividad is stocky, too—a pale brown woman with a round, pretty face, long black hair bound up in a coil atop her head. She's short, but it isn't surprising somehow that she can carry a pack and a baby and keep up a steady pace all day. I like her, feel inclined to trust her. I'll have to be careful about that. But I don't believe she would steal from us. Travis has not accepted us yet, but she has. We've helped her baby. We're her friends.

"We're going to Seattle," she told us. "Travis has an aunt there. She says we can stay with her until we find work. We want to find work that pays money."

"Don't we all," Zahra agreed. She sat on Harry's sleepsack with him, his arm around her. Tonight could be tiresome for me.

Travis and Natividad sat on their three sacks, spread out to give their baby room to crawl when he woke up. Natividad had harnessed him to her wrist with a length of clothesline.

I felt alone between the two couples. I let them talk about their hopes and rumors of northern edens. I took out my notebook and began to write up the day's events, still savoring the last of the chocolate.

The baby awoke hungry and crying. Natividad opened her loose shirt, gave him a breast, and moved over near me to see what I was doing.

"You can read and write," she said with surprise. "I thought you might be drawing. What are you writing?"

"She's always writing," Harry said. "Ask to read her poetry. Some of it isn't bad."

I winced. My name is androgynous, in pronunciation at least— Lauren sounds like the more masculine Loren. But pronouns are more specific, and still a problem for Harry.

"She?" Travis asked right on cue. "Her?"

"Damn it, Harry," I said. "We forgot to buy that tape for your mouth."

He shook his head, then gave me an embarrassed smile. "I've known you all my life. It isn't easy to remember to switch all your pronouns. I think it's all right this time, though."

OCTAVIA E. BUTLER

"I told you so!" Natividad said to her husband. Then she looked embarrassed. "I told him you didn't look like a man," she said to me. "You're tall and strong, but . . . I don't know. You don't have a man's face."

I had, almost, a man's chest and hips, so maybe I should be glad to hear that I didn't have a man's face—though it wasn't going to help me on the road. "We believed two men and a woman would be more likely to survive than two women and a man," I said. "Out here, the trick is to avoid confrontation by looking strong."

"The three of us aren't going to help you look strong," Travis said. He sounded bitter. Did he resent the baby and Natividad?

"You are our natural allies," I said. "You sneered at that last time I said it, but it's true. The baby won't weaken us much, I hope, and he'll have a better chance of surviving with five adults around him."

"I can take care of my wife and my son," Travis said with more pride than sense. I decided not to hear him.

"I think you and Natividad will strengthen us," I said. "Two more pairs of eyes, two more pairs of hands. Do you have knives?"

"Yes." He patted his pants pocket. "I wish we had guns like you."

I wished we had guns—plural—too. But I didn't say so. "You and Natividad look strong and healthy," I said. "Predators will look at a group like the five of us and move on to easier prey."

Travis grunted, still noncommittal. Well, I had helped him twice, and now I was a woman. It might take him a while to forgive me for that, no matter how grateful he was.

"I want to hear some of your poetry," Natividad said. "The man we worked for, his wife used to write poetry. She would read it to me sometimes when she was feeling lonely. I liked it. Read me something of yours before it gets too dark."

Odd to think of a rich woman reading to her maid—which was who Natividad had been. Maybe I had the wrong idea of rich women. But then, everyone gets lonely. I put my journal down and picked up my book of Earthseed verses. I chose soft, non-preachy verses, good for road-weary minds and bodies.

18

□ □ □

Once or twice
each week
A Gathering of Earthseed
is a good and necessary thing.
It vents emotion, then
quiets the mind.
It focuses attention,
strengthens purpose, and
unifies people.

EARTHSEED: THE BOOKS OF THE LIVING

SUNDAY, AUGUST 8, 2027

"You believe in all this Earthseed stuff, don't you?" Travis asked me.

It was our day off, our day of rest. We had left the highway to find a beach where we could camp for the day and night and be comfortable. The Santa Barbara beach we had found included a partly burned park where there were trees and tables. It wasn't crowded, and we could have a little daytime privacy. The water was only a short walk away. The two couples took turns disappearing while I watched their packs and the baby. Interesting that the Douglases were already comfortable trusting me with all that was precious to them. We didn't trust them to watch alone last night or the night before, though we did make them watch. We had no walls to put our backs against last night so it was useful to have two watchers at a time. Natividad watched with me and Travis watched with Harry. Finally, Zahra watched alone.

I organized that, feeling that it was the schedule that would be most comfortable to both couples. Neither would be required to trust the other too much.

Now, amid the outdoor tables, firepits, pines, palms, and sycamores, trust seems not to be a problem. If you turn your back to the burned portion which is barren and ugly, this is a beautiful place, and it's far enough from the highway not to be found by the ever-flowing river of people moving north. I found it because I had maps—in particular, a street map of much of Santa Barbara County. My grandparents' maps helped us explore away from the highway even though many street signs were fallen or gone. There were enough left for us to find beaches when we were near them.

There were locals at this beach—people who had left real homes to spend an August day at the beach. I eavesdropped on a few fragments of conversation and found out that much.

Then I tried talking to some of them. To my surprise, most were willing to talk. Yes, the park was beautiful except where some painted fools had set fires. The rumors were that they did it to fight for the poor, to expose or destroy the goods hoarded by the rich. But a park by the sea wasn't goods. It was open to everyone. Why burn it? No one knew why.

No one knew where the fad of painting yourself and getting high on drugs and fire had come from, either. Most people suspected it had begun in Los Angeles where, according to them, most stupid or wicked things began. Local prejudice. I didn't tell any of them I was from the L.A. area. I just smiled and asked about the local job situation. Some people said they knew where I could work to earn a meal or a "safe" place to sleep, but no one knew where I could earn money. That didn't mean there weren't any such jobs, but if there were, they would be hard to find and harder to qualify for. That's going to be a problem wherever we go. And yet we know a lot, the three of us, the five of us. We know how to do a great many things. There must be a way to put it all together and make us something other than domestic servants working for room and board. We make an interesting unit.

Water is very expensive here—worse than in Los Angeles or Ventura Counties. We all went to a water station this morning. Still no freeway watersellers for us.

On the road yesterday, we saw three dead men—a group together, young, unmarked, but covered with the blood they had vomited, their bodies bloated and beginning to stink. We passed them, looked at them, took nothing from their bodies. Their packs—if they'd had any—were already gone. Their clothes, we did not want. And their canteens—all three still had canteens—their canteens, no one wanted.

We all resupplied yesterday at a local Hanning Joss. We were relieved and surprised to see it—a good dependable place where we could buy all we needed from solid food for the baby to soap to salves for skin chafed by salt water, sun, and walking. Natividad bought new liners for her baby carrier and washed and dried a plastic bag of filthy old ones. Zahra went with her into the separate laundry area of the store to wash and dry some of our filthy clothing. We wore our sea-washed clothing, salty, but not quite stinking. Paying to wash clothes was a luxury we could not often afford, yet none of us found it easy to be filthy. We weren't used to it. We were all hoping for cheaper water in the north. I even bought a second clip for the gun—plus solvent, oil, and brushes to clean the gun. It had bothered me, not being able to clean it before. If the gun failed us when we needed it, we could be killed. The new clip was a comfort, too. It gave us a chance to reload fast and keep shooting.

Now we lounged in the shade of pines and sycamores, enjoyed the sea breeze, rested, and talked. I wrote, fleshing out my journal notes for the week. I was just finishing that when Travis sat down next to me and asked his question:

"You believe in all this Earthseed stuff, don't you?"

"Every word," I answered.

"But . . . you made it up."

I reached down, picked up a small stone, and put it on the table between us. "If I could analyze this and tell you all that it was made of, would that mean I'd made up its contents?"

He didn't do more than glance at the rock. He kept his eyes on me. "So what did you analyze to get Earthseed?"

"Other people," I said, "myself, everything I could read, hear, see, all the history I could learn. My father is—was—a minister and a teacher. My stepmother ran a neighborhood school. I had a chance to see a lot."

"What did your father think of your idea of God?"

"He never knew."

"You never had the guts to tell him."

I shrugged. "He's the one person in the world I worked hard not to hurt."

"Dead?"

"Yes."

"Yeah. My parents, too." He shook his head. "People don't live long these days."

There was a period of silence. After a while, he said, "How did you get your ideas about God?"

"I was looking for God," I said. "I wasn't looking for mythology or mysticism or magic. I didn't know whether there was a god to find, but I wanted to know. God would have to be a power that could not be defied by anyone or anything."

"Change."

"Change, yes."

"But it's not a god. It's not a person or an intelligence or even a thing. It's just . . . I don't know. An idea."

I smiled. Was that such a terrible criticism? "It's a truth," I said.

"Change is ongoing. Everything changes in some way—size, position, composition, frequency, velocity, thinking, whatever. Every living thing, every bit of matter, all the energy in the universe changes in some way. I don't claim that everything changes in every way, but everything changes in some way."

Harry, coming in dripping from the sea, heard this last. "Sort of

OCTAVIA E. BUTLER

like saying God is the second law of thermodynamics," he said, grinning. He and I had already had this conversation.

"That's an aspect of God," I said to Travis. "Do you know about the second law?"

He nodded. "Entropy, the idea that the natural flow of heat is from something hot to something cold—not the other way—so that the universe itself is cooling down, running down, dissipating its energy."

I let my surprise show.

"My mother wrote for newspapers and magazines at first," he said. "She taught me at home. Then my father died and she couldn't earn enough for us to keep the house. And she couldn't find any other work that paid money. She had to take a job as a live-in cook, but she went on teaching me."

"She taught you about entropy?" Harry asked.

"She taught me to read and write," Travis said. "Then she taught me to teach myself. The man she worked for had a library—a whole big room full of books."

"He let you read them?" I asked.

"He didn't let me near them." Travis gave me a humorless smile. "I read them anyway. My mother would sneak them to me."

Of course. Slaves did that two hundred years ago. They sneaked around and educated themselves as best they could, sometimes suffering whipping, sale, or mutilation for their efforts.

"Did he ever catch you or her at it?" I asked.

"No." Travis turned to look toward the sea. "We were careful. It was important. She never borrowed more than one book at a time. I think his wife knew, but she was a decent woman. She never said anything. She was the one who talked him into letting me marry Natividad."

The son of the cook marrying one of the maids. That was like something out of another era, too.

"Then my mother died and all Natividad and I had was each other, and then the baby. I was staying on as gardener-handyman, but then the old bastard we worked for decided he wanted Natividad. He would try to watch when she fed the baby. Couldn't let her alone. That's why we left. That's why his wife helped us leave. She gave us money. She knew it wasn't Natividad's fault. And I knew I didn't want to have to kill the guy. So we left."

In slavery when that happened, there was nothing the slaves could do about it—or nothing that wouldn't get them killed, sold, or beaten.

I looked at Natividad who sat a short distance away, on spread out sleepsacks, playing with her baby and talking to Zahra. She had been lucky. Did she know? How many other people were less lucky—unable to escape the master's attentions or gain the mistress's sympathies. How far did masters and mistresses go these days toward putting less than submissive servants in their places?

"I still can't see change or entropy as God," Travis said, bringing the conversation back to Earthseed.

"Then show me a more pervasive power than change," I said. "It isn't just entropy. God is more complex than that. Human behavior alone should teach you that much. And there's still more complexity when you're dealing with several things at once—as you always are. There are all kinds of changes in the universe."

He shook his head. "Maybe, but nobody's going to worship them."

"I hope not," I said. "Earthseed deals with ongoing reality, not with supernatural authority figures. Worship is no good without action. With action, it's only useful if it steadies you, focuses your efforts, eases your mind."

He gave me an unhappy smile. "Praying makes people feel better even when there's no action they can take," he said. "I used to think that was all God was good for—to help people like my mother stand what they had to stand."

"That isn't what God is for, but there are times when that's what prayer is for. And there are times when that's what these verses are for. God is Change, and in the end, God prevails. But there's hope in understanding the nature of God—not punishing or jealous, but infinitely malleable. There's comfort in realizing that everyone and everything yields to God. There's power in knowing that God can be focused, diverted, shaped by anyone at all. But there's no power in having strength and brains, and yet waiting for God to fix things for you or take revenge for you. You know that. You knew it when you took your family and got the hell out of your boss's house. God will shape us all every day of our lives. Best to understand that and return the effort: Shape God."

"Amen!" Harry said, smiling.

I looked at him, wavered between annoyance and amusement, and let amusement win. "Put something on before you burn, Harry."

"You sounded like you could use an 'amen,' " he said as he put on a loose blue shirt. "Do you want to go on preaching or do you want to eat?"

We had beans cooked with bits of dried meat, tomatoes, peppers, and onions. It was Sunday. There were public firepits in the park, and we had plenty of time. We even had a little wheat-flour bread and the baby had real baby food with his milk instead of mashed or mother-chewed bits of whatever we were eating.

It's been a good day. Every now and then, Travis would ask me another question or toss me another challenge to Earthseed, and I would try to answer without preaching him a sermon—which was hard. I think I managed it most of the time. Zahra and Natividad got into an argument about whether I was talking about a male god or a female god. When I pointed out that Change had no sex at all and wasn't a person, they were confused, but not dismissive. Only Harry refused to take the discussion seriously. He liked the idea of keeping a journal, though. Yesterday he bought a small notebook, and now he's writing, too—and helping Zahra with her reading and writing lessons.

I'd like to draw him into Earthseed. I'd like to draw them all in. They could be the beginning of an Earthseed community. I would love to teach Dominic Earthseed as he grows up. I would teach him and he would teach me. The questions little children ask drive you insane because they never stop. But they also make you think. For now, though, I had to deal with Travis's questions.

I took a chance. I told Travis about the Destiny.

He had asked and asked me what the point of Earthseed is. Why personify change by calling it God? Since change is just an idea, why not call it that? Just say change is important.

"Because after a while, it won't be important!" I told him. "People forget ideas. They're more likely to remember God—especially when they're scared or desperate."

"Then they're supposed to do what?" he demanded. "Read a poem?"

"Or remember a truth or a comfort or a reminder to action," I said. "People do that all the time. They reach back to the Bible, the Talmud, the Koran, or some other religious book that helps them deal with the frightening changes that happen in life."

"Change does scare most people."

"I know. God is frightening. Best to learn to cope."

"Your stuff isn't very comforting."

"It is after a while. I'm still growing into it myself. God isn't good or evil, doesn't favor you or hate you, and yet God is better partnered than fought."

"Your God doesn't care about you at all," Travis said.

"All the more reason to care about myself and others. All the more reason to create Earthseed communities and shape God together. 'God is Trickster, Teacher, Chaos, Clay.' We decide which aspect we embrace—and how to deal with the others."

"Is that what you want to do? Set up Earthseed communities?"

"Yes."

"And then what?"

There it was. The opening. I swallowed and turned a little so that I could see the burned over area. It was so damn ugly. Hard to think anyone had done that on purpose.

"And then what?" Travis insisted. "A God like yours wouldn't have a heaven for people to hope for, so what is there?"

OCTAVIA E. BUTLER

"Heaven," I said, facing him again. "Oh, yes. Heaven."

He didn't say anything. He gave me one of his suspicious looks and waited.

"'The Destiny of Earthseed is to take root among the stars,'" I said. "That's the ultimate Earthseed aim, and the ultimate human change short of death. It's a destiny we'd better pursue if we hope to be anything other than smooth-skinned dinosaurs—here today, gone tomorrow, our bones mixed with the bones and ashes of our cities, and so what?"

"Space?" he said. "Mars?"

"Beyond Mars," I said. "Other star systems. Living worlds."

"You're crazy as hell," he said, but I like the soft, quiet way he said it—with amazement rather than ridicule.

I grinned. "I know it won't be possible for a long time. Now is a time for building foundations—Earthseed communities—focused on the Destiny. After all, my heaven really exists, and you don't have to die to reach it. 'The Destiny of Earthseed is to take root among the stars,' or among the ashes." I nodded toward the burned area.

Travis listened. He didn't point out that a person walking north from L.A. to who-knows-where with all her possessions on her back was hardly in a position to point the way to Alpha Centauri. He listened. He laughed a little—as though he were afraid to get caught being too serious about my ideas. But he didn't back away from me. He leaned forward. He argued. He shouted. He asked more questions. Natividad told him to stop bothering me, but he kept it up. I didn't mind. I understand persistence. I admire it.

SUNDAY, AUGUST 15, 2027

I think Travis Charles Douglas is my first convert. Zahra Moss is my second. Zahra has listened as the days passed, and as Travis and I went on arguing off and on. Sometimes she asked questions or pointed out what she saw as inconsistencies. After a while, she said. "I don't care about no outer space. You can keep that part of it. But if you want to put together some kind of community where people look out for each other and don't have to take being pushed around, I'm with you. I've been talking to Natividad. I don't want to live the way she had to. I don't want to live the way my mama had to either."

I wondered how much difference there was between Natividad's former employer who treated her as though he owned her and Richard Moss who purchased young girls to be part of his harem. It was all a matter of personal feeling, no doubt. Natividad had resented her employer. Zahra had accepted and perhaps loved Richard Moss.

Earthseed is being born right here on Highway 101—on that portion of 101 that was once El Camino Real, the royal highway of California's Spanish past. Now it's a highway, a river of the poor. A river flooding north.

I've come to think that I should be fishing that river even as I follow its current. I should watch people not only to spot those who might be dangerous to us, but to find those few like Travis and Natividad who would join us and be welcome.

And then what? Find a place to squat and take over? Act as a kind of gang? No. Not quite a gang. We aren't gang types. I don't want gang types with their need to dominate, rob and terrorize. And yet we might have to dominate. We might have to rob to survive, and even terrorize to scare off or kill enemies. We'll have to be very careful how we allow our needs to shape us. But we must have arable land, a dependable water supply, and enough freedom from attack to let us establish ourselves and grow.

It might be possible to find such an isolated place along the coast, and make a deal with the inhabitants. If there were a few more of us, and if we were better armed, we might provide security in exchange for living room. We might also provide education plus reading and writing services to adult illiterates. There might be a market for that kind of thing. So many people, children and adults, are illiterate these days. . . . We might be able to do it—grow our own food, grow ourselves and our neighbors into something brand new. Into Earthseed.

OCTAVIA E. BUTLER

19

□ □ □

Changes.
The galaxies move through space.
The stars ignite,
burn,
age,
cool,
Evolving.
God is Change.
God prevails.

EARTHSEED: THE BOOKS OF THE LIVING
FRIDAY, AUGUST 27, 2027
(FROM NOTES EXPANDED SUNDAY, AUGUST 29)

Earthquake today.

It hit early this morning just as we were beginning the day's walk, and it was a strong one. The ground itself gave a low, grating rumble like buried thunder. It jerked and shuddered, then seemed to drop. I'm sure it did drop, though I don't know how far. Once the shaking stopped, everything looked the same—except for sudden patches of dust thrown up here and there in the brown hills around us.

Several people screamed or shouted during the quake. Some, burdened by heavy packs, lost their footing and fell into the dirt or onto the broken asphalt. Travis, with Dominic on his chest and a heavy pack on his back was almost one of these. He stumbled, staggered, and managed somehow to catch himself. The baby, unhurt, but jolted by the sudden shaking, began to cry, adding to the noise of two older children walking nearby, the sudden talking of almost everyone, and the gasps of an old man who had fallen during the quake.

I put aside my usual suspicions and went to see whether the old man was all right—not that I could have done much to help him if he hadn't been. I retrieved his cane for him—it had landed beyond his reach—and helped him up. He was as light as a child, thin, toothless, and frightened of me.

I gave him a pat on the shoulder and sent him on his way, checking when his back was turned to see that he hadn't lifted anything. The world was full of thieves. Old people and young kids were often pickpockets.

Nothing missing.

Another man nearby smiled at me—an older, but not yet old black man who still had his teeth, and who pushed his belongings in twin saddlebags hanging from a small, sturdy metal-framed cart. He didn't say anything, but I liked his smile. I smiled back. Then I remembered that I was supposed to be a man, and wondered whether he had seen through my disguise. Not that it mattered.

I went back to my group where Zahra and Natividad were comforting Dominic and Harry was picking up something from the roadside. I went to Harry, and saw that he had found a filthy rag knotted into a small, tight ball around something. Harry tore the rotten cloth and a roll of money fell out into his hands. Hundred-dollar bills. Two or three dozen of them.

"Put it away!" I whispered.

He pushed the money into a deep pants pocket. "New shoes," he whispered. "Good ones, and other things. Do you need anything?"

I had promised to buy him a new pair of shoes as soon as we reached a dependable store. His were worn out. Now another idea occurred to me. "If you have enough," I whispered, "buy yourself a gun. I'll still get your shoes. You get a gun!" Then I spoke to the others, ignoring his surprise. "Is everyone all right?"

OCTAVIA E. BUTLER

Everyone was. Dominic was happy again, riding now on his mother's back, and playing with her hair. Zahra was readjusting her pack, and Travis had gone on and was taking a look at the small community ahead. This was farm country. We'd passed through nothing for days except small, dying towns, withering roadside communities and farms, some working, some abandoned and growing weeds.

We walked forward toward Travis.

"Fire," he said as we approached.

One house down the hill from the road smoked from several of its windows. Already people from the highway had begun to drift down toward it. Trouble. The people who owned the house might manage to put out their fire and still be overwhelmed by scavengers.

"Let's get away from here," I said. "The people down there are still strong, and they're going to feel besieged soon. They'll fight back."

"We might find something we can use," Zahra argued.

"There's nothing down there worth our getting shot over," I said. "Let's go!" I led the way past the small community and we were almost clear of it when the gunfire began.

There were people still on the road with us, but many had flooded down into the small community to steal. The crowd would not confine its attention to the one burning house, and all the households would have to resist.

There were more shots behind us—first single shots, then an uneven crackling of exchanged fire, then the unmistakable chatter of automatic weapons fire. We walked faster, hoping that we were beyond the range of anything aimed in our direction.

"Shit!" Zahra whispered, keeping up with me. "I should have known that was going to happen. People out here in the middle of nowhere gotta be tough."

"I don't think their toughness will get them through this day, though," I said, looking back. There was much more smoke rising now, and it was rising from more than one place. Distant shouts and screams mixed with the gunfire. Stupid place to put a naked little community. They should have hidden their homes away in the mountains where few strangers would ever see them. That was something for me to keep in mind. All the people of this community could do now was take a few of their tormentors with them. Tomorrow the survivors of this place would be on the road with scraps of their belongings on their backs.

It's odd, but I don't think anyone on the road would have thought of attacking that community en masse like that if the earthquake—or something—had not started a fire. One small fire was the weakness that gave scavengers permission to devastate the community—which they were no doubt doing now. The shooting could scare away some, kill or wound others, and make the remainder very angry. If the people of the community chose to live in such a dangerous place, they should have set up overwhelming defenses—a line of explosive charges and incendiaries, that kind of thing. Only power that strong, that destructive, that sudden would scare attackers off, would drive them away in a panic more overwhelming than the greed and the need that had drawn them in the first place. If the people of the community were without explosives, they should have grabbed their money and their kids and run like crazy the moment they saw the horde coming. They knew the hills better than migrating scavengers could. They should have had hiding places already prepared or at least been able to lose themselves among the hills while scavengers were ransacking their homes. But they had done none of this. And now vast thick clouds of smoke rose behind us, drawing even more scavengers.

"Whole world's gone crazy," a voice near me said, and I knew before I looked that it was the man with the saddlebagged cart. We'd slowed down a little, looking back, and he had caught up. He too had had the sense not to try to go scavenging in the little community. He didn't look like a man who scavenged. His clothes were dirty and ordinary, but they fit him well and they looked almost new. His jeans were still dark blue, and still creased down the legs. His red, short-sleeved shirt still had all its buttons. He wore expensive walking shoes and had had, not too long ago, an expensive professional haircut. What was he doing out here on the road, pushing a cart? A rich pauper—or at least, a once-rich pauper. He had a short, full, salt and pepper beard. I decided that I liked his looks as much as I had before. What a handsome old man.

Had the world gone crazy?

"From what I've read," I said to him, "the world goes crazy every three or four decades. The trick is to survive until it goes sane again." I was showing off my education and background; I admit it. But the old man seemed unimpressed.

"The nineteen nineties were crazy," he said, "but they were rich. Nothing like this bad. I don't think it's ever been this bad. Those people, those animals back there . . ."

"I don't see how they can act that way," Natividad said. "I wish we could call the police—whoever the police are around here. The householders back there should call."

"It wouldn't do any good," I said. "Even if the cops came today instead of tomorrow, they'd just add to the death toll."

We walked on, the stranger walking with us. He seemed content to walk with us. He could have dropped back or walked on ahead since he didn't have to carry his load. As long as he stayed on the road, he could speed along. But he stuck with us. I talked to him, introduced myself and learned that his name was Bankole—Taylor Franklin Bankole. Our last names were an instant bond between us. We're both descended from men who assumed African surnames back during the 1960s. His father and my grandfather had had their names legally changed, and both had chosen Yoruba replacement names.

"Most people chose Swahili names in the '60s," Bankole told me. He wanted to be called Bankole. "My father had to do something different. All his life he had to be different."

"I don't know my grandfather's reasons," I said. "His last name was Broome before he changed it, and that was no loss. But why he chose Olamina . . . ? Even my father didn't know. He made the change before my father was born, so my father was always Olamina, and so were we."

Bankole was one year older than my father. He had been born in 1970, and he was, according to him, too damn old to be tramping along a highway with everything he owned in a couple of saddlebags. He was 57. I caught myself wishing he were younger so he would live longer.

Old or not, he heard the two girls calling for help sooner than we did.

There was a road, more dirt than asphalt, running below and alongside the highway, then veering away from the highway into the hills. Up that road was a half-collapsed house, the dust of its collapse still hanging over it. It couldn't have been much of a house before it fell in. Now it was rubble. And once Bankole alerted us, we could hear faint shouts from it.

"Sounds like women," Harry said.

I sighed. "Let's go see. It might just be a matter of pushing some wood off them or something."

Harry caught me by the shoulder. "You sure?"

"Yeah." I took the gun out and gave it to him in case someone else's pain made me useless. "Watch our backs," I said.

We went in wary and tentative, knowing that a call for help could be false, could lure people to their attackers. A few other people followed us off the road, and Harry hung back, staying between them and us. Bankole shoved his cart along, keeping up with me.

There were two voices calling from the rubble. Both sounded like women. One was pleading, the other cursing. We located them by the sound of their voices, then Zahra, Travis and I began throwing off rubble—dry, broken wood, plaster, plastic, and brick from an ancient chimney. Bankole stood with Harry, watching, and looking formidable. Did he have a gun? I hoped he did. We were drawing a small audience of hungry-eyed scavengers. Most people looked to see what we were doing, and went on. A few stayed and stared. If the women had been trapped since the earthquake, it was surprising that no one had come already to steal their belongings and set fire to the rubble, leaving them in it. I hoped we would be able to get the women out and get back on the highway before someone decided to rush us. No doubt they already would have if there had been anything of value in sight.

Natividad spoke to Bankole, then put Dominic in one of his saddlebags and felt to see that her knife was still in her pocket. I didn't like that much. Better she should keep wearing the baby so we could leave at a run if she had to.

We found a pale leg, bruised and bleeding but unbroken, pinned under a beam. A whole section of wall and ceiling plus some of the chimney had fallen on these women. We moved the loose stuff then worked together to lift heavier pieces. At last we dragged the women out by their exposed limbs—an arm and a leg for one, both legs for the other. I didn't enjoy it anymore than they did.

On the other hand, it wasn't that bad. The women had lost some skin here and there, and one was bleeding from the nose and mouth. She spat out blood and a couple of teeth and cursed and tried to get up. I let Zahra help her up. All I wanted to do now was get away from here.

The other one, face wet with tears, just sat and stared at us. She was quiet now in a blank, unnatural way. Too quiet. When Travis tried to help her up, she cringed and cried out. Travis let her alone. She didn't seem to be hurt beyond a few scratches, but she might have hit her head. She might be in shock.

"Where's your stuff?" Zahra was asking the bloody one. "We're going to have to get away from here fast."

I rubbed my mouth, trying to get past an irrational certainty that two of my own teeth were gone. I felt horrible—scraped and bruised and throbbing, yet whole and unbroken, undamaged in any major way. I just wanted to huddle somewhere until I felt less miserable. I took a deep breath and went to the frightened, cringing woman.

"Can you understand me?" I asked.

She looked at me, then looked around, saw her companion wiping away blood with a grimy hand, and tried to get up and run to her. She tripped, started to fall, and I caught her, grateful that she wasn't very big.

"Your legs are all right," I said, "but take it easy. We have to get out of here soon, and you've got to be able to walk."

"Who are you?" she asked.

"A total stranger," I said. "Try to walk."

"There was an earthquake."

"Yeah. Walk!"

She took a shaky step away from me, then another. She staggered over to her friend. "Allie?" she said.

Her friend saw her, stumbled to her, hugged her, smeared her with blood. "Jill! Thank God!"

"Here's their stuff," Travis said. "Let's get them out of here while we still can."

We made them walk a little more, tried to make them see and understand the danger of staying where we were. We couldn't drag them with us, and what would have been the point of digging them out, then leaving them at the mercy of scavengers. They had to walk along with us until they were stronger and able to take care of themselves.

"Okay," the bloody one said. She was the smaller and tougher of the two, not that there was that much physical difference between them. Two medium-size, brown-haired white women in their twenties. They might be sisters.

"Okay," the bloody one repeated. "Let's get out of here." She was walking without limping or staggering now, though her companion was less steady.

"Give me my stuff," she said.

Travis waved her toward two dusty sleepsack packs. She put one on her back, then looked at the other and at her companion.

"I can carry it," the other woman said. "I'm all right."

She wasn't, but she had to carry her own things. No one could carry a double pack for long. No one could fight while carrying a double pack.

There were a dozen people standing around staring as we brought the two women out. Harry walked ahead of us, gun in hand. Something about him said with great clarity that he would kill. If he were pushed even a little, he would kill. I hadn't seen him that way before. It was impressive and frightening and wrong. Right for the situation and the moment, but wrong for Harry. He wasn't the kind of man who ought ever to look that way.

When had I begun thinking of him as a man rather than a boy? What the hell. We're all men and women now, not kids anymore. Shit.

Bankole walked behind, looking even more formidable than Harry in spite of his graying hair and beard. He had a gun in his hand. I had gotten a look at it as I walked past him. Another automatic—perhaps a nine millimeter. I hoped he was good with it.

Natividad pushed his cart along just ahead of him with Dominic still in one of the bags. Travis walked beside her, guarding her and the baby.

I walked with the two women, fearful that one of them might fall or that some fool might grab one. The one called Allie was still bleeding, spitting blood and wiping her bloody nose with a bloody arm. And the one called Jill still looked dull and shaky. Allie and I kept Jill between us.

Before the attack began, I knew it would happen. Helping the two trapped women had made us targets. We might already have been attacked if the community down the road had not drawn off so many of the most violent, desperate people. The weak would be attacked today. The quake had set the mood. And one attack could trigger others.

We could only try to be ready.

Out of the blue, a man grabbed Zahra. She's small, and must have looked weak as well as beautiful.

An instant later, someone grabbed me. I was spun around, and I tripped and started to fall. It was that stupid. Before anyone could hit me, I tripped and fell. But because my attacker had pulled me toward him, I fell against him. I dragged him down with me. Somehow, I managed to get my knife out. I flicked it open. I jabbed it upward into my attacker's body.

The six inch blade went in to the hilt. Then, in empathic agony, I jerked it out again.

I can't describe the pain.

The others told me later that I screamed as they'd never heard anyone scream. I'm not surprised. Nothing has ever hurt me that much before.

After a while, the agony in my chest ebbed and died. That is, the man on top of me bled and died. Not until then could I begin to be aware of something other than pain.

The first thing I heard was Dominic, crying.

I understood then that I had also heard shots fired—several shots. Where was everyone? Were they wounded?

Dead? Being held prisoner?

I kept my body still beneath the dead man. He was painfully heavy as deadweight, and his body odor was nauseating. He had bled all over my chest, and, if my nose was any judge, in death, he had urinated on me. Yet I didn't dare move until I understood the situation.

I opened my eyes just a little.

Before I could understand what I was seeing, someone hauled the stinking dead man off me. I found myself looking into two worried faces: Harry and Bankole.

I coughed and tried to get up, but Bankole held me down.

"Are you hurt anywhere?" he demanded.

"No, I'm all right," I said. I saw Harry staring at all the blood, and I added, "Don't worry. The other guy did all the bleeding."

OCTAVIA E. BUTLER

They helped me up, and I discovered I was right. The dead man had urinated on me. I was almost frantic with the need to strip off my filthy clothes and wash. But that had to wait. No matter how disgusting I was, I wouldn't undress in daylight where I could be seen. I'd had enough trouble for one day.

I looked around, saw Travis and Natividad comforting Dominic who was still screaming. Zahra was with the two new girls, standing guard beside them as they sat on the ground.

"Are those two okay?" I asked.

Harry nodded. "They're scared and shaken up, but they're all right. Everyone's all right—except him and his friends." He gestured toward the dead man. There were three more dead lying nearby.

"There were some wounded," Harry said. "We let them go."

I nodded. "We'd better strip these bodies and go, too. We're too obvious here from the highway."

We did a quick, thorough job, searching everything except body cavities. We weren't needy enough to do that yet. Then, at Zahra's insistence, I did go behind the ruined house for a quick change of clothing. She took the gun from Harry and stood watch for me.

"You're bloody," she said. "If people think you're wounded, they might jump you. This ain't a good day to look like you got something wrong with you."

I suspected that she was right. Anyway, it was a pleasure to have her talk me into something I already wanted so much to do.

I put my filthy, wet clothes into a plastic bag, sealed it, and stuffed it into my pack. If any of the dead had owned clothing that would fit me, and that was still in wearable condition, I would have thrown mine away. As it was, I would keep them and wash them the next time we came to a water station or a store that permitted washing. We had collected money from the corpses, but it would be best to use that for necessities.

We had taken about twenty-five hundred dollars in all from the four corpses—along with two knives that we could sell or pass on to the two girls, and one gun pulled by a man Harry had shot. The gun turned out to be an empty, dirty Beretta nine millimeter. Its owner had had no ammunition, but we can buy that—maybe from Bankole. For that we will spend money. I had found a few pieces of jewelry in the pocket of the man who attacked me—two gold rings, a necklace of polished blue stones that I thought were lapis lazuli, and a single earring which turned out to be a radio. The radio we would keep. It could give us information about the world beyond the highway. It would be good not to be cut off any longer. I wondered who my attacker had robbed to get it.

All four of the corpses had little plastic pill boxes hidden somewhere on them. Two boxes contained a couple of pills each. The other two were empty. So these people who carried neither food nor water nor adequate weapons did carry pills when they could steal them or steal enough to buy them. Junkies. What was their drug of choice, I wondered. Pyro? For the first time in days, I found myself thinking of my brother Keith. Had he dealt in the round purple pills we kept finding on people who attacked us? Was that why he died?

A few miles later along the highway, we saw some cops in cars, heading south toward what must now be a burned out hulk of a community with a lot of corpses. Perhaps the cops would arrest a few late-arriving scavengers. Perhaps they would scavenge a little themselves. Or perhaps they would just have a look and drive away. What had cops done for my community when it was burning? Nothing.

The two women we'd dug out of the rubble want to stay with us. Allison and Jillian Gilchrist are their names. They are sisters, 24 and 25 years old, poor, running away from a life of prostitution. Their pimp was their father. The house that had fallen on them was empty when they took shelter in it the night before. It looked long abandoned.

"Abandoned buildings are traps," Zahra told them as we walked. "Out here in the middle of nowhere, they're targets for all kinds of people."

OCTAVIA E. BUTLER

"Nobody bothered us," Jill said. "But then the house fell on us, and nobody helped us either, until you guys came along."

"You're very fortunate," Bankole told her. He was still with us, and walking next to me. "People don't help each other much out here."

"We know," Jill admitted. "We're grateful. Who are you guys, anyway?"

Harry gave her an odd little smile. "Earthseed," he said, and glanced at me. You have to watch out for Harry when he smiles that way.

"What's Earthseed?" Jill asked, right on cue. She had let Harry direct her gaze to me.

"We share some ideas," I said. "We intend to settle up north, and found a community."

"Where up north?" Allie demanded. Her mouth was still hurting, and I felt it more when I paid attention to her. At least her bleeding had almost stopped.

"We're looking for jobs that pay salaries and we're watching water prices," I said. "We want to settle where water isn't such a big problem."

"Water's a problem everywhere," she proclaimed. Then, "What are you? Some kind of cult or something?"

"We believe in some of the same things," I said.

She turned to stare at me with what looked like hostility. "I think religion is dog shit," she announced. "It's either phony or crazy."

I shrugged. "You can travel with us or you can walk away."

"But what the hell do you stand for?" she demanded. "What do you pray to?"

"Ourselves," I said. "What else is there?"

She turned away in disgust, then turned back. "Do we have to join your cult if we travel with you?"

"No."

"All right then!" She turned her back and walked ahead of me as though she'd won something.

I raised my voice just enough to startle and projected it at the back of her head. I said, "We risked ourselves for you today."

She jumped, but refused to look back.

I continued. "You don't owe us anything for that. It isn't something you could buy from us. But if you travel with us, and there's trouble, you stand by us, stand with us. Now will you do that or not?"

Allie swung around, stiff with anger. She stopped right in front of me and stood there.

I didn't stop or turn. It wasn't a time for giving way. I needed to know what her pride and anger might drive her to. How much of that apparent hostility of hers was real, and how much might be due to her pain? Was she going to be more trouble than she was worth?

When she realized that I meant to walk over her if I had to, that I would do it, she slid around me to walk beside me as though she had intended to do that all along.

"If you hadn't been the ones to dig us out," she said, "we wouldn't bother with you at all." She drew a deep, ragged breath.

"We know how to pull our own weight. We can help our friends and fight our enemies. We've been doing that since we were kids."

I looked at her, thinking of the little that she and her sister had told us about their lives: prostitution, pimp father. . . . Hell of a story if it were true. No doubt the details would be even more interesting. How had they gotten away from their father, anyway? They would bear watching, but they might turn out to be worth something.

"Welcome," I said.

She stared at me, nodded, then walked ahead of me in long quick strides. Her sister, who had dropped to walk near us while we were talking, now walked faster to join her. And Zahra, who had dropped back to keep an eye on the sister, grinned at me and shook her head. She went up to join Harry who was leading the group.

Bankole came up beside me again, and I realized he had gotten out of the way as soon as he saw trouble between Allie and me.

OCTAVIA E. BUTLER

"One fight a day is enough for me," he said when he saw me looking at him.

I smiled. "Thank you for standing by us back there."

He shrugged. "I was surprised to see that anyone else cared what happened to a couple of strangers."

"You cared."

"Yes. That kind of thing will get me killed someday. If you don't mind, I'd like to travel with your group, too."

"You have been. You're welcome."

"Thank you," he said, and smiled back at me. He had clear eyes with deep brown irises—attractive eyes. I like him too much already. I'll have to be careful.

Late today we reached Salinas, a small city that seemed little touched by the quake and its aftershocks. The ground has been shuddering off and on all day. Also, Salinas seemed untouched by the hordes of overeager scavengers that we had been seeing since that first burning community this morning. That was a surprise. Almost all of the smaller communities we'd passed had been burning and swarming with scavengers. It was as though the quake had given yesterday's quiet, plodding paupers permission to go animal and prey on anyone who still lives in a house.

I suspected that the bulk of the predatory scavengers were still behind us, still killing and dying and fighting over the spoils. I've never worked as hard at not seeing what was going on around me as I did today. The smoke and the noise helped veil things from me. I had enough to do dealing with Allie's throbbing face and mouth and the ambient misery of the highway.

We were tired when we reached Salinas, but we had decided to walk on after resupplying and washing. We didn't want to be in town when the worst of the scavengers arrived. They might be calm, tired after their day of burning and stealing, but I doubted it. I thought they would be drunk with power and hungry for more. As Bankole said, "Once people get the idea that it's all right to take what you want and destroy the rest, who knows when they'll stop."

But Salinas looked well-armed. Cops had parked all along the shoulders of the highway, staring at us, some holding their shotguns or automatic rifles as though they'd love an excuse to use them. Maybe they knew what was coming.

We needed to resupply, but we didn't know whether we would be allowed to. Salinas had the look of a "stay on the road" type town— the kind that wanted you gone by sundown unless you lived there. This week and last, we had run across a few little towns like that.

But no one stopped us when we headed off the road to a store. There were only a few people on the road now, and the cops were able to watch all of us. I saw them watching us in particular, but they didn't stop us. We were quiet. We were women and a baby as well as men, and three of us were white. I don't think any of that harmed us in their eyes.

The security guards in the stores were as well-armed as the cops— shot-guns and automatic rifles, a couple of machine guns on tripods in cubicles above us. Bankole said he could remember a time when security guards had revolvers or nothing but clubs. My father used to talk like that.

Some of the guards either weren't very well trained—or they were almost as power-drunk as the scavengers. They pointed their guns at us. It was crazy. Two or three of us walked into a store and two or three guns were trained on us. We didn't know what was going on at first. We froze, staring, waiting to see what was going to happen.

The guys behind the guns laughed. One of them said, "Buy something or get the fuck out!"

We got out. These were little stores. There were plenty of them to choose from. Some of them turned out to have sane guards. I couldn't help wondering how many accidents the crazy guards have with those guns. I suppose that after the fact, every accident was an armed robber with obvious homicidal inclinations.

The guards at the water station seemed calm and professional. They kept their guns down and confined themselves to cursing people to speed them along. We felt safe enough not only to buy water and give our clothes a quick wash and dry, but to rent a couple of cubicles—men's and women's—and sponge ourselves off from a basin of water each. That settled the question of my sex for any of the new people who hadn't already figured it out.

At last, somewhat cleaner, resupplied with food, water, ammunition for all three guns, and, by the way, condoms for my own future, we headed out of town. On our way, we passed through a small street market at the edge of town. It was just a few people with their merchandise—mostly junk—scattered on tables or on filthy rags spread on the bare asphalt. Bankole spotted the rifle on one of the tables.

It was an antique—a bolt action Winchester, empty, of course, with a five-round capacity. It would be, as Bankole admitted, slow. But he liked it. He inspected it with eyes and fingers and bargained with the well-armed old man and woman who were offering it for sale. They had one of the cleaner tables with merchandise laid out in a neat pattern—a small, manual typewriter; a stack of books; a few hand tools, worn, but clean; two knives in worn leather sheaths; a couple of pots, and the rifle with sling and scope.

While Bankole haggled with the man over the rifle, I bought the pots from the woman. I would get Bankole to carry them in his cart. They were large enough to contain soup or stew or hot cereal for all of us at once. We were nine now, and bigger pots made sense. Then I joined Harry at the stack of books.

There was no nonfiction. I bought a fat anthology of poetry and Harry bought a western novel. The others, either from lack of money or from lack of interest ignored the books. I would have bought more if I could have carried them. My pack was already about as heavy as I thought I could stand, and still walk all day.

Our bargaining finished, we stood away from the table to wait for Bankole. And Bankole surprised us.

He got the old man down to a price he seemed to think was fair, then he called us over. "Any of you know how to handle a relic like this?" he asked.

Well, Harry and I did, and he had us look the rifle over. In the end, everyone had a look at it, some with obvious awkwardness and some with familiarity. Back in the neighborhood, Harry and I had practiced with the guns of other households—rifles and shotguns as well as handguns. Whatever was legal back home was shared, at least in practice sessions. My father had wanted us to be familiar with whatever weapons might be available. Harry and I were both good, competent shots, but we'd never bought a used gun. I liked the rifle, I liked the look and feel of it, but that didn't mean much. Harry seemed to like it, too. Same problem.

"Come over here," Bankole said. He herded us out of earshot of the old couple. "You should buy that gun," he told us. "You took enough money off those four junkies to pay the price I got that guy to agree to. You need at least one accurate, long-range weapon, and this is a good one."

"That money would buy a lot of food," Travis said.

Bankole nodded. "Yes, but only living people need food. You buy this, and it will pay for itself the first time you need it. Anyone who doesn't know how to use it, I'll teach. My father and I used to hunt deer with guns just like this."

"It's an antique," Harry said. "If it were automatic . . ."

"If it were automatic, you couldn't afford it." Bankole shrugged. "This thing is cheap because it's old and it's legal."

"And it's slow," Zahra said. "And if you think that old guy's price is cheap, you're crazy."

"I know I'm new here," Allie said, "but I agree with Bankole. You guys are good with your handguns, but sooner or later, you're going to meet someone who sits out of handgun range and picks you off. Picks us off."

"And this rifle is going to save us?" Zahra demanded.

"I doubt that it would save us," I said. "But with a decent shot behind it, it might give us a chance." I looked at Bankole. "You hit any of those deer?"

He smiled. "One or two."

I did not return the smile. "Why don't you buy the rifle for yourself?"

"I can't afford it," he said. "I've got enough money to keep me going and take care of necessities for a while. Everything else that I had was stolen from me or burned."

I didn't quite believe him. But then, no one knew how much money I had either. In a way, I suppose he was asking about our solvency. Did we have enough money to spend an unexpected windfall on an old rifle? And what did he intend to do if we did? I hoped, not for the first time, that he wasn't just a handsome thief. Yet I did like the gun, and we do need it.

"Harry and I are decent shots, too," I said to the group. "I like the feel of this gun, and it's the best we can afford right now. Has anyone seen any real trouble with it?"

They looked at one another. No one answered.

"It just needs a cleaning and some 30-06 ammunition," Bankole said. "It's been stored for a while, but it appears to have been well maintained. If you buy it, I think I can manage to buy a cleaning kit and some ammunition."

At that, I spoke up before anyone else could. "If we buy, that's a deal. Who else can handle the rifle?"

"I can," Natividad said. And when that won her a few surprised looks, she smiled. "I had no brothers. My father needed to teach someone."

"We never had a chance to do any shooting," Allie said. "But we can learn."

Jill nodded. "I always wanted to learn," she said.

"I'll have to learn, too," Travis admitted. "Where l grew up, guns were either locked away or carried by hired guards."

"Let's go buy it, then," I said. "And let's get out of here. The sun will be down soon."

Bankole kept his word, bought cleaning things and plenty of ammunition—insisted on buying them before we left town, because, as he said, "Who knows when we'll need it, or when we'll find other people willing to sell it to us."

Once that was settled, we left town.

As we left, Harry carried the new rifle and Zahra carried the Beretta, both empty and in need of attention before we loaded them. Only Bankole and I carried fully loaded guns. I led the group and he brought up the rear. It was getting dark. Behind us in the distance, we could hear gunfire and the dull thunder of small explosions.

20

□ □ □

God is neither good nor evil,
neither loving
nor hating.
God is Power.
God is Change.
We must find the rest of what we need within ourselves,
in one another,
in our Destiny.

EARTHSEED: THE BOOKS OF THE LIVING
SATURDAY, AUGUST 28, 2027
(FROM NOTES EXPANDED TUESDAY, AUGUST 31)

Today or tomorrow should be a rest day, but we've agreed not to rest. Last night was full of distant shooting, explosions and fire. We could see fire behind us, though not in front. Moving on seems sensible, in spite of our weariness.

Then, this morning, I cleaned the little black earring radio with alcohol from my pack, turned the thing on, and put it in my ear. I had to relay what it said since its sound could not reach the others.

What it said told us we should not only forget about resting, but change our plans.

We had intended to follow U.S. 101 up through San Francisco and across the Golden Gate Bridge. But the radio warned us to stay away from the Bay Area. From San Jose up through San Francisco, Oakland, and Berkeley, there is chaos. The quake hit hard up there, and the scavengers, predators, cops, and private armies of security guards seem bent on destroying what's left. Also, of course, pyro is doing its part. This far north, the radio reporters shorten the name to "pro" or "ro" and they say there are plenty of addicts.

Addicts are running wild, setting fires in areas that the earthquake didn't damage. Bands of the street poor precede or follow them, grabbing whatever they can from stores and from the walled enclaves of the rich and what's left of the middle class. Yeah.

In some places, the rich are escaping by flying out in helicopters. The bridges that are still intact—and most of them are—are guarded either by the police or by gangs. Both groups are there to rob desperate, fleeing people of their weapons, money, food, and water—at the least. The penalty for being too poor to be worth robbing is a beating, a rape, and/or death. The National Guard has been activated to restore order, and I suppose it might. But I suspect that in the short term, it will only add to the chaos. What else could another group of well-armed people do in such an insane situation. The thoughtful ones might take their guns and other equipment and vanish to help their families. Others might find themselves at war with their own people. They'll be confused and scared and dangerous. Of course, some will discover that they enjoy their new power—the power to make others submit, the power to take what they want—property, sex, life . . .

Bad situation. The Bay Area will be a good place to avoid for a long time.

We spread maps on the ground, studied them as we ate breakfast, and decided to turn off U.S. 101 this morning. We'll follow a smaller, no doubt emptier road inland to the little town of San Juan Bautista, then east along State Route 156. From 156 to 152 to Interstate 5. We'll use I-5 to circle around the Bay Area. For a time we'll walk up the center of the state instead of along the coast. We might have to bypass I-5 and go farther east to State 33 or 99. I like the emptiness around much of I-5. Cities are dangerous. Even small towns can be deadly. Yet we have to be able to resupply. In particular, we have to be

OCTAVIA E. BUTLER

able to get water. If that means going into the more populated areas around one of the other highways, we'll do it. Meanwhile we'll be careful, resupply every time we get a chance, never pass up a chance to top off our water and food, waste nothing. But, hell, the maps are old. Maybe the area around I-5 is more settled now.

To reach I-5, we'll pass a big freshwater lake—San Luis Reservoir. It might be dry now. Over the past few years a lot of things had gone dry. But there will be trees, cool shade, a place to rest and be comfortable. Perhaps there will at least be a water station. If so, we'll camp there and rest for a day or even two days. After hiking up and over a lot of hills, we'll need the extra rest.

For now, I suspect that we'll soon have scavengers being driven north toward us from Salinas, and refugees being driven south toward us from the Bay Area. The best thing we can do is get out of the way.

We got an early start, fortified by the good food we had bought at Salinas—some extra stuff that Bankole had wheeled in his cart, though we all chipped in to buy it. We made sandwiches—dried beef, cheese, sliced tomatoes—all on bread made from wheat flour. And we ate grapes. It was a shame we had to hurry. We hadn't had anything that good tasting for a long time.

The highway north was emptier today than I've ever seen it. We were the biggest crowd around—eight adults and a baby—and other people kept away from us. Several of the other walkers were individuals and couples with children. They all seemed in a hurry—as though they, too, knew what might be coming behind them. Did they also know what might be ahead—what was ahead if they stayed on 101. Before we left 101 I tried to warn a couple of women traveling alone with kids to avoid the Bay Area. I told them I'd heard there was a lot of trouble up there—fires, riots, bad quake damage. They just held on to their kids and edged away from me.

Then we left 101 and took our small, hilly road, our short cut to San Juan Bautista. The road was paved and not too badly broken up. It was lonely. For long stretches we saw no one at all. No one had followed us from 101. We passed farms, small communities, and shanties, and the people living in these came out with their guns to stare at us. But they let us alone. The shortcut worked. We managed to reach and pass through San Juan Bautista before dark. We've camped just east of the town. We're all exhausted, footsore, full of aches and pains and blisters. I long for a rest day, but not yet. Not yet.

I put my sleepsack next to Bankole's and lay down, already half asleep. We had drawn straws for the watch schedule, and my watch wasn't until the early morning. I ate nuts and raisins, bread and cheese, and I slept like a corpse.

SUNDAY, AUGUST 29, 2027
(FROM NOTES EXPANDED TUESDAY, AUGUST 31)

Early this morning I awoke to the sound of gunfire, nearby and loud. Short bursts of automatic weapons fire. And there was light from somewhere.

"Be still," someone said. "Stay down and keep quiet." Zahra's voice. She had the watch just before mine.

"What is it?" one of the Gilchrists demanded. And then, "We've got to get away!"

"Stay!" I whispered. "Be still, and it will pass."

I could see now that two groups were running from the highway—the 156—one group chasing the other, both firing their guns as though they and their enemies were the only people in the world. We could only stay down and hope they didn't shoot us by accident. If nobody moved, accidents were less likely.

The light came from a fire burning some distance from us. Not buildings. We hadn't camped near buildings. Yet something was burning. It was, I decided, a big truck of some kind. Perhaps that was the reason for the shooting. Someone, some group had tried to hijack a truck on the highway and things had gone wrong. Now,

OCTAVIA E. BUTLER

whatever the truck was carrying—food, I suspected—the fire would get it. Neither the hijackers nor the defenders would win.

We would win if we could just keep out of the fighting.

I reached over to feel for Bankole, wanting assurance that he was all right.

He wasn't there.

His sleepsack and his things were still there, but he was gone.

Moving as little as I could, I looked toward our designated toilet area. He must be there. I couldn't see him, but where else could he be? Bad timing. I squinted, trying to pick him out, not knowing whether to be glad or afraid because I couldn't. After all, if I could see him, so could other people.

The shooting went on and on while we lay still and quiet and scared. One of the trees we'd camped under was hit twice, but well above our heads.

Then the truck exploded. I don't know what exploded in it. It hadn't looked like an old truck—one of those that used diesel fuel, but it might have been. Would diesel fuel explode? I didn't know.

The explosion seemed to end the gunfight. A few more shots were exchanged, then nothing. I saw people, visible in the firelight, walking back toward the truck. Sometime later, I saw others—several together in a bunch—moving away toward the town. Both groups were moving away from us, and that was good.

Now. Where was Bankole? In as low a voice as I could manage, I spoke to the others. "Can anyone see Bankole?"

No answer.

"Zahra, did you see him go?"

"Yeah, a couple of minutes before the shooting started," she answered.

All right. If he didn't come out soon, we would have to go looking for him. I swallowed, tried not to think about finding him hurt or dead. "Is everyone else all right?" I asked. "Zahra?"

"I'm fine."

"Harry?"

"Yeah," he said. "I'm okay."

"Travis? Natividad?"

"We're all right," Travis said.

"What about Dominic?"

"Didn't even wake up."

That was good. If he had, his crying could have gotten us killed. "Allie? Jill?"

"We're okay," Allie said.

I sat up, keeping my movements slow and cautious. I couldn't see anyone or hear anything beyond insects and the distant fire. When no one shot me, others sat up, too. Where noise and light had not awakened Dominic, his mother's movement did the trick. He awoke and began to whimper, but Natividad held him and he quieted.

But still no Bankole. I wanted to get up and go looking for him. I had two mental images of him: One of him lying wounded or dead, and one of him crouching behind a tree holding his own Beretta nine millimeter. If the latter was true, I could scare him into shooting me. There might also be other people out there with ready guns and frayed nerves.

"What time is it?" I asked Zahra who had Harry's watch.

"Three-forty," she said.

"Let me have the gun," I said. "Your watch is almost over anyway."

"What about Bankole?" She passed both the watch and the gun over.

"If he isn't back in five minutes I'm going to go look for him."

"Wait a minute," Harry said. "You aren't going to do that by yourself. I'll go with you."

I almost said no. I don't think he would have paid any attention if I had, but I never spoke the word. If Bankole were injured and conscious, I would be useless the moment I saw him. I would be lucky to drag myself back to camp. Someone else would have to drag him back.

"Thank you," I said to Harry.

Five minutes later, he and I went first to the toilet area, then around it, searching. There was no one, or rather, we could see no one. Still, there might be other people around—others camping overnight, others involved in the shooting, others prowling. . . . Still, I called Bankole's name once, aloud. I touched Harry as a kind of warning and he jumped, settled, then jumped again as I said the name. We both listened in absolute silence.

There was a rustling off to our right where there were several trees blotting out the stars, creating a space of impenetrable darkness. Anything could be there.

The rustling came again, and with it a whimper—a child's whimper. Then Bankole's voice:

"Olamina!"

"Yes," I answered, almost limp with relief. "Here!"

He came out of the pool of darkness, a tall, broad shadow that seemed bulkier than it should have been. He was carrying something.

"I have an orphaned child," he said. "The mother was hit by a stray bullet. She just died."

I sighed. "Is the child hurt?"

"No, just scared. I'll carry him back to our camp. Will one of you get his things?"

"Take us to his camp," I said.

Harry collected the child's things, and I collected the mother's and searched her body. Between us, we gathered everything. By the time we finished, the little boy, perhaps three years old, was crying. That scared me. I left Harry to push the dead woman's pack along in her baby carriage and Bankole to carry the whimpering child. All I carried was the gun, drawn and ready. Even when we got back to our own camp, I couldn't relax. The little boy wouldn't be quiet and Dominic joined him with even louder cries. Zahra and Jill worked to comfort the new child, but he was surrounded by strangers in the middle of the night, and he wanted his mother!

I saw movement over near the burned out carcass of the truck.

The fire was still burning, but it was smaller now, burning itself out. There were still people near it. They had lost their truck. Would they care about a crying child? And if they did care, would they want to help the kid or just shut its mouth?

A lone, dark figure came away from the truck and took several steps toward us. At that moment, Natividad took the new child, and in spite of his age, gave him one breast and Dominic the other.

It worked. Both children were comforted almost at once. They made a few more small sounds, then settled down to nursing.

The shadow figure from the truck stood still, perhaps confused now that it was no longer guided by noise. After a moment, it turned and went back past the truck and out of sight. Gone. It couldn't have seen us. We could look out of the darkness under the trees that sheltered our campsite and see by firelight, by starlight. But others could only follow the baby noise to us.

"We ought to move," Allie whispered. "Even if they can't see us, they know we're here."

"Watch with me," I said.

"What?"

"Stay awake and watch with me. Let the others get a little more rest. Trying to move in the dark is more dangerous than staying put."

".. . all right. But I don't have a gun."

"Do you have a knife?"

"Yeah."

"That will have to be enough until we get the other guns clean and ready." We've been too tired and in too much of a hurry to do that so far. Also, I don't want Allie or Jill to have guns yet. Not yet. "Just keep your eyes open." The only real defense against automatic rifles is concealment and silence.

"A knife is better than a gun now," Zahra said. "If you have to use it, it will be quiet."

I nodded. "The rest of you, try to get a little more rest. I'll wake you at dawn."

Most of them lay down to sleep, or at least to rest. Natividad kept both children with her. Tomorrow, though, one of us would have to take charge of the little boy. We didn't need the burden of such a big child—one who had reached the "run around and grab everything" stage. But we had the little boy, and there was no one to hand him off to. No woman camping alongside a highway with her child would have other relatives handy.

"Olamina," Bankole said into my ear. His voice was low and soft and only I reacted to it. I turned, and he was so close that I felt his beard brush my face. Soft, thick beard. This morning he combed it more carefully than he combed the hair on his head. He has the only mirror among us. Vain, vain old man. I moved almost by reflex toward him.

I kissed him, wondering what it would feel like to kiss so much beard. I did kiss the beard at first, missing his mouth by a little in the dark. Then I found it and he moved a little and slipped his arms around me and we settled to it for a little while.

It was hard for me to make myself push him away. I didn't want to. He didn't want to let me.

"I was going to say thank you for coming after me," he said. "That woman was conscious almost until she died. The only thing I could do for her was stay with her."

"I was afraid you might have been shot out there."

"I was flat on the ground until I heard the woman groaning."

I sighed. "Yeah." And then, "Rest."

He lay down next to me and rubbed my arm—which tingled wherever he touched it. "We should talk soon," he said.

"At least," I agreed.

He grinned—I could see the flash of teeth—and turned over and tried to sleep.

The boy's name was Justin Rohr. His dead mother had been Sandra Rohr. Justin had been born in Riverside, California just three years ago. His mother had gotten him this far north from Riverside. She had saved his birth certificate, some baby pictures, and a picture of a stocky, freckled, red-haired man who was, according to a notation on the back of the photo, Richard Walter Rohr, born January 9, 2002, and died May 20, 2026. The boy's father—only twenty-four when he died. I wondered what had killed him. Sandra Rohr had saved her marriage certificate and other papers important to her. All were wrapped in a plastic packet that I had taken from her body. Elsewhere on her, I had found several thousand dollars and a gold ring.

There was nothing about relatives or a specific destination. It seemed that Sandra had simply been heading north with her son in search of a better life.

The little boy tolerated us all well enough today, although he got frustrated when we didn't understand him at once. When he cried, he demanded that we produce his mother.

Allie, of all people, was his choice for substitute mother. She resisted him at first. She ignored him or pushed him away. But when he was not being wheeled along, he chose to walk with her or demand to be carried by her. By the end of the day, she had given in. The two of them had chosen each other.

"She used to have a little boy," her sister Jill told me as we walked along State 156 with the few other walkers who had chosen this route. It was empty. There were times when we could see no one at all, or when, as we headed east and north, the only people we could see were heading west and south toward us, toward the coast.

"She called her little boy Adam," Jill continued. "He was only a few months old when . . . he died."

I looked at her. She had a big swollen purple bruise in the middle of her forehead, like a misshapen third eye. I don't think it hurt her much, though. It didn't hurt me much.

"When he died," I repeated. "Who killed him?"

She looked away and rubbed her bruise. "Our father. That's why we left. He killed the baby. It cried. He hit it with his fists until it stopped."

I shook my head and sighed. It was no news to me that other people's fathers could be monsters. I'd heard about such things all my life, but I'd never before met people who were so clearly their father's victims.

"We burned the house," Jill whispered. I heard her say it, and I knew without asking what she wasn't saying. But she looked like a person talking to herself, forgetting that anyone was listening. "He was passed out drunk on the floor. The baby was dead. We got our stuff and our money—we earned it!—and we set fire to the trash on the floor and the couch. We didn't stay to see. I don't know what happened. We ran away. Maybe the fire went out. Maybe he didn't die." She focused on me. "He might still be alive."

She sounded more scared than anything else. Not hopeful or sorry. Scared. The devil might still be alive.

"Where did you run from?" I asked. "What city?"

"Glendale."

"Way down in L.A. County?"

"Yeah."

"Then he's more than three hundred miles behind you."

". . . yeah."

"He drank a lot, didn't he."

"All the time."

"Then he'd be in no shape to follow you even if the fire never touched him. What do you think would happen to a drunk on the highway? He'd never even make it out of L.A."

She nodded. "You sound like Allie. You're both right. I know. But . . . I dream about him sometimes—that he's coming, that he's found us. . . . I know it's crazy. But I wake up covered in sweat."

"Yeah," I said, remembering my own nightmares during the search for my father. "Yeah."

Jill and I walked together for a while without talking. We were moving slowly because Justin demanded to be allowed to walk now and then. He had too much energy to spend hours sitting and riding. And, of course, when he was allowed to walk, he wanted to run all around, investigate everything. I had time to stop, swing my pack around, and dig out a length of clothesline. I handed it to Jill.

"Tell your sister to try harnessing him with this," I said. "It might save his life. One end around his waist, the other around her arm."

She took the rope.

"I've taken care of a few three-year-olds," I said, "and I'll tell you, she's going to need a lot of help with that little kid. If she doesn't know that now, she will."

"Are you guys just going to leave all the work to her?" Jill demanded.

"Of course not." I watched Allie and Justin walking along—lean, angular woman and pudgy, bumblebee of a child. The boy ran to investigate a bush near the roadside, then, startled by the approach of strangers, ran back to Allie and hung on to the cloth of her jeans until she took his hand. "They do seem to be adopting each other, though," I said. "And taking care of other people can be a good cure for nightmares like yours and maybe hers."

"You sound as though you know."

I nodded. "I live in this world, too."

We passed through Hollister before noon. We resupplied there, not knowing when we would see well-equipped stores again. We had already discovered that several of the small communities shown on the maps no longer existed—had not existed for years. The earthquake had done a lot of damage in Hollister, but the people hadn't gone animal. They seemed to be helping one another with repairs and looking after their own destitute. Imagine that.

OCTAVIA E. BUTLER

21

□ □ □

The Self must create
Its own reasons for being.
To shape God,
Shape Self.

EARTHSEED: THE BOOKS OF THE LIVING
MONDAY, AUGUST 30, 2027

There is still a little water in the San Luis Reservoir. It's more fresh water than I've ever seen in one place, but by the vast size of the reservoir, I can see that it's only a little compared to what should be there—what used to be there.

The highway runs through the recreational area for several miles. That gave us a chance to travel through on the road until we spotted an area that would make a good rest-day camp and that wasn't occupied.

There are a lot of people in the area—people who have set up permanent camps in everything from rag-and-plastic tents to wooden shacks that look almost fit for human habitation. Where are so many people going to the bathroom? How clean is the water in the reservoir? No doubt cities that use it purify the water when it reaches them. Whether they do or not, I think it's time for us to break out the water purification tablets.

Around several of the tents and shacks, there are small, ragged gardens—new plantings and remnants of summer vegetable gardens. There are a few things left to harvest: big squashes, pumpkins, and gourds still growing along with carrots, peppers, greens, and a little corn. Good, cheap, filling foods. Not enough protein, but perhaps the people hunt. There must be game around here, and I saw plenty of guns. People wear holstered handguns or carry rifles or shotguns. The men in particular go armed.

They all stared at us.

As we went past, people stopped their gardening, outdoor cooking, or whatever to stare at us. We had pushed ourselves, had been eager to arrive ahead of the crowd I believe will soon come in from the Bay Area. So we didn't arrive with the usual human river. Yet by ourselves we are enough of a crowd to make the local squatters nervous. They let us alone, though. Except during disaster-induced feeding frenzies like the ones after the earthquake, most people let one another alone. I think Dominic and Justin are making it easier for us to fit in. Justin, now tethered to Allie's wrist, runs around staring at the squatters until they make him nervous. Then he runs back to Allie and demands to be carried. He's a cute little kid. Lean, grim-faced people tend to smile at him.

No one shot at us or challenged us as we walked along the highway. No one bothered us later when we left the highway and headed into the trees toward what we thought might be a good area. We found old campsites and toilet places and avoided them. We didn't want to be within sight of the highway or of anyone else's tent or shack. We wanted privacy, not too many rocks to sleep on, and a way of reaching the water that didn't put us too much on display. We looked for over an hour until we found an isolated old campsite, long abandoned and a little higher upslope than others we'd seen. It suited all of us. Then, with hours of daylight left, we rested in enormous comfort and laziness, knowing we had the rest of today and all of tomorrow to do almost nothing. Natividad fed Dominic and the two of them drifted off to sleep. Allie followed her example with Justin, although preparing him a meal was a little more complicated. Both women had more reason to be tired and to need sleep than the rest of us, so we left them out when we drew lots for a watch schedule—one for day and night. We shouldn't get *too* comfortable. Also, we agreed that no one should go off exploring or getting water alone. I thought the couples would soon start going off together—And I thought it was just about time for Bankole and me to have that talk.

I sat with him and cleaned our new handgun while he cleaned the rifle. Harry was on watch and needed my gun. When I went over to give it to him, he let me know he understood exactly what was going on between Bankole and me.

"Be careful," he whispered. "Don't give the poor old guy a heart attack."

"I'll tell him you were worried," I said.

Harry laughed, then sobered. "Be careful, Lauren. Bankole is probably all right. He seems to be. But, well. . . . Yell if anything goes wrong."

I rested my hand on his shoulder for a moment and said, "Thank you."

The nice thing about sitting and working alongside someone you don't know very well, someone you'd like to know much better, is that you can talk with him or be quiet with him. You can get comfortable with him and with the awareness that you'll soon be making love to him.

Bankole and I were quiet for a while, a little shy. I sneaked glances at him and caught him sneaking glances at me. Then, to my own surprise, I began to talk to him about Earthseed—not preaching, just talking, testing I guess. I needed to see his reaction. Earthseed is the most important thing in my life. If Bankole were going to laugh at it, I needed to know now. I didn't expect him to agree with it or even to be much interested in it. He's an old man. I thought he was probably content with whatever religion he had. It occurred to me as I spoke that I had no idea what his religion was. I asked him.

"None at all," he said. "When my wife was alive, we went to a Methodist church. Her religion was important to her, so I went along. I saw how it comforted her, and I wanted to believe, but I never could."

"We were Baptists," I said. "I couldn't make myself believe either, and I couldn't tell anyone. My father was the minister. I kept quiet and began to understand Earthseed."

"Began to invent Earthseed," he said.

"Began to discover it and understand it," I said. "Stumbling across the truth isn't the same as making things up." I wondered how many times and ways I would have to say this to new people.

"It sounds like some combination of Buddhism, existentialism, Sufism, and I don't know what else," he said. "Buddhism doesn't make a god of the concept of change, but the impermanence of everything is a basic Buddhist principle."

"I know," I said. "I've done a lot of reading. Some other religions and philosophies do contain ideas that would fit into Earthseed, but none of them *are* Earthseed. They go off in their own directions."

He nodded. "All right. But tell me, what do people have to do to be good members of an Earthseed Community?"

A nice, door-opening question. "The essentials," I answered, "are to learn to shape God with forethought, care, and work; to educate and benefit their community, their families, and themselves; and to contribute to the fulfillment of the Destiny."

"And why should people bother about the Destiny, farfetched as it is? What's in it for them?"

"A unifying, purposeful life here on Earth, and the hope of heaven for themselves and their children. A real heaven, not mythology or philosophy. A heaven that will be theirs to shape."

"Or a hell," he said. His mouth twitched. "Human beings are good at creating hells for themselves even out of richness." He thought for a moment. "It sounds too simple, you know."

"You think it's simple?" I asked in surprise.

"I said it *sounds* too simple."

"It sounds overwhelming to some people."

"I mean it's too . . . straightforward. If you get people to accept it, they'll make it more complicated, more open to interpretation, more mystical, and more comforting."

"Not around me they won't!" I said.

"With you or without you, they will. All religions change. Think about the big ones. What do you think Christ would be these days?

A Baptist? A Methodist? A Catholic? And the Buddha—do you think he'd be a Buddhist now? What kind of Buddhism would he practice?" He smiled. "After all, if 'God is Change,' surely Earthseed can change, and if it lasts, it will."

I looked away from him because he was smiling. This was all nothing to him. "I know," I said. "No one can stop Change, but we all shape Change whether we mean to or not. I mean to guide and shape Earthseed into what it should be."

"Perhaps." He went on smiling. "How serious are you about this?"

The question drove me deep into myself. I spoke, almost not knowing what I would say. "When my father . . . disappeared," I began, "it was Earthseed that kept me going. When most of my community and the rest of my family were wiped out, and I was alone, I still had Earthseed. What I am now, all that I am now is Earthseed."

"What you are now," he said after a long silence, "is a very unusual young woman."

We didn't talk for a while after that. I wondered what he thought. He hadn't seemed to be bottling up *too* much hilarity. No more than I'd expected. He had been willing to go along with his wife's religious needs. Now, he would at least permit me mine.

I wondered about his wife. He hadn't mentioned her before. What had she been like? How had she died?

"Did you leave home because your wife died?" I asked.

He put down a long slender cleaning rod and rested his back against the tree behind him. "My wife died five years ago," he said. "Three men broke in——junkies, dealers, I don't know. They beat her, tried to make her tell where the drugs were."

"Drugs?"

"They had decided that we must have something they could use or sell. They didn't like the things she was able to give them so they kept beating her. She had a heart problem." He drew in a long breath, then sighed. "She was still alive when I got home. She was able to tell me what had happened. I tried to help her, but the bastards had taken her medicine, taken everything. I phoned for an ambulance. It arrived an hour after she died. I tried to save her, then to revive her. I tried so damned hard. . . ."

I stared down the hill from our camp where just a glint of water was visible in the distance through the trees and bushes. The world is full of painful stories. Sometimes it seems as though there aren't any other kind and yet I found myself thinking how beautiful that glint of water was through the trees.

"I should have headed north when Sharon died," Bankole said. "I thought about it."

"But you stayed." I turned away from the water and looked at him. "Why?"

He shook his head. "I didn't know what to do, so for some time I didn't do anything. Friends took care of me, cooked for me, cleaned the house. It surprised me that they would do that. Church people most of them. Neighbors. More her friends than mine."

I thought of Wardell Parrish, devastated after the loss of his sister and her children—and his house. Had Bankole been some community's Wardell Parrish? "Did you live in a walled community?" I asked.

"Yes. Not rich, though. Nowhere near rich. People managed to hold on to their property and feed their families. Not much else. No servants. No hired guards."

"Sounds like my old neighborhood."

"I suppose it sounds like a lot of old neighborhoods that aren't there anymore. I stayed to help the people who had helped me. I couldn't walk away from them."

"But you did. You left. Why?"

"Fire—and scavengers."

"You, too? Your whole community?"

"Yes. The houses burned, most of the people were killed. . . . The rest scattered, went to family or friends elsewhere. Scavengers and squatters moved in. I didn't decide to leave. I escaped."

Much too familiar. "Where did you live? What city?"

"San Diego."

"That far south?"

"Yes. As I said, I should have left years ago. If I had, I could have managed plane fare and resettlement money."

Plane fare *and* resettlement money? He might not call that rich, but we would have.

"Where are you going now?" I asked.

"North." He shrugged.

"Just anywhere north or somewhere in particular?"

"Anywhere where I can be paid for my services and allowed to live among people who aren't out to kill me for my food or water."

Or for drugs, I thought. I looked into his bearded face and added up the hints I'd picked up today and over the past few days. "You're a doctor, aren't you?"

He looked a little surprised. "I was, yes. Family practice. It seems a long time ago."

"People will always need doctors," I said. "You'll do all right."

"My mother used to say that." He gave me a wry smile. "But here I am."

I smiled back because, looking at him now, I couldn't help myself, but as he spoke, I decided he had told me at least one lie. He might be as displaced and in distress as he appeared to be, but he wasn't just wandering north. He wasn't looking for just anywhere he could be paid for his services and not robbed or murdered. He wasn't the kind of man who wandered. He knew where he was going. He had a haven somewhere—a relative's home, another home of his own, a friend's home, *something*—some definite destination.

Or perhaps he just had enough money to buy a place for himself in Washington or Canada or Alaska. He had had to choose between fast, safe, expensive air travel and having settling-in money when he got where he was going. He had chosen settling-in money. If so, I agreed with him. He was taking the kind of risk that would enable him to make a new beginning as soon as possible—if he survived.

On the other hand, if I were right about any of this, he might disappear on me some night. Or perhaps he would be more open about it—just walk away from me some day, turn down a side road and wave good-bye. I didn't want that. After I'd slept with him I would want it even less.

Even now, I wanted to keep him with me. I hated that he was lying to me already—or I believed he was. But why should he tell me everything? He didn't know me very well yet, and like me, he meant to survive. Perhaps I could convince him that he and I could survive well together. Meanwhile, best to enjoy him without quite trusting him. I may be wrong about all this, but I don't believe I am. Pity.

We finished the guns, loaded them, and went down to the water to wash. You could go right down to the water, scoop some up in a pot, and take it away. It was free. I kept looking around, thinking someone would come to stop us or charge us or something. I suppose we could have been robbed, but no one paid any attention to us. We saw other people getting water in bottles, canteens, pots, and bags, but the place seemed peaceful. No one bothered anyone. No one paid any attention to us.

"A place like this can't last," I told Bankole. "It's a shame. Life could be good here."

"I suspect that it's against the law to live here," he said. "This is a State Recreation Area. There should be some kind of limit on how long you can stay. I'm certain that there should be—used to be—some group policing the place. I wonder if officials of some kind come around to collect bribes now and then."

"Not while we're here, I hope." I dried my hands and arms and waited for him to dry his. "Are you hungry?" I asked.

"Oh, yes," he said. He looked at me for a while, then reached for me. He took me by both arms, drew me to him, kissed me, and spoke into my ear. "Aren't you?"

I didn't say anything. After a while I took his hand and we went back to camp to pick up one of his blankets. Then we went to an isolated little spot that we'd both noticed earlier.

It felt natural and easy to lie down with him, and explore the

270   OCTAVIA E. BUTLER

smooth, hard, broad feel of his body. He'd kept himself fit. No doubt walking hundreds of miles in the past few weeks had burned off whatever fat he'd been carrying. He was still big—barrel-chested and tall. Best of all, he took a lot of uncomplicated pleasure in my body, and I got to share it with him. It isn't often that I can enjoy the good side of my hyperempathy. I let the sensation take over, intense and wild. I might be more in danger of having a heart attack than he is. How had I done without this for so long?

There was an odd, unromantic moment when we both reached into crumpled clothing and produced condoms. It was funny because of the way it hit us both at once, and we laughed, then went on to the serious business of loving and pleasuring one another. That combed and trimmed beard that he's so vain about tickles like mad.

"I knew I should have let you alone," he said to me when we had made love twice and were still not willing to get up and go back to the others. "You're going to kill me. I'm too old for this stuff."

I laughed and made a pillow of his shoulder.

After a while, he said, "I need to be serious for a minute, girl."

"Okay."

He drew a long breath, sighed, swallowed, hesitated. "I don't want to give you up," he said.

I smiled.

"You're a kid," he said. "I ought to know better. How old are you, anyway?"

I told him.

He jumped, then pushed me off his shoulder. "Eighteen?" He flinched away from me as though my skin burned him. "My god," he said. "You're a baby! I'm a child molester!"

I didn't laugh, though I wanted to. I just looked at him.

After a while he frowned and shook his head. In a little more time, he moved back against me, touching my face, my shoulders, my breasts.

"You're not just eighteen," he said.

I shrugged.

"When were you born? What year?"

"Twenty oh nine."

"No." He drew the word out: "Nooo."

I kissed him and said in the same tone, "Yesss. Now stop your nonsense. You want to be with me and I want to be with you. We're not going to split up because of my age, are we?"

After a while he shook his head. "You should have a nice youngster like Travis," he said. "I should have the sense and the strength to send you off to find one."

That made me think of Curtis, and I cringed away from thinking of him. I've thought as little as possible about Curtis Talcott. He isn't like my brothers. He may be dead, but none of us ever saw his body. I saw his brother Michael. I was terrified of seeing Curtis himself, but I never did. He may not be dead. He's lost to me, but I hope he's not dead. He should be here with me on the road. I hope he's alive and all right.

"Who have I reminded you of?" Bankole asked me, his voice soft and deep.

I shook my head. "A boy I knew at home. We were going to get married this year. I don't even know whether he's still alive."

"You loved him?"

"Yes! We were going to marry and leave home, walk north. We had decided to go this fall."

"That's crazy! You intended to walk this road even though you didn't have to?"

"Yes. And if we had left earlier, he'd be with me. I wish I knew he was all right."

He lay down on his back and drew me down beside him. "We've all lost someone," he said. "You and I seem to have lost everyone. That's a bond, I suppose."

"A terrible one," I said. "But not our only one."

He shook his head. "You're really eighteen?"

"Yes. As of last month."

"You look and act years older."

"This is who I am," I said.

"You were the oldest kid in your family, weren't you?"

I nodded. "I had four brothers. They're all dead."

"Yes," he sighed. "Yes."

TUESDAY, AUGUST 31, 2027

I've spent all of today talking, writing, reading, and making love to Bankole. It seems such a luxury not to have to get up, pack, and walk all day. We all lay sprawled around the campsite resting aching muscles, eating, and doing nothing. More people flowed into the area from the highway and made their camps, but none of them bothered us.

I began Zahra's reading lesson and Jill and Allie looked interested. I included them as though I had intended to from the first. It turned out that they could read a little, but hadn't learned to write. Toward the end of the lesson, I read a few Earthseed verses to them in spite of Harry's groans. Yet when Allie proclaimed that she would never pray to any god of change, Harry was the one who corrected her. Zahra and Travis both smiled at that, and Bankole watched us all with apparent interest.

After that, Allie began to ask questions instead of making scornful proclamations, and for the most part, the others answered her—Travis and Natividad, Harry and Zahra. Once Bankole answered, expanding on something I told him yesterday. Then he caught himself and looked a little embarrassed.

"I still think it's too simple," he said to me. "A lot of it is logical, but it will never work without a sprinkling of mystical confusion."

"I'll leave that to my descendants," I said, and he busied himself, digging a bag of almonds out of his pack, pouring some into his hand, and passing the rest around.

Just before nightfall a gun battle began over toward the highway.

We couldn't see any of it from where we were, but we stopped talking and lay down. With bullets flying, it seemed best to keep low.

The shooting started and stopped, moved away, then came back. I was on watch, so I had to stay alert, but in this storm of noise, nothing moved near us except the trees in the evening breeze. It looked so peaceful, and yet people out there were trying to kill each other, and no doubt succeeding. Strange how normal it's become for us to lie on the ground and listen while nearby, people try to kill each other.

OCTAVIA E. BUTLER

22

□ □ □

As wind,
As water,
As fire,
As life,
God
Is both creative and destructive,
Demanding and yielding,
Sculptor and clay.
God is Infinite Potential:
God is Change.

EARTHSEED: THE BOOKS OF THE LIVING
THURSDAY, SEPTEMBER 9, 2027

We've had over a week of weary, frightening, nerve-wracking walking. We've reached and passed through the city of Sacramento without real trouble. We've been able to buy enough food and water, been able to find plenty of empty places in the hills where we could make camp. Yet none of us have had any feelings of comfort or well-being along the stretch of Interstate-5 that we've just traveled.

I-5 is much less traveled than U.S. 101, in spite of the earthquake chaos. There were times when the only people we could see were each other. Those times never lasted long, but they did happen.

On the other hand, there were more trucks on I-5. We had to be careful because trucks traveled during the day as well as at night. Also, there were more human bones on I-5. It was nothing to run across skulls, lower jaws, or bones of the pelvis and torso. Arm and leg bones were rarer, but now and then, we spotted them, too.

"I think it's the trucks," Bankole told us. "If they hit someone along here, they wouldn't stop. They wouldn't dare. And the junkies and alcoholics wouldn't be that careful where they walked."

I suppose he's right, although along that whole empty stretch of road, we saw only four people whom I believed were either not sober or not sane.

But we saw other things. On Tuesday we camped in a little hollow back in the hills to the west of the road, and a big black and white dog came wandering down toward our camp with the fresh- looking, bloody hand and forearm of a child in its mouth.

The dog spotted us, froze, turned, and ran back the way it had come. But we all got a good look before it went, and we all saw the same thing. That night, we posted a double watch. Two watchers, two guns, no unnecessary conversation, no sex.

The next day we decided not to take another rest day until we had passed through Sacramento. There was no guarantee that anything would be better on the other side of Sacramento, but we wanted to get away from this grim land.

That night, looking for a place to camp, we stumbled across four ragged, filthy kids huddled around a campfire. The picture of them is still clear in my mind. Kids the age of my brothers—twelve, thirteen, maybe fourteen years old, three boys and a girl. The girl was pregnant, and so huge it was obvious she would be giving birth any day. We rounded a bend in a dry stream bed, and there these kids were, roasting a severed human leg, maneuvering it where it lay in the middle of their fire atop the burning wood by twisting its foot. As we watched, the girl pulled a sliver of charred flesh from the thigh and stuffed it into her mouth.

They never saw us. I was in the lead, and I stopped the others before they all rounded the bend. Harry and Zahra, who were just behind me, saw all that I saw. We turned the others back and away, not telling them why until we were far from those kids and their cannibal feast.

OCTAVIA E. BUTLER

No one attacked us. No one bothered us at all. The country we walked through was even beautiful in some places—green trees and rolling hills; golden dried grasses and tiny communities; farms, many overgrown and abandoned, and abandoned houses. Nice country, and compared to Southern California, rich country. More water, more food, more room. . . .

So why were the people eating one another?

There were several burned out buildings. It was obvious that there had been trouble here, too, but much less than on the coast. Yet we couldn't wait to get back to the coast.

Sacramento was all right to resupply in and hurry through. Water and food were cheap there compared to what you could buy along the roadside, of course. Cities were always a relief as far as prices went. But cities were also dangerous. More gangs, more cops, more suspicious, nervous people with guns. You tiptoe through cities. You keep up a steady pace, keep your eyes open, and try to look both too intimidating to bother and invisible. Neat trick. Bankole says cities have been like that for a long time.

Speaking of Bankole, I haven't let him get much rest on this rest day. He doesn't seem to mind. He did say something that I should make note of, though. He said he wanted me to leave the group with him. He has, as I suspected, a safe haven—or as safe as any haven can be that isn't surrounded by high-tech security devices and armed guards. It's in the hills on the coast near Cape Mendocino maybe two weeks from here.

"My sister and her family have been living there," he said. "But the property belongs to me. There's room on it for you."

I could imagine how delighted his sister would be to see me. Would she try to be polite, or would she stare at me, then at him, then demand to know whether he was in his right mind?

"Did you hear what I said?" he demanded.

I looked at him, interested in the anger I heard in his voice. Why anger?

"What am I doing? Boring you?" he demanded.

I took his hand and kissed it. "You introduce me to your sister and she'll measure you for a straitjacket."

After a while, he laughed. "Yes." And then, "I don't care."

"You might, sooner or later."

"You'll come with me, then."

"No. I'd like to, but no."

He smiled. "Yes. You'll come."

I watched him. I tried to read the smile, but it's hard to read a bearded face. It's easier to say what I didn't see—or didn't recognize. I didn't see condescension or that particular kind of disregard that some men reserve for women. He wasn't deciding that my "no" was a secret "yes." Something else was going on.

"I own three hundred acres," he said. "I bought the property years ago as an investment. There was going to be a big housing development up there, and speculators like me were going to make tons of money, selling our land to the developers. The project fell through for some reason, and I was stuck with land that I could either sell at a loss or keep. I kept it. Most of it is good for farming. It's got some trees on it, and some big tree stumps. My sister and her husband have built a house and a few outbuildings."

"You might have dozens or hundreds of squatters on that land now," I said.

"I don't think so. Access is a problem. It's not convenient to any real road, and it's well away from the big highways. It's a great place to hide."

"Water?"

"There are wells. My sister says the area is getting dryer, warmer. That's no surprise. But the ground water seems dependable so far."

I thought I could see where he was headed now, but he was going to have to get there all by himself. His land; his choice.

"There aren't many black people up that way, are there?" I asked.

"Not many," he agreed. "My sister hasn't had much trouble, though."

"What does she do for a living? Farm the land?"

"Yes, and her husband does odd jobs for cash—which is dangerous because it leaves her and the children alone for days, weeks, even months at a time. If we can manage to support ourselves without becoming a drain on her few resources, we might be useful to her. We might give her more security."

"How many kids?"

"Three. Let's see. . . eleven, thirteen, and fifteen years old by now. She's only forty herself." His mouth twitched. Only. Yeah. Even his little sister was old enough to be my mother. "Her name's Alex. Alexandra. Married to Don Casey. They both hate cities. They thought my land was a godsend. They could raise children who might live to grow up." He nodded. "And their children have done all right."

"How have you kept in touch?" I asked. "Phone?"

"That was part of our agreement," he said. "They don't have a phone, but when Don goes to one of the towns to get work, he phones me and lets me know how everyone is. He won't know what's happened to me. He won't be expecting me. If he's tried to phone, both he and Alex will be worried."

"You should have flown up," I said. "But I'm glad you didn't."

"Are you? So am I. Listen, you are coming with me. I can't think of anything I want as much as I want you. I haven't wanted anything at all for a long time. Too long."

I leaned back against a tree. Our campsite wasn't as completely private as the one at San Luis had been, but there were trees, and the couples could get away from each other. Each couple had one gun, and the Gilchrist sisters were babysitting Dominic as well as Justin. We had put them in the middle of a rough triangle and given them my gun. On I-5 they and Travis had had a chance to do a little target practice. It was all of our duty to look around now and then and make sure no strangers wandered into the area. I looked around.

Sitting up I could see Justin running around, chasing pigeons. Jill was keeping an eye on him, but not trying to keep up with him.

Bankole took me by the shoulder and turned me to face him. "I'm not boring you, am I?" he asked for the second time.

I had been trying not to look at him. I looked now, but he had not yet said what he had to say if he wanted to keep me with him. Did he know? I thought he did.

"I want to go with you," I said. "But I'm serious about Earthseed. I couldn't be more serious. You have to understand that." Why did this sound strange to me? It was the absolute truth, but I felt odd telling it.

"I know my rival," he said.

Maybe that's why it sounded strange. I was telling him there was someone else—something else. Maybe it would have sounded less strange if the something were another man.

"You could help me," I said.

"Help you what? Do you have any real idea what you want to do?"

"Begin the first Earthseed Community."

He sighed.

"You could help me," I repeated. "This world is falling apart. You could help me begin something purposeful and constructive."

"Going to fix the world, are you?" he said with quiet amusement.

I looked at him. For a moment I was too angry to let myself speak. When I could control my voice, I said, "It's all right if you don't believe, but don't laugh. Do you know what it means to have something to believe in? Don't laugh."

After a while he said, "All right."

After a longer while, I said, "Fixing the world is not what Earthseed is about."

"The stars. I know." He lay flat on his back, but turned his head to look at me instead of looking up.

"This world would be a better place if people lived according to Earthseed," I said. "But then, this world would be better if people lived according to the teachings of almost any religion."

"That's true. Why do you think they'll live according to the teaching of yours?"

OCTAVIA E. BUTLER

"A few will. Several thousand? Several hundred thousand? Millions? I don't know. But when I have a home base, I'll begin the first community. In fact, I've already begun it."

"Is that what you need me for?" He didn't bother to smile or pretend it was a joke. It wasn't. I moved over closer to him and sat next to him so that I could look down into his face.

"I need you to understand me," I said. "I need you to take me the way I am or go off to your land by yourself."

"You need me to take you and all your friends off the street so you can start a church." Again, he was altogether serious.

"That or nothing," I said with equal seriousness. He gave me a humorless smile. "So now we know where we stand."

I smoothed his beard, and saw that he wanted to move away from my hand, but that he did not move. "Are you all that sure you want God as your rival?" I asked.

"I don't seem to have much choice, do I?" He covered my caressing hand with one of his own. "Tell me, do you ever lose your temper and scream and cry?"

"Sure."

"I can't picture it. In all honesty, I can't."

And that reminded me of something that I hadn't told him, had better tell him before he found out and felt cheated or decided that I didn't trust him—which I still didn't, quite. But I didn't want to lose him to stupidity or cowardice. I didn't want to lose him at all.

"Still want me with you?" I asked.

"Oh, yes," he said. "I intend to marry you once we've settled."

He had managed to surprise me. I stared at him with my mouth open.

"A genuine spur-of-the-moment reaction," he said. "I'll have to remember it. Will you marry me, by the way?"

"Listen to me first."

"No more. Bring your church. Bring your congregation. I doubt they care anymore about the stars than I do, but bring them. I like them, and there's room for them."

If they would come. My next effort would be to convince them. But this effort wasn't over yet.

"That isn't all," I said. "Let me tell you one more thing. Then, if you still want me, I'll marry you anytime you say. I want to. You must know I want to."

He waited.

"My mother was taking—abusing—a prescription drug when she got pregnant with me. The drug was Paracetco. As a result, I have hyperempathy syndrome."

He took that in with no sign of how he felt about it. He sat up and looked at me—looked at me with great curiosity, as though he hoped to see some sign of my hyperempathy on my face or body. "You feel other people's pain?" he asked.

"I share other people's pain and pleasure," I said. "There hasn't been much pleasure to share lately, except with you."

"Do you share bleeding?"

"No more. I did when I was little."

"But you . . . I saw you kill a man."

"Yes." I shook my head, remembering what he had seen. "I had to, or he would have killed me."

"I know that. It's just that. . . I'm surprised you were able to do it."

"I told you, I had to."

He shook his head. "I've read about the syndrome, of course, although I've never seen a case. I remember thinking that it might not be so bad a thing if most people had to endure all the pain they caused. Not doctors or other medical people, of course, but most people."

"Bad idea," I said.

"I'm not sure."

"Take my word for it. Bad, bad idea. Self-defense shouldn't have to be an agony or a killing or both. I can be crippled by the pain of a wounded person. I'm a very good shot because I've never felt that I could afford just to wound someone. Also . . ." I stopped, looked past him for a moment and drew a deep breath, then focused on him again. "The worst of it is, if you got hurt, I might not be able to help you. I might be as crippled by your injury—by your pain, I mean—as you are."

"I suspect you'd find a way." He smiled a little.

"Don't suspect that, Bankole." I stopped and hunted for words that would make him understand. "I'm not looking for compliments or even reassurance. I want you to understand: If you broke your leg badly, if you were shot, if anything serious and disabling happened to you, I might be disabled, too. You must know how disabling real pain can be."

"Yes. I know a little about you, too. No, don't tell me again that you aren't fishing for compliments. I know. Let's go back to camp. I've got some pain medications in my bag. I'll teach you how and when to use them on me or whoever needs them. If you can just hold on and be yourself long enough to use them, you can do whatever else may be necessary."

". . . okay. So . . . do you still want to marry me?" It surprised me how much I didn't want to ask the question. I knew he still wanted me. Yet there I was, asking him, almost begging him to say it. I needed to hear it.

He laughed. Big, full laughter that sounded so real, I couldn't take offense. "I'll have to remember this," he said. "Do you imagine for one minute, girl, that I would let you get away?"

23

□ □ □

Your teachers
Are all around you.
All that you perceive,
All that you experience,
All that is given to you
or taken from you,
All that you love or hate,
need or fear
Will teach you—
If you will learn.
God is your first
and your last teacher.
God is your harshest teacher:
subtle,
demanding.
Learn or die.

EARTHSEED: THE BOOKS OF THE LIVING
FRIDAY, SEPTEMBER 10, 2027

We had another battle to try to sleep through before dawn this morning. It began to the south of us out on or near the highway, and worked its way first toward, then away from us.

We could hear people shooting, screaming, cursing, running. . . . Same old stuff—tiresome, dangerous, and stupid. The shooting went on for over an hour, waxing and waning. There was a final barrage that seemed to involve more guns than ever. Then the noise stopped.

I managed to sleep through some of it. I got over being afraid, even got over being angry. In the end, I was only tired. I thought, *if the bastards are going to kill me, I can't stop them by staying awake.* If that wasn't altogether true, I didn't care. I slept.

And somehow, during or after the battle, in spite of the watch, two people slipped into our camp and bedded down among us. They slept, too.

We awoke early as usual so that we could start walking while the heat wasn't too terrible. We've learned to wake up without prompting at the first light of dawn. Today, four of us sat up in our bags at almost the same time. I was crawling out of my bag to go off and urinate when I spotted the extra people—two gray lumps in the dawn light, one large and one small, lying against each other, asleep on the bare ground. Thin arms and legs extended like sticks from rags and mounds of clothing.

I glanced around at the others and saw that they were staring where I was staring—all of them except Jill, who was supposed to be on watch. We began trusting her to stand night watch last week with a partner. This was only her second solitary watch. And where was she looking? Away into the trees. She and I would have to talk.

Harry and Travis were already reacting to the figures on the ground. In silence, each man was peeling out of his bag in his underwear, and standing up. More fully clothed, I matched them, move for move, and the three of us closed in around the two intruders.

The larger of the two awoke all at once, jumped up, darted two or three steps toward Harry, then stopped. It was a woman. We could see her better now. She was brown-skinned with a lot of long, straight, unkempt black hair. Her coloring was as dark as mine, but she was all planes and angles—a wiry, hawk-faced woman who could have used a few decent meals and a good scrubbing. She looked like a lot of people we've seen on the road.

The second intruder awoke, saw Travis standing nearby in his underwear, and screamed. That got everyone's attention. It was the high, piercing shriek of a child—a little girl who looked about seven.

She was a tiny, pinched image of the woman—her mother, or her sister perhaps.

The woman ran back to the child and tried to scoop her up. But the child had folded herself into a tight fetal knot and the woman, trying to lift her, could not get a grip. She stumbled, fell over, and in an instant she too had rolled herself into a tight ball. By then everyone had come to see.

"Harry," I said, and waited until he looked at me. "Would you and Zahra keep watch—make sure nothing else surprises us."

He nodded. He and Zahra detached from the cluster, separated, and took up positions on opposite sides of the camp, Harry nearest to the approach from the highway and Zahra on the approach from the nearest lesser road. We had buried ourselves as well as we could in a deserted area that Bankole said must once have been a park, but we didn't kid ourselves that we were alone. We'd followed I-5 to a small city outside Sacramento, away from the worst of the sprawl, but there were still plenty of poor people around—local paupers and refugees like us.

Where had this pair of ragged, terrified, filthy people come from?

"We won't hurt you," I said to them as they lay, still rolled up on the ground. "Get up. Come on, get up. You've come into our camp unasked. You can at least talk to us."

We didn't touch them. Bankole seemed to want to, but he stopped when I grasped his arm. They were already scared to death. A strange man, reaching out to them, might make them hysterical.

Trembling, the woman unrolled herself and gazed up at us. Now I realized she looked Asian except for her coloring. She put her head down and whispered something to the child. After a moment, the two of them stood up.

"We didn't know this was your place," she whispered. "We'll go away. Let us go away."

I sighed and looked at the terrified face of the little girl. "You can go," I said. "Or if you like, you can eat with us."

They both wanted to run away. They were like deer, frozen in terror, about to bolt. But I'd said the magic word. Two weeks ago, I wouldn't have said it, but I said today to these two starved- looking people: "eat."

"Food?" the woman whispered.

"Yes. We'll share a little food with you."

The woman looked at the little girl. I was certain now that they were mother and daughter. "We can't pay," she said. "We don't have anything."

I could see that. "Just take what we give you and nothing more than we give you," I said. "That will be pay enough."

"We won't steal. We aren't thieves."

Of course they were thieves. How else could they live. Some stealing and scavenging, maybe some whoring. . . . They weren't very good at it or they'd look better. But for the little kid's sake, I wanted to help them at least with a meal.

"Wait, then," I said. "We'll put a meal together."

They sat where they were and watched us with hungry, hungry eyes. There was more hunger in those eyes than we could fill with all our food. I thought I had probably made a mistake. These people were so desperate, they were dangerous. It didn't matter at all that they looked harmless. They were still alive and strong enough to run. They were not harmless.

It was Justin who eased some of the tension in those bottomless, hungry eyes. Stark naked, he toddled over to the woman and the girl and looked them over. The little girl only stared back, but after a moment, the woman began to smile. She said something to Justin, and he smiled. Then he ran back to Allie who held on to him long enough to dress him. But he had done his work. The woman was seeing us with different eyes. She watched Natividad nursing Dominic, then watched Bankole combing his beard. This seemed funny to her and to the child, and they both giggled.

"You're a hit," I told Bankole.

"I don't see what's so funny about a man combing his beard," he muttered, and put away his comb.

I dug sweet pears out of my pack, and took one each to the woman and the girl. I had just bought them two days before, and I had only three left. Other people got the idea and began sharing what they could spare. Shelled walnuts, apples, a pomegranate, Valencia oranges, figs. . . . little things.

"Save what you can," Natividad told the woman as she gave her almonds wrapped in a piece of red cloth. "Wrap things in here and tie the ends together."

We all shared corn bread made with a little honey and the hard-boiled eggs we bought and cooked yesterday. We baked the corn bread in the coals of last night's fire so that we could get away early this morning. The woman and the girl ate as though the plain, cold food were the best they had ever tasted, as though they couldn't believe someone had given it to them. They crouched over it as though they were afraid we might snatch it back.

"We've got to go," I said at last. "The sun's getting hotter."

The woman looked at me, her strange, sharp face hungry again, but now not hungry for food.

"Let us go with you," she said, her words tumbling over one another. "We'll work. We'll get wood, make fire, clean dishes, anything. Take us with you."

Bankole looked at me. "I assume you saw that coming."

I nodded. The woman was looking from one of us to the other.

"Anything," she whispered—or whimpered. Her eyes were dry and starved, but tears streamed from the little girl's eyes.

"Give us a moment to decide," I said. I meant, *Go away so my friends can yell at me in private,* but the woman didn't seem to understand. She didn't move.

"Wait over there," I said, pointing toward the trees nearest to the road. "Let us talk. Then we'll tell you."

She didn't want to do it. She hesitated, then stood up, pulled her even more reluctant daughter up, and trudged off to the trees I had indicated.

"Oh God," Zahra muttered. "We're going to take them, aren't we?"

"That's what we have to decide," I said.

"What, we feed her, and then we get to tell her to go away and finish starving?" Zahra made a noise of disgust.

"If she isn't a thief," Bankole said. "And if she doesn't have any other dangerous habits, we may be able to carry them. That little kid. . . ."

"Yes," I said. "Bankole, is there room for them at your place?"

"His place?" three others asked. I hadn't had a chance to tell them about it. And I hadn't had the nerve.

"He has a lot of land up north and over by the coast," I said. "There's a family house that we can't live in because his sister and her family are there. But there's room and trees and water. He says . . ." I swallowed, looked at Bankole who was smiling a little. "He says we can start Earthseed there—build what we can."

"Are there jobs?" Harry asked Bankole.

"My brother-in-law manages with year-round gardens and temporary jobs. He's raising three kids that way."

"But the jobs do pay money?"

"Yes, they pay. Not well, but they pay. We'd better hold off talking about this for a while. We're torturing that young woman over there."

"She'll steal," Natividad said. "She says she won't, but she will. You can look at her and tell."

"She's been beaten," Jill said. "The way they rolled up when we first spotted them. They're used to being beaten, kicked, knocked around."

"Yeah." Allie looked haunted. "You try to keep from getting hit in the head, try to protect your eyes and . . . your front. She thought we would beat her. She and the kid both."

Interesting that Allie and Jill should understand so well. What a terrible father they had. And what had happened to their mother? They had never talked about her. It was amazing that they had escaped alive and sane enough to function.

OCTAVIA E. BUTLER

"Should we let her stay?" I asked them.

Both girls nodded. "I think she'll be a pain in the ass for a while, though," Allie said. "Like Natividad says, she'll steal. She won't be able to stop herself. We'll have to watch her real good. That little kid will steal, too. Steal and run like hell."

Zahra grinned. "Reminds me of me at that age. They'll both be pains in the ass. I vote we try them. If they have manners or if they can learn manners, we keep them. If they're too stupid to learn, we throw them out."

I looked at Travis and Harry, standing together. "What do you guys say?"

"I say you're going soft," Harry said. "You would have raised hell if we'd tried to take in a beggar woman and her child a few weeks ago."

I nodded. "You're right. I would have. And maybe that's the attitude we should keep. But these two . . . I think they might be worth something—and I don't think they're dangerous. If I'm wrong, we can always dump them."

"They might not take to being dumped," Travis said. Then he shrugged. "I don't want to be the one to send that little kid out to be one more thief-beggar-whore. But think, Lauren. If we let them stay, and it doesn't work out, it might be damned hard to get rid of them. And if they turn out to have friends around here—friends that they're scouting for, we might have to kill them."

Both Harry and Natividad began to protest. Kill a woman and a child? No! Not possible! Never!

The rest of us let them talk. When they ran down, I said, "It could get that bad, I suppose, but I don't think it will. That woman wants to live. Even more, she wants the kid to live. I think she'd put up with a lot for the kid's sake, and I don't think she'd put the kid in danger by scouting for a gang. Gangs are more direct out here, anyway. They don't need scouts."

Silence.

"Shall we try them?" I asked. "Or shall we turn them away now?"

"I'm not against them," Travis said. "Let them stay, for the kid's sake. But let's go back to having two watchers at once during the night. How the hell did those two get in here like that, anyway?"

Jill shrank a little. "They could have gotten in anytime last night," she said. "Anytime."

"What we don't see can kill us," I said. "Jill, you didn't see them?"

"They could have been there when I took over the watch!"

"You still didn't see them. They could have cut your throat—or your sister's."

"Well. They didn't."

"The next one might." I leaned toward her. "The world is full of crazy, dangerous people. We see signs of that every day. If we don't watch out for ourselves, they will rob us, kill us, and maybe eat us. It's a world gone to hell, Jill, and we've only got each other to keep it off us."

Sullen silence.

I reached out and took her hand. "Jill."

"It wasn't my fault!" she said. "You can't prove I—"

"Jill!"

She shut up and stared at me.

"Listen, no one is going to beat you up, for heaven sake, but you did something wrong, something dangerous. You know you did."

"So what do you want her to do?" Allie demanded. "Get on her knees and say she's sorry?"

"I want her to love her own life and yours enough not to be careless. That's what I want. That's what you should want, now more than ever. Jill?"

Jill closed her eyes. "Oh shit!" she said. And then, "All right, all right! I didn't see them. I really didn't. I'll watch better. No one else will get by me."

I clasped her hand for a moment longer, then let it go. "Okay. Let's get out of here. Let's collect that scared woman and her scared little kid and get out of here."

The two scared people turned out to be the most racially mixed that I had ever met. Here's their story, put together from the fragments they told us during the day and tonight. The woman had a Japanese father, a black mother, and a Mexican husband, all dead. Only she and her daughter are left. Her name is Emery Tanaka Solis. Her daughter is Tori Solis. Tori is nine years old, not seven as I had guessed. I suspect she has rarely had enough to eat in her life. She's tiny, quick, quiet, and hungry-eyed. She hid bits of food in her filthy rags until we made her a new dress from one of Bankole's shirts. Then she hid food in that. Although Tori is nine, her mother is only twenty-three. At thirteen, Emery married a much older man who promised to take care of her. Her father was already dead, killed in someone else's gunfight. Her mother was sick, and dying of tuberculosis. The mother pushed Emery into marriage to save her from victimization and starvation in the streets.

Up to that point, the situation was dreary, but normal. Emery had three children over the next three years—a daughter and two sons. She and her husband did farm work in trade for food, shelter, and hand-me-downs. Then the farm was sold to a big agribusiness conglomerate, and the workers fell into new hands. Wages were paid, but in company scrip, not in cash. Rent was charged for the workers' shacks. Workers had to pay for food, for clothing—new or used—for everything they needed, and, of course they could only spend their company notes at the company store. Wages—surprise!—were never quite enough to pay the bills. According to new laws that might or might not exist, people were not permitted to leave an employer to whom they owed money. They were obligated to work off the debt either as quasi-indentured people or as convicts. That is, if they refused to work, they could be arrested, jailed, and in the end, handed over to their employers.

Either way, such debt slaves could be forced to work longer hours for less pay, could be "disciplined" if they failed to meet their quotas, could be traded and sold with or without their consent, with or without their families, to distant employers who had temporary or permanent need of them. Worse, children could be forced to work off the debt of their parents if the parents died, became disabled, or escaped.

Emery's husband sickened and died. There was no doctor, no medicine beyond a few expensive over-the-counter preparations and the herbs that the workers grew in their tiny gardens. Jorge Francisco Solis died in fever and pain on the earthen floor of his shack without ever seeing a doctor. Bankole said it sounded as though he died of peritonitis brought on by untreated appendicitis. Such a simple thing. But then, there's nothing more replaceable than unskilled labor.

Emery and her children became responsible for the Solis debt. Accepting this, Emery worked and endured until one day, without warning, her sons were taken away. They were one and two years younger than her daughter, and too young to be without both their parents. Yet they were taken. Emery was not asked to part with them, nor was she told what would be done with them. She had terrible suspicions when she recovered from the drug she had been given to "quiet her down." She cried and demanded the return of her sons and would not work again until her masters threatened to take her daughter as well.

She decided then to run away, to take her daughter and brave the roads with their thieves, rapists, and cannibals. They had nothing for anyone to steal, and rape wasn't something they could escape by remaining slaves. As for the cannibals . . . well, perhaps they were only fantasies—lies intended to frighten slaves into accepting their lot.

"There are cannibals," I told her as we ate that night. "We've seen them. I think, though, that they're scavengers, not killers. They take advantage of road kills, that kind of thing."

"Scavengers kill," Emery said. "If you get hurt or if you look sick, they come after you."

I nodded, and she went on with her story. Late one night, she and Tori slipped out past the armed guards and electrified fences, the sound and motion detectors and the dogs. Both knew how to be quiet, how to fade from cover to cover, how to lie still for hours. Both were very fast. Slaves learned things like that—the ones who lived did. Emery and Tori must have been very lucky.

Emery had some notion of finding her sons and getting them back, but she had no idea where they had been taken. They had been driven away in a truck; she knew that much. But she didn't know even which way the truck turned when it reached the highway. Her parents had taught her to read and write, but she had seen no writing about her sons. She had to admit after a while that all she could do was save her daughter.

Living on wild plants and whatever they could "find" or beg, they drifted north. That was the way Emery said it: they found things. Well, if I were in her place, I would have found a few things, too.

A gang fight drove her to us. Gangs are always a special danger in cities. If you keep to the road while you're in individual gang territories, you might escape their attentions. We have so far. But the overgrown park land where we camped last night was, according to Emery, in dispute. Two gangs shot at each other and called insults and accusations back and forth. Now and then they stopped to shoot at passing trucks. During one of these intervals, Emery and Tori who had camped close to the roadside had slipped away.

"One group was coming closer to us," Emery said. "They would shoot and run. When they ran, they got closer. We had to get away. We couldn't let them hear us or see us. We found your clearing, but we didn't see you. You know how to hide."

That, I suppose was a compliment. We try to disappear into the scenery when that's possible. Most of the time it isn't. Tonight it isn't. And tonight we watch two at a time.

SUNDAY, SEPTEMBER 12, 2027

Tori Solis has found us two more companions today: Grayson Mora and his daughter Doe. Doe was only a year younger than Tori, and the two little girls, walking along, going the same way, became friends. Today we turned west on State Highway 20 and were heading back toward U.S. 101. We spent a lot of time talking about settling on Bankole's land, about jobs and crops and what we might build there.

Meanwhile, the two little girls, Tori and Doe were making friends and pulling their parents together. The parents were alike enough to attract my attention. They were about the same age—which meant that the man had become a father almost as young as the woman had become a mother. That wasn't unusual, but it was unusual that he had taken charge of his child.

He was a tall, thin, black Latino, quiet, protective of his child, yet tentative, somehow. He liked Emery. I could see that. Yet on some level he wanted to get away from her—and away from us. When we left the road to make camp, he would have gone on if his daughter had not begged, then cried to stay with us. He had his own food so I told him he could camp near us if he wanted to. Two things hit me as I talked to him.

First, he didn't like us. That was obvious. He didn't like us at all. I thought he might resent us because we were united and armed. You tend to resent the people you're afraid of. I told him we kept a watch, and that if he could put up with that, he was welcome. He shrugged and said in his soft, cold voice, "Oh, yeah."

He'll stay. His kid wants it and some part of him wants it, but something's wrong. Something beyond ordinary traveler caution.

The second thing is only my suspicion. I believe Grayson and Doe Mora were also slaves. Yet Grayson is now a rich pauper. He has a pair of sleepsacks, food, water, and money. If I'm right, he took them off someone—or off someone's corpse.

Why do I think he was a slave? That odd tentativeness of his is just too much like Emery's. And Doe and Tori, though they don't look alike at all, seem to understand each other like sisters. Little kids can do that sometimes, without it meaning anything. Just being little kids together is enough. But I've never seen any kids but these two both show the tendency to drop to the ground and roll into a fetal knot when frightened.

Doe did just that when she tripped and fell, and Zahra stepped over to see whether she was hurt. Doe's body snapped into a trembling ball. Was that, as Jill and Allie supposed, what people did when they expected to be beaten or kicked—a posture of protection and submission both at once?

"Something wrong about that fellow," Bankole said, glancing at Grayson as we bedded down next to each other. We had eaten and heard more of Emery's story, and talked a little, but we were tired. I had my writing to do, and Travis and Jill were on watch. Bankole, who had an early morning watch with Zahra just wanted to talk. He sat beside me and spoke into my ear in a voice so low that if I leaned away from him, I lost words. "Mora's too jumpy," he said. "He flinches if someone walks close to him."

"I think he's another ex-slave," I said in a voice just as low. "That might not be his only problem, but it's his most obvious one".

"So you picked up on that, too." He put his arm around me and sighed. "I agree. Both he and the child."

"And he doesn't love us."

"He doesn't trust us. Why should he? We'll have to watch all four of them for a while. They're . . . odd. They might be stupid enough to try to grab some of our packs and leave some night. Or it might just be a matter of little things starting to disappear. The children are more likely to get caught at it. Yet if the adults stay, it will be for the children's sake. If we take it easy on the children and protect them, I think the adults will be loyal to us."

"So we become the crew of a modern underground railroad," I said. Slavery again—even worse than my father thought, or at least sooner. He thought it would take a while.

"None of this is new." Bankole made himself comfortable against me. "In the early 1990s while I was in college, I heard about cases of growers doing some of this—holding people against their wills and forcing them to work without pay. Latins in California, blacks and Latins in the south. . . . Now and then, someone would go to jail for it."

"But Emery says there's a new law—that forcing people or their children to work off debt that they can't help running up is legal."

"Maybe. It's hard to know what to believe. I suppose the politicians may have passed a law that could be used to support debt slavery. But I've heard nothing about it. Anyone dirty enough to be a slaver is dirty enough to tell a pack of lies. You realize that that woman's children were sold like cattle—and no doubt sold into prostitution."

I nodded. "She knows, too."

"Yes. My God."

"Things are breaking down more and more." I paused. "I'll tell you, though, if we can convince ex-slaves that they can have freedom with us, no one will fight harder to keep it. We need better guns, though. And we need to be so careful. . . . It keeps getting more dangerous out here. It will be especially dangerous with those little girls around."

"Those two know how to be quiet," Bankole said. "They're little rabbits, fast and silent. That's why they're still alive."

　　　　　　OCTAVIA E. BUTLER

24

□ □ □

Respect God:
Pray working.
Pray learning,
planning,
doing.
Pray creating,
teaching,
reaching.
Pray working.
Pray to focus your thoughts,
still your fears,
strengthen your purpose.
Respect God.
Shape God.
Pray working.

EARTHSEED: THE BOOKS OF THE LIVING
FRIDAY, SEPTEMBER 17, 2027

We read some verses and talked about Earthseed for a while this morning. It was a calming thing to do—almost like church. We needed something calming and reassuring. Even the new people joined in, asking questions, thinking aloud, applying the verses to their experiences.

God is Change, and in the end, God *does* prevail. But we have something to say about the whens and the whys of that end.

Yeah.

It's been a horrible week.

We've taken both today and yesterday as rest days. We might take tomorrow as well. I need it whether the others do or not. We're all sore and sick, in mourning and exhausted—yet triumphant. Odd to be triumphant. I think it's because most of us are still alive. We are a harvest of survivors. But then, that's what we've always been.

This is what happened.

At our noon stop on Tuesday, Tori and Doe, the two little girls, went away from the group to urinate. Emery went with them. She had kind of taken charge of Doe as well as her own daughter. The night before, she and Grayson Mora had slipped away from the group and stayed away for over an hour. Harry and I were on watch, and we saw them go. Now they were a couple—all over each other, but at arm's length from everyone else. Strange people.

So Emery took the girls off to pee—not far away. Just across the hill face and out of sight behind a patch of dead bushes and tall, dry grass. The rest of us sat eating, drinking, and sweating in what shade we could get from a copse of oak trees that looked only half dead. The trees had been robbed of a great number of branches, no doubt by people needing firewood. I was looking at their many jagged wounds when the screaming began.

First there were the high, needle thin, needle sharp shrieks of the little girls, then we heard Emery shouting for help. Then we heard a man's voice, cursing.

Most of us jumped up without thinking and ran toward the noise. In midstride, I grabbed Harry and Zahra by the arms to get their attention. Then I gestured them back to guard our packs and Natividad and Allie who had stayed with the babies. Harry had the rifle and Zahra had one of the Berettas, and in that moment, they both resented the hell out of me. No matter. For the moment, I was just glad to see them go back. They could cover us if necessary, and keep us from being overwhelmed.

We found Emery fighting with a big bald man who had grabbed Tori. Doe was already running back to us, screaming. She ran straight into her father's arms. He swept her up and ran off toward the highway, then he veered back toward the oaks and our people. There were other bald people coming up from the highway. Like us, they ran toward the screams. I saw metal gleaming among them—perhaps only knives. Perhaps guns. Travis spotted the group, too, and yelled a warning before I could.

I fell back, dropped to one knee, aimed my .45 two-handed, and waited for a clear shot at Emery's attacker. The man was much taller than Emery, and his head and shoulders were exposed except where he held Tori against him. The little girl looked like a doll that he was clutching in one arm. Emery was the problem. She, small and quick, was darting at the man, tearing at his face, trying to reach his eyes. He was trying to protect his eyes and to knock or throw her away from him. With both hands free, he might have been quick enough to bat her aside, but he wouldn't let go of the struggling Tori, and Emery wouldn't be beaten off.

For an instant, he did knock Emery back from him. In that brief window of time, my own ears ringing from his blow, I shot him.

I knew at once that I'd hit him. He didn't fall, but I felt his pain, and I wasn't good for anything else for a while. Then he toppled, and I collapsed with him. But I could still see and hear, and I still had the gun.

I heard shouting. The bald gang from the highway was almost on us—six, seven, eight people. I couldn't do anything while I was dealing with the pain, but I saw them. Instants later when the man I had shot lost consciousness or died, I was free—and needed.

Bankole had our only other gun away from camp.

I got up before I should have, almost fell down again, then shot a second attacker off Travis who was carrying Emery.

I went down again, but didn't lose consciousness. I saw Bankole grab Tori and all but throw her to Jill. Jill caught her, turned, and ran back toward camp with her.

Bankole reached me, and I was able to get up and help him cover our retreat.

We had only the scarred trees to retreat to, but they had thick, solid-looking trunks. An attacker fired several bullets into them as we reached them.

It took me several seconds to understand that someone was shooting at us. Once I did, I dropped behind the trees with the others and looked for the opposing gun.

Our rifle thundered behind me before I could spot anything. Harry, on the job. He fired twice more. I fired twice myself, barely aiming, barely in control. I believe Bankole fired. Then I was lost, no more good for anything. I died with someone. The shooting stopped.

I died with someone else. Someone laid hands on me and I came within a finger's twitch of squeezing the trigger once more.

Bankole.

"You stupid asshole!" I whimpered. "I almost killed you."

"You're bleeding," he said.

I was surprised. I tried to remember whether I'd been shot. Maybe I had just come down on a sharp piece of wood. I had no sense of my own body. I hurt, but I couldn't have said where—or even whether the pain was mine or someone else's. The pain was intense, yet defuse somehow. I felt . . . disembodied.

"Is everyone else all right?" I asked.

"Be still," he said.

"Is it over, Bankole?"

"Yes. The survivors have run away."

"Take my gun, then, and give it to Natividad—in case they decide to come back."

I think I felt him take the gun from my hand. I heard muffled talk that I didn't quite understand. That was when I realized I was losing consciousness. All right then. At least I had held on long enough to do some good.

Jill Gilchrist is dead.

She was shot in the back as she ran toward the trees carrying

Tori. Bankole didn't tell me, didn't want me to know before I had to because, as it turned out, I was wounded myself. I was lucky. My wound was minor. It hurt, but other than that, it didn't matter much. Jill was unlucky. I found out about her death when I came to and heard Allie's hoarse screaming grief.

Jill had gotten Tori back to the trees, put her down, then, without a sound, folded to the ground as though taking cover. Emery had grabbed Tori and huddled, crying with her in terror and relief. Everyone else had been busy, first taking cover, then firing or directing fire. Travis was the first to see the blood pooling around Jill. He shouted for Bankole, then turned Jill onto her back and saw blood welling from what turned out to be an exit wound in her chest. Bankole says she died before he reached her. No last words, no last sight of her sister, not even the assurance that she had saved the little girl. She had. Tori was bruised, but fine. Everyone was fine except Jill.

My own wound, to be honest, was a big scratch. A bullet had plowed a furrow straight through the flesh of my left side, leaving little damage, a lot of blood, a couple of holes in my shirt, and a lot of pain. The wound throbbed worse than a burn, but it wasn't disabling.

"Cowboy wound," Harry said when he and Zahra came to look me over. They looked dirty and miserable, but Harry tried to be upbeat for me. They had just helped to bury Jill. The group had, with hands, sticks, and our hatchet, dug a shallow grave for her while I was unconscious. They put her among the trees' roots, covered her, and rolled big rocks atop her grave. The trees were to have her, but the dogs and the cannibals were not.

The group had decided to bed down for the night where we were, even though our oak copse should have been rejected as an overnight camp because it was too close to the highway.

"You're a goddamn fool and too big to carry," Zahra told me. "So just rest there and let Bankole take care of you. Not that anyone could stop him."

"You've just got a cowboy wound," Harry repeated. "In that book I bought, people are always getting shot in the side or the arm or the shoulder, and it's nothing—although Bankole says a good percentage of them would have died of tetanus or some other infection."

"Thanks for the encouragement," I said.

Zahra gave him a look, then patted my arm. "Don't worry," she said. "No germ will get past that old man. He's mad as hell at you for getting yourself shot. Says if you had any sense, you would have stayed back here with the babies."

"What?"

"Hey, he's old," Harry said. "What do you expect."

I sighed. "How's Allie?"

"Crying." He shook his head. "She won't let anyone near her except Justin. Even he keeps trying to comfort her. It upsets him that she's crying."

"Emery and Tori are kind of beaten up, too," Zahra said. "They're the other reason we're not moving." She paused. "Hey, Lauren, you ever notice anything funny about those two—Emery and Tori, I mean? And about that guy Mora, too."

Something clicked into place for me, and I sighed again. "They're sharers, aren't they?"

"Yes, all of them—both adults and both kids. You knew?"

"Not until now. I did notice something odd: that tentativeness and touchiness—not wanting to be touched, I mean. And they were all slaves. My brother Marcus once said what good slaves sharers would make."

"That Mora guy wants to leave," Harry said.

"So let him go," I answered. "He tried to run out on us just before the shooting."

"He came back. He even helped dig Jill's grave. I mean he wants us all to leave. He says that gang we beat will come back when it's dark."

"He's sure?"

"Yeah. He's going crazy, wanting to get his kid out of here."

"Can Emery and Tori make it?"

"I'll carry Tori," a new voice said. "Emery can make it." Grayson Mora, of course. Last seen abandoning ship.

I got up slowly. My side hurt. Bankole had cleaned and bandaged the wound while I was unconscious, and that was a piece of luck. Now, though, I felt half-conscious, half-detached from my body. I felt everything except pain as though through a thick layer of cotton. Only the pain was sharp and real. I was almost grateful for it.

"I can walk," I said after trying a few steps. "But I feel like I'm walking on stilts. I don't know if I can keep the usual pace."

Grayson Mora stepped close to me. He glanced at Harry as though he wished Harry would go away. Harry just stared back at him.

"How many times did you die?" Mora asked me.

"Three at least," I answered, as though this were a sane conversation. "Maybe four. I never did it like that before—over and over. Insane. But you look well enough."

His expression hardened as though I'd slapped him. Of course, I had insulted him. I'd said, *Where were you, man and fellow sharer, while your woman and your group were in danger.* Funny. There I was, speaking a language I hadn't realized I knew.

"I had to get Doe out of danger," he said. "I had no gun, anyway."

"Can you shoot?"

He hesitated. "Never shot before," he admitted, dropping his voice to a mumble. Again I'd shamed him—this time without meaning to.

"When we teach you to shoot, will you, to protect the group?"

"Yeah!" Though at that moment, I think he would have preferred to shoot me.

"It hurts like hell," I warned.

He shrugged. "Most things do."

I looked into his thin, angry face. Were all slaves so thin—underfed, overworked, and taught that most things hurt? "Are you from this area?"

"Born in Sacramento."

"Then we need all the information you can give us. Even without a gun, we need you to help us survive here."

"My information is to get out of here before those things up the hill throw paint on themselves and start shooting people and setting fires."

"Oh, shit," I said. "So that's what they are."

"What'd you think they were?"

"I didn't have a chance to think about them. It wouldn't have mattered anyway. Harry, did you guys strip the dead?"

"Yeah." He gave me a thin smile. "We got another gun—a .38. I put some stuff in your pack from the ones you killed."

"Thank you. I don't know that I can carry my pack yet. Maybe Bankole—"

"He's already got it on his cart. Let's go."

We headed out toward the road.

"Is that how you do it?" Grayson Mora asked, walking next to me. "Whoever kills takes?"

"Yes, but we don't kill unless someone threatens us," I said. "We don't hunt people. We don't eat human flesh. We fight together against enemies. If one of us is in need, the rest help out. And we don't steal from one another, *ever*."

"Emery said that. I didn't believe her at first."

"Will you live as we do?"

" . . . yeah. I guess so."

I hesitated. "So what else is wrong? I can see that you don't trust us, even now."

He walked closer to me, but did not touch me. "Where'd that white man come from?" he demanded.

"I've known him all my life," I said. "He and I and the others have kept one another alive for a long time, now."

"But. . . him and those others, they don't feel anything. You're the only one who feels."

"We call it sharing. I'm the only one."

"But they . . . You . . ."

"We help each other. A group is strong. One or two people are easier to rob and kill."

"Yeah." He looked around at the others. There was no great trust or liking in his expression, but he looked more relaxed, more satisfied. He looked as though he had solved a troubling puzzle.

Testing him, I let myself stumble. It was easy. I still had little feeling in my feet and legs.

Mora stepped aside. He didn't touch me or offer help. Sweet guy.

I left Mora, went over to Allie, and walked with her for a while. Her grief and resentment were like a wall against me—against everyone, I suppose, but I was the one bothering her at the moment. And I was alive and her sister was dead, and her sister was the only family she had left, and why didn't I just get the hell out of her face?

She never said anything. She just pretended I wasn't there. She pushed Justin along in his carriage and wiped tears from her stony face now and then with a swift, whiplike motion. She was hurting herself, doing that. She was rubbing her face too hard, too fast, rubbing it raw. She was hurting me, too, and I didn't need anymore pain. I stayed with her, though, until her defenses began to crumble under a new wave of crippling grief. She stopped hurting herself and just let the tears run down her face, let them fall to her chest or to the broken blacktop. She seemed to sag under a sudden weight.

I hugged her then. I put my hands on her shoulders and stopped her half-blind plodding. When she swung around to face me, hostile and hurting, I hugged her. She could have broken free. I was feeling far from strong just then, but after a first angry pulling away, she hung on to me and moaned. I've never heard anyone moan like that. She cried and moaned there at the roadside, and the others stopped and waited for us. No one spoke. Justin began to whimper and Natividad came back to comfort him. The wordless message was the same for both child and woman: *In spite of your loss and pain, you aren't alone. You still have people who care about you and want you to be all right. You still have family.*

After a while, Allie and I let each other go. She isn't a chatty woman, especially not in her pain. She took Justin from Natividad, smoothed his hair, and held him. When we began walking again, she carried him for a while, and I pushed the carriage. We walked together, and there didn't seem to be any need to say anything.

On the road, there was a fair amount of foot traffic in both directions. Still, I worried that a big group like ours would be noticeable and locatable, no matter what. I worried because I didn't understand the ways of our attackers.

Sometime later when Allie put Justin back into the carriage and took the carriage from me, I moved to walk with Bankole and Emery. Emery was the one who explained things to me, and she was the one who spotted the smoke from the first fire—no doubt because she was looking for it. We couldn't tell for sure, but the fire looked as though it might have begun back as far as where we had stopped at the oak copse.

"They'll burn everything," Emery whispered to Bankole and me. "They won't stop until they've used up all the 'ro they have. All night, they'll be burning things. Things and people."

'Ro, pyro, pyromania. That damned fire drug again.

"Will they follow us?" I asked.

She shrugged. "There are a lot of us, and you killed some of them. I think they'll take their revenge on other, weaker travelers." Another shrug. "To them we're all the same. A traveler is a traveler."

"So unless we get caught in one of their fires . . ."

"We'll be okay, yeah. They hate everybody who isn't them. They would have sold my Tori to get some more 'ro."

I looked at her bruised, swollen face. Bankole had given her something for her pain. I was grateful for that, and half-angry at him for refusing to give me anything. He didn't understand my numbness and grogginess back at the copse, and it disturbed him. Well at least that had faded away. Let him die three or four times and see how he feels. No, I'm glad he'll never know how it feels. It makes no sense. That brief, endless agony, over and over. It makes no sense at all. I keep catching myself wondering how it is that I'm still alive.

"Emery?" I said, keeping my voice low.

She looked at me.

"You know I'm a sharer."

She nodded, then glanced sidelong at Bankole.

"He knows," I assured her. "But. . . look, you and Grayson are the first sharers I've known who had children." There was no reason to tell her she and Grayson and their children were the first sharers I'd known period. "I hope to have kids myself someday, so I need to know . . . do they always inherit the sharing?"

"One of my boys didn't have it," she said. "Some feelers—sharers—can't have any kids. I don't know why. And I knew some who had two or three kids who didn't have it at all. Bosses, though, they like you to have it."

"I'll bet they do."

"Sometimes," she continued, "sometimes they pay more for people who have it. Especially kids."

Her kids. Yet they had taken a boy who wasn't a sharer and left a girl who was. How long would it have been before they came back for the girl? Perhaps they had a lucrative offer for the boys as a pair, so they sold them first.

"My god," Bankole said. "This country has slipped back two hundred years."

"Things were better when I was little," Emery said. "My mother always said they would get better again. Good times would come back. She said they always did. My father would shake his head and not say anything." She looked around to see where Tori was and spotted her on Grayson Mora's shoulders. Then she caught sight of something else, and she gasped.

We followed her gaze and saw fire creeping over the hills behind us—far behind us, but not far enough. This was some new fire, whipping along in the dry evening breeze. Either the people who attacked us had followed us, setting fires, or someone was imitating them, echoing them.

We went on, moving faster, trying to see where we could go to be safe. On either side of the highway, there was dry grass, there were trees, living and dead. So far, the fire was only on the north side.

We kept to the south side, hoping it would be safe. There was a lake ahead, according to my map of the area—Clear Lake, it was called. The map showed it to be large, and the highway followed its northern shore for a few miles. We would reach it soon. How soon?

I calculated as we walked. Tomorrow. We should be able to camp near it tomorrow evening. Not soon enough.

I could smell the smoke now. Did that mean the wind was blowing the fire toward us?

Other people began hurrying and keeping to the south side of the road and heading west. No one went east now. There were no trucks yet, but it was getting late. They would be barreling through soon. And we should be camping for the night soon. Did we dare?

The south side still seemed free of fire behind us, but on the north side the fire crawled after us, coming no closer, but refusing to be left behind.

We went on for a while, all of us looking back often, all of us tired, some of us hurting. I called a halt and gestured us off the road to the south at a place where there was room to sit and rest.

"We can't stay here," Mora said. "The fire could jump the road any time."

"We can rest here for a few moments," I said. "We can see the fire, and it will tell us when we'd better start walking again."

"We'd better start now!" Mora said. "If that fire gets going good, it will move faster than we can run! Best to keep well ahead of it!"

"Best to have the strength to keep ahead of it," I said, and I took a water bottle from my pack and drank. We were within sight of the road and we had made it a rule not to eat or drink in such exposed places, but today that rule had to be suspended. To go into the hills away from the road might mean being cut off from the road by fire. We couldn't know when or where a windblown piece of burning debris might land.

Others followed my example and drank and ate a little dried fruit, meat, and bread. Bankole and I shared with Emery and Tori. Mora seemed to want to leave in spite of us, but his daughter Doe was sitting half asleep on the ground against Zahra. He stooped next to her and made her drink a little water and eat some fruit.

"We might have to keep moving all night," Allie said, her voice almost too soft to hear. "This might be the only rest we get." And to Travis, "You'd better put Dominic into the carriage with Justin when he's finished eating."

Travis nodded. He'd carried Dominic this far. Now he tucked him in with Justin. "I'll push the carriage for a while," he said.

Bankole looked at my wound, rebandaged it, and this time gave me something for the pain. He buried the bloody bandages he had removed, digging a shallow hole with a flat rock.

Emery, with Tori gone to sleep against her, looked to see what Bankole was doing with me, then jumped and looked away, her hand going to her own side.

"I didn't know you were hurt so much," she whispered.

"I'm not," I said, and made myself smile. "It looks nastier than it is with all the blood, but it isn't bad. I'm damned lucky compared to Jill. And it doesn't stop me from walking."

"You didn't give me any pain when we were walking," she said.

I nodded, glad to know I could fake her out. "It's ugly," I said, "but not too painful."

She settled down as though she felt better. No doubt she did. If I moaned and groaned, I'd have all four of them moaning and groaning. The kids might even bleed along with me. I would have to be careful and keep lying at least as long as the fire was a threat—or as long as I could.

The truth was, those blood-saturated bandages scared the hell out of me, and the wound hurt worse than ever. But I knew I had to keep going or burn. After a few minutes, Bankole's pills began to take the edge off my pain, and that made the whole world easier to endure.

We had about an hour's rest before the fire made us too nervous to stay where we were. Then we got up and walked. By then, at some point behind us, the fire had already jumped the road. Now, neither the north nor the south side looked safe. Until it was dark, all we could see in the hills behind us was smoke. It was a terrifying, looming, moving wall.

Later, after dark, we could see the fire eating its way toward us. There were dogs running along the road with us, but they paid no attention to us. Cats and deer ran past us, and a skunk scuttled by. It was live and let live. Neither humans nor animals were foolish enough to waste time attacking one another. Behind us and to the north, the fire began to roar.

We put Tori in the carriage and Justin and Dominic between her legs. The babies never even woke up while we were moving them. Tori herself was more than half asleep. I worried that the carriage might break down with the extra weight, but it held. Travis, Harry, and Allie traded off pushing it.

Doe, we put atop the load on Bankole's cart. She couldn't have been comfortable there, but she didn't complain. She was more awake than Tori, and she had been walking on her own most of the time since our encounter with the would-be kidnappers. She was a strong little kid—her father's daughter.

Grayson Mora helped push Bankole's cart. In fact, once Doe was loaded aboard, Mora pushed the cart most of the time. The man wasn't likeable, but in his love for his daughter, he was admirable.

At some point in the endless night, more smoke and ash than ever began to swirl around us, and I caught myself thinking that we might not make it. Without stopping, we wet shirts, scarves, whatever we had, and tied them around our noses and mouths.

The fire roared and thundered its way past us on the north, singeing our hair and clothing, making breathing a terrible effort. The babies woke up and screamed in fear and pain, then choked and almost brought me down. Tori, crying herself with their pain and her own, held on to them and would not let them struggle out of the carriage.

I thought we would die. I believed there was no way for us to survive this sea of fire, hot wind, smoke, and ash. I saw people—strangers—fall, and we left them lying on the highway, waiting to burn. I stopped looking back. In the roar of the fire, I could not hear whether they screamed. I could see the babies before Natividad threw wet rags over them. I knew they were screaming. Then I couldn't see them, and it was a blessing.

We began to run out of water.

There was nothing to do except keep going or burn. The terrible, deafening noise of the fire increased, then lessened, and again, increased, then lessened. It seemed that the fire went north away from the road, then whipped back down toward us.

It teased like a living, malevolent thing, intent on causing pain and terror. It drove us before it like dogs chasing a rabbit. Yet it didn't eat us. It could have, but it didn't.

In the end, the worst of it roared off to the northwest. Firestorm, Bankole called it later. Yes. Like a tornado of fire, roaring around, just missing us, playing with us, then letting us live.

We could not rest. There was still fire. Little fires that could grow into big ones, smoke, blinding and choking smoke. . . . No rest.

But we could slow down. We could emerge from the worst of the smoke and ash, and escape the lash of hot winds. We could pause by the side of the road for a moment, and gag in peace. There was a lot of gagging. Coughing and gagging and crying muddy tracks onto our faces. It was incredible. We were going to survive. We were still alive and together—scorched and miserable, in great need of water, but alive. We were going to make it.

Later, when we dared, we went off the road, unloaded my pack from Bankole's cart, and dug out his extra water bottle. He dug it out. He'd told us he had it when he could have kept it for himself.

"We'll reach Clear Lake sometime tomorrow," I said. "Early tomorrow, I think. I don't know how far we've come or where we are now, so I can only guess that we'll get there early. But it is there waiting for us tomorrow."

People grunted or coughed and downed swallows from Bankole's extra bottle. The kids had to be prevented from guzzling too much water. As it was, Dominic choked and began to cry again.

We camped where we were, within sight of the road. Two of us had to stay awake on watch. I volunteered for first watch because I was in too much pain to sleep. I got my gun back from Natividad, checked to see that she had reloaded it—she had—and looked around for a partner.

"I'll watch with you," Grayson Mora said.

That surprised me. I would have preferred someone who knew how to use a gun—someone I would trust with a gun.

"I'm not going to be able to sleep until you do," he said. "It's that simple. So let's both put our pain to good use."

I looked at Emery and the two girls to see whether they'd heard, but they seemed to be already asleep. "All right," I said. "We've got to watch for strangers and fire. Give me a yell if you see anything unusual."

"Give me a gun," he said. "If anybody comes close, I can at least use it to scare them."

In the dark, sure. "No gun," I said. "Not yet. You don't know enough yet."

He stared at me for several seconds, then went over to Bankole. He turned his back to me as he spoke to Bankole. "Look, you know I need a gun to do any guarding in a place like this. She doesn't know how it is. She thinks she does, but she doesn't."

OCTAVIA E. BUTLER

Bankole shrugged. "If you can't do it, man, go to sleep. One of us will take the watch with her."

"Shit." Mora made the word long and nasty. "Shiiit. First time I saw her, I knew she was a man. Just didn't know she was the only man here."

Absolute silence.

Doe Mora saved the situation to the degree that it could be saved. At that moment she stepped up behind her father and tapped him on the back. He spun around, more than ready to fight, spun with such speed and fury that the little girl squealed and jumped back.

"What the hell are you doing up!" he shouted. "What do you want!"

Frightened, the little girl just stared at him. After a moment, she extended her hand, offering a pomegranate. "Zahra said we could have this," she whispered. "Would you cut it?"

Good thinking, Zahra! I didn't turn to look at her, but I was aware of her watching. By now, everyone still awake was watching.

"Everyone's tired and everyone's hurting," I told him. "Everyone, not just you. But we've managed to keep ourselves alive by working together and by not doing or saying stupid things."

"And if that's not good enough for you," Bankole added, in a voice low and ugly with anger, "tomorrow you can go out and find yourself a different kind of group to travel with—a group too god-damn macho to waste its time saving your child's life twice in one day."

There must be something worthwhile in Mora. He didn't say anything. He took out his knife and cut the pomegranate into quarters for Doe, then kept half of it because she insisted that he was supposed to have half. They sat together and ate the juicy, seedy, red fruit, then Mora tucked Doe in again and found himself a perch where, gunless, he began his first watch.

He said nothing more about guns, and he never apologized. Of course he didn't leave us. Where would he go? He was a runaway slave. We were the best thing he'd found so far—the best he was going to find as long as he had Doe with him.

We didn't reach Clear Lake the next morning. To tell the truth it was already the next morning when we went to sleep. We were too tired and sore to get up at dawn—which came early in the second watch. Only the need for water made us move out when we did—at a hot, smoky 11 a.m.

We found the corpse of a young woman when we got back to the road. There wasn't a mark on her, but she was dead.

"I want her clothes," Emery whispered. She was near me or I wouldn't have heard her. The dead woman was about her size, and dressed in a cotton shirt and pants that looked almost new. They were dirty, but far less so than Emery's clothes.

"Strip her, then," I said. "I'd help you, but I'm not bending too well this morning."

"I'll give her a hand," Allie whispered. Justin was asleep in his carriage with Dominic, so she was free to help with the ordinary, unspeakable things that we did now to live.

The dead woman had not even soiled herself in her dying. That made the job less disgusting than it could have been. Rigor mortis had set in, however, and stripping her was a job for two.

There was no one but us on this stretch of road, so Emery and Allie had all the time they needed. We had seen no other walkers yet this morning.

Emery and Allie took every scrap of clothing, including underwear, socks, and boots, though Emery thought the boots would be too big for her. No matter. If no one could wear them, she could sell them.

In fact, it was the boots that yielded Emery the first cash she had ever owned. On the farm where she had been a slave, she had been paid only in company scrip, worthless except on the farm, and almost worthless there.

OCTAVIA E. BUTLER

Stitched into the tongue of each of the dead woman's boots were five, folded one hundred-dollar bills—a thousand dollars in all. We had to tell her how little that was. If she were careful, and shopped only at the cheapest stores, and ate no meat, wheat, or dairy products, it might feed her for two weeks. It might feed both her and Tori for a week and a half. Still, it seemed riches to Emery.

Late that day, when we reached Clear Lake—much smaller than I had expected—we came across a tiny, expensive store, being run from the back of an old truck near a cluster of half-burned, collapsed cabins. It sold fruit, vegetables, nuts, and smoked fish. We all had to buy a few things, but Emery squandered too much money on pears and walnuts for everyone. She delighted in passing these around, in being able to give us something for a change. She's all right. We'll have to teach her about shopping and the value of money, but she's worth something, Emery is. And she's decided she's one of us.

SUNDAY, SEPTEMBER 26, 2027

Somehow, we've reached our new home—Bankole's land in the coastal hills of Humboldt County. The highway—U.S. 101—is to the east and north of us, and Cape Mendocino and the sea are to the west. A few miles south are state parks filled with huge redwood trees and hoards of squatters. The land surrounding us, however, is as empty and wild as any I've seen. It's covered with dry brush, trees, and tree stumps, all far removed from any city, and a long, hilly walk from the little towns that line the highway. There's farming around here, and logging, and just plain isolated living. According to Bankole, it's best to mind your own business and not pay too much attention to how people on neighboring plots of land earn a living. If they hijack trucks on 101, grow marijuana, distill whisky, or brew up more complicated illegal substances. . . . Well, live and let live.

Bankole guided us along a narrow blacktopped road that soon became a narrow dirt road. We saw a few cultivated fields, some scars left by past fires or logging, and a lot of land that seemed unused. The road all but vanished before we came to the end of it. Good for isolation. Bad for getting things in or out. Bad for traveling back and forth to get work. Bankole had said his brother-in- law had to spend a lot of time in various towns, away from his family. That was easier to understand now. There's no possibility here of coming home every day or two. So what did you have to do to save cash? Sleep in door-ways or parks in town? Maybe it was worth the inconvenience to do just that if you could keep your family together and safe—far from the desperate, the crazy, and the vicious.

Or that's what I thought until we reached the hillside where Ban-kole's sister's house and outbuildings were supposed to be.

There was no house. There were no buildings. There was almost nothing: A broad black smear on the hillside; a few charred planks sticking up from the rubble, some leaning against others; and a tall brick chimney, standing black and solitary like a tombstone in a picture of an old-style graveyard. A tombstone amid the bones and ashes.

OCTAVIA E. BUTLER

25

□ □ □

Create no images of God.
Accept the images
that God has provided.
They are everywhere,
in everything.
God is Change—
Seed to tree,
tree to forest;
Rain to river,
river to sea;
Grubs to bees,
bees to swarm.
From one, many;
from many, one;
Forever uniting, growing, dissolving—
forever Changing.
The universe
is God's self-portrait.

EARTHSEED: THE BOOKS OF THE LIVING
FRIDAY, OCTOBER 1, 2027

We've been arguing all week about whether or not we should stay here with the bones and ashes.

We've found five skulls—three in what was left of the house and two outside. There were other scattered bones, but not one complete skeleton. Dogs have been at the bones—dogs and cannibals, perhaps. The fire happened long enough ago for weeds to begin to grow in the rubble. Two months ago? Three? Some of the far-flung neighbors might know. Some of the far-flung neighbors might have set the fire.

There was no way to be certain, but I assumed that the bones belonged to Bankole's sister and her family. I think Bankole assumed that, too, but he couldn't bring himself to just bury the bones and write off his sister. The day after we got here, he and Harry hiked back to Glory, the nearest small town that we had passed through, to talk to the local cops. They were, or they professed to be, sheriff's deputies. I wonder what you have to do to become a cop. I wonder what a badge is, other than a license to steal. What did it used to be to make people Bankole's age want to trust it. I know what the old books say, but still, I wonder.

The deputies all but ignored Bankole's story and his questions. They wrote nothing down, claimed to know nothing. They treated Bankole as though they doubted that he even had a sister, or that he was who he said he was. So many stolen IDs these days. They searched him and took the cash he was carrying. Fees for police services, they said. He had been careful to carry only what he thought would be enough to keep them sweet-tempered, but not enough to make them suspicious or more greedy than they already were. The rest—a sizeable packet—he left with me. He trusted me enough to do that. His gun he left with Harry who had gone shopping.

Jail for Bankole could have meant being sold into a period of hard, unpaid labor—slavery. Perhaps if he had been younger, the deputies might have taken his money and arrested him anyway on some trumped-up charge. I had begged him not to go, not to trust *any* police or government official. It seemed to me such people were no better than gangs with their robbing and slaving.

Bankole agreed with me, yet he insisted on going.

"She was my little sister," he said. "I have to try, at least, to find out what happened to her. I need to know who did this. Most of all, I need to know whether any of her children could have survived. One or more of those five skulls could have belonged to the arsonists." He stared at the collection of bones. "I have to risk going to the sheriff's office," he continued. "But you don't. I don't want you with me. I don't want them getting any ideas about you, maybe finding out by accident that you're a sharer. I don't want my sister's death to cost you your life or your freedom."

We fought about it. I was afraid for him; he was afraid for me, and we were both angrier than we had ever been at each other. I was terrified that he would be killed or arrested, and we'd never find out what happened to him. No one should travel alone in this world.

"Look," he said at last, "you can do some good here with the group. You'll have one of the four guns left here, and you know how to survive. You're needed here. If the cops decide they want me, you won't be able to do a thing. Worse, if they decide they want you, there'll be nothing I can do except take revenge, and be killed for it."

That slowed me down—the thought that I might cause his death instead of backing him up. I didn't quite believe it, but it slowed me down. Harry stepped in then and said he would go. He wanted to anyway. He could buy some things for the group, and he wanted to look for a job. He wanted to earn some money.

"I'll do what I can," he told me just before they left. "He's not a bad old guy. I'll bring him back to you."

They brought each other back, Bankole a few thousand dollars poorer, and Harry still jobless—though they did bring back supplies and a few hand tools. Bankole knew no more than he had when he left about his sister and her family, but the cops had said they would come out to investigate the fire and the bones.

We worried that sooner or later, they might show up. We're still keeping a lookout for them, and we've hidden—buried—most of our valuables. We want to bury the bones, but we don't dare. It's bothering Bankole. Bothering him a lot. I've suggested we hold a funeral and go ahead and bury the bones. The hell with the cops. But he says no. Best to give them as little provocation as possible. If they came, they would do enough harm with their stealing. Best not to give them reason to do more.

There's a well with an old-fashioned hand pump under the rubble of an outbuilding. It still works. The solar-powered electric pump near the house does not. We couldn't stay here long without a dependable water source. With the well, though, it's hard to leave— hard to walk away from possible sanctuary—in spite of arsonists and cops.

Bankole owns this land, free and clear. There's a huge, half ruined garden plus citrus trees full of unripe fruit. We've already been pulling carrots and digging potatoes here. There are plenty of other fruit and nut trees plus wild pines, redwoods, and Douglas firs. None of these last were very big. This area was logged sometime before Bankole bought it. Bankole says it was clear-cut back in the 1980s or 1990s, but we can make use of the trees that have grown since then, and we can plant more. We can build a shelter, put in a winter garden from the seed I've been carrying and collecting since we left home. Granted, a lot of it is old seed. I hadn't renewed it as often as I should have while I was at home. Strange that I hadn't. Things kept getting worse and worse at home, yet I had paid less and less attention to the pack that was supposed to save my life when the mob came. There was so much else to worry about—and I think I was into my own brand of denial, as bad in its way as Cory's or Joanne's mother's. But all that feels like ancient history. Now was what we had to worry about. What were we going to do now?

"I don't think we can make it here," Harry said earlier this evening as we sat around the campfire. There should be something cheerful about sitting around a campfire with friends and a full stomach. We even had meat tonight, fresh meat. Bankole took the rifle and went off by himself for a while. When he came back, he brought three rabbits which Zahra and I skinned, cleaned, and roasted. We also roasted sweet potatoes that we had dug out of the garden. We should

OCTAVIA E. BUTLER

have been content. Yet all we were doing was rehashing what had become an old argument over the past few days. Perhaps it was the bones and ashes just over the rise that were bothering us. We had camped out of sight of the burned area in the hope of recovering a little peace of mind, but it hadn't helped. I was thinking that we should figure out a way to capture a few wild rabbits alive and breed them for a sure meat supply. Was that possible? Why not, if we stay here? And we should stay.

"Nothing we find farther north will be any better or any safer than this," I said. "It will be hard to live here, but if we work together, and if we're careful, it should be possible. We can build a community here."

"Oh, god, there she goes with her Earthseed shit again," Allie said. But she smiled a little as she said it. That was good. She hadn't smiled much lately.

"We can build a community here," I repeated. "It's dangerous, sure, but, hell, it's dangerous everywhere, and the more people there are packed together in cities, the more danger there is. This is a ridiculous place to build a community. It's isolated, miles from everywhere with no decent road leading here, but for us, for now, it's perfect."

"Except that someone burned this place down last time," Grayson Mora said. "Anything we build out here by itself is a target."

"Anything we build *anywhere* is a target," Zahra argued. "But the people out here before . . . I'm sorry, Bankole, I gotta say this: They couldn't have kept a good watch—a man and a woman and three kids. They would have worked hard all day, then slept all night. It would have been too hard on just two grown people to try to sit up and watch for half the night each."

"They didn't keep a night watch," Bankole said. "We'll have to keep one, though. And we could use a couple of dogs. If we could get them as puppies and train them to guard—"

"Give meat to dogs?" Mora demanded, outraged.

"Not soon." Bankole shrugged. "Not until we have enough for

ourselves. But if we can get dogs, they'll help us keep the rest of our goods."

"I wouldn't give a dog nothing but a bullet or a rock," Mora said. "I saw dogs eat a woman once."

"There are no jobs in that town Bankole and I went to," Harry said. "There was nothing. Not even work for room and board. I asked all over town. No one even knew of anything."

I frowned. "The towns around here are all close to the highway," I said. "They must get a lot of people passing through, looking for a place to settle—or maybe a place to rob, rape, kill. The locals wouldn't welcome new people. They wouldn't trust anyone they didn't know."

Harry looked from me to Bankole.

"She's right," Bankole said. "My brother-in-law had a hard time before people began to get used to him, and he moved up here before things got so bad. He knew plumbing, carpentry, electrical work, and motor vehicle mechanics. Of course, it didn't help that he was black. Being white might help you win people over faster than he did. I think, though, that any serious money we make here will come from the land. Food is gold these days, and we can grow food here. We have guns to protect ourselves, so we can sell our crops in nearby towns or on the highway."

"If we survive long enough to grow anything to sell," Mora muttered. "If there's enough water, if the bugs don't eat our crops, if no one burns us out the way they did those people over the hill, if, if, if!"

Allie sighed. "Shit, it's if, if, if anywhere you go. This place isn't so bad." She was sitting on her sleepsack, holding the sleeping Justin's head in her lap. As she spoke, she stroked the boy's hair. It occurred to me, not for the first time, that no matter how tough Allie tried to seem, that little boy was the key to her. Children were the keys to most of the adults present.

"There are no guarantees anywhere," I agreed. "But if we're willing to work, our chances are good here. I've got some seed in my pack. We can buy more. What we have to do at this point is more like gardening than farming. Everything will have to be done by hand—composting, watering, weeding, picking worms or slugs or whatever off the crops and killing them one by one if that's what it takes. As for water, if our well still has water in it now, in October, I don't think we have to worry about it going dry on us. Not this year, anyway.

"And if people threaten us or our crop, we kill them. That's all. We kill them, or they kill us. If we work together, we can defend ourselves, and we can protect the kids. A community's first responsibility is to protect its children—the ones we have now and the ones we will have."

There was silence for a while, people digesting, perhaps measuring it against what they had to look forward to if they left this place and continued north.

"We should decide," I said. "We have building and planting to do here. We have to buy more food, more seed and tools." It was time for directness: "Allie, will you stay?"

She looked across the dead fire at me, stared hard at me as though she hoped to see something on my face that would give her an answer.

"What seed do you have?" she asked.

I drew a deep breath. "Most of it is summer stuff—corn, peppers, sunflowers, eggplant, melons, tomatoes, beans, squash. But I have some winter things; peas, carrots, cabbage, broccoli, winter squash, onions, asparagus, herbs, several kinds of greens. . . . We can buy more, and we've got the stuff left in this garden plus what we can harvest from the local oak, pine, and citrus trees. I brought tree seeds too: more oak, citrus, peach, pear, nectarine, almond, walnut, a few others. They won't do us any good for a few years, but they're a hell of an investment in the future."

"So is a kid," Allie said. "I didn't think I would be dumb enough to say this, but yeah, I'll stay. I want to build something, too. I never had a chance to build anything before."

Allie and Justin were a yes, then.

"Harry? Zahra?"

"Of course we're staying," Zahra said.

Harry frowned. "Wait a minute. We don't have to."

"I know. But we are. If we can make a community like Lauren says and not have to hire out to strangers and trust them when they shouldn't be trusted, then we should do it. If you grew up where I did, you'd know we should."

"Harry," I said, "I've known you all my life. You're the closest thing to a brother that I have left. You aren't really thinking about leaving, are you?" It wasn't the world's best argument. He had been both cousin and lover to Joanne, and he'd let her go when he could have gone with her.

"I want something of my own," he said. "Land, a home, maybe a store or a small farm. Something that's mine. This land is Bankole's."

"Yes," Bankole said. "And you'll be getting the use of it rent free—and all the water you need. What are those things going to cost you farther north—if you can get them at all farther north—if you can get yourself out of California."

"But there's no work here!"

"There's nothing but work here, boy. Work, and a lot of cheap land. How cheap do you think land will be up where you and all the rest of the world are heading?"

Harry thought about that, then spread his hands. "What I'm worried about is spending all our money here, then discovering we can't make it here."

I nodded. "I've thought about that, too, and it bothers me. But it's a possibility anywhere, you know. You could settle in Oregon or Washington, not be able to get a job, and run out of money. Or you could be forced to work under the conditions that Emery and Grayson found. After all, with rivers of people flowing north, looking for work, employers can take their pick, and pay what they feel like paying."

Emery put her arm around Tori, who sat drowsing next to her. "You might be able to get a job as a driver," she said. "They like white

OCTAVIA E. BUTLER

men to be drivers. If you can read and write, and if you'd do the work, you might get hired."

"I don't know how to drive, but I could learn," Harry said. "You mean driving those big armored trucks, don't you?"

Emery looked confused. "Trucks? No, I mean driving people. Making them work. Pushing them to work faster. Making them do . . . whatever the owners says."

Harry's expression had dissolved from hopeful to horrified to outraged. "Jesus God, do you think I'd do that! How could you think I'd do anything like that?"

Emery shrugged. It startled me that she could be indifferent about such a thing, but she seemed to be. "Some people think it's a good job," she said. "Last driver we had, he used to do something with computers. I don't know what. His company went out of business and he got a job driving us. I think he liked it."

"Em," Harry said. He pitched his voice low and waited until she looked at him. "Are you telling me you believe I'd like a job pushing slaves around and taking away their children?"

She stared back, searching his face. "I hope not," she said. And then, "Sometimes jobs like that are the only jobs—slave or slave driver. I heard that just on this side of the Canada border there are a lot of factories with jobs like that."

I frowned. "Factories that use slave labor?"

"Yeah. Workers make things for companies in Canada or Asia. They don't get paid much, so they get into debt. They get hurt or sick, too. Their drinking water's not clean and the factories are dangerous—full of poisons and machines that crush or cut you. But people think they can make some cash and then quit. I worked with some women who had gone up there, taken a look, and come back."

"And you were going up there?" Harry demanded.

"Not to work in those places. The women warned me."

"I've heard of places like that," Bankole said. "They were supposed to provide jobs for that northward-flowing river of people. President Donner's all for them. The workers are more throwaways than slaves. They breathe toxic fumes or drink contaminated water or get caught in unshielded machinery. . . . It doesn't matter. They're easy to replace—thousands of jobless for every job."

"Borderworks," Mora said. "Not all of them are that bad. I heard some pay cash wages, not company scrip."

"Is that where you want to go?" I asked. "Or do you want to stay here?"

He looked down at Doe who was still nibbling at a piece of sweet potato. "I want to stay here," he said, surprising me. "I'm not sure you have a hope in hell of building anything here, but you're just crazy enough to make it work." And if it didn't work, he'd be no worse off than he was when he escaped slavery. He could rob someone and continue his journey north. Or maybe not. I'd been thinking about Mora. He did a lot to keep people away from him—keep them from knowing too much about him, keep them from seeing what he was feeling, or that he was feeling anything—a male sharer, desperate to hide his terrible vulnerability? Sharing would be harder on a man. What would my brothers have been like as sharers? Odd that I hadn't thought of that before.

"I'm glad you're staying," I said. "We need you." I looked at Travis and Natividad. "We need you guys, too. You're staying, aren't you?"

"You know we are," Travis said. "Although I think I agree more than I want to with Mora. I'm not sure we have a prayer of succeeding here."

"We'll have whatever we can shape," I said. And I turned to face Harry. He and Zahra had been whispering together. Now he looked at me.

"Mora's right," he said. "You're nuts."

I sighed.

"But this is a crazy time," he continued. "Maybe you're what the time needs—or what we need. I'll stay. I may be sorry for it, but I'll stay."

Now the decision is acknowledged, and we can stop arguing about it. Tomorrow we'll begin to prepare a winter garden. Next week, several of us will go into town to buy tools, more seed, supplies. Also, it's time we began to build a shelter. There are trees enough in the area, and we can dig into the ground and into the hills. Mora says he's built slave cabins before. Says he's eager to build something better, something fit for human beings. Besides, this far north and this near the coast, we might get some rain.

SUNDAY, OCTOBER 10, 2027

Today we had a funeral for Bankole's dead—the five people who died in the fire. The cops never came. At last Bankole has decided that they aren't going to come, and that it's time his sister and her family had a decent burial. We collected all the bones that we could find, and yesterday, Natividad wrapped them in a shawl that she had knitted years ago. It was the most beautiful thing she owned.

"A thing like that should serve the living," Bankole said when she offered it.

"You are living," Natividad said. "I like you. I wish I could have met your sister."

He looked at her for a while. Then he took the shawl and hugged her. Then, beginning to cry, he went off by himself into the trees, out of our sight. I let him alone for an hour or so, then went after him.

I found him, sitting on a fallen log, wiping his face. I sat with him for some time, saying nothing. After a while, he got up, waited for me to stand, then headed back toward our camp.

"I would like to give them a grove of oak trees," I said. "Trees are better than stone—life commemorating life."

He glanced back at me. "All right."

"Bankole?"

He stopped, looked at me with an expression I could not read.

"None of us knew her," I said. "I wish we had. I wish I had, no matter how much I would have surprised her."

He managed a smile. "She would have looked at you, then looked at me, then, right in front of you, I think she would have said, 'Well, there's no fool like an old fool.' Once she got that out of her system, I think she would have gotten to like you."

"Do you think she could stand. . . or forgive company now?"

"What?"

I drew a deep breath and wondered about what I meant to say. It could go wrong. He could misunderstand. It still needed to be said.

"We'll bury your dead tomorrow. I think you're right to want to do it. And I think we should bury our dead as well. Most of us have had to walk away—or run—away from our unburned, unburied dead. Tomorrow, we should remember them all, and lay them to rest if we can."

"Your family?"

I nodded. "Mine, Zahra's, Harry's, Allie's—both her son and her sister—maybe Emery's sons, maybe others that I don't know about. Mora doesn't talk about himself much, but he must have losses. Doe's mother, perhaps."

"How do you want to do it?" he asked.

"Each of us will have to bury our own dead. We knew them. We can find the words."

Words from the Bible, perhaps?

"Any words, memories, quotations, thoughts, songs. . . . My father had a funeral, even though we never found his body. But my three youngest brothers and my stepmother had nothing. Zahra saw them die, or I wouldn't have any idea what happened to them." I thought for a moment. "I have acorns enough for each of us to plant live oak trees to our dead—enough to plant one for Justin's mother, too. I'm thinking about a very simple ceremony. But everyone should have a chance to speak. Even the two little girls."

He nodded. "I don't have any objection. It isn't a bad idea." And a few steps later: "There's been so much dying. There's so much more to come."

"Not for us, I hope."

He said nothing for a while. Then he stopped and put his hand on my shoulder to stop me. At first he only stood looking at me, almost studying my face. "You're so young," he said. "It seems almost criminal that you should be so young in these terrible times. I wish you could have known this country when it was still salvageable."

"It might survive," I said, "changed, but still itself."

"No." He drew me to his side and put one arm around me. "Human beings will survive of course. Some other countries will survive. Maybe they'll absorb what's left of us. Or maybe we'll just break up into a lot of little states quarreling and fighting with each other over whatever crumbs are left. That's almost happened now with states shutting themselves off from one another, treating state lines as national borders. As bright as you are, I don't think you understand—I don't think you can understand what we've lost. Perhaps that's a blessing."

"God is Change," I said.

"Olamina, that doesn't mean anything."

"It means everything. Everything!"

He sighed. "You know, as bad as things are, we haven't even hit bottom yet. Starvation, disease, drug damage, and mob rule have only begun. Federal, state, and local governments still exist—in name at least—and sometimes they manage to do something more than collect taxes and send in the military. And the money is still good. That amazes me. However much more you need of it to buy anything these days, it is still accepted. That may be a hopeful sign—or perhaps it's only more evidence of what I said: We haven't hit bottom yet."

"Well, the group of us here doesn't have to sink any lower," I said.

He shook his shaggy head, his hair, beard, and serious expression making him look more than a little like an old picture I used to have of Frederick Douglass.

"I wish I believed that," he said. Perhaps it was his grief talking. "I don't think we have a hope in hell of succeeding here."

I slipped my arm around him. "Let's go back," I said. "We've got work to do."

So today we remembered the friends and the family members we've lost. We spoke our individual memories and quoted Bible passages, Earthseed verses, and bits of songs and poems that were favorites of the living or the dead.

Then we buried our dead and we planted oak trees.

Afterward, we sat together and talked and ate a meal and decided to call this place Acorn.

> *A sower went out to sow his seed:*
> *and as he sowed, some fell by the*
> *way side; and it was trodden down,*
> *and the fowls of the air devoured*
> *it. And some fell upon a rock; and*
> *as soon as it was sprung up, it*
> *withered away because it lacked*
> *moisture. And some fell among*
> *thorns; and the thorns sprang up*
> *with it, and choked it. And others*
> *fell on good ground, and sprang up,*
> *and bore fruit an hundredfold.*

THE BIBLE
Authorized King James Version
St. Luke 8: 5-8

OCTAVIA E. BUTLER

A writer who darkly imagined the future we have destined for ourselves in book after book, and also one who has shown us the way toward improving on that dismal fate, OCTAVIA E. BUTLER (1947–2006) is recognized as among the bravest and smartest of contemporary fiction writers. A 1995 MacArthur Award winner, Butler transcended the science fiction category even as she was awarded that community's top prizes, the Nebula and Hugo Awards. She reaches readers of all ages, all races, and all religious and sexual persuasions. For years the only African-American woman writing science fiction, Butler has encouraged many others to follow in her path.

GLORIA STEINEM is a feminist, journalist, activist, and author. She is well known for her contributions to the women's rights movement, and for her tireless advocacy for equality ever since. Her most recent book is *My Life on the Road*, published in 2015 to wide acclaim.

ABOUT SEVEN STORIES PRESS

Seven Stories Press is an independent book publisher based in New York City. We publish works of the imagination by such writers as Nelson Algren, Russell Banks, Octavia E. Butler, Ani DiFranco, Assia Djebar, Ariel Dorfman, Coco Fusco, Barry Gifford, Martha Long, Luis Negrón, Hwang Sok-yong, Lee Stringer, and Kurt Vonnegut, to name a few, together with political titles by voices of conscience, including Subhankar Banerjee, the Boston Women's Health Collective, Noam Chomsky, Angela Y. Davis, Human Rights Watch, Derrick Jensen, Ralph Nader, Loretta Napoleoni, Gary Null, Greg Palast, Project Censored, Barbara Seaman, Alice Walker, Gary Webb, and Howard Zinn, among many others. Seven Stories Press believes publishers have a special responsibility to defend free speech and human rights, and to celebrate the gifts of the human imagination, wherever we can. In 2012 we launched Triangle Square books for young readers with strong social justice and narrative components, telling personal stories of courage and commitment. For additional information, visit www.sevenstories.com.